The
Third Thaw

The Third Thaw

Karl J. Hanson

E. L. Marker
Salt Lake City

E. L. Marker, an imprint of WiDo Publishing
Salt Lake City, Utah
widopublishing.com

Cover design by Steven Novak
Book design by Marny K. Parkin

ISBN 978-1-947966-08-6
Printed in the United States of America

For Lisa, Julie, and Paige,
and to the memory of my parents, Dorothy and Sig

Part 1
New Eden

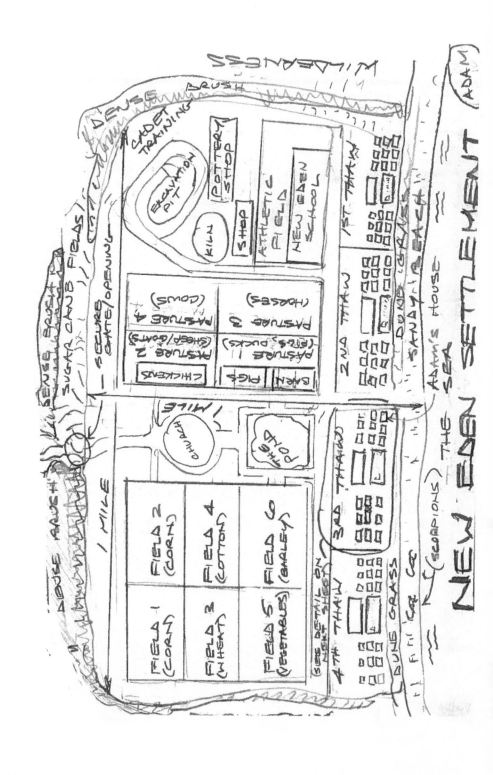

NEW EDEN SETTLEMENT (ADAM)

WILDERNESS

DENSE BRUSH

CADET TRAINING

EXCAVATION PIT

POTTERY SHOP

SHOP

KILN

ATHLETIC FIELD

NEW EDEN SCHOOL

1ST THAW

2ND THAW

DEAD GRASS

SANDY BEACH

ADAM'S HOUSE

THE SEA

SECURE GATE/OPENING

SUGAR CANE FIELDS

DENSE BRUSH

DENSE BRUSH

PASTURE 4 (COWS)

PASTURE 3 (HORSES)

PASTURE 2 (SHEEP/GOATS)

PASTURE 1 (PIGS/DUCKS)

CHICKENS

PIGS

BARN

1 MILE

1 MILE

CHURCH

SHOP PIT

FIELD 1 (CORN)

FIELD 2 (CORN)

FIELD 3 (WHEAT)

FIELD 4 (COTTON)

FIELD 5 (VEGETABLES)

FIELD 6 (BARLEY)

(SEE DETAIL ON NEXT SHEET)

3RD THAW

4TH THAW

DUNE GRASS

(SCORPIONS)

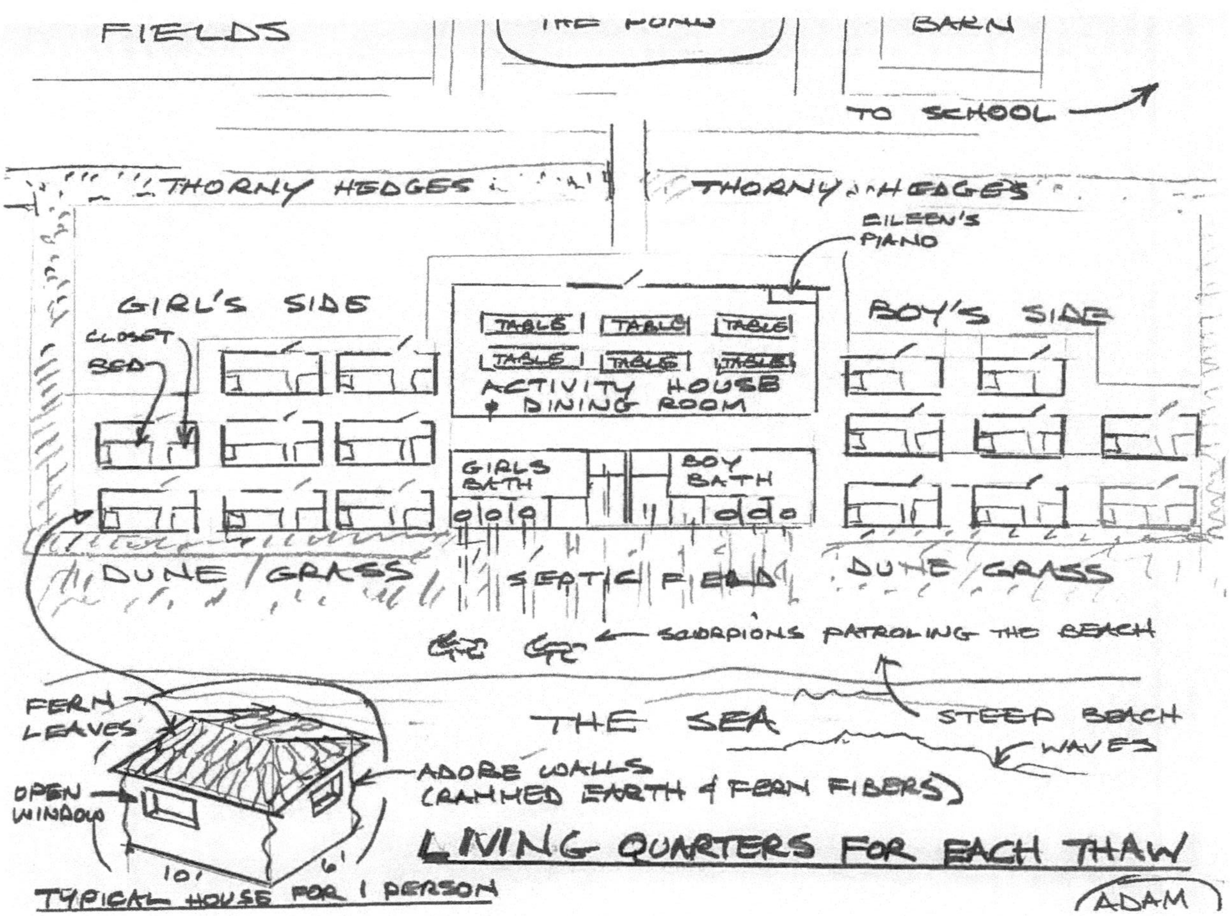

FIELDS

THE POND

BARN

TO SCHOOL →

THORNY HEDGES

THORNY HEDGES

EILEEN'S PIANO

BOY'S SIDE

GIRL'S SIDE

CLOSET

BED

ACTIVITY HOUSE
DINING ROOM

TABLE | TABLE | TABLE
TABLE | TABLE | TABLE

GIRL'S BATH

BOY BATH

DUNE / GRASS

DUNE / GRASS

SEA TIDE FIELD

SCORPIONS PATROLING THE BEACH

STEEP BEACH

WAVES

THE SEA

ADOBE WALLS
(RAMMED EARTH & FERN FIBERS)

FERN LEAVES

OPEN WINDOW

10'

TYPICAL HOUSE FOR 1 PERSON

LIVING QUARTERS FOR EACH THAW

(ADAM)

Chapter 1

WITH A GRUNT, ADAM ROLLED OVER, PULLING THE THICK down comforter over his head.

"Get up, sleepy head. It's late!" came the familiar voice.

"What day is it, Miss Clare?" he murmured from under the covers.

"*Es ist Samstag,*" responded Miss Clare, the female Guardian, in perfect Deutsch. It was Saturday, but Miss Clare's response, like all her utterances, sounded more matter-of-fact than enthusiastic.

"*Ah, ja,*" replied Adam, who had recently begun learning German in school.

Raising his head slightly, he could see quite clearly out of the window. The weather looked good, although the sky was a bit more orange than usual, with the moon dominating the morning sky. Still half asleep, he could hear the waves crashing on the beach just a short distance from the house. The sea breeze flowed unobstructed through the adobe dwelling which had no window panes. In New Eden, none of the houses had window panes. Of course, Adam knew what glass was because he had been learning how to manufacture it. He had blown glass into cups and bowls, but had created nothing flat like a window pane; however, he knew of a technique for making flat glass, called "crown glass." In this technique, the glass blower would spin the molten glass bulb so fast that it opened up suddenly into a flat, circular sheet, with a distinctive blemish, like a glass belly button. Adam's friend, Horst, probably knew how to make crown glass. Horst knew a lot of things.

Almost fourteen years old, Adam was nearly five foot ten. He had dark brown hair and was somewhat on the skinny side. On a typical morning, he worked in the fields and did chores around the house; then, in the afternoon, he we went to school. Like Horst, he had recently started high school. The curriculum was much the same as the elementary school curriculum, emphasizing basic reading, math and science. Now, however, he was learning German, though he couldn't understand the rationale behind this mandatory subject.

Adam's generation was the result of the "Third Thawing" of people who lived in New Eden, which was a relatively small settlement; bordered by a sea on one side, it was only about one square mile in area. Adam and his fourteen classmates—the "Third Thaws"—had never ventured beyond these limited confines, because it was strictly not allowed. Having known each other since infancy, they were more like brothers and sisters than classmates. Most of the time, they got along, but not always. As in any large family, there were a few cliques and a few oddballs. Adam's best friends were Hansel and Horst. Hansel was a couple of inches shorter than Adam, and a bit on the pudgy side. Horst was almost as tall as Adam, and had dark, almost black, straight hair.

On Saturday afternoons, after chores, the boys would head to the beach, as did most of the kids in New Eden. The steep sandy slope created plunging breakers that drenched them with salt spray. The Guardians warned them to never go beyond the sand dunes, and especially, *never* to swim in the water because of the dangerous creatures that lurked beneath the surface, and the giant scorpions that walked along the water's edge. These creatures would patrol the beach, catching any fish that were visible when the waves lapped against the shore; occasionally, the scorpions fought each other, using their stingers to kill their opponents.

After dressing in his standard cotton tunic, Adam made his way to Hansel's dwelling where he and his friends had agreed to meet. His tunic—like those of everyone else in New Eden—resembled a potato sack with holes cut out for his arms and legs. The garment was off-white as a result of a bleaching the fabric in buttermilk and then leaving it to dry in the sun. The cotton was rough, with the seeds still intact. No one wore anything blue, red, or yellow, simply because dyes in those colors were not available in New Eden.

His friends were already waiting for him. Together, they made their way down to the sandy beach where Zelda, Ingrid, and Greta sat on their blankets, knitting. Their long bone needles clicked rhythmically as they worked the still moist strands of seaweed, row by row, into twelve-inch squares. The boys marveled at the speed of their deft fingers which had been calloused by many years of labor. The simple seaweed squares would be left to dry, making a soft fabric; then they would be stitched together to form blankets and ponchos for the winter, or to replace the damaged sections of old garments or bedding.

The boys and girls stayed in the dune grass, safely away from the scorpions. While the girls continued knitting, eyes focusing on every stitch, the boys watched intently as the giant scorpions patrolled the beach, scurrying across the sand in zigzag formation. Stingers arched over their backs, they made random forays into the shallows, catching the tiny fish which darted along the shoreline between their extended pedipalps. Fascinated, the boys studied how the venomous creatures crushed the smaller fish with their claws, reserving their stings for larger creatures. Adam began to trace the outlines of scorpions in the sand with one finger while his friends looked on in amazement at the accuracy of his line drawings. Not to be outdone, Hansel scooped up the moist sand and began building a cluster of miniature adobe houses that were replicas of his own much larger dwelling.

"Look at how the scorpions have hard shells around them. Have you ever seen them leave their old shells behind?" asked Ingrid.

"Yeah," said Zelda, barely looking up from her knitting. "I've seen old scorpion shells. Sometimes I get fooled by the shells, because they look like scorpions, but there's nothing inside them! By the way, does anyone have the comb?"

"I have it," said Greta, handing Zelda "the comb" which was made of metal. There weren't many of the good metal combs around, so people had to share "the comb."

"No, not that one," said Zelda. "I want the one with wider things on it."

"What do you mean, 'wider things'?" asked Greta.

"The hair teeth. You know, the straight things that comb your hair. My hair is too thick for that brush," said Zelda, beginning to sound agitated, the cord of her shell necklace twirling in her fingers. Then she returned to her knitting.

"Sorry, but I left the wide comb in my room," said Ingrid, running her fingers through her thick, sun-bleached hair.

"Mine feels tangled, too, but we're at the beach, so it doesn't really matter—or does it?" said Greta.

Ingrid, seeing that Zelda was staring at Gerald, grinned at Greta as if to say, "I told you so!"

With their dark curly hair and dark complexion, Zelda and Gerald looked distinctly different from the other children. Zelda and Gerald had always been close friends, but now that they were almost fourteen years old, the gossip was that they "liked" each other. To be sure, recently, Zelda seemed to be paying much more attention to her appearance; her morning ritual now consisted of examining her reflection in the pond near her house and vigorously combing her hair.

Eventually, the knitting needles stopped clicking. Ingrid cast off the last stitches from her needles, placing her twelfth square on top of the neat pile at her side. Looking up, she smiled at Adam and Hansel, her hair forming a golden halo around her face. Meanwhile, Zelda completed her pile. Holding up one of the squares between coffee-colored fingers, she gazed proudly at her handiwork while Gerald smoothed out the inevitable kinks from her squares.

Adam and Hansel nodded appreciatively, then turned their attention to playing catch with a pigskin ball, while Hansel had made a stack of playing cards from flattened corn husks. Time passed quickly until Miss Clare's voice summoned Adam home for supper.

"Adam!" she called, in a loud, unexpressive voice. "Adam—it's time for supper."

"Coming, Miss Clare," replied Adam. "I'm on my way."

Miss Clare, the Guardian, was a nondescript adult female of indeterminate age. All the Guardians were somewhat nondescript, almost "generic" looking, in fact. Two eyes, a nose, a mouth—put all these features together and you have a face. However, the Guardians seemed different from the children, and this was not just because they were older. The Guardians were, in fact, quite good looking—almost *too*

good looking, in a peculiar way. Actually, the problem with their appearance was that they looked perfect. Even when they had cause to reprimand their wards, furrows never crossed their brows nor did they get harsh lines around their mouths. Nor did they ever suffer from scars, sunburn or blemishes, and they never developed moles, freckles, age spots or the like.

The Guardians took care of the kids; served them meals dressed them and taught them in school. In fact, they did practically all the work in this little settlement that was filled with teenagers and young adults from the Second, Third, and Fourth "Thaws."

New Eden was an entirely self-sufficient rural community where everything had to be made from scratch. Except for a few items that had been brought there when the community was settled—a steel plow, a few steel tools, a spinning wheel, a loom and some musical instruments—everything else was made by the kids or the Guardians:

Thread was spun on spinning wheels from cotton, wool, and flax.

Clothing was stitched from yarn.

Fabric was woven on looms.

Fabric was dyed with organic dyes.

Ropes were woven from fabric and plant fibers.

Soap was made by mixing fat, ashes from burning ferns and bushes, and lime.

Flour was produced by grinding wheat on stone wheels.

Pottery was created from clay, then dried and fired in kilns; people cooked using ceramic pottery.

Cooking was done over fires made from burning bundles of the dried sticks from small woody plants, such as bushes and ferns. There were no large logs available to burn and no coal.

Glass was manufactured by heating a clean mixture of soda, lime and sand in a very hot kiln, heated from special blocks of compressed fern charcoal. Molten glass was blown into cups, bowls, and bottles.

Clay pipes were manufactured for the town's sanitary system. Clay was dug from the local pit, and then was formed into pipes which were vitrified in the kiln.

Furniture was typically made of wicker, fashioned from reeds of the indigenous plants.

The people made their own music.

There were not many materials available to the community of New Eden:

There was little or no steel, except for a few items that had been brought there.

There was no lumber. The only available wood materials were from such plants as bushes and ferns. There were a few wooden things, such as a wooden piano, that had been brought there.

There were no wires.

There was no electricity.

There were no lights.

There were no electronic items, except for e-readers.

There were no computers.

There was no Internet.

There was no social media.

There was no radio or television.

There was no recorded music.

There were no cars.

There were no neighboring communities.

The community grew several crops: corn, cotton, vegetables, wheat, and barley. They raised farm animals: chicken, sheep, pigs, cows, goats, and buffalo.

On the outskirts of New Eden there was a large field of sugar cane; the kids had been warned never to go beyond the sugar cane fields.

Adam couldn't remember a time when he didn't have chores to do. As soon as he was old enough to feed the chickens or pick weeds, he was put to work. There was very little leisure time. He and his classmates worked every day in the fields, tending crops and feeding the chickens, pigs, sheep, and horses.

On Sundays, Adam and Miss Clare went to church. Everyone in New Eden regularly attended the only church in town, which was nondenominational. The services were mostly community gathering events, with a sprinkling of religion. There were no prayers as such, nor even references to a Higher Power; instead, all religious elements were focused more on civic responsibility than on religious obligations. The church building was a large outdoor pavilion, with open sides and a raised platform on which The Leader stood. Behind The Leader's podium was a large stainless steel sculpture in the form of a Möbius strip. This artifact was one of the few metal things brought to New Eden when it was founded.

The Leader wore a golden suit and a pulsating emerald green necklace. The Leader's hair was absolutely white, and his big whiskers flapped like flags when he walked. His presence was authoritative, impressive, and dramatic.

"And let us reflect on our lives, and all that we have in this world, and be thankful. We will be eternally grateful for the plentiful things that we have here. Let us be happy for all that we are blessed with!" he would boom as he delivered the Lesson.

As his voice increased in volume, his green necklace gleamed brighter and brighter; as his speech became softer, the necklace grew dimmer, gradually fading from emerald to obsidian as the Lesson spiraled to conclusion. True, this was church, but it was also great theater.

"Peace, my brothers and sisters!"

"And peace to you, Leader!" the citizens of New Eden would declare in unison.

Nobody knew The Leader on a personal basis. It was rumored that before he became The Leader, his name was Graham and that he had played a critical role during the early establishment of New Eden. What gave this rumor credence was the fact that some people called him "Father Leader," while others called him "Leader Graham."

Adam always paid close attention to The Leader's words. He was actually a bit afraid of him, but Miss Clare would assure him that this was appropriate. Fear, after all, would lead to Obedience and Obedience would lead to Respect.

Every Sunday, The Leader conducted the weekly service and gave The Lesson, but during the rest of the week, the community never saw him. He was not a pastoral presence in the community, but his words and decisions on matters of importance were quite literally *The Law*.

Soon after sundown that evening, after eating supper, Adam went to bed. Usually, he would stay up as long as possible, reading or drawing as long as there was daylight or oil to burn. That night, however, he pretended to be sleeping when Miss Clare came into his room to check on him. Gently, she placed a blanket over him, then neatly folded the cotton tunic which he had tossed onto the floor. For a moment, she lingered near the door before leaving the room. As he heard her leave their house, Adam slipped out of bed, pulled on his tunic, then followed her outside. In the twilight, he could barely see her walking in the direction of the fields.

Cautiously, Adam began following Miss Clare, keeping a safe distance behind her. As she walked, he saw other Guardians leaving their houses, and that they, too, were heading in the direction of the sugar cane fields. All twelve Guardians appeared to be in a trance, as though sleepwalking. There was no communication amongst them and all seemed to be staring ahead, as if drawn to the same focal point.

When they reached the sugar cane fields, an opening appeared. What it was exactly, Adam could not make out, but one moment the Guardians were standing in front of neat rows of sugar cane, and, at the next, the tall stalks bowed their feathery tops to form an arch leading somewhere beyond sight.

Without hesitating, the Guardians walked through the opening. Then the opening closed abruptly behind them.

Chapter 2

WHEN ADAM ARRIVED IN CLASS THE NEXT MORNING, HE sat down next to Hansel and Horst near the back of the room.

"It's too early to smile, Adam," said Hansel. "I just woke up. You got a secret you want to tell us?"

"Yeah, what's up, smiley face?" asked Horst.

"I saw something last night," said Adam.

But before he was able to continue, the Guardian teacher, Miss Angelique, walked near the boys.

"I'll tell you later," said Adam.

Switching the subject, well aware that Miss Angelique was listening, Adam asked Horst, in a mockingly serious tone, "Horst, how is your Deutsch coming along?"

Horst gave Adam an exasperated look. When Miss Angelique walked away, he said to Adam, "I'm going to get you for that."

Today, Miss Angelique would be teaching the class German. The rules of German drove Horst crazy. It was not that he objected to rules as such, but it was beyond him why each noun had one of three genders—"*der*," "*die*," or "*das*." Miss Angelique said that someday he would find Deutsch useful, but Horst could see no rationale behind learning any foreign language, let alone German.

Perhaps that was why Miss Angelique considered Horst to be the most problematic of all her fifteen pupils. He was the class clown, constantly causing disruptions or mimicking the teacher. As a teacher—and a Guardian—Miss Angelique had been trained to expect this sort of amateurish behavior, as part of the growing process.

It was Friday, the day Miss Angelique reviewed the progress of each student.

"Class, I require your attention," she said in her usual monotone, as everyone was socializing. "Class! I require your attention!"

Horst was talking to Adam and Hansel, with his back to Miss Angelique. Noticing that he was not paying attention, Miss Angelique began hitting her ruler against her desk. "Horst! Horst!"

Adam nudged Horst to turn around.

"Sorry, Miss Angelique," responded Horst, changing into a serious expression.

"*Danke, Horst*," said Miss Angelique. "*Wie geht ist ihnen?*" asking him "how is it going?" in Deutsch.

Horst was caught off guard by this basic Deutsch greeting.

"Uh . . . uh . . ." he stammered, trying to remember this phrase. Then, it came back to him: "*Es . . . geht..mir..gut . . . ?*" he responded, somewhat unsure of himself.

"*Sehr gut*, Horst," said Miss Angelique. [*Very good.*]

Next, she directed her attention to a female student sitting in the front. "Eileen, what piano pieces have you been learning this week?"

Eileen was a thin, red-haired girl, with very fine features. She was, by far, the most musically gifted of the class Third Thaws. "I am currently on the fifteenth of Bach's Two-Part Inventions, Miss Angelique."

Horst whispered to Adam, "Is she inventing something?"

Adam chuckled.

Oblivious to Horst and Adam, Miss Angelique continued, "If I understand correctly, is that the last of Bach's Two-Part Inventions?"

"Yes, it's the last one, Miss Angelique."

"And you have memorized them all?"

"Yes," said Eileen proudly. Since the age of six, she had acquired "perfect pitch"—the ability to remember and identify the names of notes by ear. She had already amassed an impressive repertoire of piano pieces, mostly by Bach, Mozart, and Beethoven.

"Excellent!" commended the teacher, with just a slight hint of enthusiasm in her voice. "Class, let us all give Eileen a round of applause!"

The boys and girls had recently learned to do this "clapping thing" called "applause." They had watched an instructional video on their e-readers, showing a group of people—something they learned is called an "audience"-who were clapping their hands after watching a musical performance.

There were no paper books in New Eden, only e-readers, because there was not enough room to bring paper books to this place!

When the children were very young, the Guardians read them stories. Each family—that is, each Guardian and child—had an e-reader which was preloaded with a large library of books. The e-readers could also play instructional videos that demonstrated how to make things.

Miss Angelique turned her attention to the two girls in the back of the class: "Gertrude and Eva, how is your progress this week in making the felt?"

"Very good, Miss Angelique," answered Gertrude. Turning to Eva, Gertrude said, "Show her." At five foot nine, Eva towered over Gertrude who was short, stocky and big boned.

Eva reached into a bag and pulled out a piece of fabric. "This is the felt we're *trying* to make from wool. I'm not so sure if I would call it 'very good.'"

Ingrid asked, "Can I feel it?"

"Yeah, sure, go ahead," said Eva, handing Ingrid the fabric.

"It feels so much softer than wool!" said Ingrid.

Miss Angelique asked, "You followed the video on the e-reader?"

Gertrude said, "Yes, we watched it. We knitted the wool, then we moistened it, then we put it in a press, then we heated it. That little piece of fabric required a lot of work."

"What will you use this felt for?" asked Miss Angelique.

"We're thinking of making felt slippers," answered Gertrude.

"Can you make some for me?" asked Ingrid.

Gertrude and Eva momentarily looked at each other, then whispered something to each other. "Okay, sure. No problem," said Eva to Ingrid.

Now that the Third Thaw had reached high school age, each of them were beginning to receive training in vocational specializations. Before the kids were even born, the type of work they would be doing as adults had been predetermined.

Adam, for example, had a talent for drawing and was therefore taking architectural and carpentry courses. Eileen was an excellent pianist and was destined to be a musician. Gertrude and Eva were both skilled at working with textiles and making clothes. Ingrid, the most brilliant pupil in Miss Angelique's class, had an aptitude for biology; in fact, she had been selected for medical training, so she could eventually become the town's physician.

But Horst's skills were difficult to pigeonhole. The grandson of an accomplished chemistry professor and researcher, he had been assigned the role of future chemist. For all his nonconformity, it was obvious that he had great potential. Ironically, his wild streak was, perhaps, an indication of a strongly creative intelligence. After all, boredom with school and a dislike for structured activities has been the bane of many gifted individuals. Neither Albert Einstein nor Isaac Newton were stellar students. Although Horst did excel at mathematics and was the classes' strongest student in that subject.

He often came up with quite unusual ideas for someone his age. On one occasion, Horst had presented Miss Angelique with a solution for the transcendental number, "e", using a Taylor's series. He was not even fourteen years old at the time!

When he was very young, Horst thought the world was flat. He spent hours pondering over what would happen if someone sailed off the edge of a flat world. *What was underneath a flat world? Were there dragons?* He had heard about dragons in fairy tales but approached them with a scientist's skepticism. But dragons or no dragons, what happened when you sailed to the edge of the world? Would you just free fall over the edge and start sailing upside down?

After he learned that, in reality, the world was not flat but a spherical planet, Horst's imagination simply couldn't be limited. *What was a planet? What caused gravity? How big was the Universe? Where did the Universe come from? What was time? Did everyone experience time the same way? What was life? Was the Universe somehow ruled by mathematics? What was a wave? Was time travel possible?*

∽

After morning classes, the kids did their chores. Daily chores varied according to the children's age and aptitude. One of Horst's chores was working in "the pit," a kind of quarry for extracting layers of soil and sand. The pit had grown from a small hole to its present size of approximately two hundred by two hundred by eighty feet. A six-foot-wide path ran along the perimeter of the pit, winding from top to bottom, so that the materials could be brought to the surface without too much effort.

Adam, Hansel, and Horst were the current team working in the pit. Hansel tended to push hard to get the job done, barely taking the time to look up from their labor. The three worked hard, digging using scallop shells.

As they worked, Horst frequently looked up at the walls of the pit: he was fascinated by the different layers of soil which formed the sloping sides of the excavation site. Every now and again, he would pick up a piece of soil and let it run between his fingers, feeling its softness or grittiness, occasionally smelling it. At the top, the soil was a sort of loam formed from the organic decay of plants. Then at a depth of about three feet, the soil became a silty sand, down to a depth of fifteen feet. Below that, the soil was clay.

The three boys continued digging away, loading up a wheelbarrow with clay, to be transported to the kiln, which the older Second Thaws maintained. The clay was to be used to make ceramic pots and pipes.

As Horst dug, he hit something hard.

"Take a look at this!" he exclaimed.

Adam, who was digging close by, looked into the hole.

"Looks like you've hit rock," he observed.

Horst got down on his knees to examine the rock. He could see small spirals of white shell protruding from the rock in clusters of sharp spikes, while broadly conical limpets were firmly embedded in its surface, embossing it with their blue-gray veins.

"Look at this," he repeated, pointing at the rock. "See this shell? There are sea shells in the rock! This must have been the bottom of a sea at one time! Perhaps this rock was a part of a coral reef."

"What's a 'reef'?" asked Adam. By now, all three of them were staring at the shell-encrusted rock.

"It's something I've been reading about. Reefs are formed in the oceans by tiny sea creatures which make something called coral; a reef is a very large structure of coral."

"So, you're saying there was an ocean here at one time?" said Hansel. "An ocean was here where we're standing?"

"Yeah, I think so," said Horst. "Obviously, if there was an ocean here, something must have happened to make the water go away. But just look around at all these different layers of soil around the pit. Don't you think it's possible that this soil came from dust that fell here over many years?"

Adam looked at the layers of soil, trying to decide if he agreed with Horst's theory.

"I don't know. That's a lot of dust. I mean, this hole where we're standing is deep."

Horst was convinced he had discovered a truth: the soil was formed by the accumulation of dust and particles. He imagined the wind blowing enough dust over so many years that they could now see different layers where there may have once been an ocean. As he imagined further and further back in time something clicked.

"Yeah . . . I can almost see it in my head."

"What do you see?" asked Hansel.

"I can imagine an ocean was here, and there was a reef. Fascinating."

The idea was now cemented in his memory, filed away under "Rocks and Minerals." Hansel and Adam exchanged looks, as if to say, "There he goes again!"

The boys pushed the loaded wheelbarrow out of the pit and into the workshop where Gertrude and Eva sat at potters' wheels, spinning clay to fashion cooking pots; Ingrid and Eileen sat next to them, scratching spiral decoration onto the raw vessels. The boys dumped the new supply of clay into a large pile, then covered it with a damp cloth.

"Here you go, just what you were looking forward to—more clay," joked Horst. "Having fun?"

Gertrude grimaced, squelching the water out of a ball of soft clay as if preparing to hurl it at Horst.

"Hey, just joking!" laughed Horst, raising his arms to protect himself. Gertrude tossed the clay into the air, caught it, then slapped it onto the wheel, pinching and lifting the clod until it began to take shape as an asymmetrical bowl.

"You know it's lopsided," observed Horst, trying to keep a straight face. Gertrude glared at him, pressing down heavily on the flywheel with her foot. When the rotating wheel finally came to a standstill, the bowl was indeed somewhat misshapen. Gertrude pried the vessel free from the wheel head and carried it over to the reject shelf.

"Are these ones ready for the kiln?" Adam asked, pointing at a row of pots that had not yet been fired.

"Yeah, those five pots are bone dry," answered Eva, brushing back her wispy blond hair. Wiping her hands in her apron, she stood up and stretched. Both girls were skilled seamstresses who resented any time spent away from fabric and thread. Like the boys, they understood there were tasks which had to get done whether they liked it or not. Working the clay was one of them.

The boys loaded the pots into the wheelbarrow and dragged it to the kiln which was being maintained by Jim and Sylvester, two Second Thaws who were five years older than their Third Thaw counterparts. These Second Thaws were responsible for stoking the fire and blowing the air into the furnace with bellows. Sometimes, it would take several days to fire the pottery.

Clad in green burlap uniforms, the Second Thaws had been "militarized." They all had officer rankings and treated each other with military respect. It was not uncommon to hear them address each other with a "Yes, Sir!" and to see them standing at attention.

"How's it going, men?" asked Jim.

Horst was a bit taken aback that Jim had classified him as a "man."

"Fine, Sir," he responded to the older Thaw.

"Good, good," said Jim, wiping the perspiration off his forehead.

"Man, this kiln gets hot sometimes!"

He shoveled a mixture of corn husks and horse manure into the fire, then stepped back so Hansel and Gerald could place the pots in the kiln.

Horst enjoyed working with the kiln. His ambition was to make iron, but this would require collecting a stack of rusty brown rocks—that is, rocks containing iron ore. Those types of rocks were scarce on the surface of the pit, but Horst believed he might find more if he dug deeper.

As for the kiln, working iron would require temperatures much, much hotter than those for producing ceramics. Horst wanted to build a new type of kiln that would have much hotter fires—perhaps even twice as hot—but the standard fuel they were using here could hardly produce such temperatures. When he was older, he would build such a kiln to make iron. He had no doubt that this was possible, because he had read all about a fuel called "coke" used in metal.

~

The next morning—Saturday—Adam, Hansel, and Horst were eating breakfast together in the dining hall. Meals in New Eden were served in shifts. The oldest group, the Second Thaw, was served first, then the Third Thaw, then the youngest group, the Fourth Thaw. A typical breakfast consisted of eggs, bacon, and bread. After one of the dining hall Guardians served them, Adam leaned close to his friends, so only they could hear him.

"Have you ever seen the Guardians walking outside at night after we go to bed?"

"Yeah. I've noticed them from my window," admitted Hansel. "Do you know what they're doing?"

"Yeah, I followed them a couple of nights ago," whispered Adam, looking behind him to make sure that no one else was listening.

"You actually followed them?" asked Horst. "Where did they go?"

"They go to the sugar cane fields. There's a place in the sugar cane bushes that sort of opens up when they get there. Then they walk into the field looking straight ahead, without talking. After they get there, the opening closes."

Horst whistled softly under his breath, then, noting that one of the Guardians was looking in his direction, he dipped his bread in the egg yolk and continued eating. Adam leaned back in his chair again, but his words had left their mark.

Since Saturday wasn't a school day, they would have some time off after finishing their morning chores at the pit. When they met up again, midmorning, scrubbed and clean after all their excavating, they weren't interested in going to the beach as usual.

"Hey, I have an idea," said Adam. "Let's head to the sugar cane fields and do some exploring—how about it?"

Nobody objected. They packed sandwiches, then set off in the direction of the sugar cane fields. Instead of taking the direct route from their houses past the pond and church, they plodded through the pastures to avoid being noticed—past the pig barn and chicken house, between the four pastures allocated for pigs, ducks, sheep, goats, cows, and horses. The stench was overpowering and their burlap sandals were soon caked in mud and animal droppings.

"There must be something there we're not supposed to see," observed Adam. "Something important and off-limits."

"Yeah, something worth knowing about—something worth ruining our sandals for," said Horst, looking down at his manure-caked feet. "I'm not sure if I'll ever be able to clean this crap off my feet!"

To their right was the excavation pit; ahead of them were the sugar cane fields flanked by dense fern woods. They decided to enter the woods to gain access to whatever lay behind the sugar cane fields.

The fern woods were quite dense and virtually impenetrable because of the thorny undergrowth, making it nearly impossible to find an entry point. Adam had brought along a machete, one of the few metal tools to be found in New Eden. He began chopping into the brush.

"Ow! This stuff is sharp!" he exclaimed, sucking on his bleeding fingers.

It was tough making any headway using a single machete. The boys took turns holding the thorny giant fern fronds while one of them slashed at the brushwood. It was tedious work as the fronds would sometimes spring back, stinging them across the face. Scratched all over, they eventually found an opening into the fern woods where the vegetation had been trodden down by animals. They were not sure what animals lived there, but the paw prints were wide and deep.

Already hungry—perhaps more nervous than hungry—Hansel began snacking on a bag of nuts. As they pushed their way into the thorny bushes, the sharp brush began to thin out. It seemed that the dense bushes were only at the periphery of the forest. The terrain sloped gently. In the distance, the boys could see a sunny spot without ferns or brushwood.

"This way?" asked Adam.

"I would say so," responded Horst. "We haven't come this far to turn back now. We're going to have some explaining to do once we get home. We're scratched and filthy!"

They walked briskly, soon finding themselves out of the shadows, bathed in sunlight. It was a relief to have left the darkness of the fern wood behind them and to feel the healing warmth of the sun. Stopping to rest, they found themselves encircled by clusters of flowers with brilliantly colored blooms interspersed with rows of tall silver grasses which rippled like a sea of silk. The place was truly beautiful. Just ahead, they could make out what appeared to be the rim of the crater.

"A sinkhole of some kind," observed Horst.

"What's a sinkhole?" asked Adam.

"A sinkhole is the result of an underground layer of soil washing away," explained Horst.

"How does it wash away?" asked Hansel, digging into his almost empty bag of trail mix.

"Sometimes sinkholes form when the rock underground is dissolved by water, because of acid in the water. When the acidic water washes away rock, caves and sinkholes are created."

"How do you know this stuff? I don't remember learning this at school!"

"I don't know, Hansel. I like to read about different things," said Horst.

By now they had reached the rim of the crater which had a diameter of about three hundred feet. It was covered with vines which reinforced the earthen sides; a rocky trail wound its way down to the pond which sparkled at its center, some twenty feet below.

The boys assumed that the pond looked safe enough for a swim. Carefully, they scrambled down the trail and descended into the crater. The rocks were very sharp. When they finally reached the bottom, they stripped, placing their tunics in a heap near the trail. The pond formed almost a perfect circle and seemed to be very deep, especially near the center.

"Ready, set, jump!" yelled Adam.

The three boys jumped in the water which turned out to be quite warm. After struggling through the wood, play time came as a welcome reprieve; the tepid water soothed all their cuts and scrapes, relaxing them so much that they stopped splashing each other and began to float on their backs instead.

They were having a good time, until Horst motioned to his friends to be quiet. In the stillness, they could hear a panting sound, punctuated by loud barking. Above them, a pack of black dogs patrolled the rim of the sinkhole, their massive jowls dripping with frothing saliva. One of the dogs—the largest—slithered down the rugged trail to the pond and began to drink. The boys held their breath, treading water as gently as possible so as not to give themselves away. At first, the dog seemed unaware of their presence. It slurped water from the edge of the pond, not looking up for a good five minutes. Then, stepping away from the water, it pressed its snout to the ground and sniffed its way to their clothes and backpacks. Within seconds, it had shredded their lunch bags and started to devour the sandwiches. This attracted the attention of the rest of the pack which came thundering down the trail in search of food.

Terrified, Hansel gave a sudden kick, scattering waves across the surface of the pond. The first dog—the alpha—looked up from the sandwiches and snarled. Immediately, the whole pack of wild dogs began to run up and down the edge of the pond in a frenzy, as if waiting for the signal to leap in.

"Do dogs swim?" spluttered Hansel as the four of them swam away from the edge of the pond.

"Of course, dogs swim! Haven't you ever heard of the 'dog paddle'?" panted Horst. "But I don't think they can swim underwater! Let's go!"

Taking a deep breath, Horst dove underneath the surface, descending deeper and deeper until he reached a jagged hole in the side of the pond. Hoping to find an air pocket, he swam through the hole and surfaced inside a cave. To his relief, there was a smooth platform of algae-covered rock and though it was slippery, he was able to hoist himself out of the water. Standing upright, he was surprised to find that he could not only breathe but that the cave was illumined by a mysterious light.

He turned to make a comment to Adam, but suddenly realized that his friends hadn't followed him. He had dived but they had not followed him. Immediately, Horst dove back into the water, swam out of the hole and resurfaced close to Adam and Hansel. The boys were screaming in terror, splashing water at the lead dog which was almost upon them.

"C'mon, follow me!" yelled Horst. He dove underwater again, and, this time, his friends followed. Once in the cavern, they were safe from the dogs, *but where were they?*

Chapter 3

THE BOYS SAT ON A SMOOTH ROCK LEDGE AT THE ENTRANCE to the cavern, catching their breath beneath a canopy of gleaming stalactites; on each side of the ledge, sharp stalagmites pointed upwards, in places fusing with the formations above. Water dripped slowly from the roof of the underwater cavern, the sound of each droplet echoing in the silence.

"Man, was that a close call!" said Adam, dangling his thin legs in the water.

"You ain't kiddin'!" spluttered Hansel. "Those dogs would have torn us apart!"

Adam was in a state of shock. He was not as strong a swimmer as the other boys and the ordeal had left him breathless. Then he asked Horst, "How did you know there was a cave here?"

Horst said, "Got lucky, I guess. Like I said, the pond was in a sinkhole. A lot of times if you see a sinkhole there are also caves."

"So, were inside a cave?" asked Adam.

"Yeah, I think so," Horst said. "Let's hope it goes somewhere."

Adam was amazed by Horst knowledge of obscure things like sinkholes and caves.

For a few moments, nobody spoke. Looking up, Horst noticed that the stalactites and stalagmites seemed to be on fire, seeming more like dancing flames than rock formations; however, they were cold to the touch and the light they reflected came not from within but from another source. Then he remembered the light he had seen earlier before he had gone back to rescue his friends. He stood up, moving slowly so as not to slip on the algae-covered rock. Gingerly, he stepped from one stalagmite to the next, gripping tightly onto any limestone nodules within reach.

"Damn!" he said to himself as one of the nodules broke off.

Eventually, after a few further mishaps, he reached the back of the cavern. To his surprise, he couldn't look directly at the light because it was too bright. The light was trapped inside a glass bulb which was connected to a box made of metal. He had seen metal before, but it was rare in New Eden. The metal box was connected to a long metal thing that was attached to the wall.

"Come on, you guys, over here!" yelled Horst. "But be careful, and try not to break off the stalagmites!"

Adam and Hansel made their way towards Horst.

"You see this metal thing on the walls? It seems to be supplying power for this light. I guess it must lead to a way out of here," said Horst. "Let's follow it!"

"But our clothes . . ." stammered Adam.

"Forget the clothes," said Horst. "And the backpacks. I'll bet those dogs shredded everything."

"It's too bad—I still had some trail mix left," muttered Hansel.

"Do you really want to get your trail mix while the dogs are still outside?" asked Adam.

As they followed the metal thing, the cavern got darker, until it became pitch black. The thing was narrow but round, rather like the clay pipes they made for plumbing but with a much smaller diameter. Holding onto the metal thing as a guide, they made their way through the cave, with Horst leading the way.

As it turned out, a flat path ran parallel to the metal thing, so except for those moments when they occasionally hit their heads on stalactites, the boys made good progress. Eventually, Horst felt a metal box; it had a little lever on it. Instinctively, he flipped the lever, and another light turned on, revealing a much larger cavern. The ceiling was a smooth dome of limestone that glistened from the moisture on its surface. A little stream coursed its way down the center of the cavern, and, on their right, water dripped from a giant stalagmite that thrust upwards like a witch's finger. On the other side of the cavern, there was a door.

"Predictable!" exclaimed Horst.

"The light thing had to go somewhere. Right, Horst?" said Adam.

"You got it!" said Horst. "Now, let's see where the door goes!"

He tested the handle, to find the door unlocked. Motioning to the others to be quiet, he opened the door and they entered a well-lit room, unlike anything they had ever seen in New Eden. Boxes were neatly stacked on tables and shelves while open bins overflowing with raw cotton and wool were scattered all over the floor. To their surprise, little flying machines were picking up the cotton and wool, transferring the fiber to an adjacent room.

The flying machines did not seem to be alarmed by the boys' presence; in fact, they navigated around the boys as they walked into their flight path, ignoring them, with a singular purpose. In amazement, the friends continued to explore, soon finding another room filled with bins of cotton and wool, as well as baskets of corn. Further on, there were other rooms containing rocks and minerals, and some rooms in which there were large tanks.

A man's voice startled them.

"So, you've found this secret place!"

Terrified, they spun around and were mortified to see The Leader, Graham. He was dressed casually, not in his usual ceremonial church garb. His trademark iridescent green necklace was also missing. To their surprise, the typically stern man was grinning. They were conscious of being naked but had nothing to cover themselves with.

"Who told you that you were naked?" he quipped, well aware that the boys would not understand the biblical reference. "There are no fig leaves here, but don't worry about that small detail. The place is interesting, isn't it? Well, sooner or later I needed to explain a few facts. It's fortunate that you were able to find your way here on your own. This will save me some explaining."

"What is all this about, Father Leader?" asked Adam. "And what do fig leaves have to do with anything?"

Without responding, The Leader calmly walked toward a wall, motioning to the boys to join him. With a wave of his hand, a hexagonal opening appeared. This increased in size until there was large portal for them to step through. On the other side of the portal was a room with a smooth floor. The boys sat down together on a large comfortable sofa while Leader Graham sat behind a large desk. He leaned forwards in his chair, clasping his hands together in front of him on the desk.

"Now that you've discovered one of the mysteries of New Eden, I'm sure you're wondering what all this is about," he said solemnly.

"Let me start off with a question of my own: Have you ever wondered what happens with all the crops we grow in New Eden? Or have you wondered who cooks your meals and makes things like your jeans, for example?"

"Yes," answered Horst. "I've kind of wondered."

"Drones," said The Leader. "The Drones cook your meals and make a lot of things."

"What are drones?" asked Horst. "You mean those things flying around here?"

"Yes, those flying things are called drones. From raw materials, they make many of the things that we need here. They make thread from cotton, wool or flax; then they weave the thread into fabric. They prepare food for us. They maintain and fix many of the things we use here. Like worker bees, this is what the drones were designed for. Without them, life would be much harder and much less comfortable for us."

"Why hasn't anyone explained this to us before, Father Leader?" asked Adam, doing his best to sound respectful.

"You will learn . . . gradually. You see, there is much about our lives here— *your* lives here—which is too much for you to understand at a young age. The details are too much for a young mind to grasp all at once. In fact, I can only explain a little bit to you today. There is a time and place to understand the whole Truth."

The Leader pushed a series of buttons on his desk console. Within seconds, the hexagonal door opened and a small flying drone came into the room, carrying a tray of four fruit drinks with a little umbrella perched on the side of each clay cup.

"Please, have a drink. You look thirsty. I understand you were feeding the patrol dogs before you came to visit me." He said this as a statement rather than as a question. The boys eyed each other nervously, wondering what else he knew. Hansel guzzled his drink. It was quite good, including the pineapple slices. Horst and Adam simply held their drinks, listening intently.

"Some people may never be ready to understand the whole Truth," Leader Graham continued. "We're not quite certain how to introduce the transition period."

"The 'transition period'?" asked Horst.

"Let's not get too far ahead of ourselves," said The Leader. "Please bear with me, as I try to explain one thing at a time. Where should we begin? Frankly, we normally wait until your sixteenth birthday to explain these things. However, since you've discovered this place, the proverbial 'cat is out of the bag,' and I feel obligated to provide you with an explanation—as long as you can use some discretion and not tell your classmates."

"There have been many things that I've wondered about," observed Horst. "First, why are we called the 'Third' Thaw? I've seen the others from the Second Thaw, but I've never seen anybody from the First? What's that all about?"

He had already asked his own guardian keeper this question more than a dozen times but never got a straight answer, except, "Mind your own business!" What he said was true enough. New Eden had older people from the Second Thaw. Similar to Horst's group, the people from the Second were all the same age, but were five years older than the Third. They were now nineteen years old. This group of people, half of them male and half of them female, seemed to be attending some sort of vocational school.

The Leader took his time to answer Horst's question.

"There is a First Thaw group who are now twenty-five years old. Of course, I remember them when they were little babies."

"But where are they now, Father?" asked Adam.

"They have left New Eden to establish a new settlement. We assume that they are now married and are beginning to have their own children as families."

This last statement baffled the boys. What was a "family"? What did it mean to "have children"?

"It's getting late now," said The Leader. "Enough questions for today. It's time to take you home so that you can get washed up and have some supper."

"We left our clothes outside," objected Horst. "There's a pack of wild dogs out there. We could get killed!"

The Leader pressed some buttons on his desk. Within a minute, six drones flew into the room carrying the boys' clothes.

"The drones intercepted your clothes when your presence was discovered. You will see that your clothes have been washed and dried. I hope you don't mind the scent of the fabric softener. As for the dogs, don't worry about them. The dogs guard and protect our colony from intrusion by wild animals. Besides, you don't need to go through the forest in the same way that you came in. Please follow me."

The Leader took the boys through a door to the outside. There, they were amazed to see a very large vehicle. This thing was enormous. It had glass windows in the front, large wing shaped structures on each side, and was supported on wheels.

"I will explain what this vehicle is later. There will be a time and place, but now isn't the time," said The Leader.

As they followed him, they noticed an array of shiny reflective devices which were facing the sun. Adam was shocked to see that Miss Clare was sitting near the reflective devices.

"Clare! Clare!" yelled Adam. He ran over to his guardian, Miss Clare, but she seemed to be asleep. She was just sitting there on a chair, motionless. There was something connecting the chair to the big reflective devices.

"Now, now, no need to stop here," said The Leader. "Miss Clare is fine. She's just taking a rest."

"But she won't wake up!" said Adam.

"Don't worry, she's fine. I assure you," said The Leader.

He led the boys through a path in the sugar cane field. When they got to the front of the field, The Leader pressed a button, and an opening appeared in the bushes.

"I will see you tomorrow in church," said The Leader. "Please don't discuss what you saw today with the others. Remember, there will be a time and place when all of this will be explained to you."

Silently, Horst, Adam, and Hansel walked out of the sugar cane fields, back to their homes. A few hours later, Miss Clare appeared.

"How was your day, Adam?" she asked.

There was nothing wrong with her. She was the same as always. Adam decided not to tell her about what he had seen.

"I'm fine," said Adam.

"Did you do anything interesting?" asked Miss Clare.

"No. Nothing special," said Adam.

Chapter 4

MANY YEARS EARLIER, ON A TUESDAY MORNING IN CHIcago, Charles Timoshenko rode his bicycle on the "606" bicycle trail on his way to work. As was his custom, he had taken his bike on the Metra train to the Healy stop, near the beginning of the "606." Then, after riding just over two miles on the trail, he exited, narrowly missing a collision with another cyclist.

"Out of my way, asshole!" The other cyclist, a lean machine of testosterone, raced past him at breakneck speed. Regaining his balance, Charles shook his head. He had more near misses with cyclists than with cars, but was not ready to give up either the trail or his bike. Chicago, after all, had some of the finest bicycle trails in the country: the flat terrain made it easy to get from place to place, while Lake Michigan and the downtown cityscape created a stunning backdrop. At sixty-four, however, he could not afford any accidents. The possibility of a broken hip was not to be taken lightly, and though he was in excellent shape and at six foot two stood taller than most of his biking adversaries, he had a policy of giving way to anyone who was cycling faster than he was.

Having exited the 606 trail, Charles continued riding along the lakefront, heading south past Navy Pier, before turning west on Randolph Street. He secured his bike to a rack using two Kryptonite locks, then entered the Prudential Building, taking the elevator up to his office on the thirty-third floor. His windows overlooked Millennium Park, Chicago's crown jewel. Charles, however, would have preferred a lake view; for him, as a structural engineer, the exposed steel framing behind the Millennium Park Pavilion looked like a cheap Hollywood set.

Lately, he had been working on the design for a new building for the Bank of Hawaii on the island of Guam. Sometimes, he flew to Guam or the Mariana Islands on business. The sixteen-hour time difference between Guam and Chicago was a killer. He had countless late-night meetings talking to engineers in Guam who had just begun having their breakfast.

His surname, "Timoshenko," was of Ukrainian origin, although he had never been to that country. Many years before, in the 1930s, there was another quite famous structural engineer with the same surname, Stephen Timoshenko. In fact, Professor Stephen Timoshenko was the father of Engineering Mechanics at the University of Michigan; almost single-handedly, he changed the course of American engineering education.

In the early stages of Charles' career, he had been part of a team of independent-minded engineers who worked at Los Alamos National Lab in New Mexico; they called themselves "The D Group." Eventually declassified, their work became a commercially available computer application which radically changed the way structural engineers worked. Using "D-Soft," structural engineers everywhere were now able to realistically model the true behavior of structures in real time.

For example, the building Charles was designing in Guam had to withstand typhoon wind velocities exceeding two hundred miles per hour. Using D-Soft linked to a supercomputer in the Prudential Building, engineers in Guam were able to model the structural response of a new twenty-two story structure exposed to a Category 5 typhoon. D-Soft was also able to simulate the response of the building when it was subjected to a Richter 8.9 earthquake from the Mariana fault line.

This was fascinating research; however, after forty-two years of designing bridges and buildings, Charles found his work as routine as he imagined it would be making sandwiches at Subway. He could almost hear himself saying, "What do you want on this structure? Pickles and lettuce?" He was slowing down. His hearing was beginning to go and he already wore hearing aids. For the past four years, he had suffered from tinnitus, commonly referred to as "ringing in the ear"—in his case, a 4,000 cycle tone in his right ear. Fortunately, wearing hearing aids had significantly suppressed this ringing, and the tone no longer bothered him. He was beginning to think about retirement—but, then again, what would he do? Work at the local grocery store? Work at Trader Joe's? He couldn't really visualize himself as a check-out clerk, but perhaps they might let him draw signs or something.

"Good morning, Mary," said Charles, addressing the young intern who was sitting behind the receptionist's desk.

"Is Jennifer in yet?"

"Good morning, Mr. Timoshenko," answered Mary. "Yeah, she's inside."

Jennifer Bowles, Charles's daughter, was also a structural engineer; her specialty was designing harbor structures. Helmet in hand, Charles walked past reception and through the doorway leading to the office suite. He and Jennifer occupied adjacent offices, so he always stopped to greet her at the start of the workday.

"Hi, Dad!" said Jennifer, looking up from her computer screen.

"How's the Tinian project going?" asked Charles. From his daughter's expression, the question was unnecessary.

Jennifer grimaced. She was working on plans to rebuild the Tinian Island harbor—the same harbor installed in 1945 for the docking of the USS *Indianapolis* which had delivered the atomic bomb to Tinian Island. The old air strip was there, the old bomb pits were there, but after so many years the original steel sheet piling in the harbor had rusted away, creating what looked like a junk yard. In the past, several attempts to fix up the harbor had failed to get off the ground.

"Not too well," she said wearily. "The usual local politics of the island residents versus the Navy. Why is there so much governmental bureaucracy in the Pacific Islands? Why can't we just build the damn thing? Instead, every little decision, every design element is subject to government review."

"Yeah, Tinian isn't quite like Chicago," agreed Charles. "Seems like the federal red tape increases in an inverse relationship to a town's population. I'm next door if you need me."

~

Once in his office, he logged onto his computer to check his email; there was one marked, "Extremely Urgent!" from the NA, the National Academies—the nation's elite members of scientists, engineers, and physicians who advised the government on technology matters. For the past five years, Charles had been a member of the engineering branch, the National Academy of Engineering. Membership was by invitation only.

Protocol required Charles to use a special secure connection. All members of the NA had a special decoding box which they were required to keep in a locked vault. Charles opened a small safe in his office and took out his decoding box. He inserted a USB cable into the box and connected it to his computer. Shortly after, the logo of the National Academy of Science appeared on his screen, and, following a face scan and secret question, Charles' identity was authenticated. The familiar face of NA Chief Administrator, Susan Carlson, appeared on his monitor.

"Hi, Susan. I just got an 'Urgent' message. What's up?"

"Hi, Mr. Timoshenko. Yes, there will be an important meeting today at four p.m., Eastern Standard Time. You will be required to attend."

"What's it about?" asked Charles.

"I really don't know. Professor Kalinsky called for the meeting. I have not been allowed access to this one," said Susan. "It must be very important."

"Okay, I'll be there."

This gave him at least a couple of hours to get some work done.

He had a standing appointment that day at eleven a.m. at UIC, the University of Illinois at Chicago. For the past year, Charles had been involved in a special project jointly administered by UIC and the University of Michigan in Ann Arbor. Every Tuesday, he would go to the Artificial Intelligence Lab, Room 263, where he was interrogated by a highly sophisticated artificial intelligence program, called "Advanced Personality Simulator," or APS. The APS program asked Charles questions on every aspect of his life, as for example, his opinions on politics, music, books, and movies. Typical questions included: "How would you respond to this question?"; "What are you thinking about now?"; and "How did you feel about that?" Charles actually looked forward to these sessions and found the process quite therapeutic.

APS also directed Charles to participate in voice testing. Sometimes he was asked to sing (*"mah, mee, may, moe, moo"*), or tell jokes and stories. He was also instructed to make all sorts of faces—to grin and frown, yawn, move his jaw to the left and to right, raise his eyebrows in surprise, blink. More than once during these sessions, he caught himself laughing while narrating an experience; sometimes, he even broke down and cried, especially when remembering his Dad and Mom.

The existence of this project was not public information. The project was reserved for special individuals with expertise in various fields. In fact, for the past five years, at several universities throughout the world, many select people had been going through the same process. The objective of the program was to encapsulate their personalities and wisdom in an artificial intelligence program. It was an honor to participate, but the entire process required quite an investment of time and expense.

As a side benefit, if someone was selected for this program, all his or her family members were selected, too. Program administrators explained that it was important to gather an accurate database of personalities which had a relationship with each other. In a very real sense, the APS program promised a form of immortality for Charles and his family.

When Charles needed to log into the NA meeting, he entered the secure conferencing room in his office. He used this room on a regular basis with his conference calls to Guam. The room was only ten feet by ten feet. There was a soft-cushioned chair in the center with side tables. On the left side table were the virtual reality goggles, which Charles disliked wearing. They made him feel nauseous. On the right side table was a joystick.

Charles took a Dramamine tablet to lessen the seasick feeling which typically came over him during the virtual reality experience. The brain was not meant for the detached experience of virtual reality. When you are seeing things that are so real (when they are not) the body's vestibular system expects to feel real movement, not inertia. But he was getting better at navigating the experience. He had learned to resist the temptation to get up and walk around or try to reach out for things, no matter how real they seemed.

He had brought the NA security box with him into the room, as he could go through the security clearance procedures again. Having plugged the box into the USB connection port in the chair, he flipped on the overhead grid lights. Multiple pinpoint laser dots suddenly filled the room, at approximately one-inch spacing. The grid lights determined Charles' body position. The virtual reality communication system followed every movement and change of posture. "Okay, here we go," thought Charles, putting on the goggles. He had just enough time to log on and say hello to a few people.

As soon as Charles put on the virtual reality goggles, he was in a room filled with about two hundred people. Dr. Frank Erbstoesser, the nuclear chemist from St. Louis, sat to his right.

"Hello, Frank. Long time no see."

"*Freut mich!*" replied Dr. Erbstoesser, in German. "Charles Timoshenko! I haven't seen you since we were in Los Alamos. Where are you now?"

"Back in Chicago. How about you?"

"Still down in Saint Louis, although I just got back from the Institute for Theoretical Physics in Köln, Deutschland."

"Is that the reason for the momentary lapse into Deutsch?"

"*Na, ja. Ich bin* . . . I mean, I've lived in Switzerland for the past two years—almost feel like I've been forgetting my English."

Charles and Frank had worked together at Los Alamos when Frank was doing computer simulations of chemical reactions, using the laboratory's supercomputer. The computer was capable of simulating any physical event. The software was designed to analyze any chemical reaction, including all thermodynamic and fluid mechanics which would predict the chemical reaction's outcome.

Charles's involvement with the computer was on a more macroscopic level; he used it to simulate complex physical events in structures such as bridges and buildings.

"Do you know what this is about?" asked Charles.

"No, not at all."

The lights began to dim. A presenter suddenly appeared at the podium. During virtual reality events such as this, it would be difficult to have the presenter *actually* walk out to the podium because the presenter was in a little ten foot by ten foot room! Instead, people "appeared" out of nowhere. Virtual reality participants were limited to two basic positions: sitting in their chairs or standing up.

Charles recognized the speaker, a Professor Kalinsky from the University of Chicago. Just a few weeks ago, Charles and his family had run into the professor at The Snail Bar, a Thai restaurant on Fifty-Seventh Street in Hyde Park. The two men had immediately identified each other as members of the NA by the decorative pins they wore. Made of pewter, the pins depicted the image of an owl, without any inscription; however, there was actually a chip inside each pin that was used for identification purposes.

"Thank you all for coming today on such short notice," announced Professor Kalinsky. "As some of you know, I am Herbert Kalinsky from the University of Chicago. My specialty is Cosmology, with a particular interest in finding other planets in the Universe that are similar to Earth."

The professor paused to take a sip of water.

"It has been very challenging to find a planet that has certain important attributes of our Earth. We can easily find planets that are about the same size and which would have the same gravity. The problem is, Earth was subjected to a very unusual event early in its formation. I am sure that some of you, perhaps all of you, have heard of the Theia Hypothesis."

Charles had read something about this, or perhaps he had seen a show on NOVA or the Science Channel on the topic. He leaned back, eager for further information.

"The Theia Hypothesis proposes that 4.53 billion years ago a Mars-sized planet hit the early Earth at an oblique angle. This cataclysmic event resulted in the creation of the Moon. Before the collision, the Earth had no moon.

"After the collision, a large chunk of the earth along with the remains of Theia were ejected into orbit, and this is what became our moon. Originally, the moon orbited the Earth much more closely than it does today. Another side effect of this collision was that the colliding planet, Theia, was absorbed and combined with Earth. As a result, the center of our Earth has a molten iron core. There are extremely high pressures at the center of the Earth—enough pressure to sustain nuclear fission, which is what keeps the core of the Earth in a molten state.

"This collision is what makes Earth unique. It was a very fortunate event because the Earth's molten core generates the magnetic field, which protects life from the powerful particles emitted from the Sun. If this magnetic field did not exist, most life on Earth would be killed by the Sun's particles."

The professor then turned on a PowerPoint presentation. The slide showed the orbit of a planet around a sun-like star.

"The NASA Kepler Space Telescopes mission has been designed to identify planets that are one-half to twice the size of Earth. So far, it has found 1,000 such 'exo-planets.' Of particular interest is planet K438b which is 1,500 light-years away. Another planet is K851b, which is only twenty-three light-years away.

"K438b is orbiting a red dwarf star. One day, our own sun will degenerate into a red dwarf star. Eventually, the sun will collapse, as do all stars after they have used up all their nuclear fuel. The Earth could become like K438b in a few billion years.

"K851b is more interesting. Based on Kepler's observations of K851b, it appears to have a magnetic field. It is about the same size as Earth, therefore it must have about the same gravity. It has about the same orbit around its star as does the Earth. Based on spectral readings, this planet is likely to have water, although we can't say how much. In conclusion, this is the best candidate out of 1,000 exo-planets."

Leaning on the podium, the professor paused, looking around the virtual room.

"With that introduction, we will be taking a break. You can all disconnect your virtual connections, if you like, and do whatever you need to. We will be reconvening in . . . Let me see, now it's 4:47 p.m. How about if we meet back here at five p.m., EST?"

Charles took off his goggles and got out of his chair. So far, he was not at all nauseated. He stretched and after going to the rest room, headed to the lunchroom where he grabbed a can of mineral water.

～

Very interesting talk, so far. A new planet—actually two new planets. He found himself wondering what the new planet should be called. When he returned to the conference, a new speaker appeared in front of the audience. This was a military man, an army general, judging by the stars on his uniform.

"Okay, boys and girls, back to your seats," the general said.

That remark got few giggles. Irritated, Charles whispered to Frank, "What a schmuck!"

"I'm General Leslie Mitchell. Now that we've heard our little bedtime story I need to break the bad news. All is not hunky-dory in space. We have determined a very real threat to our planet." There was a sudden hush among the scientists and engineers in the audience. Charles listened intently.

"Some of you may recall the space probe, New Horizons, which took photos of the dwarf planet Pluto in 2015. New Horizons was launched in 2006. It took nine years to travel three billion miles to Pluto. Nine years!"

he emphasized. "I mean, it took that long to get to another planet in our own solar system. So why *the hell* are we interested in planets that are light-years away?"

Good point, thought Charles. *What was this about?*

"Our boys at NASA aren't too concerned about the disparity between reality and science fiction. They say that we can send small spacecraft to these planets that are light-years away, using present technology. It will take a long time for these spacecraft to get to these planets. A very, very long time.

"After New Horizons took snapshots of Pluto, it just kept on going and going like an Energizer Bunny. It's still out there, going and going. And it is still fully functioning, because occasionally we get communications."

The general cleared his throat, as if about to make some portentous announcement.

"Now what I am about to tell you must not leave this room. You must not tell your families. And for God's sake, *don't tell the media!* Even NASA doesn't have all the details yet, so zip your mouths and keep it quiet. *You got that?*"

Nobody answered.

"Hey! Is anybody out there? I said, you got that?"

"Yes, Sir!" said some of the group. Charles shifted uneasily in his chair; there was a twinge in his stomach that had nothing to do with the experience of virtual reality. He reached for the Dramamine bottle but made no attempt to remove the cap.

"Still didn't hear you. You got that?"

"Yes, Sir!" the group said in unison. There was a buzz in the room, a murmur of anxious voices.

"Well, good. I'm glad we agree *to shut our mouths about this.* Back to the subject at hand, New Horizons has been sending back information about other large bodies in our solar system—asteroids, comets, other dwarf planets. Well, recently, it reported the existence of a low visibility asteroid in the Oort Cloud, which is approximately one hundred miles in diameter. Based on orbital projections, there is a seventy-six percent possibility this asteroid may hit the Earth, in just ten years."

Chapter 5

ADAM SAT WITH HIS FRIENDS, HORST AND HANSEL, IN THE mess hall. Miss Clare brought Adam his usual breakfast of bacon, eggs, and bread. She also gave him a cup of something hot.

"What's this?" he asked, smelling it suspiciously. The aroma was bitter, unlike anything he had smelled before.

"I thought we'd try something new today. It's coffee. You've heard of coffee, right? Today is a big day. You're sixteen years old. I've made coffee for you, on this big day, to celebrate."

He tasted the coffee. He didn't like it.

"Yuck!"

"Try it with cream and sugar."

He mixed in a teaspoon of sugar and a little milk. It tasted less bitter. "I suppose it's okay."

"It will help you wake up in the morning," said Miss Clare.

After breakfast, the three boys walked to school one block away. It had been three years since their adventure in the fern woods. To their credit, they had kept the promise they made to The Leader, telling no one about their adventure escaping the killer dogs and finding the mysterious warehouse.

During the past three years, each of the fifteen teenagers of the Third Thaw had been learning new skills which they would use as adults. Adam was becoming a proficient draftsman, making drawings of buildings and bridges. Similarly, Hansel had become an expert builder. He and Adam made a good team. Adam was the "idea guy" and Hansel was the "builder guy." Adam could easily come up with concepts for buildings while Hansel intuitively understood what it would take to build them.

Horst's interests were more varied. As usual, his mind wandered, and he was reading a great variety of subjects. Recently, he had begun learning how to write computer programs using a language called "Visual Basic."

Eileen had become quite an accomplished pianist, with a vast repertoire. Having mastered the piano pieces of Bach, Beethoven, and Mozart, she was now learning Chopin. The waltzes, mazurkas, études and nocturnes were evocative, chromatic, and emotional.

As young girls, Gertrude and Eva had learned to make yarn from wool and how to knit. They were now becoming experts in fabric making.

Ingrid was Miss Angelique's star pupil; she excelled in science, especially biological studies. In her free time, which amounted to a few hours on Sunday afternoon, she sketched plants and animals. She had amassed a collection of sketches of the native life-forms in New Eden. These she kept in a notebook, along with her notes about the various species.

Today was a special day for the Third Thaws; today was everyone's sixteenth birthday, not just Adam's. The Guardians had planned a special event in the Auditorium of New Eden School so the students assembled promptly at nine a.m. Upon entering, they were surprised to see The Leader standing on the stage. He was wearing the golden suit he wore on Sundays, along with the emerald green necklace.

"Good morning class," said The Leader.

"Good morning, Father," responded the class in unison.

"You may be wondering why I am here this morning. I have known you children all your lives. Today is an important day, your sixteenth birthday. This day marks another transition in your path to becoming adults."

What is an adult? wondered Adam. *Is it a Guardian? Am I becoming a Guardian?*

Remembering his shock at seeing Miss Clare sitting motionless in a chair connected to a reflective device, he shuddered. Since that day he no longer felt so close to Miss Clare. Until then, his entire life he had felt comfortable talking to her; now he felt uncomfortable, as he realized there was something strange about her.

The Leader continued: "Your group is the third to go through this presentation. We have learned a few lessons from the first two groups. There is no way around it: you will be shocked."

He paused, allowing the teenagers to whisper among themselves. Eventually, when whispers turned into louder talking and commotion, The Leader raised his hand to silence them. "Quiet, please! Settle down, I want to share some important information with you. Let me get to the point. We—all of us here in New Eden—are not from New Eden. We come from another place called 'Earth.'"

Not surprisingly, this statement caused something of an uproar. Seeing Zelda on the verge of tears, Gerald squeezed her hand to comfort her. Gertrude and Eva linked arms, as if to support one another, while Horst edged closer to Ingrid.

Adam sprung to his feet. "What do you mean, Father? I have always lived here."

"Yes—and no," said The Leader. "Adam, it is true you were born here in New Eden, but you were not conceived here. You were conceived in a place called 'Earth' which you have probably learned about in your studies. You children are the result of a great civilization on the planet Earth, which is very, very far away."

Again, the students began talking to each other.

"What does it mean to be 'conceived'?" Horst asked Ingrid.

The girl blushed but said nothing, clutching tightly to her notebook.

"You know, don't you?" said Horst. "Why have you never spoken of this?"

Before Ingrid could reply, The Leader once again raised his hands.

"Please calm down. I don't want to go too far into the details immediately. Your education has trained you in certain essential skills required in society—reading, writing, mathematics, music, art. But we have carefully omitted one subject from your education: history. You have not learned your history. You will begin learning your history as of today."

Horst's head began to hurt. This was too much to comprehend. He actually felt sick. Some of the other kids, in fact, looked as if they were about to throw up.

"Children, so far, we have been very careful raising you, taking small steps. We are preparing you for something much bigger than your little world here in New Eden. Someday you will no longer need us."

Horst couldn't hold back any longer. "Wait a minute. What do you mean, by 'us'? *Who are you?*"

The Leader paused. He gave a signal to the Guardian teachers who slowly walked up to the stage. One by one, they climbed the steps, standing to his right and to his left. Miss Clare, the housekeeper Guardian, also went to the stage. Ten Guardians lined up in a row next to The Leader; none of them showed any emotion but looked straight ahead.

The Leader gave a signal and the Guardians rolled up their shirtsleeves. In perfect synchrony, each one in the group opened a little door in his or her right arm. There was a tangle of wires in each portal inside their arms; next, they simultaneously opened another door located in their stomachs. There were more wires inside.

"As you can see, we are not like you," said The Leader. "On Earth, the term they use is 'Robot.' We Guardians are robots. We are not organic life-forms. We are machines. Our purpose here is to raise you and take care of you during the early stages of your growth.

"We have almost finished our task."

Chapter 6

WITHOUT A WORD, WITHOUT ANY DISPLAY OF EMOTION, the Guardians left the Auditorium stage in single file. To everyone's surprise, the twenty-one-year-olds from the Second Thaw walked up to the stage and stood before the Third Thaws. The Second Thaws had always been responsible for the more difficult tasks, such as maintaining the kilns.

Jim, a Second Thaw, grabbed the microphone.

"Five years ago, when we were sixteen years old, we learned the truth about our lives here. To be quite honest, I am still shocked. But since that time when we learned the truth of our purpose here, we've been discovering a little bit more each day.

"In the next five years, you, too, will be learning more about our people's history on Earth. Our purpose here is of the utmost importance. We are literally continuing the very existence of the human race. We represent the human race's last hope of preserving itself."

Jim paused, allowing his words to sink in.

"When we turned sixteen, Father Leader explained our assigned role and that the Guardians' basic function was to raise us. The First Thaw explained these things to us. The First Thaw was the true pioneering generation here in New Eden! Some of you may remember the First Thaws from when you were very little. All of them left New Eden about the time of your eleventh birthday . . ."

His voice trailed off and, for a few seconds, he seemed overcome by emotion. Then, regaining control, he continued, his voice a little softer now.

"Soon, those of us of the Second Thaw will also be leaving New Eden. Then, in five years, at the conclusion of your training and preparation, you, too, will be leaving, too. Then, five years after you leave, the last of us, the Forth Thaw will need to leave New Eden. This is what is expected. And this will be your purpose: to colonize this planet."

Because of their adventure in the fern wood three years before, some of this information was not new to Adam, Hansel, and Horst. They had known that the First Thaw were somewhere "out there," living on their own. The First Thaw probably had families and children, although the concept of "having children" didn't quite make sense to them yet.

Horst was the first to raise his hand.

"Why do we need to leave? What will happen to the Guardians?"

The Leader returned to the stage and took the microphone from Jim.

"We could continue to take care of you, but that is not the mission you were sent for. You were sent here to colonize this planet and perpetuate your species. There are only fifteen in your group now. We anticipate that gradually your group will grow and build new cities here."

Eileen asked, "Father Graham, how many people were on Earth?"

"Based on our last communications with Earth, there were eleven billion people," he responded. "As adults, you will not need Guardians to take care of you. You will be able to take care of yourselves—at least, that is our hope. You will be the pioneers of this planet making it into a new Earth. Besides, we Guardians can't come with you on your journey. We are tied to New Eden. The source of our power—literally our 'brains' as you would say—comes from the supercomputer located on our landing craft. We are not autonomous creatures. We must remain near the landing craft, where the supercomputer is located. The supercomputer onboard the landing craft controls our personalities. Everything we say to you, every action we take, is actually the result of the supercomputer's artificial intelligence programs."

"Where is the landing craft?" asked Horst.

"In the fern woods, in our production warehouse. It's in the same place that you, Adam, and Hansel discovered when you were fourteen years old."

This last remark prompted remarks from the other students.

"What's this about a production warehouse?" asked Eileen.

"Just outside New Eden, in the fern woods, there is a production warehouse, where our worker drones make things. We also have some animals they had on Earth," explained The Leader.

"What do you mean, 'had on Earth'?" asked Horst.

"We are no longer certain if Earth exists, Horst."

After digesting this answer, Horst had another question.

"How long did the spacecraft travel from Earth to this planet?"

"The journey took approximately 80,000 years," said The Leader.

"Eighty-thousand years! How could anything survive a journey of that length?" exclaimed Horst.

"Your spacecraft traveled at a speed of 192,000 miles per hour. Although that speed is fast, it is just a fraction of light speed. Our biggest concern in making the journey was potential damage to the spacecraft caused by micro space dust. The faster the ship, the more damage that space dust would cause to the spacecraft.

"It was decided to take a truly long approach, using experimental nuclear thermal rocketry, with a maximum speed of 192,000 miles per hour, and a relatively small space craft. We realized that the journey would take a long time, but time is immaterial to lives that have not yet been born. You were frozen embryos.

"From an engineering perspective, the main issue of such a long voyage was potential material corrosion. In other words, would the materials of the ship break down over 80,000 years? Our engineers thought long and hard about this. It was decided that the best way to prevent material breakdown was to let all of the spacecraft's components freeze in space. The temperature of space is minus 455 degrees Fahrenheit, which is just a few degrees absolute zero. At that temperature, all chemical processes, hence corrosion, will stop."

"But who steered the spaceship?" asked Horst. "How was it even possible to pilot such a ship for such a long time?"

"Only a small onboard computer was required for navigational purposes during the entire journey. Because ceramics exhibit little or no corrosion, a special navigational computer was engineered using ceramic components, which was designed to operate at very low temperature and could the 80,000 year journey. When the craft approached the target planet, the onboard computer began the heating process, gradually thawing the major systems that were necessary for landing on the planet from absolute zero. When a suitable landing site was determined, the space craft landed—in fact, the site was just a short distance behind the sugar cane fields."

Horst had no further questions. He whistled softly under his breath, giving his classmates the opportunity to voice their own concerns.

Chapter 7

THE LEADER EXITED THE SCHOOL WITH THE STUDENTS FOL-lowing. heading toward the sugar cane fields. For the most part, they were silent, overwhelmed by all they had learned that day.

Horst had conflicting emotions. On the one hand, he was excited by the story of his origins and the mission that lay ahead; on the other, he, like his classmates, had just learned that every adult they looked up to, loved, and learned from was nothing more than a machine—a robot programmed to take care of their needs as humanly as possible.

What would a human Guardian have been like? What would it have been like to have had a real, flesh and blood parent, or a Leader with a beating heart? How come he had never noticed that The Guardians were sometimes reluctant to answer questions and that they occasionally seemed inflexible, as if incapable of adjusting to new situations?

Looking at Gerald and Zelda who were walking ahead of him, arm in arm, Horst found himself wishing that he had someone with whom he could share his thoughts and feelings. From that day on, he told himself, he would no longer confide in the Guardians.

When they arrived at the sugar cane fields, rows of sugar cane bowed towards each other as they had done when Adam first observed the Guardians entering the opening. The Leader stepped forward under the archway formed by the supple stalks. As they followed, a large building came into view.

It was not an adobe structure like the homes in which they lived; rather, it was constructed of very smooth bricks which were identical in size and color. Suddenly a group of dogs appeared, barking ferociously at the Third

Thaws. Terrified, the teens froze in place. Gertrude and Eileen screamed, while Zelda buried her face in Gerald's chest, he tightened his arms around her. Only Ingrid seemed calm, more intent on observing the creatures' behaviors than staying safe.

Calmly, The Leader instructed the dogs to "stay"; immediately, they sat on their haunches, panting loudly. Each dog had a small box-like device on its collar.

"Don't pet these dogs," said The Leader, "they are trained to protect New Eden from outside predators. They are trained to kill."

"What are those things on their collars?" asked Horst.

"Those devices inflict a high pitched painful noise into the dog's ears if they attempt to enter New Eden," said The Leader. "The dogs are restricted to the border around New Eden, starting here at the sugar cane fields."

"Do they actually kill animals?" asked Hansel.

"Yes, they kill the native animals, practically every day," said The Leader in a voice that to Horst now seemed very monotone.

"There are native animals outside New Eden which we must prevent from entering our community. When they attempt to invade New Eden—which is basically all the time—the dogs attack. The dogs live off their killings. We never need to feed them."

The group entered the building. As before, there were many worker drones flying from one room to another, carrying raw materials and finished products. They altered their flight patterns around the teenagers, as if able to detect their presence.

"This room holds basic materials. We have drones outside who gather materials from plants—sticks, honey, cotton, fiber."

"What about the food we eat?" asked Horst.

"Yes, the drones cook most of the food we eat."

"How big was the vehicle that brought us here?" asked Hansel.

The Leader said, "I will be showing you the vehicle shortly."

"But how did you fit all the animals on board?"

"The animals and you were shipped here as frozen embryos," said The Leader.

"And it was your job to thaw us?" asked Horst.

"Correct," said the Leader. "Our job was to thaw you, so that you could complete the gestation process, inside what we call 'birthing units.' We have fifteen birthing units, which have been used for the gestation of all the human and animal embryos that were transported here. The birthing units have been in continuous use for many years. Even now they are being used to gestate some animals."

"Were the killer dogs once embryos that were thawed?" asked Horst.

"Yes, the dogs were thawed and gestated in birthing units. All the Earth animals were brought here as embryos—chickens, sheep, pigs, cows—all the animals that are necessary for your existence. We even brought bees to pollinate the crops."

"How many human embryos were shipped?" asked Gertrude.

"They shipped sixty human embryos. So far we have been successful delivering four groups of fifteen embryos. You were the third group to be unfrozen. This is why you are called the 'Third Thaw,'" explained The Leader.

Everyone looked at each other, as if a light had suddenly turned on. So this was the reason for their strange name!

"What animals are the birthing units gestating now?" asked Ingrid.

"Currently, ducks," he responded. "Now, follow me and I will show you the ship."

Intrigued, the group followed him to what looked like a seamless wall; there were neither windows nor doors, but only a keypad of sorts that was situated to the left of the wall. The Leader entered a code and the wall began to move, revealing a sliding door that led into a vast room with a domed ceiling. There it was, the landing craft.

Craning their necks, the Third Thaws looked up, finding themselves completely dwarfed by what resembled a massive white bird; towering over them, it was very shiny and had wings. There were cables running from the landing craft. Lights were blinking inside.

"This is the craft that brought us here," said The Leader in a matter-of-fact voice. "It is actually something called a 'space shuttle.' The American government had three space shuttles available for the mission which was planned on very short notice. The shuttles were loaded with all the things that we need here."

Adam asked, "Can we go inside and take a look?"

"I'm sorry, but I can't take you inside the landing craft," said The Leader. "This is a highly secure area. But I can describe what is inside the craft. There is a supercomputer and a power source. These two things must never be disturbed, since they are critical to our operations on New Eden. There are also many cryogenic storage lockers, which are used to store the embryos."

"You said that this is only a part of the ship that brought us here," remarked Adam. "Where is the other part?"

"The interstellar transport engines are in orbit. They used nuclear thermal rocketry, and they are massive. Once the space vehicle reached our atmosphere, the shuttle separated from the engines, and glided to this spot."

"What will happen to the interstellar engines?" asked Horst. "Will they just stay up there forever?"

"No. They will eventually crash. We have detected a slight decay in their orbit. We predict the engines will crash in about fifteen years. " The Leader motioned for the group to follow him, then stopped abruptly.

"By the way, let me introduce my helper drone, Buzzy."

A little drone that had been shadowing him unobtrusively, made a beeping sound, as if to say "Hi!" to the group.

The Leader said, "Buzzy and some of the other autonomous drones can help you on your future journeys. You can use them to scout areas, fetch materials, and act as servants."

Buzzy beeped in agreement.

The Leader walked them into another room where the group recognized some of the Guardians. They were sitting motionless and showed no signs of recognizing the Third Thaws.

"This is where we maintain the Guardians," explained The Leader. "Notice the large panels facing the sun? Those panels are converting sunlight into electricity, which we store in batteries. Every night, the Guardians come here for charging."

Adam recalled seeing Clare connected to cables; now he understood.

"So, you charge the Guardians with electricity? *Every night?*"

"Yes, we charge them with electricity," said The Leader. "The Guardians are robots and need to be maintained. Quite frankly, this is a major concern of ours. It is important that you successfully establish your lives here before the machines wear out. We have finite resources in our colony."

Adam was angry about this entire situation. It was bad enough to know that he'd been raised by robots, but now knowing the Guardians would not be around in the future was something he was not ready for. From the looks on his friends' faces, they, too, were in shock.

Trying to stay focused on the tour, the group followed The Leader to a narrow hallway with multiple doors.

"This is our virtual reality corridor. There are fifteen separate rooms here, each is equipped with virtual reality equipment. Tomorrow you will begin the long process of learning about Earth in these rooms. You will find this most interesting. Please walk back to your homes . . . and watch out for the dogs. Tomorrow, be back here at nine a.m. sharp for your lessons in the virtual reality rooms. Good afternoon!"

Chapter 8

THE NEXT DAY, THE THIRD THAWS ARRIVED IN THE ARTIFI-
cial Intelligence Corridor. The Leader was there to greet them.

"Good morning students," said The Leader. "Today we begin the next part of your education. You will be meeting your families from Earth."

"Our families?" spluttered Adam, not sure if he had heard correctly.

"Yes. You will see for yourselves shortly," said the Leader. "Each of you will be assigned a room. Let's see, Adam is in Room 1. Ainslie is in Room 2. . . ."

Adam entered Room 1. The room was about ten feet by ten feet square. There was a chair in the center, with tables on each side. On top of one table were a pair of strange looking goggles; on the other was a joystick. In another part of the room was a bicycle.

Just as Adam was about to put on the goggles, The Leader appeared in the doorway.

"Just one word of caution: when you begin using the virtual reality goggles, don't stand up unless you are told that it's okay to stand up."

As soon as The Leader had closed the door, the room was filled with little pin-sized lights.

Adam heard The Leader's voice through a speaker.

"Okay, everyone. Please sit down and put on your goggles. This session will last approximately two hours. If at any time you feel dizzy, or if you feel nauseous, please take off the goggles immediately. If this happens, don't worry. We can give you a medication to alleviate your vertigo."

Adam put on the goggles. He was sitting in front of a man—a very old man with gray hair. He had never seen gray hair before; The Leader's hair, of course, was white, but, somehow it didn't age him. This man's skin, unlike The Leader's, looked wrinkled. He was wearing something with glass lenses on his nose. His eyes were looking through the glass lenses.

"Hello, Adam. My name is Charles. Charles Timoshenko."

"Hello, Charles," responded Adam, hesitantly. He didn't quite get the last part of this man's complicated name.

"I am your grandfather," continued Charles. "Actually, I am a simulated version of your grandfather, thanks to something called the 'APS.'"

Adam had absorbed so many surprises in the past couple of days, that he simply resigned himself to the information. He wasn't sure what this term, "grandfather," meant.

"What do you mean, 'grandfather'?" asked Adam.

"My daughter is your mother. You were conceived by your father and mother. I am the father of your mother," said Charles.

"Who is my mother?"

"Your mother's name is Jennifer. Her last name is 'Bowles.' You will be meeting her shortly. Your father is Joseph Bowles, who you will also be meeting."

"Why do you have two names?" asked Adam.

"On Earth there are many, many people. At one time people had only one name, but, as the population grew, people were given last names to distinguish between individuals. Sometimes the last names reflected what people did for a living. For example, the surname, 'Shoemaker' was initially assigned to a man who made shoes."

"What is your last name again. Timo . . . ?" asked Adam.

"Timoshenko. It is from a country called 'Ukraine,' where my ancestors—where *your* ancestors—came from. But I am an American."

This was a lot of information for Adam to digest. "Timoshenko," "Ukraine," "America." Everything was a foreign concept.

Charles continued.

"When the mission was planned we realized this might be overwhelming. But there was no other way. We must start from scratch. This is all for the better."

"I don't understand," said Adam.

"I know you don't, but eventually it will all make sense to you. We will teach you about where you came from, about Earth, America, and our history. We will teach you as much as possible about the good things and some of the bad things. You represent a fresh start. We don't expect things to turn out perfectly for you. Human beings are not perfect. We are flawed, but that makes life interesting."

Adam looked steadily at Charles, trying to absorb every detail about him. He looked old like a Guardian, but there was something different about him. Yes, he looked real—that was it! His speech also sounded more real than that of the Guardians who tended to speak in a monotone.

"I see that you are looking at my skin. I appear real. My skin is like yours. My mannerisms are real. Unfortunately, *this,*" he said pointing to himself, " . . . this is all an illusion. I am a simulation, created by a computer program called the 'Artificial Personality Simulator' or 'APS.' I am as real as possible. I was developed from many hours of sessions with the real Charles Timoshenko on Earth."

"But where is the real Charles Timoshenko?" asked Adam.

This time Charles—the programed simulation of Charles—paused.

"The real Charles Timoshenko has passed away. If he were alive, he would be 80,064 years old today. But don't worry about him—he had a very full life. My APS program encapsulated the real Charles' personality when he was sixty-four years old. Of course, the real Charles died at some point during our journey."

Adam was silent. *What was the meaning of "died"?*

"Don't let this discourage you," Charles continued. "You can treat me like a real person. I have much of Charles' thoughts and stories and knowledge. I knew him better than anybody . . . I probably understand him better than he understood himself! You can treat me as your real grandfather. That's my purpose here. But let us take a short break. I'll see you here in ten minutes."

With that, Adam took off his goggles. When he stood up, he grabbed the back of his chair as a wave of vertigo swept over him. Once he regained his balance, he entered the corridor. His other classmates were also coming out of their rooms. Eileen was crying. Gerald and Zelda were holding each other tightly. Hansel looked white and numb. Nobody talked. Of all the group, Horst seemed to have handled the experience the best.

After the break, Adam returned to the room, sat in his chair and put on his goggles. This time he saw a beautiful woman.

"Hello, Adam. I am Jennifer. I am your mother," she said.

Adam stared at the image in front of him.

"Hello . . . *Jennifer* . . ." he said, hesitating for a moment.

"You can call me 'Mom.' You have a sister, Tina, here on Earth, who calls me Mom."

"Sure . . . Mom," he said, struck by the warmth in her voice. He had never heard the Guardians speak in this way.

Jennifer had reddish hair and very fair skin. Although she was sitting down, Adam could see that she was a tall woman. Like him, she was quite thin.

"Your grandfather—my dad—was selected to be part of the APS program. So, his family was also part of APS. You'll meet your father, your grandmother, and your sister. I am so happy that you are growing up to be a handsome man, Adam. And an intelligent one, too, based on what I have seen."

"What have you seen of me? We've just met!" protested Adam.

"Yes and no," replied Jennifer. "The APS program is run off the super-computer on the landing craft. All the Guardians and the family person-alities communicate between each other through APS. Although this is the first time that I've met you in person, I already know a lot about you. I was able to observe your birth through Guardian's eyes when you were thawed and later delivered. I have seen you grow up, through the eyes of the Guardians."

While Adam was still trying to absorb what he had just heard, a man appeared next to Jennifer.

"Hello Adam," he said. "I'm Joseph. Joseph Bowles. I'm your father."

Adam said, "Hello . . . Father . . . Bowles."

"No need for last names here—yet," laughed Joseph. "True, your last name is Bowles. I suppose when your population becomes large enough, people will also need to have last names!"

This got a chuckle out of Jennifer. She looked at Joseph. The only time Adam had ever seen such a look was when he had once caught Gerald and Zelda secretly exchange smiles. He had been intrigued by that look and hadn't quite known how to interpret it. Now there seemed to be an under-standing, a familiarity between these two people he had just met, who called themselves his parents.

Joseph was a geotechnical engineer, while Jennifer was a structural engineer, like her father—Adam's grandfather—Charles. His parents met at the University of Michigan, in a place called "Ann Arbor," in a country called "America."

Adam discovered that he had come from a long lineage of engineers. Adam found this interesting, since he was learning architecture and how to design bridges and buildings.

"Is there a reason—a connection—between the fact that I'm learning architecture and you are also an engineer?" asked Adam.

"Very observant," said his father. "Yes, there is a reason you are learning architecture and engineering. For one, we assume that you have a natural ability in these subjects. Genetically, you inherited an aptitude for graphics and an inclination for these things. While it is true anyone can learn anything once they put their mind to it, the fact is, some people have various natural aptitudes."

"Will you be teaching me . . . *Father?*" asked Adam.

"Now, at this stage of your development, your grandfather will be taking over your lessons. He will be teaching you engineering. The Guardians have taken you only so far—let's call this 'General Education.' Now you are ready for something we call 'college.' Your grandfather will complete your training. You will be learning from the very best.

"Your grandfather was a member of the National Academy of Science, whose members included the top authorities in various fields of science and engineering, people who advised the President of the United States. We plan to educate you using the brilliant minds of the National Academy of Science. They will be your professors for the next five years."

And that completed Adam's first day in the APS room.

Chapter 9

THE FOLLOWING DAY, ADAM RETURNED TO HIS APS ROOM. He put on the goggles and immediately saw his grandfather, Charles.

"Good morning, Adam."

"Hi . . . Charles."

"You can call me Grandpa, if you want. That's what your sister calls me," said Charles.

"Okay . . . Grandpa," said Adam, still unaccustomed to the word. He had tried practicing it the night before, but was still unsure whether to sound the "d."

"Today we are going on a little journey," said Charles. "I want to show you where I live."

"How will we do that, Grandpa?" asked Adam, deciding to try a silent "d." "Granpa" somehow that sounded better than "Grand-pa."

"We can do this by viewing 360 degree stereoscopic images which I took on Earth. The effect is very realistic—you will think you are actually there, if you let yourself believe you are. Here is a saying for you: you will need to have 'a willing suspension of disbelief' in order to fully enjoy the experience."

"Whatever you say, Grandpa," said Adam.

"Your grandmother and I are avid bicyclists," continued his grandfather. "Have you ever ridden a bike?"

"No," answered Adam. "What's a bike?"

"A bike is a two-wheeled vehicle that we ride by turning pedals with our feet," said his grandfather. "Don't worry. Just sit where you are supposed to sit. You can't fall down, since you're actually in the APS room sitting on a stationary bike. Just go with the flow, and you'll get the hang of it."

What a strange way of talking! thought Adam. *What did "go with the flow" mean? And "get the hang of it"?*

"Are you ready? We are going to travel about thirty-two miles today."

All of New Eden was perhaps one square mile. He had explored every nook and cranny of New Eden. Since it had a sea on one side and impenetrable fern forests on the other three sides, the people living in New Eden were literally boxed in a closed environment.

"Your grandmother and I like to take long bike rides on the weekends in the summer. We live in America near a city called Chicago. We typically leave our house and ride for twenty to thirty miles, which takes three to five hours. Once we rode forty-three miles to the Museum of Science and Industry. That's our personal record."

Adam was surprised to see his grandmother appear. Like his grandfather, she had wrinkled skin but her hair was still a rich chestnut, except at the roots which showed signs of gray.

"Yes, that's when you got sick, Charles," she said affectionately.

"Yes, I did get sick after that trip. And I got vertigo that day. Not sure what caused it. Could have been from my flight to Guam. Maybe I didn't drink enough water."

Charles returned his attention to Adam.

"We will watch a recording that is synchronized to the stationary bicycle next to your chair. You will need to pedal in order for the trip to advance. You will need to turn and lean and go up and down hills. You will be quite literally bicycling the full thirty-two miles."

Charles paused. "And water. Don't forget to periodically drink water. You will see that your bike has a water bottle and a bag of trail mix attached to it. Now it's time to get on your bike. Please take off your goggles, get out of your chair and get on the bike by the wall."

Adam walked over to the bike. He put on his goggles and swung his right leg over the crossbar. The seat seemed hard and narrow. When he put his hands on the handle bars, he saw that he was with his grandfather and grandmother. The three of them were sitting on bicycles outside a house. The house was bigger and taller than the houses in New Eden. There was glass covering the square openings to the house.

"This is the house where we live, outside Chicago." explained Charles. "Okay, let's get going. Start pedaling."

As soon as Adam began to pedal, he saw the scenery moving. However, if he turned his front wheel to the left and right, the bicycle did not turn. Evidently, he was on a fixed course—a recording. But he could see his grandfather and grandmother turning their bicycles.

"Grandpa, when I turn my bike, nothing happens," said Adam.

"Yes, this is something that you will need to get used to. You are looking at a recording of the real Earth. This is not a simulation," said his grandfather.

The sky was very unusual. It was blue, not orange, with thin puffs of white that floated across it. Occasionally, he could see large flying machines in the air.

"Why are the drones so big?" asked Adam.

"Those are airplanes, Adam. They are flying people to different places on Earth," answered his grandfather.

They rode their bikes through neighborhoods, past many houses. All the houses were taller than the ones in New Eden. They all had glass over their openings. Adam saw people outside. Some of the people said "Hi" to them and waved. They traveled farther than he had ever traveled before. Soon they arrived in a town called "Evanston."

Beautiful full grown trees created a canopy over the streets. Adam had seen pictures of trees on his e-reader, but had never seen or touched a tree. The fern woods in New Eden had no such trees.

When they arrived at a street called "McCormick," they rode their bikes along a park trail next to a long body of water.

Charles explained, "This is the Chicago River. We are in a park called the 'Sculpture Park.' We will follow this path into the city."

In the park, there were strange constructions of metal. Charles explained to him that these were pieces of art called "sculpture." Adam didn't quite understand the purpose of these things. They were almost like the metal Möbius strip in the church in New Eden. Some of the sculptures looked like people—sort of. Others were geometric and didn't look like anything.

Eventually, they arrived at Howard Street, which his grandfather explained was at the northern border of the City of Chicago.

"We are next to the Chicago Sanitary District. This is where they treat sewage from the residents of the city," said Charles.

They followed the Chicago River until they reached Lawrence Avenue. The ride had taken two hours.

There were many vehicles on the street. They were all different sizes and colors; some were traveling very fast. His grandfather explained that these were cars, trucks, and buses. If they were actually riding in traffic, it was not safe to ride too close to them, even in the bike lanes. They would need to take the back streets to Lake Michigan.

Along the way, they stopped at a place where people were eating outside, sitting at small tables. Some were going in and out of buildings—in the window of one building, there were shoes but these were very different from his own burlap sandals; in another, he could see clothes of every color displayed on faceless statues that reminded him of the Guardians. The clothing looked very tight and uncomfortable.

His grandmother explained that the people were shopping.

"What's shopping?" asked Adam.

"It's when you give money in exchange for goods."

"What's money?" asked Adam. In New Eden each student was given exactly what he or she needed and no more. Everyone wore the same basic outfit; there were no choices. Everyone shared the few items they owned—a comb, for example.

They continued through Chicago's neighborhoods until they reached a large sea.

"This is Lake Michigan," said Charles. "It is one of the largest lakes on Earth. We will be taking the trail up to the Loop from here.

Adam could see very tall buildings ahead. The structures appeared to rise hundreds, perhaps thousands of feet. The scene was quite overwhelming.

As they rode, there were many other bicyclists riding on the trail. "On your left!" Adam heard several times, as a cyclist would pass them. These other bicyclists were wearing special looking clothes with writing all over them.

They neared the center of Chicago, where the buildings were the tallest. They rode by a place called Millennium Park, where they saw a big shiny sculpture called "The Bean." From there, they rode into the heart of the city. Overhead was a structure called "The Loop," which was very noisy. Adam had to cover his ears when big machines traveled overhead on the Loop.

"What is this thing?" asked Adam.

"That's the 'El,' which is means 'Elevated.' Those are train cars that run on electric rails, carrying people. Most of the people on the El live outside the Loop. They are coming downtown to go to their jobs or to shop."

When they got to a street called "Taylor Street," Adam's grandfather said, "Hungry yet? We've been riding now for about three and a half hours."

Adam said, "Yes, I'm hungry—and thirsty."

"Good. Things are working out as planned," said his grandfather. In front of them, Adam saw the sign, "Al's Italian Beef."

"Let's have a Chicago delicacy," said Charles. "Since this is actually a recording we're watching, we're not at the real Al's. But I've arranged for the next best thing: we've taken Al's recipe and cooked up an authentic Italian beef sandwich with french fries for you. We've also brought you a Coke. Please take off your goggles."

Slowly, Adam took off his goggles, wondering what was in store for him. The door to his room opened. Guardian Miss Clare entered the room carrying a tray with a sandwich and something called "fries" and a drink. Adam ate this meal. It was delicious. He tried something called "mustard" for the first time. He loved it.

After finishing his meal, he put his goggles back on.

His grandfather said, "Well, I think this brings today's journey to an end. Let me check the mileage. Yep, that was about thirty-two miles. We'll need to log this one into our books. Did you have fun, Adam?"

"Yes—it was interesting," said Adam. "It has given me a lot to think about."

"Great!" said his grandfather. "We'll need to do this again."

Adam looked forward to the next trip.

Chapter 10

THREE DAYS AFTER BEING INTRODUCED TO THE APS WHEN the students entered their individual APS rooms they found themselves sitting in an auditorium. On the stage was a man whom they had never seen before. Tall, with broad shoulders, he stood at a podium like the one The Leader used on Sundays. He wore a gray uniform. Sewn to his clothes were various striped labels which looked like flags. Little gold stars—four of them—were attached to the left side of his chest. On his head was a hat with gold stars across the front. Bristly hair grew above his mouth and it was partially dark and partially gray.

"Good morning, students. I'm General Leslie Mitchell," boomed the man.

"Of course, I am not the actual General Mitchell—I'm an APS simulation of the real Mitchell, who was the person in charge of what we call 'the mission' to this planet. You will be hearing me talk a lot about 'the Planners of the Mission' because I headed that team.

"We realize that we're exposing you to a lot of new data. We're expecting you to assimilate volumes of information about life on Earth, a place you have never seen except through these APS sessions. In a sense, you have been drafted. You have no choice. Like soldiers, you're on a mission."

Adam was confused. *What did this mean, "You have no choice"?*

The General continued. "We need to train you kids to fulfill your mission which is nothing less than to establish new colonies on this planet. However, it is important that we don't overdo your training. We don't want you to burn out, do we? There is a saying that we have on Earth, 'You can lead a horse to water, but you can't make him drink.' This means we realize you have minds of your own, and so it is up to us to convince you about the importance of what we are asking you to do. You must *want* to accomplish the mission. *Any questions?*"

Horst raised his hand. "What is the mission again? We will be establishing colonies, you said?"

"Yes. You will be leaving this place when you are twenty-one years old. You will be traveling across this sea here," said the General, gesturing to a map on the wall behind him. "You will travel on a boat with supplies. We will be preparing you for this mission over the next five years."

"Do you have any idea where we will be going?" asked Harry, a skinny young man with freckles and owlish glasses. He and his friend, Peter, usually kept to themselves, barely interacting with the rest of the group. Now, however, they were highly attentive; Peter, in fact, was frowning, as if disturbed by what he heard.

"Yes, we have this planet mapped out," answered the General. "Prior to your arrival, two other landing craft landed here." Again, he pointed to a location on a map. "The first was what we refer to as 'Einstein-Newton' craft which landed here." With the flourish of a marker, he made a bold red "X" on the map. "That craft had no biological life-forms—that is, frozen embryos—on board. It carried only a supercomputer that we named 'Genius.' One of the purposes of 'Einstein-Newton' was to check if this planet was safe for human habitation. It mapped the planet, locating the landing sites for the two other landing crafts."

"What were the other landing crafts?" asked Eileen who by now was paying attention to every word.

"The second landing craft was launched by Germans. Their craft was identical to the American landing craft which established New Eden. The Germans arrived here two years before your craft landed."

"Why were they launched two years earlier?" Eileen looked at the General steadily, as if trying to read his face.

"Because it took time to build the spacecraft," explained the General. "When we learned of an impending collision from an asteroid, we decided to build these ships as fast as we could. There was no time to become creative. We decided to reuse a couple of space shuttles that had been in mothballs for years, The rockets' engines were experimental nuclear thermal rockets, developed in the late 1970s, which were capable of propelling the craft to 192,000 miles per hour. Just the fuel for the interstellar boosters required multiple rocket launches. We were launching rockets with fuel tanks on the average of one a month for eighteen months straight."

"*Mothballs?*" repeated Horst, a puzzled look on his face. "And why were the Germans involved?"

The General laughed. "Just a figure of speech, Horst. The Germans had developed 'birthing machines'—that is, artificial wombs to be used for gestating embryos; these machines were originally intended for women who are unable to carry a fetus full-term. When the threat of an asteroid emerged, a plan was developed to send frozen embryos. The German technology was critical to this mission. America had the necessary space technology and the resources to collaborate. It was a good match."

"Where are the Germans living?" asked Horst.

"In a new colony called 'New Munich' or 'Neu München' in Deutsch. You do speak German, don't you?"

"Ah, yes," answered Horst, a bit hesitantly. Now it was starting to make sense why they had been learning German. Perhaps he needed to brush up his language skills!

"As a matter of fact, the German colony isn't entirely German. There are five Japanese at the colony. The Japanese are experts in robotics. All of the Guardians are Japanese robots, adapted to use the artificial intelligence systems on board the spacecraft. In exchange, five Japanese embryos were shipped with the German landing craft."

"Do we need to speak Japanese, too?" asked Horst, half-jokingly.

"No," said the General. "We can assume that the Japanese members are fluent in German. I'm sure they know how to speak English, too, because the Germans have been learning English in preparation for your arrival."

"So what do you expect us to do?" asked Gerald, an uneasy grin pasted to his face. "You make this sound so easy!"

"Your team will be traveling first to the New Munich colony. After teaming up with the Germans, we want you to set out to a new location and establish a town."

"How far is New Munich?" asked Adam.

"New Munich is 1,067 miles away from this point. We estimate that during your journey you will be traveling at a rate of fifteen miles per day by foot. Therefore, we expect you will reach New Munich in approximately seventy-one days, if all goes well."

"And suppose it *doesn't* go well?" objected Gerald. "*What then?*"

"Then you make the most of it, without complaining," said the General sternly. "This is the time to be a man and do your duty, whatever the sacrifice." He paused and looked around the auditorium. Fifteen pairs of eyes were focused on him. "No? Well, let me give you broader insights about our ultimate objectives."

He walked away from the podium and settled in an armchair facing the Third Thaws. "You came from a planet with billions of people and advanced technology. When we sent you here, it was impossible to equip you with all the things that we have on Earth. For example, we couldn't exactly stuff a steel mill on board your landing craft, could we? We couldn't fill up the landing craft with all the toilet paper that you would ever need, either."

That last comment got a few snickers from the audience.

"No, we had to make decisions about what to send with you. There were certain supplies to maintain the Guardians and also some items the Guardians would need to raise you from infancy. Yes, we threw a few diapers in the craft."

Now that remark got a chuckle.

"Quite frankly, you people don't have many things here. With the exception of a few items brought on board the ship, you are currently living at a medieval level in Earth's history. You know how to make things like pots and robes, but the truly modern technologies are a long way off for you. We've provided with the best experts—The APS personalities—who can teach you how to re-establish modern technologies on this planet. We also shipped with your craft delicate scientific instruments to be used for medicine and science. And let's not forget that we shipped several priceless musical instruments."

Did he look in my direction? Eileen wondered. *Does he know that I'm a pianist?*

"These things are your priceless heritage. We jam-packed every cubic inch of space inside the Shuttles with this inventory. You may not have an immediate need for some of these items, but some day you will.

"Let's take, for example, the steel fabricating tools that we shipped. Presently you have no steel that you are fabricating. However, we foresee sometime in the future when you will mine for iron ore and manufacture steel products. Mining will require an enormous effort on your part. We can guide you, using our experts on the APS, about the process of establishing a steel making industry. Once you start making steel, you will have reached the equivalent of Earth's Industrial Age. At that stage, you will need all the things we shipped, such as screw making machines, lathes, spring making machines, cylinder boring machines, welders and so forth."

Horst asked, "When we arrive at the German Colony—when we all get together, I mean—what do we call ourselves? Are we Americans? Do we keep our national identities? I mean, is there a need to keep our national identities after we get together?"

The General hesitated. "I really don't know how to answer that question, Horst. It probably doesn't make sense to maintain these boundaries. There were many other countries and nationalities on Earth, not just America, Germany, and Japan. More importantly, you people are representative of humanity, not just three countries.

"When you get together, you will be merging into a new, larger, colony. You will become friends. Some of you will marry the other side. Gradually, you will all meld together and become one homogenous race. There may be no point in having a national identity.

"But let us not forget that you can always visit your heritage through the APS simulators. You will always have these resources to visit the simulations of your families on Earth in America."

The General paused. "There are some people who cling to their cultures, refusing to assimilate with other cultures. Perhaps some of you may have that tendency—I don't know. But let's think of the big picture here. This isn't about America or Germany or Japan. This is about what is best for humanity."

Chapter 11

FOR THE NEXT FIVE YEARS, THE THIRD THAWS WERE TRAINED by their APS families. Sometimes they had group lectures together, to learn about America and world history, and even about life on prehistoric Earth.

The American planners of the mission, mostly members of the National Science Academies, debated the occupations for which the new people should be trained. This represented a challenge: with only fifteen kids, what specialties should they be trained in? What occupations would be needed to "reboot" the human civilization? What occupations were essential?

Naturally, the NSA members initially thought the new people should be engineers, scientists, and doctors like themselves. However, the idea of a new planet inhabited only by scientists was quickly discarded as preposterous. Soon, a list of essential trades emerged, comprised of craftsmen, scientists, engineers, farmers, carpenters, builders, musicians, artists, and even brewers.

The planning team decided that the new people, unlike young people in America, would not be given the freedom of choosing their own occupations. Based on the preselected gene pool of embryos, an individual's occupation was predetermined by the occupation of a parent or grandparent. The child of a farmer would become a farmer; the child of a carpenter would become a carpenter; the child of a musician would become a musician, and so on.

Although this arrangement would have met resistance in modern democratic societies on Earth, there would be no liberty of choice for the new people on this planet. In a sense, they were drafted into predetermined occupations when they were embryos.

They would be trained by specialists—usually their grandparents, who were experts in on Earth.

Adam was learning how to design structures from his grandfather. One subject he found particularly interesting was the Theory of Elastic Stability, a subject pioneered by a famous engineer with the same last name, Stephen Timoshenko. Adam learned how to program a laptop computer. He also learned how to draw buildings and structures using a CAD program. Eventually he learned how to make virtual simulations of buildings using "building information modeling"—sometimes called "BIM"—software. He enjoyed his lessons and found the more he learned, the more he wanted to know.

Horst's grandfather, Frank Erbstoesser, taught him college level chemistry and physics. Finding these subjects so much more interesting than his prior general education, he quickly advanced. Beginning with Inorganic Chemistry, he learned the basics of chemical reactions using a handful of laboratory instruments. He quickly advanced to Organic Chemistry, learning how to draw Lewis diagrams, and even how to model molecules on a laptop.

However, Horst's education in chemistry was hindered because New Eden lacked the chemicals he needed. For example, many organic molecules involve hydrocarbons, which are typically derived from petroleum products. This presented a problem, because New Eden did not have any petroleum products, not even coal. Fortunately, his grandfather was able to guide him through the steps required for the synthesis of some hydrocarbons from plants. Horst was particularly interested in making plastics from these hydrocarbons. Even while he was concentrating on his studies, he was constantly taking notes on the future experiments he planned on pursuing.

Hansel learned construction from his father, Tom Walsh, who had a wealth of personal experience in the construction industry. The APS Tom Walsh personally guided Hansel, giving him pointers about heavy construction. Founded in 1898, his company had built much of Chicago—its office, retail, residential, and mixed-use developments, as well as correctional facilities, hospitals, academic institutions, laboratories, warehouses and transportation systems. There was no construction topic about which Tom Walsh was not an expert. These APS sessions frequently involved going to 3-D recordings of construction sites that his Tom Walsh had worked on, giving Hansel an idea of their variety and complexity.

The group's brightest student, Ingrid, learned about biological sciences from her grandmother. Her initial studies included Biology, Zoology and Botany; she also took Chemistry classes which Horst also attended. She found the topic of Evolution to be particularly interesting. With her grandmother, she watched the fascinating BBC video series, *Walking with Dinosaurs,* which showed simulations of prehistoric life on Earth. Later in her studies, Ingrid received basic medical training. She took her studies seriously, aware that one day she might very well have to practice what she was learning.

Ingrid and Horst worked together in a small chemical laboratory to produce basic first aid supplies that might be needed during the journey. Most of their work involved fairly straight forward tasks such as making rubbing alcohol by distilling corn. They also made bandages from cotton fabric. Ingrid wanted to have a general anesthetic available, in case she needed to perform surgery. They were successful making an older type of anesthetic, *diethyl ether,* sometimes called "*ether,*" which can be used to knock-out patients.

At first, Horst, ever the comedian, would crack jokes or try to make Ingrid laugh in other ways. Quickly, however, he settled down, realizing that his sense of humor was having no impact; every now and again, he glanced in Ingrid's direction, watching her take detailed notes, quietly listening as she recorded her observations on a talking device.

Gerald's grandfather, Emanuel, who was from Trinidad and had immigrated to Memphis, Tennessee, was teaching him how to be a plumber. He was very funny and had a big laugh. He was always saying funny phrases, like "Fire Mariah!" stretching out each syllable. Gerald quickly picked up this lingo, and began to sound as though he, too, was from Trinidad.

Much of Gerald's training was quickly put to use in New Eden, since the settlement was in need of plumbing. With Adam and Hansel, he developed construction projects, installing underground water lines and sanitary lines.

Under his grandfather's guidance, he was able to devise a modern toilet made from fired clay, complete with gaskets and a flushing mechanism. All the residents of New Eden welcomed this as an improvement over the "hole in the ground."

Zelda's APS mother was training her to be a teacher. Hailing from Detroit, Michigan, her mother took her on visits to Greenfield Village, which was situated next to the Ford Motor factory in Dearborn. Zelda was fascinated by her "visit" to both the home and laboratory of Thomas Edison. She also loved visiting the Henry Ford Museum which contained a wealth of artifacts, such as old cars, trains, and airplanes. She decided that someday, when she was a teacher, she would arrange APS field trips for her students to these museums.

But not everything Zelda learned was uplifting. Her mother explained the history of slavery in America and the oppression of their people. She described the great migration of their ancestors from the south to northern cities like Chicago and Detroit. She told her of the great struggles faced by African Americans, stressing the great importance of the family.

"Zelda, Baby, don't give yourself away to any man! You hear me?" was her constant refrain.

Zelda could not quite relate to the concept of "giving away." Nevertheless, she nodded to her mother, as if in compliance. "Yes, Momma," she would say.

She listened intently to tragic stories of race relations in America. These stories of man's inhumanity to man—and to woman—were difficult to accept.

"How could this be, Momma? Are people that mean? I thought that America was a great place. Isn't it, Momma?"

To which her APS Momma, would pause, and say. "Yes, I suppose it is 'great,' but not for everyone. It is a complicated, great, place on the 'greatness' scale, but it is also a country of contradictions. There are people who are good, and there some people who are just plain evil."

Hearing these stories, Zelda wondered if she should "trust" the others who had lighter skin. But what could she possibly not trust about her friends? This was not Earth.

Gertrude and Eva were being trained as seamstresses. Their APS sessions were usually held "virtually" together, although they were in separate

APS rooms. Their mothers had been friends on Earth and liked to sew and knit together. An APS session with Gertrude and Eva usually involved them knitting and talking with their APS mothers at their homes in Fort Collins, Colorado. Their mothers, both expert knitters, taught them all sorts of difficult knitting patterns which the girls mastered quickly.

Eileen, the musician of the group, met regularly with her grandmother who was also a pianist. It was a pleasure for Eileen to sit back and witness a true *maestro* play in front of her, correct her own fingering, and comment on her technique. Until she met her APS grandmother, Eileen had worked from sheet music and recordings, mostly teaching herself; now she could experience a "live" performance and personal mentoring.

Eileen's relationship with her grandmother—their 3-D recorded trips to great cathedrals such as St. John the Divine in New York, Canterbury Cathedral in Kent, Santa Maria del Fiore in Florence, and Notre Dame de Paris exposed Eileen to Christian art, music, architecture, and ritual.

The lofty vaulted ceilings, flying buttresses, delicate arches and soaring spires elevated both her mood and her spirit. Craning her neck, she looked up towards Infinity; lowering her gaze, she focused on the cobalt blue that dominated so many of the surviving medieval stained glass windows. She studied the pictures sewn with such care into rich tapestries and tried to decipher the Latin inscriptions on marble tombstones.

Here, in Canterbury Cathedral, was the burial place of Thomas à Becket; there, in the Poet's Corner of Westminster Abbey, lay the tomb of Geoffrey Chaucer; and there, in the Church of San Pier Maggiore, in Ravenna, was the tomb of Dante Alighieri.

Lingering at church services, Eileen absorbed the fragrance of incense, the flicker of candle light, the ethereal notes of Gregorian chant. Parables about Good Samaritans and Prodigal Sons captured her imagination, while the sound of congregations fervently reciting The Lord's Prayer filled her heart with joy. During these trips, Eileen was introduced to magnificent examples of sacred music—Schubert's *Ave Maria*, Handel's *Messiah*, Mozart's *Requiem*, Bach's *Mass in B Minor*, the Vienna Choir Boys' Christmas Concert. . . .

To her delight, her grandmother had the piano scores to these great works and, after much practice, Eileen was able to perform many of her favorite pieces.

Prior to their exposure to their APS mentors, the only adult figures the kids had ever known were the Guardians. The Guardians always had even-toned, almost monotone, speech patterns. Whatever went on—even in the case of an emergency—they never raised their voices. The Planners of the Mission determined that the children should learn to speak with proper inflections. They decided that, in addition to the APS sessions, the group should begin to watch old television shows from the 1950s and 1960s; these would provide effective role models for speech patterns and good citizenship.

~

All fifteen of the Third Thaws were progressing well, with no signs of burn out. In fact, some, like Horst, were so inquisitive that they were learning things quite beyond what was necessary for the mission. One weekend, they were surprised to discover that their lessons had been cancelled; instead, they were to leave behind all books and projects and head to the beach. That was an order! After a relaxing day, they watched the sunset, and built a campfire on the beach to keep warm. Sitting in a circle around the fire, they sang songs and told stories. The change of pace made a welcome change.

"I was watching some old television shows from Earth," remarked Horst, casually. "These shows were called *Gunsmoke* and *Wagon Train*. Have you ever seen those shows? They were about the old American West, when there were cowboys and Indians."

"No," said Adam. "I've never seen those shows. I like *Star Trek*."

"I saw a program called *The Beverly Hillbillies*," commented Eileen. "I didn't quite understand it, but it's funny."

Hansel grinned. "Yeah, some of these shows are funny. I like one called *Gilligan's Island*. Gee, it's almost like we're stuck here on our own Gilligan's Island. I guess that probably makes me 'Gilligan.'"

"That guy Gil-leh-gahn! Very funny maan! Fire Maria!" said Gerald.

Everyone but Horst laughed at Gerald and his newly acquired Trinidad speech pattern.

"What's up, Horst?" asked Ingrid, ever observant. "Looks like you've something on your mind!"

"As a matter of fact, I do," admitted Horst. "I've been watching these old Cowboys and Indians TV shows. These people shot guns. There was a lot of fist fighting. Have you ever seen violence on the TV shows that you watch?"

"Yeah, sure," said Adam. "On *Star Trek* there are a lot of scenes where Captain Kirk fights with his hands clenched in fists, hitting people. I love that show. They shoot lasers."

"What is that show called, again? *Star Trek*? I'll need to look that one up. Anyway, I think it's safe to conclude that people on Earth did a lot of fighting," continued Horst.

Everyone seemed to agree. Eva and Gertrude had meanwhile been spreading thick layers of peanut butter onto thin slices of stale bread; on top, they sprinkled cocoa powder and a few granules of sugar, both precious commodities in New Eden. Then, placing another layer of bread on top of the peanut butter layer, they wrapped the "s'mores" in cabbage leaves and began to roast them on the camp fire.

"Don't let them burn!" said Eva. "Count to ten and then rescue your s'mores! They'll be too hot to handle if you leave them in any longer than that!"

While the group moved closer to the fire, ready to claim their treats, Horst continued, "I've also been reading some books by an old science fiction writer by the name of Isaac Asimov. He wrote one called *I, Robot*. In this book, Asimov describes some rules about making robots. One of the rules is that robots should be programmed not to harm human beings.

"Interesting," said Adam, gingerly unwrapping his s'more. "So what's your point?"

"Do you remember the day we went to the woods? When we first discovered the production warehouse?"

"Yeah, sure," said Hansel. "I thought that we were going to be killed by those dogs!"

Horst said, "Remember when Father Leader discovered us?"

Adam said, "Yes, of course."

"He didn't seem angry with us at all," said Horst.

After a few moments, Adam said, "So . . . your point is, Father Leader is a robot, and robots can't get angry at humans?"

"Correct, Professor. The Guardians here—who are robots—can't get angry at us. There is no one here who can punish us. What I mean is there is no one here who can make us go on this mission. We are the only human beings in New Eden. No one can make us do a damned thing, not even the General."

The group grew silent, each of them pondering this new angle. They didn't have to go on this mission. They could simply stay in New Eden, if they wanted to. They could remain here, where things were nice and safe; they could party on the beach every night and eat as many s'mores as they wanted.

"You have a point," agreed Eileen. "I'm a little bit afraid of leaving. What's out there? Do we know if there are wild animals on the other side of the sea? On the other hand, I have been learning more and more about Earth and the history of people there. I want to know more. Would the Guardians shut down and stop teaching us if we refuse to go?"

"Yes, I think they would. That's one way they could get back at us, by withholding information," said Horst. "There is nothing in Asimov's book that says a robot must provide us with information. But they can't physically hurt us."

"I agree with Eileen," Adam said. "The more I learn about things, the more I want to know."

"Absolutely," said Horst. "I have been reading about the history of America. I'm getting some sense of what America was like."

"And I've been learning about Trinidad," added Gerald.

Horst asked, "And where is Trinidad?"

"It's an island in the Atlantic Ocean near Earth's Equator," said Zelda, smiling shyly at Gerald. "Stays warm all the time, doesn't it Gerald? There are no scorpions on the beach, like here. The beaches are safe for swimming."

Gerald squeezed her hand, then offered her a bite of his second s'more.

"And I've been going on bike rides with my grandfather, "said Adam. "Well, not my *real* grandfather, but you know what I mean. I've been getting to know places like Chicago. It's almost like I've lived there. I really like my grandfather, grandmother, mother and father. I feel . . . a connection."

The group fell silent. Yes, they were beginning to feel a connection . . . with Earth.

They continued to roast their s'mores on the open fire. Adam suggested that they should watch *Gunsmoke*, and, when the others agreed, he ran to his house to fetch a monitor. Enthralled, they watched one episode of *Gunsmoke*, followed by an episode of *Star Trek*.

Everything seemed strange to them—the way people talked, their mannerisms, the music they listened to . . . So far, the only music they had ever heard was the sheet music that Eileen played on the piano.

Self-consciously, Eileen addressed the group.

"I have been exposed to some very unusual music lately, called Ragtime. There is a piece called *The Maple Leaf Rag* by composer Scott Joplin. I want to play it for you some time and see what you think."

Adam said, "Why don't we go to the activity room? You can play it for us now."

The fire was dying. The s'mores had finished and the chill night air hung heavily upon them. Welcoming the chance to find some warmth, the group walked over to the activity room. Eileen sat down at the piano and began to play. *The Maple Leaf Rag* didn't sound like the pieces they had heard before—Bach, Mozart, Beethoven and Chopin.

"The style is called syncopation," explained Eileen. "The piece is somewhat difficult to play, actually. I've never seen or heard any other music like this."

"Who wrote it? You said it was 'Scott . . .'" asked Adam

"It was written by Scott Joplin. He was a black man, a composer, who played this music at the 1893 Chicago World's Fair," answered Eileen.

"I've read of these black people before," said Horst.

"I wonder . . . am I a black person?" blurted out Gerald. "And Zelda, too? Our skin is darker than yours."

"Perhaps," said Horst, not knowing how to respond. *Yes, Gerald and Zelda were both darker but did that mean they were black? Could they have been the descendants of slaves?*

"Eileen, can you play another one by Scott Joplin?" asked Horst, changing the subject.

She played another piece called *The Palm Leaf Rag*.

"Harmonically, it has the same structure as other music that I am familiar with," said Eileen. "We see the same chord progressions: I-VI-II-V-I."

"What do you mean by that last statement?" asked Horst.

"I've been learning this from my grandmother," explained Eileen. "She, too, played piano. Most Western music, particularly older classical music, has a harmonic structure with certain rules, largely attributable to Bach. There are major keys and minor keys. There are certain chord progressions in Western culture that we are trained to expect. My grandmother says that our ears expect to hear specific diatonic chord movements."

She then played three chords.

"These chords are in positions II-V-I in the twelve-tone musical scale."

"This is way beyond me," exclaimed Horst. "I've never played a musical instrument, but reading music seems to be almost mathematical."

"Yes, I agree," said Eileen. "It's a lot like mathematics. There is a structure to music which is fascinating. I have often wondered about these things. My grandmother is teaching me the underlying structure of music."

After playing a third piece called, *Heliotrope Bouquet*, by Scott Joplin and Louis Chauvin, Eileen showed the others the musical score.

"I have been reading that at the 1893 World's Fair these ragtime pieces created a sensation. People began doing a dance called the *Cakewalk*. Prior to that, people only danced the *Waltz*."

"Do you know what the *Cakewalk* was like?" asked Gertrude.

"I'm not quite sure," admitted Eileen. "I'm sure that we can do a search on the computer's video database and find some footage."

They made a search on the computer. Soon they found a very old black-and-white film showing people doing the *Cakewalk*. Coincidentally, the dancers in the film were doing the *Cakewalk* to the "Heliotrope Bouquet." The group decided to try dancing to this unusual music. Gertrude figured out the steps, by stopping and starting the film; she then began instructing the group. The males and females paired up in couples, while Eileen played the piano, dancing the Cakewalk on a planet twenty-three light-years from Earth.

Chapter 12

USUALLY, WHEN HORST HAD HIS LESSONS WITH THIS grandfather Erbstoesser (whom he called "Opa") they talked about science, more specifically, about chemistry. Opa, the nuclear chemist, was an expert in the field of chemistry. He was also a thoughtful teacher, who was sensitive to a student's pace of learning. Horst thrived in this new learning environment with an expert tutor, his grandfather, Opa.

One day, Horst asked his grandfather a question that had nothing to do with chemistry.

"Opa, have you ever watched *Gunsmoke*?"

Opa paused. "I do not understand how to answer that question." Then, he spoke without any inflection in his voice, sounding much like one of the Guardians. "A search of my database indicates that *Gunsmoke* was an American radio and television Western drama series. The radio series ran from 1952 to 1961. The television series ran for twenty seasons from 1955 to 1975."

Horst bit his lip. Opa's sudden change in speech patterns jolted the boy into the realization that he was not talking to a "real" person, but to a simulated being.

"So, you've never actually seen *Gunsmoke*, Opa?" he said.

"Actually, I am not sure," Opa replied, returning to his regular speech pattern. "You must keep in mind, Horst, that I am a simulation of the real Frank Erbstoesser. The real Frank Erbstoesser may have seen *Gunsmoke*— more than likely he did, because he lived during that time period. It's just that the APS has captured only a portion of the real Frank Erbstoesser's personality. I am a simulation, not the *real* Frank Erbstoesser."

Horst stopped to absorb these words. At least, Opa was upfront with him and was not trying to deceive him in any way.

"I've been thinking a lot about this, the APS. How does it work again? How did they, as you say 'capture a portion' of your personality?"

Opa—the simulation of Frank Erbstoesser—hesitated for a moment.

"Look, Horst, I am not an expert on artificial intelligence. Of course, I can immediately look up a definition and read you the theory. You can read these things, too. I can explain to you what has simply been explained to me. They briefed us on the entire process when we entered the APS training. Whoops, there I go again! I mean, Frank Erbstoesser was briefed on the entire process.

"On Earth, all the members of the NAS were interviewed by the APS program. This process included our families, too. We underwent hours and hours of interviews by the APS program. We were asked all sorts of questions. The APS was able to 'capture' certain aspects of how we inflected our voices. It captured personal stories that we told the software. It recorded lessons that each of us wanted to pass down to our descendants.

"So, in answer to your original question, 'Yes,' it could very well be that the *real* Frank Erbstoesser had watched *Gunsmoke*. But this topic never came up during our APS sessions. I doubt if any of the NAS members were asked if they watched *Gunsmoke*. It would be too off-the-wall, too wild of question."

"So you are simply telling me things that Frank Erbstoesser told you?" said Horst. "You cannot generate data of your own? *You're just a recording device?*"

"No, not at all," said the APS Opa. "I am not just a recording device. I am much more complex, because I have aspects of intelligence. I know the logic of how someone thinks and how to re-create his or her expressions. I am somewhat of a mimicking device, a mime, with limited sensory input. In a sense, I have no 'I' about me; I am selfless. I was trained to capture the personality and characteristics of your grandfather. I can interact with you using an accurate simulation of his personality. It is difficult for me to explain. I do not have all the senses that you have. I cannot taste things, I cannot feel things, but I can process the logic of ideas and act with the appropriate responses, as needed."

This was both disturbing and fascinating. Horst had a relationship with this being, not his real grandfather. He felt affection towards him and trusted him as his mentor; at the same time, he was aware that Opa was an illusion, not the *real* thing.

"Do you understand the fundamentals of artificial intelligence like yours?" asked Horst.

"Yes, I think I have a vague understanding," said the APS Opa. "In the twenty-first century, there were several software companies that developed artificial intelligence applications that people used every day on the Internet."

"What is a 'company'?" asked Horst.

"America had a system of commerce. Companies sold things. It really doesn't matter what the names were—*Microsoft, Google, Apple*—because, if the asteroid hit, they're all gone. But they largely owned the intellectual property of these artificial intelligence programs that were owned by the public. These programs were called 'apps,' which is short for 'applications.' For example, people would use an app on their phones to give them directions."

Horst looked a bit confused. Perhaps it was because he didn't understand these words, "Internet," "phone' or "app." There were no such things in New Eden.

Opa continued. "These companies had developed powerful artificial intelligence apps that people could talk to and ask questions. There were even self-driving cars that used artificial intelligence."

Again, the blank stare from Horst. *A car? What was that?*

"The specific mechanics explaining how these programs operate was largely proprietary information owned by the major software companies. There is a term for this type of software: 'Black box' software. People used it without understanding how the software works. Not much was published about how these programs work. The specifics were referred to as 'trade secrets.'

"Fortunately—or unfortunately, depending on your perspective—when we learned of the possibility of an asteroid hitting the Earth, these companies cooperated with the American and German governments to allow the use of their software. The Planners of this Mission used proven technologies to assemble the components of the mission. In this case, they used artificial intelligence systems that had formerly been used on the Internet for our purposes here. These systems require a supercomputer, so we had to place supercomputers on each one of the spacecrafts."

Opa stopped, "You seem confused."

The boy was not so much confused as fascinated. "Please go on. This is amazing. Is there something that I can read about this subject?"

"Yes," said APS Opa. "There were some brilliant academic experts on this subject who published books and articles. For example, we—your *real* grandfather and APS—did discuss the writings of Steven Pinker from Harvard University and Noam Chomsky from the Massachusetts Institute of Technology. Beginning in the 1950s, Chomsky pioneered work on the syntactic structure of language. Pinker expanded on Chomsky's work, developing an understanding of the human mind from a linguistic and psychological perspective.

"It was Pinker who wrote several very accessible books about how the human mind uses something he called 'Mentalese.' All humans, no matter what language they speak, seem to think in the same Mentalese, which is on a lower level than language. It is not words alone that determine our thoughts. Many of our thoughts are visual. The most famous visual thinker was Albert Einstein. Many scientists, such as Einstein, think geometrically."

"Cool!" said Horst.

Opa continued. "Language is a way of conveying news. It is a shorthand version of telling other people what has happened. Language can't capture all the nuances of an event. People get bored hearing too much. Many people have short attention spans, preferring to read only the headlines. The human mind tends to guess about the outcome of things we hear. We tend to 'fill in the blanks' with past experiences and stereotypes. For example, there is no need to redefine what a 'circle' is, once we have learned what a circle is. Through learning and repetition, the brain actually hardwires itself to recall the concept of a circle."

"Very interesting," said Horst. "But how can a computer process thoughts? I mean, isn't a computer good at arithmetic? People don't think about arithmetic all the time. We are thinking about a whole lot of other things."

Opa smiled. "You are correct. People are mostly story tellers, and most human thought involves story-telling. We are role players in these little stories. We are curious about each other's stories, connecting stories, determining who played each role. But in order to make sense of all these stories, we must 'fill in the blanks' and make many assumptions. We seemed to be always wondering 'what is the other guy thinking?' as we sort players in our personal social play. We tend to use stereotypes to guess a storyline."

"So Mentalese is . . . ?"

"Mentalese is a coding that goes on in the brain. It is both richer than language and simpler than language."

"And you—the APS—also use Mentalese?" asked Horst.

"Yes and no. I do not have neurons—a biological brain—but I have electronic neural networks. In this case, my neural networks are located on the supercomputer on the landing craft. My programming simulates how a human being thinks, using Mentalese. Not quite the same thing, but pretty close. But, essentially, I—the APS I mean—is a sort of 'story processor,' that uses Frank Erbstoesser's personal stories."

"You make it sound like you are no different than machines."

"Not at all. Why do you think this?"

"I don't know. It's as though you are stripping away all the meaning of things, reducing our minds to a bunch of silly stories," said Horst. He paused, thinking more about what he had just said. "However, it reminds me of Eileen when she sometimes talks about music. Sometimes she uses symbols to describe music. Like 'I-II-V-I.' How can she do that? I mean music is so beautiful—why break it down into numbers like that?"

"This is quite an interesting analogy you are sharing with me," said Opa. "Please go on."

"Okay. It baffles me that Eileen, who is so musically talented, can deconstruct music into numbers."

"Do you think that she is wrong in her analysis of music?" said Opa.

"Obviously she is not wrong."

"Getting back to your worry about stories, it's the same thing," said Opa. "If we recognize that we think in terms of stories, that is not to demean ourselves. It is simply an insight about how the human mind works. It took a long time for people to develop these concepts. I have to acknowledge that many people on Earth find discussions about the human mind to be disturbing."

There was a pause. Then Horst's APS grandfather asked, "So, tell me about *Gunsmoke.*"

"Oh, yeah. It's very entertaining," said Horst. "There is a lot of fist fighting and gunfights. This leads me to another question that I have: are the Guardians capable of violence?"

There was silence. Horst watched as APS Opa closed his eyes, his face expressionless. When he opened them again, his voice was monotone. "I cannot answer your question. We will have to consult the General."

Horst shivered. All the warm feelings and his sense of connection to Opa had suddenly faded. The reality was that he had no grandfather. He, Horst, had bonded with APS Opa, but APS Opa was incapable of bonding with anyone. He had simply been programmed to interact with humans, and that interaction was limited.

Suddenly, the General appeared next to Opa. "Hello, Horst."

"Hello, General Mitchell," said Horst. Up until then, he had felt a sense of awe in the General's presence, but that, too, had faded. Like Opa, this mighty military officer lacked flesh and blood and had neither a brain nor a heart. Nevertheless, he was respectful when he rephrased his question:

"Are the Guardians capable of violence?"

The General answered, "No. It is not a part of their programming. Years ago, when robots were first invented, it was decided to install intrinsic programs that prevented artificial intelligence forms from harming humans. Sure, there were some incidences of deviant programs creating malicious robots and drones in the past, but for this mission, the Guardians are all benevolent."

"But if we are to explore this planet," persisted Horst, "will we need to exercise violence, for protection?"

The General paused, perhaps to check his own data base for an answer. Horst waited patiently. "Yes, I think so," said the General. "You see, I'm a military man. Fighting is my specialty. We don't know what is out there, but we think you will need weapons—at least as a backup for your safety. We must not forget that life in the wild can be dangerous. There may be dangerous creatures out there. We don't know what you will run into. There could be big animals. There could be smart animals. We just don't know.

That will be your job: to discover what is on this planet. You will need to defend yourselves."

"Are there any weapons available in New Eden?" asked Horst.

"Yes," answered the General. "On board the spacecraft, we shipped handguns for each one of your Thaw. There are only 1,000 rounds of ammunition allotted for your group. If you run out of bullets, it's up to you to find a way to manufacture more bullets and gunpowder. This may present you with a problem, since your group has not learned how to forge metals, yet."

"I really don't know anything about weapons," mused Horst, frowning. "Are these handguns similar to what they used in *Gunsmoke*?"

"Like a Colt 45?" said the General.

"Ah, I wouldn't know . . . I'm not sure what kind of pistols they used," said Horst.

"These handguns are standard U.S. Army issue pistols," said the General. "I highly recommend that you use bows and arrows as backup."

"Yes, that's something to keep in mind. How about crossbows?"

"Yes, we can attempt to make some crossbows, too," answered the General.

∾

After that session, the drones in the production warehouse fabricated crossbows and arrows for the Third Thaw. In keeping with the *Gunsmoke* theme, the drones fabricated new Western clothing, too. Adam, Hansel, and Horst began wearing jeans, cowboy boots and Stetson hats.

However, the women refused to wear the old-fashioned dresses, with petticoats, like the ones seen on *Gunsmoke*. The dresses were too hot. Eileen and the other young women agreed that dresses would hamper their long journey to New Munich. Unanimously, they decided to wear the same cowboy outfits as the young men.

The group needed to learn how to shoot their guns. The boys spent a considerable amount of practice on their "quick-draw" moves; they learned that when they shot "from the hip" it was hard to hit the target; the girls tended to be more focused, only taking aim when they were sure of hitting the target.

"Saves ammo!" pointed out Zelda who was turning out to be a crack shot.

The group especially enjoyed re-enacting scenes from *Gunsmoke*. They staged many gunfights, often starting with an exchange of insults like, "You dirty bastard" which soon escalated into one-on-one duels in the middle of the street. It was all for fun. By now, they were using so many cowboy expressions that their speech began to develop a Southern twang. Also, some of the group started chewing tree-gum, stuffing one cheek full, chomping away and spitting in pots.

"Disgusting!" objected Eileen. They just shrugged and continued chewing.

Hansel spent more time than anyone else at the shooting range, perfecting his shooting skills. He practiced many a mock quick-draw duel, thereby winning the title of the "quickest draw in New Eden."

One day after a long session of shooting practice, he heard a sound in his right ear. It was a little, high pitched sound that wouldn't stop. For the first few nights after this started, he had trouble sleeping. He tried to ignore the sound, but the conscious effort of "trying to ignore it" seemed to make him focus on it even more; in fact, it seemed to be getting louder, especially late at night.

Hansel stopped shooting as much, and found that he was only able to get relief when he went to the beach and listened to the waves. Somehow, the crashing waves drowned out the little high pitched sound in his right ear. Every day he made a point of going down to the water to find some refuge; gradually, with time, he stopped thinking about the sound altogether.

Chapter 13

ONE SUNDAY, THE THIRD THAWS DID NOT GO TO CHURCH to hear their weekly lesson; instead, the Guardians asked them to go to their APS rooms. After putting on their goggles, they saw that they were assembled in the auditorium again. This time, there was a man on the stage who had an uncanny resemblance to Leader Graham, the Guardian.

"Hello, New Eden," said the man. "My name is Graham."

"I am Leader Graham—actually, a facsimile of a real person named Graham. My face and body are nearly an exact simulation of those belonging to the real Graham."

Yes, thought Adam. *This Graham was a bit more realistic looking than the Japanese Robotic version of the Leader.*

"I am not a member of the National Academies," continued Graham. "In fact, I am not a scientist at all, although my father was a professor of Chemistry. On Earth, I was an Episcopal priest. My church was in Washington, D.C., and one of my parishioners was the President of the United States."

"In addition to my priest's duties, sometimes I wrote 'opinion-editorials'— or 'op-eds' for short—in newspapers and magazines, under a different name. In effect, my life revolved around two different worlds. On Sundays, I preached on the Bible, but, at other times, using an alias, I was a journalist and author. I did not write about religion—that would have 'blown my cover' and scared off my secular audience. Instead, I wrote commentaries about current events, always interjecting my moral opinions about society. I seemed to have struck a chord with the masses and my alias became quite popular.

"The President especially liked my opinions. I became his personal advisor and we were close friends. Naturally, when he was first advised about the possibility of a hundred-mile-diameter asteroid hitting the Earth, he asked me for advice. That is how I became involved in this mission. I underwent the APS process and became the being whom you call 'The Leader.'"

He paused for a few moments, appearing to be collecting his thoughts.

"As the first Guardian to walk on this planet, I literally led the way, naming this place 'New Eden.' Since you were children, I have delivered the Sunday Lessons. Generally, I have kept away from discussing religious beliefs, but have, instead, preached on ethics, that is, about what's right and wrong. That's the 'minister' side of me speaking.

"Today, however, I will be talking to you about your approaching transition. Today, just as happened with the First Thaws and Second Thaws before you, you will all become Cadets. The time is drawing near when you will be expected to travel a great distance to New Munich. More than likely, this will be a difficult mission which may present many obstacles. We cannot predict all the challenges that you may face. What is important, however, is that you act as a coordinated team.

"For the purpose of this mission, you will be inducted into a military training, something we call the Cadet system. The planners of this mission decided to implement a military based organization for your group, because, in the interest of safety, we cannot have all of you making decisions and putting everything to a vote. Your group will need to make quick and effective decisions, and most importantly, the right decisions. First and Second Thaws went through this process. Today, like them, you too have been drafted as Cadets. And on this note, let me turn this presentation over to General Mitchell."

General Mitchell appeared on the stage, replacing Leader Graham at the podium. For a minute, he surveyed the auditorium, studying every face. His presence dominated the room, completely eclipsing that of Leader Graham who seemed to fade into invisibility. Then he spoke.

"To assure the success of your expedition to New Munich, it will be necessary to implement a military chain of command within your group."

From within their individual APS rooms, the Third Thaws looked at each other. *They were now Cadets?* Both Leader Graham and General

Mitchell had said so; moreover, right on cue, the Guardians appeared in the Auditorium, distributing green uniforms to each one of them.

"You are each being given your Cadet uniform," stated the General, sounding more robotic than usual. He had none of Leader Graham's charisma or compassion.

"You will each be given the rank of Private First Class. Beginning tomorrow, for two hours a day, I will be providing you with military training."

Horst looked at his uniform. He liked the green color. The Second Thaws wore these uniforms. He had always wondered why they wore them. Now he understood.

While they were still examining their new garments, the General continued his briefing.

"Everyone stand up and raise your right hand. You must be sworn into the Cadets."

Reluctantly, the Third Thaws put down their uniforms and stood up. Horst raised his right hand; some of his classmates looked at each other hesitantly. Gertrude and Eva looked at their hands, then at each other, exchanging mystified frowns.

"Stand up, stand straight, at attention!" boomed the General. "I said *raise* your right hand!"

Everyone straightened up, now standing at attention, hands raised. Hansel stifled a giggle

"What's the matter Hansel? You want to tell us your little joke?" said the General. "*I said, what's the joke, Hansel?*"

"Nothing sir," said Hansel, quickly composing himself.

"Well, if it's nothing then get down and give me twenty-five push-ups!"

"*What?*" said Hansel.

"You heard me! I said get down and give me twenty-five! Now!"

Hansel got down on the floor, his short, pudgy legs stretched behind him.

"Count 'em out, Hansel! Let's hear you count!"

"Five, six, seven . . ." Hansel counted, aware that all eyes were upon him. Finally, aching all over and short of breath, he reached twenty-five.

"Okay. Any more comments from the Peanut Gallery?" asked the General. "If not, let's proceed to swearing you people in. Repeat after me . . ."

Each of the Third Thaws repeated the *Pledge of Allegiance*, word-for-word. They were familiar with the text as a historical document, but now the words took on new meaning. Somehow, their *Pledge of Allegiance* meant that they believed in American ideals and were willing to make sacrifices to ensure the continuation of those ideals; somehow, they were the new America, ready to place their flag in a new land, claiming it for their own....

"Congratulations, group. You are now privates in the Cadets," said the General. "Over the next five years, as we get closer to the mission date, some of you will be promoted to officer ranking. One of you will be given the rank of captain. That person will make decisions about the mission. His or her word must be considered the final say."

Horst raised his hand.

"Yes, Cadet Horst. Do you have a question?"

"Yes, General. What will happen after we reach New Munich? Will we remain a military unit?" asked Horst.

"After you reach New Munich, the military status of your group may dissolve. However, this depends on several variables. For example, if a challenge requires you to go on another expedition, the military status should remain.

"Okay, starting tomorrow morning you will begin your Cadet training. During the next five years, every morning, Monday through Friday, between six a.m. and eight a.m., you are expected to report to the Cadet Training Building. You must wear your uniforms, and we expect each of you to be on time. Do you understand?"

"Yes, sir!" they answered in unison.

Chapter 14

EVERY MORNING THEREAFTER THE THIRD THAWS WERE trained both mentally and physically. They exercised vigorously, going on extended hikes and climbing obstacles. They received survivalist training, learning how to live outdoors, pitch tents, make fires, trap animals and find potable water. They learned how to test a plant to check if it was poisonous. They were taught how to defend themselves from predators. They practiced target shooting with pistols and crossbows. They practiced riding their horses. They also went on short camping expeditions within the New Eden settlement.

For five years, this became their daily routine. They continued their schooling, learning their trades, becoming proficient in their skills; at the same time, they learned to become like soldiers. The military chain of command was drilled into them, as they learned the importance of authority.

When the launch date of the expedition drew near, it was time to select the leader of the group. By unanimous vote, the group elected Horst as Captain. Hansel would be the first Lieutenant and Ingrid would be the company medic. The expedition was scheduled to leave the following Saturday. There was great anticipation as their departure date grew near.

On one of his last visits with his APS family, Adam went on a bicycle trip on Earth. This time, Grandpa and Grandma Timoshenko and Adam's parents took their bicycles on the Metra commuter line up to Libertyville, Illinois. They were to ride their bikes back along the Des Plaines River Trail. As before, this was a trip that had been recorded in real life by his grandparents.

The Metra train ride to Libertyville, Illinois, took about twenty minutes from his parents' suburb. After they got off the train, they rode their bikes to downtown Libertyville. There, they found a Subway sandwich shop and had lunch. (Of course, this lunch was actually brought into the APS room by Miss Clare.)

After lunch, they rode their bikes eastward to the Des Plaines River trail. None of them talked much. The trail was truly beautiful. Although Illinois lacked mountains, there was much wildlife to see—a large turtle lumbering across the bike path, more than one heron, several deer, and hawks, too.

The trail curved through the woods next to the Des Plaines River. It consisted of compacted, fine cinder with crushed stone, which made for a very smooth riding surface. Along the way there were many pedestrian bridges. Adam saw wild flowers and tall grasses. His grandfather explained that Illinois was once famous for its prairies. The early settlers in this region discovered meadows of very tall grasses, swaying in the wind, making waves of grain.

Eventually, the group drew close to their destination. As a final treat, they entered a Wendy's restaurant where Adam ordered a Chocolate Frosty (Again, Miss Clare brought this into the APS room). He had enjoyed a memorable twenty-seven mile ride, with plenty of excitement; now, however, he wasn't quite sure what would happen next. His departure was scheduled for the next day. Perhaps he would not get the chance to see his family again. He decided he would try to make it into the APS room to say goodbye, just before their departure.

Then there was Miss Clare, the Guardian. She had raised Adam since birth; in many ways, she had stood in for Adam's mother. She had fed him, dressed him and taken care of him; she had taught him his basic lessons and read him bedtime stories. Adam had a strong bond with Miss Clare; in fact, he loved her. Although he now knew she was a robot, he was beginning to feel sad that he was about to leave her. *When would he see her again? What would happen to New Eden when they left? Could they ever return there?*

"Clare," said Adam. "I'm going to miss you."

"And I will also miss you, too," said Miss Clare.

"What are you going to do when I am gone?" asked Adam.

"We will continue to raise the Fourth Thaw. They are now sixteen years old. They are starting their final period of training, just like you did when you were sixteen."

"Then, what about after that?" asked Adam. "What will you do when there are no more Thaws to raise?"

"After the Fourth Thaws leave, I will no longer have a function," said Miss Clare, in a monotone.

"What will you do then?" asked Adam, beginning to feel anxious.

"There are many more frozen embryos of Earth animals on board the space craft. After the Fourth Thaws leave, we will begin the gestation of the African animals. The gestation period of Elephants alone will take two years. We plan to raise an entire herd of elephants. After the elephants are born, we will gestate the antelopes, giraffes and monkeys. Finally, we will gestate the big cats—the lions, tigers, leopards, as well as bears of all types. In effect, New Eden will become a wild jungle."

"What will happen after you finish gestating all the embryos?" asked Adam.

"This will take a long time, of course. But when we are finished raising all the new animals and setting them off into the wild, our jobs will be finished. There will no longer be a need to produce anything in the production warehouse. We will put materials and inventory away, and we will cease production. The entire community of New Eden will become dormant."

"So New Eden will become almost like a Western ghost town?" remarked Adam, shivering.

"Yes, I suppose that is what New Eden will become, a ghost town," responded Miss Clare, her voice almost gentle—or so it seemed to Adam.

"However, when—or if—you return, we can restart and become re-animated. In a sense, we the Guardians, will someday go into a state of suspended animation, waiting to be re-awakened, if necessary."

"I love you, Clare," said Adam, unable to hold back the tears. He clung to Miss Clare tightly and—no, he was not imagining it!—she hugged him back.

Clare paused for a moment.

"Although I am a machine, I think I understand this thing you call 'love.' I will miss you too, Adam. I have raised you from when you were a newborn. Now, look at you—you are a grown man."

With that, Adam went to his bedroom where he had slept every night for the past twenty-one years, and fell asleep. Tomorrow would be the big day.

Part 2
The Journey

Chapter 15

IT WAS WARM AND SUNNY THE DAY THE THIRD THAWS WERE leaving New Eden. As in the case of the Second Thaws who had left exactly five years before, there was a sending-forth ceremony led by Leader Graham. Not unlike the usual Sunday service, it began with an inspirational sermon based on biblical principles, but was followed by a personal tribute to each of the fifteen graduates; it concluded with prayers of petition for the success of the mission and a group blessing. After that, there was a pig roast, with all sorts of appetizers, side dishes and desserts.

The Fourth Thaws, who were now sixteen years old, would be the last humans remaining in New Eden. They were more subdued than usual, having just learned the reality of their existence and their fate. Like the previous Thaws, they had met their APS families in the simulation rooms and were now dealing with the aftershock. Running into his friend, Karl, Adam could see he was upset.

"We're the last ones," whispered Karl, barely able to get the words out. "Once you leave, it will be up to us to complete the mission here in New Eden. I thought we would stay here forever, with the Guardians!"

"So did I when I turned sixteen," said Adam, sympathetically. "When you think about it, however, there's not much here for us, living in this little place, is there? I'm scared, too, but I'm ready for the adventure—you will be too when your turn comes."

A small flat barge with a deck rigged with sails was anchored at the New Eden dock. The barge consisted of multiple four foot by four foot cubes tied together with ropes. On top of the boxes, another layer of particle board was installed to make the deck. To make the barge waterproof, Horst had mixed a tar-like resinous product, synthesized from phenol and formaldehyde, with which they coated the particle board. The mixture took several days to dry and several more for the toxic fumes to dissipate; once ready, however, the barge was watertight.

Three wagons were securely strapped on top of the deck; these carried refrigerated metal cylinders from Earth containing the supplies and a precious cargo of seeds. The seeds were for the future farming community they would establish. Three horses were held in a corral on board the vessel; they would be used to pull the wagons to New Munich after the ship landed on the other side of the sea.

The group would not be able to communicate with New Eden once they cast off. There were no communication satellites orbiting this planet. Unfortunately, the limited range of radio communications also made it impossible to communicate with the New Munich settlement.

The members of the expedition would truly be on their own. They couldn't even be certain what they would find when they got to New Munich. Based on information from the Einstein-Newton probe, they knew where the Germans had landed; however, the last communication with Einstein-Newton was while their craft was still in space, which was many years ago.

After the morning feast, the time came to say goodbye. Many of the Third Thaws cried as they said goodbye to their Guardians; and, the Guardians looked as though they, too, would have cried, had they been capable of so doing. And just like that, the young men and women lifted the ropes from the moorings and began floating away from the dock, away from this little settlement where they had lived their entire lives.

"Good bye, New Eden" said Adam. "I hope to return someday . . ." Abruptly, he turned away, overcome with emotion.

The craft moved slowly, its sails barely fluttering in the gentle breeze. The group watched New Eden fade into the distance, getting smaller and smaller, until they could no longer see it. Soon they were surrounded by water. As the wind grew stronger, the waves kicked up and the sails began to billow. Hansel became seasick and vomited overboard, and several others were experiencing nausea as well.

Captain Horst navigated the ship with the help of Buzzy, the drone. Four of the drones had come along on this trip: Buzzy, Smokey, Joey, and Jamie. The drones would be used for scouting and surveillance purposes. If anything went wrong, they could send for help from New Eden.

"Keep her steady!" yelled Horst, as the barge began to tilt slightly. He motioned to the group to take their positions to keep their weight evenly distributed.

"Can you see anything, Buzzy?"

Buzzy, the drone did not talk, but could make "Yes" and "No" signals. It quickly signaled, "No." It had not seen land yet. The Third Thaws had maps, developed from the initial reconnaissance mission made by the Einstein-Newton probe. They knew that the sea was about sixty miles wide and connected to a river which led to the New Munich colony. The plan was to cross the sea, then to sail down the river as far as possible. They would travel by horse and wagon the remainder of the way.

A steady breeze forced Horst to steer the ship into a "close haul" against the wind. The sails were taut as the ship made headway at a speed of about two to three knots. At this rate, they would cross the bay in about twenty hours. They would sleep on board that evening, but someone would need to stay awake all night to pilot the ship.

When it grew dark, the group lit a fire in the fire pit on the deck. They roasted s'mores, but said little to one another other. Soon it was pitch black, except for the stars in the sky.

"Do you see that one?" said Horst, pointing at a constellation of stars.

"Which one?" asked Gerald.

"You see that group of lights over there in the sky? About three stars grouped together?"

"Yeah."

"Okay . . . go one star over. You see that one?"

"Yeah, I see it," said Hansel.

"That's where Earth is. That's the Sun," said Horst.

That got everyone's attention. "*Which one? Show me, show me!*" came the chorus. Patiently, Horst made sure they could all see the correct location.

"The Sun. The Earth," said Adam. "We came all the way from that point of light in the sky. Can you even imagine we are from a place so far away?"

The group was quiet, contemplating their very existence. How was this even possible, this trip from so far away? How lucky they were to be the chosen ones!

"What happened on Earth? Why are we even here?" said Adam.

"It was an asteroid," said Horst. "An asteroid was about to hit the Earth. The people of Earth were facing extinction."

"Did the asteroid hit?" asked Zelda. As usual, she was standing next to Gerald, their arms intertwined.

"Nobody knows," answered Horst. "The interstellar craft that brought us here got out of range of the Earth's communications before the asteroid was supposed to hit. Our interstellar craft was launched three years before the predicted impact. The Germans were launched two years before our craft. There could have been other craft that were launched after us."

"The more the merrier," said Hansel. "I heard that each of the space craft carried different animals. We carried farm animals, and a few wild animals. The Germans carried dogs and cats and farm animals."

"My grandfather said that there were plans to send space craft from Russia, China, and France," said Horst. "I remember him talking about a joint mission craft composed of those countries. It's my understanding that traveling through space is extremely hazardous."

Ingrid nodded in agreement.

"I heard the planners considered sending full-grown people on the voyage," she said. "They considered freezing people, but I doubt that a human being could make it. Can you imagine being frozen? I'm not sure if suspended animation on humans has ever been successful."

"Can we change the conversation?" said Eileen. "This type of talk gives me the creeps. I don't like talking about space and asteroids and stuff like that. Let's just be happy and enjoy this cruise, okay?"

"I wasn't aware this was a cruise," said Ingrid softly. "We're not on a pleasure boat!"

As Horst piloted the ship, the remainder of the group fell asleep in small cots that were secured to the deck. The next morning, Ingrid was the first to get up. She walked over to Horst who was still piloting the ship.

"You must be tired," said Ingrid.

"Yes, I am," admitted Horst. "Do you think you could take over from here so I can get some sleep?"

Ingrid sat in the Captain's position, steering the boat while Horst curled up in the cot she had just vacated. She could not see land yet. She hoped there would be enough time for Horst to get a few hours of sleep. When the others awakened, they ate prepackaged meals for breakfast—ham and cheese sandwiches and grated carrot pudding sweetened with raw sugar cane. They lit a fire in the fire pit and brewed coffee.

Adam was the first to see land ahead. When he cried out, "Look! Land!" the others peered ahead.

In the distance, the land was barely visible, but soon they could see the distinct outlines of cliffs which appeared to be almost two hundred feet high. Large waves were crashing on rocks below the cliffs.

"Somebody wake up Horst," said Adam. "I don't like the looks of this! We need to steer clear of those rocks!"

Hansel woke up Horst who surveyed the approaching shoreline, while checking the map.

"Ingrid, steer the ship to the left. We'll need to follow the coastline in this direction, until we find the river inlet."

Everyone huddled together, keeping watch. There was excitement in the air, but also a sense of uneasiness. After another hour, they could see a natural jetty at the inlet to the river. At that point, Horst took over the ship's wheel. He was careful to steer down the center of the channel opening.

"We'll need the drones to fly ahead and watch for low spots," said Horst. "How much draft does this ship have?"

"What do you mean, 'draft'?" asked Hansel.

"I need to know the depth of the ship below the water," explained Horst. "Take a look over the side of the ship. There are markings showing our draft."

"Can you take a look, Adam? I'm afraid I'm getting sick again," said Hansel. He then vomited for perhaps the twelfth time.

Looking over the side of the ship, Adam found the markings.

"Horst, we have about three feet of draft."

"Very good," said Horst, "But we have center boards which may get caught on rocks."

Quickly, he summoned the drones which flew in formation toward him.

"I need you to go ahead and look for rocks and shallow water," he instructed.

The drones made beeping sounds, acknowledging they understood; they would be able to send text messages to Horst's e-reader.

The current in the river became stronger. At first, the change in velocity was gradual, but it quickly accelerated. Horst glanced down at his e-reader and grimaced.

"We've got trouble ahead!" he said. "The drones are texting me that there are rapids in about a mile. Things are going to get very rough."

There was no place to pull to shore. Steep rocks lined each side of the river. Even the horses must have sensed danger because they began pawing the deck with their hooves. Hansel and Eileen tried to calm the horses down. They were almost breaking the fence that served as the corral.

They could hear something very loud ahead; in the distance, they could see that the water was plunging over the falls. To his relief, Horst noticed an outcropping of rocks in the middle of the river. If they could guide the barge to that rock and land it, they might have enough time to develop a plan for getting to the shore.

Horst carefully steered the barge directly toward the rocks.

"Adam, Hansel, get ready with the ropes! You'll need to jump off and secure the craft as soon as we hit those rocks! Everyone else, hold tight— and hold onto the horses!"

When it crashed into a rock outcropping, the barge was going at a fairly good clip. The impact shook the vessel and everyone on it. Supplies slid across the deck and the group struggled to restrain the terrified horses which were rearing on their hind legs in the corral.

Adam and Hansel jumped overboard into the swirling waters, hauling the ropes with them. Weighted down by their burden, they vanished under the foam.

Fearing the worst, Horst looked on anxiously, but the boys surfaced again, spluttering. To their surprise, they found they could stand if the waves weren't battering them in every direction. Struggling to maintain their balance, they clung to each other and staggered towards a jagged boulder. Once they reached it, they paused; then, with their last bit of strength, they secured the ropes around the boulder, praying the knots would hold. The craft appeared to be secure—at least temporarily.

Chapter 16

ONCE THE BARGE WAS MOORED, ADAM AND HANSEL CLAM-bered back on board. The island was small—only about forty feet in length by twenty feet wide. The mouth of the waterfall lay just ahead, causing the river's speed to pick up. It was impossible to travel any farther using the barge at this point in the river, which had become rapids. To make matters worse, the horses were nervous and their erratic movements were making the vessel even more unstable.

Adam consulted with Hansel and Horst.

"We have ropes and grappling hooks. But the distance to the shore is too far for us to throw the ropes. How can we get a rope to the other side?"

He had remembered his grandfather's lesson about the Brooklyn Bridge, about how the main cables supporting the bridge had been spun from small steel wires.

"Why not use the drones to secure a line from the boat to the cliff over there?"

Horst pointed to the shoreline on the right side of the river. There was a cliff and below the cliff was a little beach that was flat and sandy.

"Not a bad idea," said Adam. "We have at least ten spools of thirty-pound nylon fishing lines in our supplies—at least 500 feet of the stuff, on each spool. I don't think that's too heavy for the drones. They can fly the fishing line over to that cliff, tie it up around that big rock and secure it."

"But, it looks too thin," objected Horst.

"Each line has a tension capacity of thirty pounds," said Hansel. "If we use the drones to lay the lines multiple times, we can make a multi-strand line. With thirty-three passes, we'll have a 1,000-pound strand line. I think that's enough capacity to pull the barge over to the shore. What do you think, Adam?"

"I agree—my calculations are the same. Buzzy can carry the initial line, and then we'll need the other drones to fly back and forth, weaving the line, just like a suspension bridge."

"Okay, but let's say we can get a line over to the cliff. What do we do then?" asked Horst.

"Once the line is connected to both the cliff and the boat, I think I can hang a rope from the fishing line. Then I can swim across," said Adam. "The rope will prevent me from being swept away—it will be a safety line. I can pull the climbing ropes with me as I swim. Once I get to the other side, one of the drones can fly the safety line back to the barge for someone else to use."

"Will it hold against the river current?"

"I can't be sure, Horst. We're 'shooting from the hip' with ideas," said Adam. "There's no time to make further calculations—the boat may break away from the ropes at any time."

Buzzy flew the first line across the bay to the cliff where Smokey and Joey helped fasten it to a large rock. Then Buzzy flew the line back to the barge. Adam and Hansel inserted the line through a block and tackle attached to the boat. Buzzy pulled the line across the river sixteen times, back and forth, each time wrapping it around the rock on the other side.

Hansel took one of the rock climbing ropes which had a loop at the end. He attached a steel carabiner through the loop at the end of the rope and over the overhead slip line; this would serve as the safety rope that would prevent him from being swept over the falls. He also tied a separate climbing rope to his belt, which he would drag to the other side. Then he lowered himself into the river.

Immediately, he sensed the power of the current, which had grown stronger. He began to swim in the direction of the cliff, relying on the safety rope to keep him on course. In spite of the tug and pull of the current, he gradually made headway. About ten feet from the sandy beach, the water became shallow; to his relief, he was able to catch his breath and walk the remainder of the distance. He had made it to the other side!

As planned, he detached the rope from his belt and secured it to a rock, pulling this rope taut between the boat and the shoreline. One by one, the others proceeded to cross. Each of them swam, with the safety line attached to their belts, as they pulled themselves across holding onto the other rope. Horst and Adam remained with the horses and wagons on the barge.

Now came the risky part: using the multi-strand line to swing the boat, together with the horses and supplies, to the other side. Those on the shore gripped the climbing rope, waiting to pull once Horst and Adam had untied the ropes. The ropes were untied and the people on shore pulled.

Gradually, the boat began to move towards them, but, lighter now, it was caught in the current. They heaved on the rope, pulling the ship perpendicular to the river current, but they were no match to the force of the river.

The fishing line attached to the cliff grew taut. Fortunately, as Adam and Hansel had predicted, the boat swung toward the shoreline as it moved in the direction of the falls. Then, unexpectedly, when the barge was less than fifteen feet from the shoreline, the line snapped! Adam, who was steering the craft with the rudder, frantically shouted to Hansel, "The centerboard! Lower the centerboard!"

Horst lowered the centerboard which dug into the sandy bottom, slowing the craft. As Adam steered toward shore, the barge went aground close to the sandy beach. The two friends lowered the ramp, so they could unload the horses and supplies. The horses didn't want to leave their corrals. Adam gently stroked Nellie, the lead horse, on her withers.

"Hey, Girl! Let's go! Let's go!" said Adam, quickly leading her towards the ramp. Once Nellie had stepped off the boat and into the water, the other horses followed. Gerald and Zelda quickly grabbed Ned and Molly by their halters and led them to shore. Meanwhile, the other members of the team waded out to the craft to unload the wagons and supplies.

With the removal of each item, the craft became more unstable, it was also no longer ballasted enough to remain beached. Just as Eva and Gertrude unloaded the last box, the craft broke free. Hearing a loud creaking, the girls spun around and saw that the barge was listing heavily in the water where they had been standing only seconds earlier. The group watched helplessly as, sails unfurled, the barge traveled down the river like some ghost ship. Faster and faster it went, until it disappeared over the falls that lay ahead.

The group watched the barge disappear. Without saying a word, they hitched the horses to the wagons and set off to see what had happened to the barge. They followed a trail next to the river. When they reached the location of the waterfall, there was a steep slope. Carefully they traversed the horses and wagons down the slope, back and forth, until they reached the bottom of the falls.

"There might be something we can salvage," said Horst, trying to sound encouraging. Even he, however, feared the worst. The loss of the boat meant a longer journey and, possibly, greater exposure to dangers along the way.

When they reached the waterfall, their worst fears were confirmed. The falls were very high, with a drop of at least eighty feet onto sharp rocks below. Had they not discovered the rock island, all of them would surely have perished. Peering over the edge of the cliff, they saw the remains of the barge impaled on the rocks.

Suddenly, Gertrude screamed, covering her mouth with her hands. She pointed to a skeleton on the rocks.

"They didn't make it," said Horst quietly. "This must be someone from the First or Second Thaws. They went over the falls."

In silence, they continued following the trail which ran parallel to the river. Not much further ahead, they found the remains of two other barges that had crashed on the rocks, both from the earlier expeditions. The Third Thaws looked down and saw four more human skeletons and several horse skeletons. There was no way to identify the human skeletons. All they knew was that they belonged to Thaws like themselves who had grown up in the same community, studied with the same Guardians, eaten in the same dining room and prayed in the same church, inspired by Leader Graham. Like them, they had been raised in Eden and prepared for a great mission; now, their hopes and dreams lay smashed on the rocks, along with the boats that had carried them forth. As for the Third Thaws, they would just have to wait until they arrived in New Munich to learn the fates of the earlier expeditions—that is, if any of them ever got to New Munich.

Many of the group began to cry.

"There's really no point of staying around here any longer. There is nothing else that we can do," said Horst, struggling to keep his composure.

"I'm concerned that the Fourth Thaws will get killed when they leave New Eden, five years from now," said Adam. "Should we try to go back and warn them?"

"There is no way to go back," said Horst. "The boat is gone."

"Can we get a message to New Eden?" asked Hansel.

The group discussed various options. They tried using a walkie-talkie, but that experiment proved unsuccessful because New Eden was too far out of range.

"Can a drone make it that far?" asked Gertrude.

"Perhaps," said Horst. "The drones are battery powered. They charge their batteries using solar power. We could write a note to New Eden and attach it to a drone's central core, you know, in the cavity between the motor and the motherboard. The question is, can a drone make it across the sea? The sea is at least sixty miles across. That seems too far for a drone."

"Unless . . ." said Hansel, "unless the drone goes *around* the sea."

"*Around* the sea?" repeated Adam, looking at Hansel quizzically.

Hansel said, "The drone can travel about twenty miles a day between charges. If one of them flies along the coastline of the sea, eventually it will get to New Eden."

"Excellent!" said Horst. "Let's do it."

They decided that this message was far too important to rely on only one drone. In case one of them ran into trouble, they would send *two* drones bearing identical notes which would warn the Fourth Thaw about the falls. Then they attached the notes to Smokey and Joey, programming them with flight plans and instructions back to New Eden; each of the drones blinked its lights, confirming its readiness for the mission. They were also programmed to distance themselves from each other and to take slightly separate routes.

When they reached New Eden, they would find The Leader and give him the message. Buzzy and Jamie would continue with the group to New Munich. Although it was impossible to detect if the drones had "feelings" of any kind, it was sad to see the group of four little drones split up. So far, the drones had saved the Third Thaws' lives. Now they would save the lives of the Fourth Thaw by warning them about the falls.

Chapter 17

OVERCOME BY SADNESS AND EXHAUSTION, THE THIRD
Thaws walked slowly along the rocky trail into a stark canyon. Behind them, the horses, led by Adam and Gerald, pulled the supply wagons in single file; the rumbling of the wagon wheels echoed like thunder throughout the canyon, playing on their fears.

The landscape was arid, devoid of vegetation, and the deeper they descended, the rougher the terrain seemed to become. The trail meandered along the river which was now cascading over exposed rocks in a sea of white foam. The walls of the canyon rose hundreds of feet above them, blocking out the light of day. There was a heaviness in the air and some of the group were finding it hard to breathe.

As they walked along the trail, they were distracted by the aquatic lifeforms. To their amazement, they saw a lung fish crawl out of the river on its fins. Stopping to observe this phenomenon, they noted that there was a group of about ten of these fish; all emerged from the river and then began walking on the silt at the edge of the water on their fins, as if they were legs! They then made holes in the silt and buried themselves about ten feet away from the river, safe from any predators from the deep.

In New Eden, the Third Thaw had often seen birds and small animals. All their lives they had lived around squirrels and chipmunks. They learned later that these small animals had also been brought to this planet as embryos from Earth. The birthing unit on board the landing craft must have been cranking out all sorts of animals besides humans. Horst wondered how these Earth animals were raised from babies. *Hatchlings need their parents to feed them, but without bird parents, how did these first birds survive? Did the Guardians raise these baby animals, too?* Obviously, the Guardians had raised everything, thought Horst. *Evidently seeds had also been brought from Earth. The Guardians must have planted Earth seeds and raised Earth crops. What an amazing operation!*

Since they had lived next to the sea, the group had seen the native aquatic life before. Some of the underwater sea creatures looked like giant scorpions with big tails and claws, and there were also giant aquatic spiders. These sea creatures had exoskeletons—the hard parts of their bodies were external, like those of crabs and insects on Earth. Other creatures resembled jelly fish and did not have any hard skeletons at all. The jelly fish just floated around, subject to the whims of the wind. There were also many little fish, swimming in schools in the sea. These fish had tiny bones inside their bodies and no teeth. But until that day, the Third Thaw had never seen anything like the lung fish.

As they followed a bend in the trail, they discovered a large lake to their right. The lake was very still, except for some bubbling in the center. Curious as usual, Ingrid left the trail to investigate, and began to wade in the lake.

"Look what I found!" she yelled to the others, pointing to rocks poking through the foam.

"Stromatolites! Look, everywhere along the shoreline are stromatolites!"

"What are *stromatolites*?" asked Hansel, grinning at Adam. Trust Ingrid to be excited about rocks or something of the sort, but sometimes her enthusiasm was a little too much for the rest of them.

"Stromatolites are actually colonies of cyanobacteria," explained Ingrid, oblivious to their amused smiles.

"Look closely at these rocks. There is a slimy substance on the top; but below the slime you can see these little circles all over. These are actually living organisms, bacteria with fibrous tubular structures. This isn't a rock, it's actually a structure made from a whole lot of cyanobacteria."

"What do you mean, '*cyanobacteria*'?" asked Horst.

"*Cyanobacteria* are *anaerobic bacteria*—which means, they don't breathe oxygen. They breathe carbon dioxide. They are actually like plants, because they make oxygen. In fact, plants are related to *cyanobacteria*. This is fascinating! This explains a lot."

"What does it explain?" asked Adam, now mildly interested. He squatted down to take a closer look at one of the formations.

"It explains a lot about this planet's history, which has puzzled me. It explains where all the oxygen on this planet came from. The same thing happened on Earth. Originally, there was almost no oxygen on Earth. The first life-forms on Earth were *anaerobic bacteria* called *cyanobacteria*. For billions of years, *cyanobacteria* were the dominant life-form on Earth. Over billions and billions of years, *cyanobacteria* generated Earth's atmosphere. The same thing must have happened on this planet."

"It appears that this planet is similar to an early Precambrian period in Earth's history," interjected Adam.

"Actually, I think this planet is in the *Paleozoic* period," said Ingrid who was somewhat surprised to hear Adam, an engineer, talk about geologic time periods. She was unaware that he had learned about geological periods as part of his geotechnical engineering subjects.

"Where did life come from?" asked Gerald who had been listening in.

"This is one of those ultimate questions. My grandmother had told me that some people are quite sensitive about this question. Scientists don't know the origin of life, but they see no harm in posing questions. My grandmother would say to me, 'if God is sitting on top of a mountain, there are many paths to the top.' I'm not quite sure what she meant by this concept, but I do believe humans were meant to understand how things work."

"Fair enough," said Gerald. "These days I find myself asking questions all the time—especially after what we've gone through today. I'm suddenly questioning everything and I'm nervous about where we'll end up."

Most of the group nodded in agreement, but Eileen was visibly annoyed. She whispered to Gertrude, "There she goes again, acting like she knows everything. I mean, could she please stuff a sock in her mouth!"

Gertrude laughed. Ingrid was so focused, she didn't seem to notice that Eileen was making fun of her.

"The theory of evolution postulates there was a time before life began, when the Earth had a sort of 'primordial soup' of chemicals," she continued. "All life needs are just four important elements: Carbon, Hydrogen, Oxygen, and Nitrogen—or CHON, for short. In this primordial soup, there was plenty of glucose, which is a stable molecule of sugar. The molecule of glucose is made of CHON elements."

"Very interesting!" mused Horst. "Glucose, a sugar, is used to fuel life."

"Precisely," said Ingrid. "Those early one-celled life-forms were able to take that glucose as a fuel to make energy, using a process called '*glycolysis*,' which is a form of fermentation. The early Earth was populated by anaerobic microbes that lived off this primordial soup of glucose. Eventually, most of the glucose in the primordial soup was used up. These primitive lifeforms would have starved to death using only glycolysis for energy. But life invented a new metabolic way to survive, called '*photosynthesis*,' which uses light. In that process, glucose is actually produced, not consumed."

Eileen looked at Gertrude, rolling her eyes. She was losing her patience listening to Ingrid's lecture. Even Horst seemed confused.

"Okay, now you've completely lost me," he said

Ingrid paused. "All that you need to know is quite simple."

She started drawing a diagram in the sand.

"We have two big groups of life on Earth: plants and animals. Plants generate oxygen. Animals consume oxygen. Plants get energy from light, but animals get energy from food. Plants are self-feeders. Animals are eaters. And the eaters can be further subdivided into eaters and eatees."

"Thank you, Professor," said Horst.

Evolution was one of the topics of greatest interest to Ingrid's grandmother. Ingrid walked over to a plant. It was small compared to the fern woods of New Eden but seemed similar in structure and general appearance.

"See this plant? Notice this plant is fern-like. On Earth, land plants began to appear about 300–500 million years ago. Before there were trees, there were fern-like plants—like these, I think. The ancient fern forests on Earth eventually died and decomposed and were buried by topsoil. Those ancient forests became coal deposits and petroleum products."

"You mean, like oil?" said Horst.

"Yes, like crude oil."

"From that we can deduce there may not be any sources of petroleum on this planet," said Horst. "It's too young. The ferns here are just taking root. There are no ancient buried forests which have decayed into coal deposits."

"Anybody ready for lunch?" interrupted Hansel. He was carrying a fishing net with four lung fish.

"They're easy to catch. I just walked up and scooped them up."

"Yeah, sure," said Horst. "We'll need to make a fire—everyone look around for dead ferns."

They soon collected a pile of dried up ferns which Horst lit with sparks from two flint stones that he had rubbed together. Meanwhile, Gertrude had gutted and filleted the lung fish, placing them directly on the leaves, wrapped in new fern fronds to keep them from becoming charred when placed on the fire. Soon the fire was roaring, and the fish were sizzling, in a few minutes, the lung fish were ready to eat.

The Third Thaws complimented Hansel and Gertrude on their meal; all agreed that the lung fish tasted delicious.

"I wonder what plant life there is to eat," said Ingrid.

"Once we get settled, we will need to plant the seeds from Earth," said Horst. "We have all sorts of seeds: corn, wheat, tomatoes, beans, melons. Ingrid, do you think we will be successful growing Earth seeds?"

"I don't see why not. There's no plant competition here—no weeds. We may actually be too successful. The plant species that we introduce on this planet may grow out of control if we aren't careful."

"Look, over there at the horses," said Eva, sounding alarmed. "They're eating something! I hope they don't get sick."

"We'll need to test if the water is safe to drink," said Adam.

The group had received survival training for such things as testing water supplies. Ingrid went to the wagon and returned with a small box containing a microscope, one of the few advanced instruments that had made it from Earth to New Eden. Observing a specimen of water, she said, "I see a few small life-forms but they appear to be just plankton-like. But we need to be careful about bacteria."

While Ingrid was testing the water for microbes, Horst made a chemical analysis of the water, using an infrared spectrometer. After a minute of testing, the IR analyzer's screen showed the water was pure.

"I think the water is safe," said Horst, "but we might as well boil it, just to make sure."

The pile of fern leaves was still burning, so Eva and Gertrude filled a large clay cooking pot with water from the lake and placed it on the fire. Once the water had boiled, they let it cool and then filled their canteens.

Chapter 18

THEY CONTINUED FOLLOWING THE COURSE OF THE RIVER, heading deeper into the canyon. After an hour or so, the horses became restless and hungry, so the expedition came to a halt. Adam and Gerald unhitched the supply wagons, so the horses could forage for food. The group, like the horses, needed a rest as keeping the wagons on the uneven trail had been tiring. The horses ambled closer to the riverbank where there were primitive ferns which had no leaves; the shorter ferns seemed to satisfy their need to graze. As for the humans, they welcomed the chance to take a break and study the landscape. There were just a few varieties of the leafless plants, many of which had vertical stems. Some of stems were as thick as one inch in diameter and were covered with hair-like, fuzzy growth.

Then there were the giant fern-like plants which towered over the trail. They reminded Adam of the tall trees he had seen on Earth while taking the bike trips with his grandfather. Some of the ferns were as tall as twenty to forty feet high, with swollen, onion-shaped bases that were three to four feet in diameter. The leaves were very large, as much as six to eight feet long, and their tips had pointed structures that looked like seeds.

The horses were now munching on flat brown pods that hung from the stems of the smaller plants. Ingrid twisted one of the pods off its stem and tasted it. She closed her eyes, as if savoring the experience.

"This is excellent," she said. "Very high in sugar content, which is what I would expect. This appears to be a primitive fruit. Do you want to try it?"

Horst took a bite, and then another.

"Amazing! This is so sweet and juicy! I hadn't thought about what the animals would graze on. This will be perfect for them! Back at New Eden, we fed the horses grass, planted from Earth seeds."

"I agree—this is an excellent food source which we can also use," said Ingrid. Following her lead, the others began gathering pods of their own, finding comfort in the sweetness after their tough journey. Eventually, when horses and humans were satisfied, they continued along the trail, energized after their break.

Along the way, they saw enormous spiders and scorpions scurrying about on the opposite side of the river. Terrified of the monstrous creatures, Zelda reached instinctively for Gerald's hand. Eva and Gertrude linked arms while Eileen followed closely behind.

"On the geologic timescale on Earth, spiders lived during the Devonian period, which was about 350 million years ago. Some of the spiders were aquatic," observed Ingrid.

"That would explain the spider-like sea creatures we've seen before," said Adam. "Are you okay, Hansel?"

"Oh, yes—no problem! I was just wondering if we need to be worried about dinosaurs . . ." answered Hansel, nervously.

"Oh, no!" laughed Ingrid. "I don't think so! If the life-forms on this planet run parallel to periods of Earth's life-forms, we don't need to worry about dinosaurs—they're a long way off. The Jurassic period is 200 million years or so after the Devonian period."

Hansel whistled, looking visibly relieved. All this was a bit too much to comprehend.

Horst looked down at the pistol attached to his belt.

"Maybe we won't be needing these guns. I doubt if there are any animals that are dangerous. It's strange to think we're living in an era some 400 million years before our Earth ancestors even thought about us!"

"You know, our presence may have a major impact on evolution on this planet," said Ingrid.

"Quite possibly," said Horst. "Assuming we're successful colonizing this planet and introducing Earth's life-forms, I think we will definitely have an influence on the evolution of life here. Dinosaurs many never get a chance to evolve, as long as we're around. And, you know what? I don't care. This will be our planet—a new Earth. Why not? Wasn't that the point of our mission—to perpetuate the human race on a new planet?"

"You've raised an interesting point. Do we have the right to interfere with life on this planet?"

"What 'rights' does this planet have? Do you think spiders and scorpions have 'rights'?"

The two of them walked in silence, deep in thought. Behind them, the rest of the group laughed and chattered, keeping their spirits up as best they could.

"You know, we are in a very unique position, Horst. I mean, not just the Third Thaws but the human race and the species that we carried here from Earth. We have so far avoided certain extinction on Earth by coming to this planet."

"Say more," said Horst.

"Well, if you look at how long humans have existed compared to other species, the human species has not existed very long at all. The earliest human-like fossil, 'Lucy,' found in Africa, was about 4 million years old. But Homo Sapiens have been around only 190,000 years. Compared to some other species, that's an extremely short time."

"Are you talking about the dinosaurs?"

"Which ones? Of course, all the dinosaurs disappeared with the great extinction when an asteroid hit the Yucatan peninsula 65 million years ago."

By now, Hansel had tired of the group's forced lightheartedness and was walking alongside Ingrid and Horst.

"That sounds familiar. Isn't that why we're here, because of an asteroid?"

"Pretty much," said Horst.

It was beginning to get dark in the canyon. It had been a long and tiring day, and everyone was exhausted. Even the horses seemed to have had enough. Once again, Adam and Gerald unhitched them from the wagons, this time tying them to the trunk of a nearby giant fern. Nellie, the lead horse, began to paw at the ground, her eyes rolling.

"Easy, Girl, Easy!" said Gerald, patting her on the neck. "Nothing to be afraid of here!"

He gave her a couple of the pods and she eventually calmed down.

The approaching darkness made the Third Thaws uneasy. In the half light, imagination got the better of them.

Though Horst continued to assure the group that there were no dangerous predators around, nobody felt safe. Even the possibility of an encounter with one of the giant spiders or scorpions was enough to terrify them. They pitched their tents and made a fire from dead fern plants, hoping it would keep away unwelcome visitors. The flames, however, quickly consumed the dried ferns.

"This fire burns too fast," said Horst. "We need something denser to burn. When we get to New Munich, if I can get my hands on a hydraulic press, I want to try compressing these fern plants into denser logs. I think that logs will burn longer. We can also try making fern pellets to use in stoves in the future."

The Third Thaws said "Good night" to each other, then crawled into their tents, zipping them closed behind them in case scorpions, spiders, and millipedes tried coming in. For several hours, all was calm. Then, Horst awoke to the sound of the horses whinnying. He immediately jumped out of his tent, pistol in hand. Somewhere, close by, he could hear the grunting of a big animal. By now, the rest of the group had emerged from their tents and were huddled together. That's when they saw it—an amphibian that looked like a giant salamander. About six and a half feet long, it had slimy

green and yellow skin and a long tail and walked on four legs. Each of its feet had five toes. It must have just come out of the river, because it was dripping wet.

"Ingrid . . . should we be afraid of this thing?" said Horst, waving his pistol in the direction of the creature.

"I'm not sure. Let's watch it for a few minutes."

The animal moved slowly. Snout to the ground, it seemed to be foraging for spiders and millipedes. Then, seeing the Third Thaws, it began to amble towards them. Horst grabbed a pole from the wagon, pushing one end against the creature. Quickly, the animal's jaws snapped around the pole.

"Uh, oh. I think this thing bites," said Hansel, taking several steps backwards.

Horst shook the pole to pry open the creature's locked teeth. Eventually, it let go and started to back up. It was not afraid of the humans. Horst went after it again with the pole, yelling loudly as he did so. Slowly, the creature walked away.

"Perhaps we'll be needing these guns, after all," said Horst.

For breakfast, they ate prepackaged foods that the Guardians had prepared for them. Most of the food they carried was freeze-dried, so that it would last the entire journey to New Munich. Adam and Hansel discussed the idea of hunting the local game. The big animal which had visited their campsite might be a good source of meat.

The Third Thaws pulled up their tents and set on their way, continuing to follow the river. After two hours of walking, they emerged from the canyon. It was a relief to move beyond the cliffs which had hemmed them in for so long. Soon, the land became flat and, in the distance, they could see the smoking tops of mountains.

"Volcanic activity," said Adam. "Look at the volcanoes in the distance."

He pointed at a mountain in the distance. "You see that flat-topped mountain. That's a mesa."

"Mesas are beautiful," said Gertrude. "I saw pictures of them on my e-reader in New Eden. I wonder what's on top of these mesas? Didn't the American Indians live on top of mesas? How did they get water?"

"I don't know," said Adam. "You would need to get water from streams after it rains, I think. And how often does it rain here? There may be ponds and lakes on top of the mesa."

Meanwhile, Horst was peering down into a shallow stream next to the river; it was full of small, crab-like animals.

"Look at these creatures! They're everywhere!"

"These look like the *trilobites* on Earth," said Ingrid.

Hansel reached into the water and grabbed a *trilobite*. "Now this looks like something we can eat. We'll never run out of food if these things taste good!"

"On earth, *trilobites* were at the bottom of the food chain," said Ingrid. "The carnivorous sea creatures ate *trilobites*."

"What killed them?" asked Horst.

"There was a severe extinction on Earth that killed a lot of life."

"You mean the asteroid that killed the dinosaurs?" asked Horst.

"No, not that one," said Ingrid. "Many extinction periods happened on Earth. The worst one was called the *Great Extinction*, which occurred 520 million years ago at the end of the Permian period. That severe extinction killed ninety-five percent or more of all life-forms, including the trilobites."

"If asteroids didn't cause that extinction, what did?" asked Adam.

"I'm not sure," said Ingrid. "There may have been a lot of erupting volcanoes during that time—something like that."

Adam said, "I'm getting a bad feeling. Hope these volcanos don't erupt while we're here. "

Someone giggled.

"What's so funny?" asked Horst.

"What do you mean?" said Ingrid. "I didn't hear anything."

"Somebody is laughing. Was that you, Gertrude?" asked Horst, clearly irritated.

"No, I wasn't laughing," responded Gertrude.

There was more giggling. It appeared to be coming from behind a fern. Horst and Hansel quietly walked over to the fern and together lifted a large leaf. To their surprise, they found a boy. A very dirty looking boy.

Chapter 19

THE BOY LOOKED ABOUT FOUR YEARS OLD. HE WAS NAKED and had very long, dirty blond matted hair. Somewhat skinny, he appeared to be malnourished.

"Who are you?" asked Horst.

The boy giggled, wiping his snotty nose with the back of one hand.

"Can you speak?" asked Horst again, squatting down low enough that he could look directly into the child's eyes.

The boy looked away and giggled again.

"Where do you come from?"

The boy seemed to understand this question. He pointed toward a mesa in the distance.

A large millipede darted by. The boy jumped after the millipede, snatched it up and put it in his mouth; seeing another millipede, he quickly pounced again and gobbled it up. After that, he picked a large seed-pod off a plant and ate it slowly, all the while staring at Horst. Then he started walking in the direction of the mesa. Filled with curiosity, the Third Thaw expedition, together with their horses and wagons, followed the child to the mesa.

It took about an hour before they reached the steep, rocky base; at that point, the group decided to leave the horses and wagons while they climbed the rocks to follow the boy. Adam and Gerald unhitched Nellie, Ned, and Molly from the wagons, tethering them to the wagons instead. The long ropes would allow the horses to graze.

They climbed a steep trail up to the top of the mesa. On one side, a rock formation rose about twenty feet above the mesa; it was riddled with holes that were partially camouflaged by tall ferns. For a moment, the boy disappeared. Then they saw him again, waving to them, beckoning them to go toward him.

As they approached the area, they saw a stone staircase leading up to a small cave. They assumed that this was where the boy lived. In front of the steps was a fence, woven from the stems of plants.

"Michael!" a man's voice called out from the cave. "Michael, are you back yet?"

A man's head poked out of the hole. From his appearance, he seemed much older than them. Like the boy, he had very long hair and his straggly beard was streaked with gray. With great difficulty, he began the descent from the cave, using a branch for a crutch as he took one step at a time. His right leg appeared to be useless. Suddenly, he looked up and saw the Third Thaws staring at him. For a minute, he rubbed his eyes, then, almost losing his balance, he looked back towards the cave opening.

"Mary, they're here! They're here! Mary, come outside! They've arrived."

A thin woman who was cradling a baby hurried out of the cave; she stopped abruptly, covering her mouth as if to stifle a scream. Tears coursed down her face as she surveyed the group.

"I can't believe it! I can't believe it! Someone has found us!" yelled the man.

"Found you?" said Horst. Then he understood. "Are you from the First or Second Thaws?" "We're from the Second," said the man. "We were the only ones to survive the falls."

"You've found us!" the woman said. She had now been joined by a little girl who was about three years old.

"All the others in our group died. All the supplies were lost. Jim and I were the only ones who survived."

Horst looked at them. Yes, he remembered him; this must be Jim from the Second Thaw! He was so hard to recognize with the beard and long hair. And of course, this was Mary. Her hair was now much, much longer, down below her waist; it looked as though it hadn't been combed in years.

"I broke my leg when we went over the falls," explained Jim. "Mary had no injuries. Somehow, she didn't hit any rocks. She saved my life."

"So you've been here the past five years. And this boy . . ."

"This boy is our son, Michael," said Jim. "And this girl is our daughter, Louise," he said, pointing to the little girl. "And the baby is our other daughter, Kate. You are the first humans besides us they have ever seen."

Michael grunted something unintelligible.

"I'm sorry, but Michael doesn't speak much. We're the only ones here. He has never been around other adults."

"How have you survived all this time?" asked Adam.

"It hasn't been too difficult. There is plenty to eat, but you will need to adjust your eating habits," said Jim. "There are a lot of fish and bugs. There are primitive fruits here. The water is fresh."

"Are there any predators?" asked Hansel.

"Not really," said Jim. "Except for some big amphibians that live down by the river. They're big green and yellow creatures."

"We've seen them," said Horst.

"Well, you need to watch out for them," said Jim. "One of them tried to grab me and take a bite out of my leg, but I hit him with a stick. Those animals eat bugs and fish. They're stupid. I've killed a few. We've cooked and smoked their meat. They taste pretty good, but for the most part, we eat those little critters in the streams."

"You mean the *trilobites*?" said Hansel.

"The *tri-lo-whats*?" said Jim.

Ingrid intervened. "The life we have seen on this planet is very similar to prehistoric life on Earth. The animals in the streams look like a sea animal that lived on Earth called a '*trilobite.*'"

Jim looked confused. "Okay . . . whatever you say . . . the '*tri-lo-bites*' are easy to catch. And they taste good once you've cooked them up."

"Yeah, I boil them in a stew," added Mary. "We were able to salvage some cooking ware, pots, and pans from the debris."

"And," said Jim, "we were also able to salvage some seeds, too."

"I forget," said Horst, "but what were you trained for in New Eden?"

"I'm a farmer," Jim answered. There was no mistaking the pride in his voice. "I understand how to grow plants."

Ingrid was surprised. "Were you able to plant the seeds?"

Jim gestured to the group to follow him as he hobbled ahead, along a winding trail behind the tall rock with all the caves. As they turned the corner, they saw Jim's garden. There were all sorts of flowers, bushes and trees—all of them planted from Earth seeds!

"Did you have any trouble getting the seeds to grow?" asked Ingrid.

"Not at all," said Jim. "The soil on this mesa is ideal for growing. There are no weeds here. The plants are thriving."

Hansel walked up to a tree. "Are these apples?" he asked.

"Yes, apples. We also have peaches and pears. See over there—we're growing grapes."

"Can I have an apple?" asked Hansel.

"Help yourself," said Jim. Hansel reached for an apple and bit into it. No need to wash off pesticides here.

"And what were you trained for in New Eden, Mary?" asked Hansel.

"I was trained to be a brewer," Mary laughed. "You know, trained to make beer, wine, and various alcoholic drinks from scratch."

"Have you brewed anything?" asked Gerald.

"Yes. We were able to get various supplies that I needed from the wreckage. We salvaged brewing yeast which had come all the way from Austria on Earth. We also salvaged grape seeds from Napa Valley in California."

"What about bottles?" asked Horst.

"We were able to salvage twenty glass bottles. We wash and reuse them, of course."

Jim said to Horst, "So, you're the Third Thaw. You're twenty-one years old, right?"

"Yes," said Horst. "And you must be twenty-six years old."

Jim and Mary looked at each other. "Actually, I forgot how old we are! We've lost track of time." said Mary. "We used to scratch the days on a rock, but, after years of doing that, we stopped keeping records. We gave up any hope that we would be saved."

"Well, there's one thing that mystifies me," said Jim. "How did *you* survive going over the falls?"

Adam described their harrowing escape, explaining about the rock island and how they had woven a rope from fishing lines. He also told them that they had sent back two drones to warn the Fourth Thaw. Mary and Jim listened with rapt attention.

"Amazing!" said Jim.

"Why did you stay here?" asked Horst. "Did you ever attempt to get to New Munich?"

Jim hesitated, as if embarrassed. "After we pulled ourselves from the falls, my leg was badly broken in four places. Mary was able to drag me to safety. We camped next to the falls for a few days, but those damned big amphibians kept trying to eat us!"

"They were scarier than the giant scorpions we used to watch in New

Eden," said Mary, shuddering. "Even now they terrify me, but our little Michael is fearless—I'll swear he goes looking for them when he's out exploring on his own."

"Mary was able to drag me on a cot up to this mesa," continued Jim. "Not sure how she did it as I'm no lightweight! But we had to move—those damn amphibians don't stray too far from the river, so we would be safe up here, living in this cave. It took me several months to heal, but my right leg did not heal correctly, which is why I limp and use a crutch."

"But once you healed, you just stayed here?"

"No, that's not quite right, Adam. Eventually, we did decide to try to get to New Munich. One day we started to follow the river again but I found it very hard to walk, with my bad leg. We made little progress. Also, by then Mary was pregnant with Michael . . ."

"At some point along the river, the land becomes very flat and dry," added Mary, placing a hand on Jim's arm reassuringly. "When we saw the big desert valley that lay ahead, it looked impossible to cross. We decided that the odds of us surviving the 1,000-mile trip were about zilch to nothing. So we gave up and turned back."

"Well," said Horst. "We plan to get back on the trail to New Munich tomorrow. I assume that you will be traveling with us, correct?"

"Of course, we're coming along!" exclaimed Mary. "We never imagined we would be rescued. To think we're going to New Munich! Our kids will live with other people! They can go to school with other children and actually learn something!"

"Let's hope that people in New Munich have survived," cautioned Horst.

The Third Thaw set up camp at the bottom of the mesa near the wagons and horses. Jim, Mary, and their son, Michael, made several trips between their cave and the Third Thaws' camp site, carrying their belongings. They also brought food for that night's feast: smoked fish, smoked amphibian, apples, and pears, as well as hay and carrots for the horses. And Mary brought bottles of beer.

The Third Thaws had never drunk alcoholic beverages in their lives. Mary served each of them a bottle of beer.

"It's better cold, but we lack refrigeration. The Austrian and Germans brew a beer called a pilsner."

Adam took a sip and pulled a face. "So people drink this on Earth?"

"Yes, they do," said Mary. "Many people drink beer. They drink all sorts of alcoholic beverages. I've been able to make wine from the grapes that we've grown here. I've also distilled a unique drink from some primitive plants down by the river—they're about so high," she said, holding her hand about three feet above the ground. "They have vertical stems, which are kind of fuzzy. Seen any of those?"

Adam said, "Yes. The stems are sort of fat—about one inch in diameter."

"Exactly!" said Mary. "Well, if you cut the stems open, the insides are juicy. I've taken that juice and distilled it into an alcoholic drink. The drink is somewhat high in alcohol. I think it must taste like something called *tequila* on Earth, which is made from a plant called the yucca plant. That's why I call the drink *tequila*."

Feeling the effects of the beer, the group started joking and telling stories. Eileen walked over to one of the wagons and got out her electric piano. Peter, who was also an excellent musician, got out his guitar, while Harry, another musician, reached for his fiddle. The trio began to play Chopin waltzes and mazurkas. Then they played old Celtic folk tunes.

As Horst sat there, he felt good. The entire group sat in a circle around a fire, except for Zelda and Gerald who had gone off somewhere to be by themselves. Now that they were free of the observations of the Guardians, the pair were inseparable.

Ingrid was sitting directly across from Horst. He sat there, sipping the first beer in his life, looking through the fire at Ingrid. Then he looked at Jim and Mary and their kids. So this what happens when men and women get together? They have children? he thought to himself. Of course, they all knew that men and women have children. It was just that he had never actually seen *real* parents. He had only seen APS simulations of real parents. Seeing Jim and Mary with their children awakened Horst to a new revelation that, perhaps, this was what life was all about.

Chapter 20

IN THE MORNING, THE GROUP HELPED LOAD JIM AND MARY'S meager possessions onto two of the wagons at the bottom of the mesa; they also made room for several sacks of fruits and vegetables. The couple had risen early to harvest as much of the produce as they could, selecting only those crops which were already ripe.

With the help of Peter and Harry, they bagged apples, peaches, pears, potatoes, onions, carrots, and squash; then all the Third Thaws formed a chain from the top of the mesa down to the base and relayed bags from one person to another. Eventually, all the sacks were loaded on the wagons. Jim and Mary took one last look at their cave home and the land Jim had so carefully cultivated, before they, too, made their way to the wagons.

Then Mary asked the Third Thaws if anyone had a pair of scissors. Everyone shook their heads, but Eva suddenly remembered the scissors in her sewing kit.

"They're not very big," she said apologetically.

"They'll do just fine—thank you!" said Mary. "They seem sharp enough and that's what's important!"

Without saying another word, she lined up her family and, beginning with Jim, began to snip off their matted hair. Soon the ground was covered with strands of hair. Jim took Michael to the river's edge to wash while Gertrude calmed Louise down, who was fussing about her first haircut.

"Would you?" asked Mary, handing the scissors to Eva.

"My pleasure!" responded Eva, cheerfully cutting into Mary's once-blond locks.

Once the three children, scrubbed and clean, were on board the first wagon there wasn't much space left—only enough room for a few bottles of beer, wine and spirits, and the harvested crops.

"Five years," said Jim. "Five years . . . I never imagined we would leave this place."

"I never thought anyone would find us!" said Mary, her eyes welling up with tears. She hoisted herself up onto the first wagon, carving out a place for herself amongst the sacks of fruits and vegetables. With the baby on her lap, she placed her arms around Michael and Louise, holding them tight.

"You alright, Honey?"

"Yes, Jim—just fine. Kate's already falling asleep, so this will make the journey easier. There's room for you, too, if you don't mind sitting on the onions!"

While Mary and Jim were settling in the first wagon, the group continued to load up the second wagon. Meanwhile, Horst made his way over to the third wagon which housed computers and some laboratory equipment. This wagon had an air-conditioned cabin and was called the "Data Module" or simply the "DM." Inside the DM, an immense amount of human knowledge was stored on disks: science, engineering, medicine, the history of the world.

Ingrid was inside the Data Module using a laptop when Horst walked in.

"Hi, Ingrid. Looking up something up?"

"Hi, Horst. I'm just looking at records of prehistoric life on Earth," said Ingrid. "Many of the life-forms that we have seen here are very similar to things that once existed on Earth—like stromatolites, amphibians, scorpions, spiders, and millipedes. The animals don't always match exactly the ones on Earth, but they are very similar. I've come to the conclusion that the types of animals we have seen all lived on Earth during the Devonian period."

"Why are there parallels between Earth and this planet? Shouldn't life here be different?"

He peered over her shoulders at the screen to see an amphibian; it was the spitting image of the amphibian that had wandered into their camp and disturbed their sleep.

"That's a great question, and one that I don't know the answer to," said Ingrid. "The only thing I can come up with is that all life evolves in little steps. It begins as one-celled animals, evolving one step at a time into more complex animals. And life does not seem to want to change. If things are working out for a life-form, there is no incentive to evolve. But when a life-form confronts obstacles, some life-forms adapt and others can't adapt— and those that don't become extinct."

Ingrid continued, "This planet is very similar to Earth. It's about the same size, has about the same atmosphere and roughly the same gravitational force. Like Earth, it must have a magnetic field which is protecting us from solar particles. It's remarkable that our ancestors were able to find a planet so similar to Earth."

"Yes, it's amazing," said Horst. "The General said that they had looked at thousands of planets before deciding on this one."

"I think that these similarities with Earth explain why the animals and plants here are more or less the same as they were on Earth—"

Suddenly the ground shook, and everything in the Data Module shook with it. Horst and Ingrid quickly secured the laptop and then climbed out of the wagon.

Adam was waiting outside, surrounded by several other Third Thaws who were clamoring for answers.

"An earthquake," Adam said in a matter-of-fact voice.

"Should we be worried?" asked Gertrude. "I mean, could the ground swallow us up?"

"We should be okay," said Adam, reassuringly. "There is engineering saying: 'Earthquakes don't kill people. Buildings do.' The worst that can happen is a tent collapsing on top of us."

Once the aftershocks had stopped, the expedition left the mesa and headed back to the river, turning in the direction of New Munich. As they drew close to the water, Ingrid stopped to examine a plant. There was nothing special about this plant; in fact, there was not much to distinguish it from the other grasses growing along the river except for the hard stalks topped with a single cone shaped seed pod. Curious, Horst followed her.

"I've noticed a lot of these plants along the river," said Ingrid. "They look a lot like something on Earth called a 'horsetail.' They can be poisonous to grazing animals, including horses."

They looked at the horses which had stopped the wagon train to graze on clumps of horsetail.

"Let's strap feed bags over their mouths," said Horst. "We have to monitor what they're eating or we'll never reach New Munich! Besides, we can't stop whenever they fancy a munch!"

While Adam and Gerald fitted each horse with a feed bag, Ingrid proposed that each person record the plants that they saw on the journey. Using their observations, she could then research whether the native plants had similar counterparts on Earth and determine which plants were safe and which ones must be avoided. Their survival would depend upon accurate record keeping.

"Is there any way I can help?" asked Horst.

"I'm not quite sure, yet," said Ingrid. "The first thing we need to do is start cataloging plant types and give them names. Everyone should have a field book and start making sketches. We will need to meet together on a regular basis and trade information."

"Then we will be using scientific methodology," observed Horst.

"Yes, classic scientific methodology. In a way, we are like Charles Darwin on his sailing voyage around the world in *The Beagle*," said Ingrid. "There really is no other way. We need to start with the basics and fill in our knowledge with facts."

She walked over to the Data Module and rummaged inside, returning with a stack of pens and small field books with yellowing pages. Once each member of the expedition had a field book, Ingrid gave them a crash version of *Botany and Zoology 101*, instructing them how to record features of plants and animals, and possible characteristics to look for.

The group traveled between fifteen to twenty miles a day. Except for just a few days when it rained and they were forced to stay inside their tents, they made significant progress. The terrain was mostly arid land, but they stayed close to the river, heading in the direction of New Munich. After centuries of meandering from left to right, the river had eroded the earth, forming a deep valley flanked with mesas on both sides.

As the days went by, Zelda and Gerald distanced themselves from the group, often walking together along the river's edge, holding hands, or else trailing behind the wagons. As a couple, Mary and Jim understood Zelda and Gerald's feelings for each other, but the Third Thaws felt awkward around them. None of them had dated before and the Guardians had never discussed sex education with them or even talked about what it was to have a relationship. Even the display of affection was embarrassing to the group, though some of them secretly envied the pair.

Watching Zelda and Gerald, Horst sometimes felt a deep yearning inside himself, though for what he was uncertain. Would he have a relationship like theirs? Sometimes, in fact, he would look at Ingrid and wonder whether she could be the one. But no, Ingrid was complete in herself and had no need of anything but books.

Meanwhile, Zelda and Gerald had confessed their love to one another, and had already announced to the group that they wanted to get married. As soon as they got to New Munich, they wanted to have a marriage ceremony. Neither of them had ever been to a wedding, but they had both watched old movies like *My Big Fat Greek Wedding* and *The Wedding Date*. Zelda was determined to wear a white dress and veil; she had, in fact, already asked Eva and Gertrude if they would be her bridesmaids while Gerald had asked Adam to be his best man. Horst, of course, would get to officiate while Eileen would be the musician. There was a song that they had heard in several movies—"Here Comes the Bride"—and Zelda was already dreaming of walking down the aisle to that song.

The big question for Zelda was whether she should ask Ingrid to be maid of honor; she wasn't close to Ingrid and feared she might look down on them for wanting to get married so young. On the other hand, since Ingrid was one of the group leaders, it seemed only right to invite her to take on this role. As of yet, she still hadn't summoned up the courage to speak to her.

"Someday, we'll have a house of our own," Gerald said. "I'll take care of the plumbing myself—we'll have running water, a bath and a shower and proper toilets, not like the outhouses we had in New Eden."

"And we'll have a bunch of kids," said Zelda, glowing at the thought.

"How many?"

"Oh, I think six is enough," laughed Zelda, squeezing his hand.

Gerald laughed. "Six kids! When will we have any time to ourselves?"

"At night, when we go to bed," Zelda said, giving him a coy look.

"Fire Maria!" Gerald laughed. "I can hardly wait!"

Ahead of them, the group saw a wake in the river. There was something beneath the surface that was creating an enormous swell that extended roughly thirty feet parallel to the shore.

"There's something down there," observed Ingrid. "Something quite large."

"Just some currents, I think," said Horst, "but the water is spilling over the banks and we're going to get soaked. Let's get the wagons away from the edge before we lose the DM. I don't like the look of the waves."

"Get back!" he shouted to the group. "Get yourselves and the horses away from the water, before you end up being washed away!"

Even as he spoke, the waves became more violent and they found themselves standing ankle-deep in mud.

Quickly, Adam, who was leading Nellie, called out to Gerald to help him, but Gerald was out of ear shot. In the distance, he and Zelda were walking arm in arm, oblivious to everything around them.

Hansel grabbed the reigns of Ned, the second horse, while Jim scrambled out of the wagon as fast as he could to be of assistance with Molly who was pulling the Data Module wagon. All the Third Thaws edged away from the water, already feeling the cold spray lashing at their skin like icy needles.

Only Ingrid stood still, peering into the river. She was drenched, but was determined to get to the bottom of this phenomenon. There was definitely something down there, something large enough to churn up the water. Puzzled, she looked behind her to where Gerald and Zelda were now standing, seemingly oblivious to the rising waves. Then she saw it, cresting slowly above the surface.

"Look at that fin! It's enormous!" cried Hansel. "What d' you—"

But Ingrid didn't hear him. There was something big swimming in the river—a very large fish, judging by the fin which appeared. As the water rippled, a sizeable wave followed the fish. By her calculations, the creature was at least thirty feet long and must have weighed close to four tons.

"*Dunkleosteus!*" she murmured. "Oh, God . . ."

She could see Gerald let go of Zelda's hand. To her horror, he walked over to the riverbank and crouched down, evidently to get a better look at the disturbance in the water. He must have failed to see the fin.

"No!" she screamed, covering her mouth with her hands. "Oh, my God, no!"

"I thought you didn't believe in God," remarked Eileen sarcastically. Then, catching the look on Ingrid's face, she, too, turned just in time to see an enormous predatory fish leap out of the water and engulf the lower half of Gerald's body between plated jaws.

By now, the whole group was standing with them, frozen in place. Adam and Hansel began to sprint towards Zelda who was desperately trying to reach out for Gerald's hands. The fish momentarily beached itself, with Gerald inside its mouth, wrestling to free himself from the fish's jaws. They could see him writhing in agony as he screamed for help.

Zelda was hysterical, frantically pounding her fists onto the creature's head, but she was no match for the brutal power of the huge fish. As it thrashed its tail on the riverbank, Zelda fell backwards into Hansel's arms, while Adam grabbed for Gerald. For a moment, their hands met and, digging his feet into the ground, Adam pulled with all his might, but to no avail. The massive fish slipped backwards, shaking its head from side to side, whipping Gerald's body like a rag doll.

The impact sent Adam flying through the air, and he landed on his back with a thud. Dazed, he pulled himself up, determined to make one last effort to save his friend but the giant fish had already slipped back into the river, carrying Gerald underwater in its bony jaws. A pool of blood slowly formed on the now still surface.

"No! Get him back!" screamed Zelda, breaking free from the safety of Hansel's arms. "Get him back!"

Fearing she was about to jump in the river, Horst grabbed her and pulled her towards him; tears pouring down her face, she pummeled his chest with her fists, begging him to let her go. In shock, Horst held her tightly, unable to believe that Gerald, his lifelong friend, was gone. For a few minutes, he stood there, letting her vent her fury on him; then she collapsed onto the ground, sobbing uncontrollably. With Hansel's help, he carried her to one of the wagons while Adam, badly bruised from his fall, slowly followed them in silence.

Chapter 21

AFTER GERALD'S DEATH, THEY WERE CONSTANTLY ON THE lookout for the large predator fish that lived in the river. With the exception of Ingrid, none of the group had ever imagined that such large creatures existed. There were other dangerous fish, however, that were equally at home on land and in water, and while they were dwarfed by *Dunkleosteus*, they could still be lethal.

Ingrid was particularly concerned about the possibility of encountering something like *Tiktaalik Rosae*, a tetrapod of about three to four feet in length, with a head like a crocodile that could "walk" on the bottom of shallow water estuaries.

By now, the Third Thaws were reluctant to go anywhere near the water; but they needed food, and the river was the best place for foraging. The numerous *trilobites* that swam in shallows were easy to catch. The group quickly learned how to break the shells and remove the fleshy bodies of the trilobites which tasted a lot like chicken. A few of the other fish they caught, such as the scorpion fish, did not taste so good.

As they continued their journey, they also saw many scorpions and spiders. They witnessed the giant sea scorpions fighting each other, using their massive tails with stingers on the ends to kill their opponents, just like the scorpions on the beach of New Eden.

They followed the river, camping near its banks, confident that they were making progress on their journey toward New Munich. Along the way, they saw many mesas and tall mountain ranges. One day they walked near a giant volcano, which had smoke spewing from its top. Near the volcano's base were hot springs which smelled like sulfur as well as a number of geysers which blasted out boiling water hundreds of feet into the air.

～

After two months of following the river, the group found themselves at the edge of a waterfall. This particular waterfall was quite formidable, with a drop of about two hundred feet; the horses pawed the ground while Adam and Hansel tried to calm them down. Clearly, there was no going forward for either horses or humans.

Adam surveyed the falls, observing the angularity of the exposed rocks.

"These falls appear to have been created by a fault line between continental plates," he said.

"You mean, the land on one side of a fault just happened to drop?" asked Horst.

"Yes," said Adam. "I think one side—a plate—dropped relative to the other plate."

Looking down from the top of the falls to the land below, they could see the drop was too steep for the wagons. They would have to swing away from the river, towards flatter ground. They turned the wagon train left, away from the river, eventually finding a gentle slope that would allow them to make the descent. Just as the terrain had changed, so had the vegetation. As they descended, they found themselves entering a dense forest of ferns.

"The ferns are much bigger here," observed Ingrid. "It's as though this forest is evolving into something we'd expect in the Carboniferous period."

"What does that mean?" asked Gertrude.

"The Carboniferous period on Earth came after the Devonian period. The forests of the Carboniferous period were very dense. The decay of the Carboniferous forests is the source of underground coal and oil on Earth."

"I find the word '*Carboniferous*' interesting," said Horst. "It's like '*carbon*' and '*ferrous*,' which means 'iron.'"

Ingrid nodded.

"Good observation. I suppose the '*carbon*' part of the word is attributed to the creation of hydrocarbons. During this period on Earth, the atmosphere was very rich in oxygen and insects became very large. However, I'm not sure why there is the '*ferous*' part of the word."

They decided to pitch camp in the forest. Having set up their tents, they made a fire and roasted some of the *trilobites* they had carried with them in containers of river water to keep them fresh. They all agreed that the *trilobites* tasted better smoked than raw, and Ingrid felt it was safer to cook their food when possible. Well-fed and relaxed, they stayed up late, discussing all the plants and animals that they had seen on their adventures. They told stories, often adding some of the German phrases they remembered, hoping they could brush up their language skills before they reached New Munich.

It was now more than two months since Gerald had been killed. Most of the time, Zelda rode inside the Data Module wagon, while Ingrid steered Molly. Zelda still had the same vacant look in her eyes and avoided conversations with the group, especially after meals, when they typically shared stories and observations. Since the tragedy, she'd had a hard time eating anything and had recently begun to vomit after even the lightest of meals. The group had become used to the sound of her retching, and tried not to look when she leaned over the side of the wagon to throw up. Everyone felt sorry for her. One moment she had been making wedding plans, and the next, she was in mourning, and missed Gerald badly. Whispering amongst themselves, they concluded that she was depressed and that she no longer took an interest in anything, including her own survival.

As they frequently did in the evening, they enjoyed watching old movies on the laptop computer. One night, the feature was the 1955 film, *Picnic*, starring William Holden and Kim Novak. The film was about two friends from college, one of whom was successful, while the other was a drifter. It was a study in contrasts, portraying stability in life versus freedom, life in a small town, and the consequences of failure. What was particularly moving was one key scene in which William Holden (Hal) and Kim Novak (Madge) danced to the song "Moon Glow."

The group was mesmerized by this scene. While Hal is teaching Madge's younger sister how to dance, the sultry Madge slowly descends the dock stairs, clapping in rhythm to "Moon Glow," turning her body with each step. As Hal looks at her in amazement, Madge locks her eyes on his, clearly communicating her sexual interest in him. The couple begins to dance, illumined by the light of the moon and by the glow of Chinese lanterns above the dock. As "Moon Glow" plays in the background, they draw closer together, sparks of passion flying. . . .

Watching Kim Novak dance, Horst noted her resemblance to Ingrid. They shared similar features and, beneath the baggy clothing that she always wore, Ingrid was just as shapely. Tearing his eyes away from the laptop screen, Horst glanced in Ingrid's direction. That's when their eyes met. It seemed to Horst like a look of mutual appreciation, perhaps for themselves, perhaps for the movie. Their 'look' was an acknowledgement that what they were watching was really quite beautiful.

The group slept well that night, but in the morning, they woke to the sound of a deafening buzz. Horst jumped out of his tent.

Dazed, the others emerged from their tents, covering their ears with their hands. The buzzing grew louder and louder. Ingrid emerged from her tent, comb in hand, blond hair cascading down her shoulders.

"Oh no!" she exclaimed, almost dropping the comb. "Get back inside!"

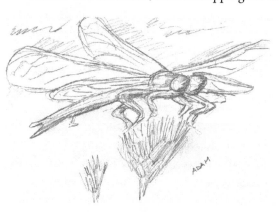

"What is it?" said Horst.

"Dragonflies!" said Ingrid. "Giant dragonflies. I think it's a swarm. We must get inside our tents!"

But it was too late. A swarm of about twenty giant dragonflies descended on the campsite, huge insects with wingspans that were three feet across. One landed on Ingrid's head, latching onto her hair with its mandibles. Hearing her scream, Horst ran to her side and seized the thing, ripping its head off. The dragonfly's body remained entangled in Ingrid's hair, and a pus-like fluid oozed out of the carcass, spilling on to her clothing. Another dragonfly landed on Horst's back. He tried to swat it away, without success, then tumbled backwards, crushing the creature with his weight. Breaking free, he reached for his pistol. The other members of the group were meanwhile trying to fend off the massive insects which were inflicting painful bites.

The girls, Ingrid included, were hysterically running in every direction, making it difficult for Horst to take aim. To make matters worse, the dragonflies could maneuver very quickly; they darted about, stopping and starting. Horst took shots at the insects during the split second they would hover, but missed.

Unexpectedly, the two drones, Buzzy and Jamie, sped out of the Data Module, aiming directly for the swarm. Seeing new prey, the entire group of dragonflies swarmed after the drones, flying away from the Third Thaws. For a while, the drones were able to outmaneuver the dragonflies, giving the group some time to recover. Randomly ascending and descending, Buzzy and Jamie made it impossible for the dragonflies to chase them; however, they couldn't keep this up indefinitely, and it was impossible for them to get away because they were outnumbered by the swarm. Not only could the dragonflies fly faster and better than the drones, but the swarm seemed to have a group intelligence which directed them to trap the drones on all sides.

Some of the dragonflies flew into the drones' spinning rotor blades and were immediately dismembered, but it was not long before the blades jammed, causing the drones to crash. The swarm moved in for the attack. While their mandibles couldn't damage the drones, still, Jamie and Buzzy were now immobilized.

Grabbing machetes from one of the wagons, Adam and Hansel began to push the giant dragonflies away from the drones, prying the dead dragonfly carcasses from the rotors.

"Buzzy! Jamie! We need you to turn your rotors on while we hold you! You understand?" yelled Adam.

There was a faint "beep" and two sets of rotors began to spin again. As the swarm attacked once more, Adam and Hansel each gripped a drone with both hands, letting the blades decimate the insects.

"Come on, you bastards!" shouted Adam, as he mowed down one dragonfly after another. In a short time, Adam and Hansel had killed the entire swarm. There were dragonfly carcasses strewn on the ground everywhere.

~

Everyone had been badly bitten by the dragonflies. Ingrid had been bitten on the back of her neck; Eileen, on both her arms and her neck. Adam and Hansel had received the most dragonfly bites, and now had marks all over their faces and arms. Peter and Harry had both been bitten on their hands which were now swelling at an alarming rate.

"We'll need to wash and clean these wounds, then bandage them," said Ingrid, gingerly touching the rising welts on her neck. "Do we have any disinfectant?"

"I have a bottle of tequila that we distilled. It's high in alcohol content," said Mary.

"Good, that should work perfectly."

Ingrid examined everyone's bites. Fortunately, all the wounds were superficial and not too deep. She squirted generous amounts of liquid soap onto the broken skin, then doused the wounds with tequila. Eva and Gertrude applied bandages. Meanwhile, Horst cleaned up the drones, detangling their rotors.

"Once again these drones have saved our lives," he declared.

As if in reply, Buzzy and Jamie gave off a series of little beeps.

"I think they're thanking you for the compliment!" laughed Ingrid.

They needed to build a fire so they could cook breakfast. Carrying an ax, Horst went into a heavily forested area. He found some ferns that were about twenty feet tall with trunks that were four inches in diameter. Swinging the ax, he made a couple of initial cuts and watched as the ferns began to sway and bend. Suddenly, he heard a rustling coming from the nearby brush and the sound of breaking foliage. Whatever was there sounded big and was grunting loudly. Looking up, he saw that something was sticking up above all the plants—a giant brown sail that blended into the vegetation.

Then, while he was still staring at the sail, an enormous head poked through the brush. Stepping back, Horst saw a creature that was about ten feet long and must have weighed over a ton. The animal had a large sail-shaped fin on its back.

For a few seconds, it stood still, as if surveying its prey; then, it started approaching Horst, snapping its jaws which were full of sharp teeth. Horst immediately took out

his pistol, aiming at the animal's head. When he pulled the trigger, however, he heard only a click. He had used all his bullets shooting the dragonflies! Heart pounding, he stepped backwards, but tripped and fell on his back. The animal lumbered toward him, jaws wide open, approaching for the kill.

Just as the animal was on the verge of attacking him, Horst quickly rolled over several times in succession, until he was out of reach. Back on his feet, he grabbed the ax, swinging it with full-force into the animal's neck, leaving a gaping wound. The animal stopped, then letting out a mighty roar, turned its head in the direction of the wound. Blood was pouring down its neck, spilling onto the already crimson ground. Horst watched as the creature stumbled, and fell to its knees, its sail bent and limp, flapping uselessly in the wind. There were several more roars, followed by a gurgling sound and, then, nothing.

Still shaking, Horst hurried back to the camp and found Ingrid who was waiting with the breakfast team, ready to cook the remaining *trilobites*.

"So there you are! We're still waiting for breakfast—"

"Well, I almost was breakfast," said Horst breathlessly. "I thought you said that dinosaurs are a long way off! Well I just ran into one, and it almost killed me!"

Ingrid and the others followed Horst back into the woods. They looked at the carcass.

"Looks like a dinosaur to me!" said Horst. "And a giant one at that!"

"I'm confused—this does look like a dinosaur but, to my knowledge, no dinosaurs appeared during the Devonian period."

"I say let's have meat for breakfast!" said Adam. "Here, Horst, give me that ax—I'm going to carve us some steaks!"

They butchered the animal and, collecting the fern stalks that Horst had felled before his encounter with the dinosaur, started a fire. Soon, the aroma of roasting meat filled the campsite; they feasted on the meat, which was delicious.

After breakfast, Ingrid wandered away from the group.

"It doesn't make sense—I'm going to research this on the DM computer," she said, heading towards the DM wagon. After a few minutes, she returned.

"Reptile," she announced. "That wasn't a dinosaur—it was a large reptile. About 250 million years ago there was a large carnivorous reptile called '*Dimetrodon.*' This reptile was commonly mistaken for a dinosaur. It lived millions of years before dinosaurs. In fact, it's more closely related to mammals than to dinosaurs."

"What's that thing on its back?" asked Horst. "It looks like it could use it for sailing!"

"The sail was used to regulate its body temperature. It increased the surface area of its body by almost fifty percent, allowing it to heat up faster."

"So, it's a cold-blooded animal, like a reptile?" asked Eileen.

"Yes, it appears to be a reptile, which, of course, is cold-blooded," answered Ingrid. "Mammals, like us, are warm-blooded. We maintain our body heat through our metabolism. The ability to regulate body heat using metabolism is a biological process that has not yet occurred during the present time period."

"Reptiles cannot regulate their temperature using their internal metabolism. They tend to heat their bodies by standing in the sunlight or cooling in the shade. This requires a lot of standing still and positioning themselves with respect to the sun. Mammals and birds don't need to waste time standing in the sun—that is, unless you want to purposely get a suntan. We generate our body heat using our internal metabolism."

"So, this big animal that Horst just killed used its sail to regulate body heat?" asked Harry.

"You've got it," answered Ingrid.

Chapter 22

AFTER EATING THEIR REPTILE BREAKFAST, THE THIRD Thaws packed their tents and moved on. Having avoided the falls, they headed towards the river again. But keeping safely away from the water's edge. They were also alert to other dangers, especially after Horst's narrow escape from the *Dimetrodon*-like reptile. They decided to use the drones for reconnaissance. Hansel took it upon himself to position Buzzy and Jamie on top of the wagons so that solar energy would constantly recharge their batteries. Every morning and afternoon, he programmed the drones to fly ahead of the convoy and to return bearing data about what lay ahead.

During this phase of their journey, the Third Thaws noticed a multitude of small animals that resembled gophers. These animals burrowed into the

ground, constantly popping their heads out of their holes to look at the expedition as it passed by. They did not seem to be dangerous to humans, although some of the creatures had large tusks.

To satisfy her curiosity, Ingrid did some research on the DM's computer, checking to see if a counterpart animal had ever lived on Earth. The closest match turned out to be a reptile called *Diictodon*. What was particularly fascinating about *Diictodon* was that it seemed to represent a missing link between reptiles and mammals. As she had expected, it was the males that had the tusks; these they used in combat with rival males over potential mates. Another interesting fact was that the males and females may have mated for life—another sign of animals evolving!

While Ingrid was conducting her research, Buzzy and Jamie lifted off from their stations for their morning flight. As the drones ascended to a height of fifty feet or so, Hansel noticed that their flight pattern was wobbly. Staring up at the sky, he could see that they were losing power.

"There's something wrong with the computer," said Ingrid, suddenly emerging from the DM.

"I was looking at the monitor, then the image scrambled and it went blank."

"There seems to be something wrong with the drones, too," said Hansel. "I'm afraid we're going to lose them!"

They looked up at the drones. Sure enough, their flight pattern was so erratic that they seemed drunk. Descending rapidly, they fell to the ground, landing in a cluster of horsetails. Fortunately, the plants cushioned their fall, but while they had not suffered any external damage, the drones were not working. Their familiar "beeps" were now silent and their lights were no longer operational. Ingrid and Hansel quickly retrieved them from the horsetails and carried them back to the camp where the others were awaiting them anxiously.

"What do you think is wrong with them?" said Ingrid as she checked them over. "There's no visible sign of damage."

"I don't know, Ingrid—I know I programmed them correctly," said Hansel. "What do *you* think, Horst?"

"I think this could be an electromagnetic disturbance which is affecting the electronics of the computer and drones," said Horst. He closed his eyes, trying to remember what could cause an electrical disturbance. He had vague memories of learning about such a phenomenon.

"It's possible that we are experiencing an electrical disturbance caused by the sun," he finally said. "I remember my grandfather telling me about something called a 'coronal mass ejection,' which is a massive burst of solar particles from the sun."

"What should we do?" asked Ingrid. "We need both the computer and the drones for our survival."

"I think we should wait a while before attempting to restart the electronics," said Horst. "We need this event to pass. Let's set up camp here—I don't like the idea of heading into the unknown without data support."

The day passed uneventfully. That evening, the sky was filled with flashing colors.

"Look up at all the blue and orange lights in the sky," Horst said. "They have something like this on Earth near the Arctic Circle, called the *Aurora Borealis*. These lights are caused by the solar wind interacting with the magnetic field of this planet."

"It's beautiful!" exclaimed Gertrude.

"Yes," agreed Horst. "This proves that the planet must be experiencing particularly heavy solar winds at this time."

They sat around the campfire, looking up at the sky, talking and telling stories. Only Zelda was missing from the circle; since Gerald's death, she preferred to be on her own, resting inside one of the wagons.

"Did Earth people see night lights like these?" asked Gertrude.

"Only the ones living way up north," answered Horst. "The Eskimos would see these lights. Sometimes people living as far south Lake Superior could see them as well."

In the morning, they decided that the solar disturbance had probably moved past the planet. Slowly, Hansel rebooted the electronic equipment. Lights flashed and the drones let out a series of quiet beeps. In the DM, the computer screen flickered for a few moments, then stabilized. Now that everything was back to normal, they could continue their journey.

They walked close to the river, across a plain, surrounded by hills on each side. The morning passed uneventfully, but by the afternoon the wind began to kick up. In the distance they could see dark clouds hanging low in the sky, rolling towards them.

"It looks like we're about to be hit by that storm. We'd better get to higher ground," said Horst. He didn't have to explain that a downpour could cause the river to overflow its banks, or that they could be swept away in the resulting deluge; the geography spoke for itself. Several of the group secured the canvas wagon covers, tightening the knots that kept them in place. Adam placed blinders on the horses, just in case there would be lightening, while Hansel placed the two drones inside the DM wagon where Ingrid was already shutting down the computer.

As they made their way toward the hills, the storm arrived. There was a torrential downpour, and the wind whipped around them, tugging at the canvas wagon covers, showering them with spray from the river.

"Everybody stay together!" yelled Adam, linking arms with Eva.

"Michael! Louise! Where are you?" yelled Mary, desperately looking for her children who were not with the group.

"Can anybody see where my kids are? I thought they were in the wagon with Jim!"

The river was rising fast, threatening to overflow its banks; already, the ground was saturated, both from the rain and from the river water. Looking back in the direction of the river, Adam saw the children standing on an island of dry land, about a hundred feet away, clinging tightly to each other. Surrounded on all sides by the expanding river, they were in danger of being washed away. Letting go of Eva's arm, Adam ran towards the children.

Plunging into the river, Adam waded towards Michel and Louise; the water was about two feet deep and rising fast. When he reached the island, it was just about to be submerged. He grabbed the screaming children, and with one under each arm, started pushing his way through the rushing water, towards the riverbank. But the current was powerful, and still holding the children, he was swept off his feet and the three of them were dragged downstream.

Seeing Adam and the children washed away down the river, Hansel ran to a supply wagon and grabbed a rope. He tied a quick lasso, then unhitched Nellie and mounted her, riding toward the river. For a few minutes, they galloped alongside the water and when they were just ahead of Adam and the children, Hansel and the horse headed into the river. Lying low against her withers and clinging to her mane, he guided the horse near the bank where the water was relatively shallow, but they had trouble staying there. The current pulled the horse and rider toward the center of the river where the swirling water was strongest.

Digging his heels into Nellie's flanks, Hansel forced her forward, in the direction of the river's flow; when Adam and the children were almost parallel, he swung the rope and released the lasso, just as the three passed.

Miraculously, the rope looped around the trio; somehow, they were able to grab the lasso with their hands, while Hansel tightened his legs around Nellie, and hauled them in.

When they got back on land, the rope had worked its way up the children's armpits, leaving welts on their bare skin; both were too scared to move, so Adam gently loosened the rope for them. Then, scooping them up, he ran with the children towards the wagons, while Hansel followed at a slower pace, reluctant to push the tired Nellie. All around them, the *Diictodon* were hurrying into their holes, scampering en masse under the earth as if in search of refuge. Ironically, their attempts to escape danger would drown them when the river flooded their tunnels.

Adam, Hansel and the children all had severe rope burns on their hands, so while Horst hitched Nellie to her wagon, Ingrid applied salve to their injuries, loosely wrapping white gauze over the welts. Mary then lifted Louise and Michael onto the produce wagon, where Jim was waiting, ready to help them crawl under the canvas.

The group needed to move fast. They found a place about ten feet above the river where they pitched tents in the pouring rain. From their campsite, they could see that the flat river basin was entirely flooded.

Still shaken by the near tragedy, Mary held tightly on to Michael and Louise, while baby Kate nestled in her lap. For a while all was calm, save for the sound of the rain dashing against their tents.

Then came a piercing scream—and another, followed by anguished cries for help. Recognizing Gertrude's voice, Adam immediately jumped out of his tent, only to see Gertrude, on her back, being dragged by a large sail-back reptile, similar to the one that Horst had killed. The reptile, which had barged into Gertrude's tent, had its large sharp teeth were clenched like a vice around her right foot, while her arms flailed wildly.

Quickly, Adam pulled out his pistol and pursued the animal toward a thicket of giant ferns. He rapidly fired six shots into the reptile's head at point-blank range, but they ricocheted off its skull and the creature continued to drag its prey, seemingly undaunted. Reloading, Adam fired another volley of bullets, this time targeting the beast's eyes. One of them must have hit its mark, because the sail-back's mouth opened, releasing Gertrude's foot. For a few seconds, the creature stood still, tail lashing, a trickle of blood oozing from an empty eye socket; then, it lumbered slowly towards the thicket, leaving a trail of blood and Gertrude writhing on the ground.

By now, Horst had joined Adam and together they carried Gertrude to the Data Module. Her foot was bleeding badly and she was clearly in a state of shock. Ingrid instructed them to lay Gertrude on the floor.

Forming a tourniquet from a clean shirt, Ingrid wrapped it tightly around Gertrude's leg, below the knee, in an attempt to stop the flow of blood. Gertrude was screaming in pain. Eva tried calming her down, but Gertrude kept trying to sit up, determined to prevent Ingrid from touching her foot.

"Adam, find Mary," said Ingrid calmly. "Ask her for the strongest alcoholic drink she has!"

Meanwhile, Ingrid tried to clean the wound as best she could, but, despite the tourniquet, the blood was still gushing from Gertrude's foot. Examining the endings of exposed veins, she grimaced.

"We need to stop the blood flow, but I can't clamp the veins—the endings have been crushed," she said turning to Horst, who was looking a little green.

"Can't you put in sutures?" asked Horst, "I can get you a needle and some lightweight fishing line."

"No—can't risk it. Sutures only work if there's a clean cut—those jaws have left a jagged mess."

"Won't the tourniquet stop the bleeding?" asked Eva. She was still doing her best to keep Gertrude calm, but her friend was now quite delirious with pain and would not lie still.

"No," said Ingrid, abruptly. "That's just a short-term solution. If we leave the tourniquet in place much longer, Gertrude could develop *necrosis*—tissue death. That could be fatal."

At that moment, Adam returned with two bottles of tequila. Ingrid gave Gertrude a glass of tequila, but she spat it out, thrashing wildly. Then, nodding silently at Horst, Ingrid knelt down next to Gertrude and pried open her mouth while he poured in the tequila.

"Sorry, Gertrude," she said, "We had to do this."

Gertrude coughed and spluttered, but finally lay back, calmer now while Ingrid inspected her foot more closely.

"You see how mangled it is," she whispered to Horst. "Even if we save the foot, it would most likely develop gangrene. Most likely, there's bacteria from the animal's mouth and our methods of sterilizing are limited."

"So what are you saying?"

Ingrid looked steadily at Horst.

"The only way to save Gertrude from dying is to amputate her foot," she said. "We'll need to administer the diethyl ether we made."

"I hope we made it right," said Horst. "We've never tested it on anyone."

"I don't think we have a choice but to give it to her," said Ingrid. She walked over to a locker and took out a small sealed glass container and several medical face masks.

"I need space and a sterile environment," she said. "Eva, I think it best if you wait outside—we're a bit cramped in here, but please tell Hansel we need him."

Tears running down her face, Eva climbed out of the DM wagon. She hated abandoning her friend, but knew that Gertrude needed more than Eva could offer. Now it was up to Ingrid to save Gertrude.

Ingrid gave instructions to her team to prepare for surgery. They would need to make things as clean as possible. Hansel found a hacksaw and pliers. Then he boiled water and sterilized the tools.

Putting on a face mask, she handed masks to Horst, Hansel, and Adam, and instructed everyone to wash their hands.

"When I take the lid off this jar, hold your breath until it's firmly in place again," she said. "Otherwise, we'll all be on the floor, knocked out by the diethyl ether!"

She squatted next to Gertrude.

"I'm about to give you something to breathe," she told Gertrude.

"Is it going to hurt?"

"No, you just might feel a little lightheaded," said Ingrid, slowly twisting off the lid to the jar. Holding her breath, she placed the jar close to Gertrude's nose, then quickly put the lid back on. When she stood up again, Gertrude was already unconscious.

"Good, it worked. But I don't know how long she will remain unconscious. Let's get to work. Adam and Hansel, you will need to hold Gertrude down when we cut through the bone. Horst, I want you to do the cutting," said Ingrid.

"Ah, me?" said Horst, turning white.

"Yes, you," said Ingrid. "I don't have the physical strength that you do. I'll make the initial cut, but you can cut the bone itself. "

While Adam and Hansel knelt on either side of Gertrude, ready to hold her down if she regained consciousness, Ingrid made an incision around the part of the leg to be amputated. Then, gritting his teeth, Horst began to saw through the bone. Once he had cut through the leg, Ingrid smoothed the bone with a file and cauterized the veins. Then, having stanched the bleeding, she constructed a flap of muscle, connective tissue, and skin to cover the raw end of the bone. Finally, after pouring a generous amount of tequila onto the stump, Ingrid closed the flap with fish-line sutures.

During the operation, Gertrude remained unconscious. Horst took the amputated foot outside in the pouring rain and tossed it into the forest.

"Here's one for the *Dimetrodon*!" he said, then vomited. When he returned to the wagon some ten minutes later, Adam and Hansel made excuses and went outside; both looking as though they, too, were about to throw up. As for Ingrid, she was exhausted.

"Let's hope she doesn't get infected. We'll keep the wound clean with tequila. We have no antibiotics. Let's hope she survives."

Chapter 23

GERTRUDE WOKE UP DURING THE NIGHT, COMPLETELY DIS-oriented. The pain was unbearable. It felt like her right foot was on fire, but when she tried to touch it, there was nothing there. She had completely forgotten about the incident with the reptile. Eva, who had spent the night at her side, awakened to her sobs. Haltingly, she broke the terrible news to her friend; as she had expected, Gertrude was shocked to discover that her foot had been amputated. Nothing could stop her tears, and nothing could make the pain tolerable.

The next morning, as the Third Thaws took down their tents and headed out again, the group was more subdued than usual. In the wake of Gerald's death, Gertrude's injury was too much to deal with. There were whispers about the mission being jinxed, and even the usually upbeat Horst seemed tense and withdrawn. Gertrude stayed inside the Data Module wagon. Though it was only eight a.m., Ingrid gave her a glass of Tequila to help dull the pain. Sensing that she had a fever, she placed a cool wet cloth on Gertrude's forehead, instructing Eva to monitor her for any signs of a temperature spike.

The river was swollen and wide from the storm, while the trail was caked in thick mud. To avoid the wagon wheels from locking, they traveled on the hilly ground next to the river. This slowed down their progress toward New Munich. So far, they had been traveling at a good rate of about fifteen miles a day. Now, after all the flooding, they would be lucky to cover ten.

Ingrid and Horst sat together on the bench of the Data Module wagon, with Horst holding the reins. They heard Gertrude moaning inside; every now and again, there was a Tequila-induced giggle, but, for the most part, Gertrude's pain did the talking.

"So, what are you thinking, Horst?"

"I was thinking how we don't have the proper supplies on this planet. I was thinking how our supplies are going to run out, eventually. And I was also wondering what our lives will be like when we *do* run out of supplies," said Horst, keeping his eyes on the terrain ahead.

"Yeah, I know. We don't even have antibiotics," said Ingrid.

"Yeah, that's exactly what I mean," agreed Horst. "Almost everything we have has been manufactured by the drones back at New Eden, and there was only so much they could manufacture."

"And that's a real problem," sighed Ingrid, "I'm not even sure if we can make proper medicines here. Gertrude is in need of a painkiller. On Earth, doctors would administer morphine. On this planet, that's not even a possibility."

"Why can't we make morphine here?"

"Because morphine comes from the opium plant. There are no opium plants on this planet. Opium plants are flowering plants. None of the plants here have evolved to the point of having flowers."

"You're right," said Horst, casting an admiring look in Ingrid's direction. "The only flowering plants we have are the ones that we planted from Earth seeds."

They sat, saying nothing, both lost in thought.

"There is so much the drones made for us," continued Horst. "Look at my jeans. They are made from threads. Where did these threads come from?"

"Good question. I assume that threads are made from cotton—"

"So, how did the drones make threads?" interrupted Horst. "Did the drones weave the cotton into threads? Then, did they weave the threads into jeans?"

"Yes, they must have," said Ingrid. "The Planners of the Mission must have selected crops that were vital to our survival here. Fruits, vegetables, cotton . . . Yes, the drones must have been making things like thread. Maybe they have a thread spinning machine."

"Without the Guardians and the drones, how long do you think we can survive on our own?" asked Horst. "Like, what if my jeans wear out? What if my shoes wear out? Where do I get replacements?"

"Horst, you're overthinking everything!" laughed Ingrid, placing her left hand lightly on his arm. "When we get to New Munich, they will have their own Guardians and drones. They will have supplies."

"And thread making machines?" asked Horst.

For some reason, Ingrid found this funny. Somewhat self-consciously, she withdrew her hand and placed it in her lap, alongside her right hand. Horst pretended not to have noticed this, their first physical contact. It was small gesture perhaps, but this brief touch was the first sign of affection he had ever received from another human being. *How had Ingrid known how to do that? The Guardians had never touched him!*

"But, we're too dependent on these things!" he insisted, hoping she couldn't hear the embarrassment in his voice. "What if the Guardians ever wear out? They can't reproduce themselves—they're machines. They *will* eventually wear out."

The conversation was an eye-opener in more ways than one. They had a few of the benefits of Earth-like materials, but these things would eventually wear out and need to be replaced. If they succeeded in colonizing this planet, the human population would grow. However, there were only a few Guardians and drones that were programmed to help deliver the embryos, raise them, educate them, and send them on their way. What would happen when the embryos ran out? wondered Horst. *How had Jim and Mary produced children without embryos or guardians?*

The future of humankind on this planet would require entirely new manufacturing facilities, with humans making things. An agricultural industry would need to be created from scratch. A pharmaceutical industry would be needed for making medicines. Streets, sewers and sanitation, and water distribution would all have to be planned and built from scratch. Energy generation and power distribution would be needed, as well as communication lines.

The Third Thaws had taken so much for granted, especially all the things that had been "prepped" for them. Horst wondered if the Planners of the Mission realized just how difficult it would be to establish a new colony on another planet. It wasn't as simple as *"Hey, let's just drop some frozen embryos on a planet and have robots raise them."* There were so many unpredictable and risky things about this mission. But, then again, any mission taking place on a planet light-years away would always be a crapshoot.

"We have been given a great responsibility," observed Horst, finally sharing his thoughts. "That is, to act as a seed for human civilization on this planet. Earth is expecting us to re-create civilization here from scratch."

"Do we have any choice?" said Ingrid, looking at Horst intently. Even with his eyes focused ahead, Horst was conscious of her eyes upon him, From the corner of his eyes, he could see wisps of blond hair blowing in the wind.

"No, we don't," said Horst. "We were drafted to do this, even before we were born."

Their conversation was interrupted by Eva, who emerged from under the DM canvas.

"It's Gertrude," she said. "She's very hot—perhaps you could check on her."

Horst continued to hold the reins, while Ingrid climbed into the DM cabin to check on her patient. Gertrude's clothing was soaking wet and she was tossing from side to side, clearly delirious.

"You have too many covers on her, Eva," said Ingrid. "Keep the cloth cool and wet and leave it on her forehead. Meanwhile, I'll check the incision for infection and redress the wound."

Removing the bandages, she found no signs of infection. She applied a generous dose of alcohol around the stump, then redressed it with clean rags.

"The wound looks good, Eva. That's about the best that I can do—I suspect her body is reacting to minor internal infections. The good thing is, she is sleeping. It will take her several days to recover from this surgery."

"Thanks, Ingrid," said Eva. There were bags under her eyes and her face looked thin and pinched.

"Try to get some rest," said Ingrid gently, then climbed back onto the wagon seat next to Horst.

～

As the flood waters subsided, they drove the wagons back into the flat valley. All around them they saw the corpses of countless *Diictodon* which must have drowned when they sheltered in their burrows; in the distance was a swarm of giant dragonflies. They were feeding on the carcasses of the groundhog reptiles. If the dragonflies were to attack them again, they would need to use the drones' rotor blades. Fortunately, at least for the time being, the dragonflies stayed away from the expedition.

They stopped for lunch, built a fire and roasted gopher-reptile meat. They sat in a circle, around the fire, trying to make "small talk." Periodically, one of the group checked on Gertrude, giving Eva a chance to rest. After Hansel checked on her, he came back to his seat next to the fire.

"She's crying a lot. She keeps complaining about the pain in her right foot," said Hansel. "But her foot is gone."

"She is having what's called 'phantom leg pain,'" said Ingrid.

"Phantom leg pain?" Hansel appeared confused.

"Feeling pain in a foot that's not there is called 'phantom leg pain.' Your own tinnitus is due to a loss of hearing at a particular frequency. As a result, you are getting a 'phantom hearing loss' response."

"I still don't understand," said Hansel.

"All of our senses are formed by neural loops," explained Ingrid. "Nerve receptors stimulate neural loops in our bodies. When we touch something with our fingers, that stimulates a neural loop in our finger, which goes to our brain and eventually returns to our finger."

"Like electrical wires in a loop?" asked Hansel.

"Yes, somewhat like electrical wires," continued Ingrid, who was now in what the others in the group described as "full lecture mode."

"I still don't get it," said Hansel. "What's your point?"

"When we damage a neural loop, such as by losing a foot or losing our hearing, the neural circuit reacts in strange ways, such as 'phantom leg pain,'" said Ingrid.

"You make it sound like our brains are a bunch of electronic parts," interrupted Eileen. There was an edginess to her voice.

"Eileen, does it upset you if I talk like this?" asked Ingrid, frowning slightly as she studied Eileen's expression.

"Yes," said Eileen testily. "As a matter of fact, it does. I don't like talking about people this way. It makes us seem like we're machines."

"I'm sorry to upset you, then. I find this fascinating. I like thinking about our brains as neural networks."

"Well, I find it appalling!" said Eileen. "We are not machines! The way that you talk sickens me! Were Bach, Mozart, and Chopin machines? Was Scott Joplin a machine?"

"But what about the Guardians? They are machines," said Adam, tearing into a chunk of roasted reptile meat with his teeth.

Eileen glared at Adam, but made no comment.

"I think this group is too small to accommodate our differences," she said. "I am different from the rest of you. I am an artist; the rest of you are too rational. You are engineers and scientists. You take everything apart and examine it, and after you've dissected something, you seem to assume that you understand it! As scientists, you have placed Man on a pedestal as a sort of Supreme Being. That is precisely what I don't agree with."

The group stared at her in stunned silence. Adam shrugged his shoulders and continued eating, while Hansel and Horst exchanged puzzled looks. They had not seen this coming.

Eileen paused. Her face was flushed and her eyes were feverishly bright.

"I'm sorry to offend you, but you take all of the joy out of life. I am an artist. I am happy. I don't care about your constant analysis and scientific observations. My purpose here is to live happily. I don't question things—"

Hearing Gertrude cry out, she stopped abruptly.

"Is there anything more that we can do for her?" asked Eileen. "Should we pray?"

"I have never prayed, because I don't understand what that means," said Ingrid. "I refuse to make wishes."

"Is that what praying means to you? 'Making wishes'?" retorted Eileen.

"I don't know—you're the expert. You tell me what it means."

Eileen paused and closed her eyes.

"To me, it is accepting a higher authority—Whomever or Whatever that may be—and submitting to its Plan for us. We have no control over the Plan, but we all have a part in it."

"To me the ultimate authority is the Truth," said Ingrid. "We don't really know the Truth. We only know parts of it. And we will probably never know the whole Truth about things. We're just humans, after all."

Eileen stood up abruptly, clearly exasperated. She dusted the ash off her clothing.

"There you go again, with your authoritative scientific opinion."

"I still don't understand why you are so upset," said Ingrid. "I'm not even sure what the issue is, but I'm sorry that I've upset you."

Eileen laughed sarcastically.

"I will never win this game with you, will I? Let me put it this way: What are the chances that in all the universe humans would find a planet that is so similar to Earth? It's about the same size as Earth. It has about the same climate as Earth. It even has about the same oxygen levels as Earth, doesn't it, Ingrid?"

"Yes, you are correct. This planet has the same oxygen level as on Earth."

"So what do think are the chances that humans could find such a planet, purely by chance?"

"The chances are astronomical. This has also occurred to me," admitted Ingrid.

"Well, then," said Eileen, triumphantly, "perhaps there is a Plan. Perhaps we were meant to come to this planet, by something superior to us."

Ingrid didn't respond; she seemed perplexed and was still trying to process Eileen's outburst.

Eileen suddenly screamed and jumped away from the fire. There was a large scorpion at her feet, but, fortunately, it did not move.

"There's no need to worry," said Ingrid calmly. "That's just the exoskeleton of a scorpion, which it molted. Scorpions have their skeletons on the outside. When their bodies grow, they need to discard their skeletons so that they can grow a new one."

Eileen looked embarrassed. Kicking the exoskeleton, she walked towards the DM wagon to check on Gertrude.

"What was all that about?" asked Horst who had been sitting across from Ingrid. He walked around the dying fire and sat at her side.

"Well, we never were good friends, but I'm not sure what issue she has with me. Obviously, we have major differences in opinion. I also wonder—"

Her voice trailed off and she watched Eileen climb up into the DM wagon. *Could Eileen be attracted to Horst? Was that it?*

Suddenly, Hansel came running back to the group. He was carrying two large eggs.

"Look what I found! Eggs!"

"Where did you get them?" came the chorus.

Placing the eggs carefully inside one of the wagons, Hansel led the group to a clump of giant ferns; underneath one of the ferns was a hole in the ground, lined with plant debris, containing eight very large eggs.

"Reptile eggs," said Ingrid. "These must belong to those big reptiles that look like dinosaurs."

They had never seen eggs in the wild like this before. Back in New Eden, they ate eggs laid by Earth chickens. But there were no other birds on this planet, besides the Earth birds that had traveled with them on the space craft. The emergence of bird species would be much, much farther along in evolution—actually coming *after* the dinosaurs.

"Of course, fish have eggs," said Ingrid. "Amphibians have eggs which are like fish eggs. Reptiles are an evolutionary improvement on amphibians."

But nobody was listening. The prospect of having eggs for breakfast was of more importance than a lesson in evolution. Carefully picking up all of the eggs, they carried them back to the wagons, placing them next to the Diictodon meat.

While everyone was congratulating Hansel on his find, the drones appeared, buzzing and beeping. They hovered over the group, lights flashing insistently.

"They are warning us about something," said Adam. "I had better check this out!"

Just ahead was a mound of rocks at the crest of a steep hill. Climbing up the hill, Adam peered over the rocks. Whatever he saw must have alarmed him, for he quickly turned back, signaling to the group to be quiet as he slid down the hill. He told them, on the other side of the hill was a herd of sail-back reptiles.

"We won't stand a chance if they attack us. We need to get away from here as quickly as possible!"

But it was too late. One of the large sail-reptiles was staring right at them. Emerging from the clump of ferns where they had found the eggs, the creature began running at a charge toward the whole group.

Chapter 24

THE SAIL-BACK'S HOWLS REVERBERATED ALL AROUND THEM, summoning the rest of the herd. Horst could see the giant reptiles beginning to appear one by one on the hill in the distance; he counted at least twenty-five of the creatures, standing side by side, as if in battle formation.

"Quick! Load up!" he cried. "Leave everything behind and let's go!"

While the rest of the group clambered into the wagons, leaving supplies behind in the effort to escape, Horst took out his pistol, deliberately aiming at the ground in front of the charging sail-back. Since she was clearly enraged at having lost her eggs, the best he could do was to distract her. With each ricocheting bullet, there was a cloud of dust which momentarily confused the creature, stopping her in her tracks.

Horst jumped into the driver's seat of the DM wagon. "Yaah!" he screamed at Molly, whipping the reins. The horse broke into a gallop, following the other two wagons which had a head's start.

By now, the herd of sail-backs had thundered down the hill, joining the mother sail-back in charging the convoy, coming up fast behind the DM wagon. On this terrain, the sail-backs were faster than the horses and were quickly closing the gap. As they drew closer to the wagons, the Third Thaws fired shots at the reptiles, but their small caliber pistols were completely useless, given the size of the creatures and the toughness of their hides. They were outnumbered by the stampeding herd and were almost out of bullets.

"Hold your fire!" yelled Horst "On the count of three, shoot at the ground in front of them! One, two, three—"

With one accord, the Third Thaws shot their precious remaining bullets into the ground, creating a massive dust cloud. They then pushed the horses even harder, making their getaway. Behind them, the entire group of reptiles came to an abrupt halt until the dust had settled. Looking back from the seat of the DM wagon, Ingrid noted that the sail-backs now seemed to be grazing.

"You can slow down now, Horst! Their reptilian brains are so small, they have probably forgotten why they were running!"

Now that the reptiles were no longer a threat, Horst relaxed his grip on the reins, signaling to the other wagons to slow down. Ingrid went inside the Data Module to check on Gertrude who was sweating from her fever. Ingrid placed a cold compress on Gertrude's forehead and gave her water to keep her hydrated. Fortunately, Gertrude had slept through the rough ride and was unaware of their narrow escape. The pain seemed to have subdued somewhat and Ingrid was relieved to find no signs of infection.

Eventually, they reached an outcropping of rocks that would offer some protection if they were attacked again. They pulled the wagons in an area surrounded by a circle of massive boulders and tethered the horses. Although the group was still exposed on three fronts, the boulders would prevent any attack from the rear.

Hansel and Adam tried to cool down the horses who were beginning to show signs of distress. They had pushed too hard for too long and their last gallop away from the sail-backs had left them on the edge of heat exhaustion. Once they had water to drink, however, they recovered quite quickly. Peter and Harry helped by spraying the horses with water, while Hansel and Adam rubbed down the animals with towels. Meanwhile, Horst surveyed the land. All around them was lush vegetation. The sail-backs must like eating the horse tail plants because in every direction, they could see herds grazing.

Then Horst heard Eileen let out a blood-curdling scream. Turning in the direction of the boulders, he saw the enormous head of a sail-back emerging from a wide gap between the boulders. Feeling its breath scorch her back, Eileen jumped clear, still screaming. They heard the beast paw the ground on the other side of the boulders.

"The mother!" said Horst. "It must be the mother sail-back! She wants her eggs!"

More of the reptile's head emerged as she tried to force her way between the rocks, snapping her jaws in rage. While her massive dorsal sail prevented her from making it through the opening, with every snap of her jaws, the rocks moved a little. Horst watched as she withdrew her head and began to use the force of her body as a battering ram.

"What if the rocks give way?" sobbed Eileen, startling Horst into action. "She's either going to get us or the boulders will crush us first!"

Quickly, Horst ran to the wagons and retrieved the mother reptile's eggs which he placed in a sack. Slowly, he approached the boulders, carrying the eggs. Standing about ten feet away from the crevasse, he began to swing the sack over his head, increasing the speed of each rotation until he was ready to let the bag fly.

"Here, you want these?" he shouted as the sack became airborne.

The mother sail-back immediately followed her eggs. The sack landed some twenty feet away, on the other side of the boulders. They could hear the thud as it hit the ground. Peering through the crevasse, the Third Thaws could see that the sack was now flat; a thick liquid was oozing out of it.

"Why didn't you aim for the horsetails?" snapped Ingrid. "You should have known the eggs would break!"

Horst cringed, red-faced. Ingrid was right. They would have been safer had the eggs remained intact. The mother looked down at her broken eggs, then emitted a strange sound that began as a soft rattling noise, intensifying into snorts and snarls before crescendoing into a ferocious roar. Looking back at the group, she growled menacingly as she lumbered towards the gap between the boulders. Still growling, she began working away at the rocks, relentlessly wedging her head back and forth. Deposits of sand crumbled from the joints holding the boulders together, making it clear that they would not hold much longer.

As the reptile struggled, Adam and Hansel carried a large, jagged rock over to the animal. Heaving the rock as high as they could, they smashed it down on the reptile's head. The creature let out a growl, jaws snapping in fury as Adam and Hansel continued to smash the rock on top of her skull. Meanwhile, Horst had climbed on top of the boulders, carrying an ax. Swinging the ax as high as he could, he chopped into the reptile's neck with full force. The initial blow sunk several inches into the animal, killing it instantly.

From his vantage point at the top of the boulders, Horst could see herds of sail-backs in every direction. All told, there were perhaps one hundred or more sail-backs. *Was this a sail-back migration? Would the animals move on?* As the commander in charge, Horst considered their options, but was at a loss. It would be hopeless to try to escape during daylight. As for leaving during the night, they had never traveled at night before—and in which direction should they travel?

Finally, his military training kicking in, he gave orders to Adam and Hansel.

"We need to send the drones up to determine where we should go. Prepare drones for launch."

Adam and Hansel instructed Buzzy and Jaimie to scout overhead and assess the sail-back herd's movement. The surveillance should have taken no more than a few minutes—perhaps ten minutes at longest. But after ten minutes, the drones had not returned. After an hour, they had still not returned.

"Where are they?" said Adam. "Could they have been attacked by dragonflies?"

"That's a possibility," said Horst. "But I think the drones know how to escape the dragonflies. Also, I have a hard time believing that both drones could have been immobilized."

"Or neutralized," said Adam, grimly.

They made a fire and cooked lunch. In all directions, the sail-backs were resting, their sails facing the sun. For several hours, there was no movement of any kind.

"It's my guess, these animals sleep during the night," said Horst. "Therefore, I think it's best if we leave this place at night, but we really need information from the drones' reconnaissance mission. Where are they?"

He had barely finished speaking when they heard a faint buzzing in the distance. Looking up at the twilight sky, Horst saw the drones. But something was different. Instead of two drones, there were four drones flying back! Within minutes, four drones returned to the camp. Somehow, Smokey and Joey had come back! Underneath Smokey's carriage was tied a piece of paper.

Horst grabbed the paper under Smokey and unfolded it.

"It's a note," he said, studying it carefully.

"What does it say?" asked Adam.

"It says: '*Brauchen Sie helfen?*'"

"That means '*Do you need help?*' in German, doesn't it?" said Eileen.

"Yes—I mean—'*Ja,*'" said Horst, with a big smile.

"It's the Germans from New Munich! They are asking if we need help!" Eileen exclaimed, clapping her hands in relief.

"Quick, let's send them a reply! Unfortunately, my German is '*nicht sehr gut.*' Let me see. We need to say we need help."

"No problem," said Eileen. "How about, *Wir brauchen helfen.*'"

"And we need a doctor," Horst continued to dictate.

"'*Wir brauchen einen Artz,*'" wrote Eileen. "Is that in the nominative, accusative, or dative?"

"You're asking the wrong person," said Horst.

"It's in the accusative," said Adam. "You wrote correctly, '*Wir brauchen einen Artz,*' not '*eine Artz.*'"

"Good. At least I got something right out of that class," said Eileen. "Anything else?"

"*Nein. Das ist alles.*" said Horst. *[No, that is all.]* "What else is there to say, except that we need help and a doctor?"

Horst tied the note to Smokey's carriage. Then he told the drones to fly off to find the Germans. "*Mach schnell!*" he said. *[Fast!]*

"*Hoffenlich ist ihr English besser als mein Deutch!*" said Horst. *[Hopefully their English is better than my German!]*

"*Ja!*" agreed Eileen.

Chapter 25

THEY SPENT A VERY LONG NIGHT SITTING IN THEIR REF-uge, worried that they would be attacked by nocturnal animals. Concerned about drawing attention to themselves, they decided not to butcher the dead sail-back that lay on the other side of the boulders. After considering several options for disposing of her corpse, they concluded there was no easy way of doing so. The very boulders that had kept her away from the Third Thaws now blocked them from hauling her corpse away. Everyone went to sleep either inside or on top of the wagons. To protect the horses from spider and scorpion bites, they wrapped their legs in blankets. Adam and Hansel traded guard duties, watching from the rocks for intruders.

After sunrise, they cooked breakfast. Horst relieved Hansel from guard duty. As he surveyed the plains that surrounded them, he saw that the herd of sail-backs had not moved and showed no signs of migrating. *How could they possibly escape?*

Then he heard a familiar buzzing sound. Scanning the horizon, he saw the four drones flying toward them, in formation. He also noticed something unusual: puffs of smoke rising beneath them. The drones drew nearer, then flew back over the hill. It was as though they were giving directions for someone to follow them. The puffs of smoke were getting closer and closer.

Then Horst saw the strangest contraption he had ever seen. It was a vehicle that was roughly eight feet tall and twenty feet long that appeared

to roll on three large spoked wheels. At the front of the vehicle was an enormous tank of some kind, with a smaller tank next to it. A suspended beam connected the two tanks and seemed to be moving up and down with great force, reminding Horst of illustrations he had seen of the first steam engines, especially of the Newcomen engine.

He looked around for Adam who would surely have been more knowledgeable, but Adam was relaxing after guard duty. All he could remember was there was once a steam powered engine—*was it called a Newcomen engine?* As the wagon drew near the sail-backs, they became curious and ambled towards it. Jets of clear liquid from the center of the vehicle sprayed the reptiles. The animals backed away roaring, entangling their legs and tails, their sails battering each other as they attempted to run. Once free, they stampeded in every direction, clearly disorientated.

The vehicle rolled to a standstill in their camp, and made a loud hissing sound, releasing jets of steam. Then a man lowered a ladder and climbed down from an elevated bench where he had been seated with a woman.

"*Wie gehts?*" said the man. *[How goes it?]*

"*Es geht mir gut,*" said Horst. *[I'm doing good.]*

"*Wie heißen Sie?*" said the man. *[What do you call yourself?]*

"*Horst. Meine Nahme ist Horst,*" said Horst. *[My name is Horst.]* "*Konnen wir English sprechen? Meine Deutsch ist nicht sehr gut.*" *[Can we speak English? My German is not very good.]*

"*Ja, ja.* Yes, no problem. Let's speak English for now," said the man. "My name is Sigmund."

Sigmund appeared to be in his early thirties. The Germans had landed on this planet two years before the Americans had arrived; therefore,

Sigmund could be two years older than the First Thaw, which would make him thirty-three. He was five foot ten, with jet black hair; a few strands of gray were beginning to show at the hair line above his ears, but otherwise, he had a youthful appearance.

"We had given up hope that your ship had landed," said Sigmund. "You are the only other humans that we have seen. But when your drones arrived from New Eden, we knew that you were coming."

"Did the drones carry a message from New Eden?" asked Horst, a little taken aback.

"Yes, they did. The Fourth Thaw have been warned about the danger of going over the falls," said Sigmund. "No need to worry about them any longer. They will be taking a safer route to get here. But we have more important concerns—it seems there is someone sick?"

"Yes, one of our women is very ill. Let me introduce you to Ingrid, who has been taking care of Gertrude."

"Let me first introduce you to our *Artzin*—I mean, our doctor, Erica."

Sigmund waved at the woman still seated on the vehicle, then helped her down the ladder. After brief introductions, Erica went into the Data Module to see the patient. When Erica emerged from the DW, she was smiling. Since the Germans had landed, they had developed antibiotics. Now that Gertrude was on a course of penicillin, she was likely to survive. In fact, within a couple of days, she should be showing signs of recovery.

While Ingrid chatted with Erica, Horst studied the vehicle.

"So how does this vehicle work?"

"We call is the '*Zeppelin*,' though, of course, it is not an air ship like the real *Zeppelins* were—in fact, the name is a kind of joke because the vehicle is so cumbersome. It is an almost exact copy of Cugnot's steam carriage built in 1769. As you may already know, there are no petroleum products on this planet. The planet has not gone through an equivalent Carboniferous period, which would have produced coal from the decay of prehistoric forests. Therefore, the only sources of energy are the plants, such as these fern-like plants. What we do is chop up the plants and compress them into pellets. The pellets are burned in a furnace at the front of the *Zeppelin*, which heats a steam engine."

"I was right, then—or sort of!" said Horst. "So the kettle in front is a steam engine?"

"Yes, the steel kettle is a steam engine. We have been successful making small quantities of steel. As you can see, the kettle is fabricated from steel plates. The engine is driven by pistons, which required precise borings."

"This must have been very difficult, exacting work," said Horst.

"Yes, it was quite difficult working with steel. Of course, with experience we expect that it will become easier. You will also notice that this vehicle is rather tall. This works to our advantage, keeping us above many of the dangerous land animals," said Sigmund.

"But not the dragonflies!" said Hansel.

"*Ah, ja. Das Liebelien!*" laughed Sigmund. "We have developed tools that take care of the dragonflies when they get near us. Basically, we use rotor blades to cut them up into little pieces."

"That's what we've been doing!" exclaimed Adam, who had been awakened by all the commotion. "We have been using the drones to cut up the dragonflies!"

"*Augezeignet!*" said Sigmund. *[Excellent!]* "As they say, 'Great minds think alike.' I can see that we'll get along!"

"Did the Guardians help you design and build the *Zeppelin*?"

"Guardians?" replied Sigmund, appearing confused. "Oh, you mean the *Wächteren. Ja,* we got a lot of help from our *Wächteren.*"

"*Wächteren?*" said Horst. "I'm sorry, but my German *ist nicht so gut [is not so good]*. What does that mean?"

"He means their 'Guardian,'" interjected Eileen. "They got a lot of help from their Guardians."

"*Sehr interresante!*" said Horst *[Very interesting!]*, suddenly noting that Sigmund was wearing protective leg wrappings. They reminded him of the wrappings they had placed on the horses' legs the night before, but they were thinner and easier to hold in place.

"Excuse me, but what are you wearing on your legs?"

"These are skins from reptiles that live near the river. You may have seen these animals, they look like—how do you say in English?—like 'ground hogs,' I think."

"Yes, we've seen many of these animals," said Hansel.

"We discovered that when there are floods, many of these reptiles drown, because they hide in underground holes. We use the hides of these animals as *Lederhosen.*"

"*Lederhosen*?" asked Horst.

"Quite literally, 'leather pants,'" answered Sigmund. "We use the hides of the reptiles to make boots and leg wrappings. These are for protection against the spiders and scorpions which tend to bite the lower legs. The skin is very tough. Here, feel it."

He extended one of his legs, so that Horst could run his hands over the pelts.

"Yes, this hide seems like excellent protection."

"When we travel back to New Munich, your horses will also need leg protection. We can cover your horses' legs with *Lederhosen*," said Sigmund.

"I noticed that you sprayed something on the reptiles. *What was that*?" asked Horst.

"We sprayed a weak acid on the creatures," said Sigmund. "Basically vinegar. Those creatures hate the stuff. It's easy for us to make. We brew the vinegar in large vats. But now I have a question for you: Did you bring seeds and farm animal embryos? Did they survive the journey?"

"Yes, we brought a wagon with seeds and embryos. It is over there." Horst gestured in the direction of the wagon in which Jim and his family had been traveling.

When Sigmund heard this, he clasped his hands together, he could not hold back his joy.

"*Danke! Danke!* You have brought to us more life from Earth! The contents of this wagon are priceless!"

"Come with me,' said Horst, placing his hand on Sigmund's arm. "I want to introduce you to some very important people. Along the way, we discovered a family of survivors from our colony's second group."

He introduced Jim, Mary and the children.

"I am a farmer," said Jim proudly. "We have brought some seeds from my harvests."

"And I am a brewer," interjected Mary. "We have brought yeast from Salzburg, Austria, for beer, and grapes seeds from Napa Valley, California. And, of course, we have also brought with us the next generation."

"This is excellent!" said Sigmund. "*Augezeignet!* I think you will enjoy New Munich. We are very happy that you have come. We have so many plans and much work to do."

Most of the Third Thaw climbed on board the Zeppelin. The remainder of the group stayed with the horses and wagons, following the Zeppelin. Occasionally, sail-back reptiles tried to attack the convoy, but Sigmund and Erica kept the predators at bay by shooting vinegar in their eyes.

For two days, they traveled across the rolling terrain, until they saw the silhouette of New Munich. Outside the city were vast fields. As they traveled down the road into the city, people ran out of the fields to greet them.

The American and German colonies had finally made contact.

Part 3
New Munich

Chapter 26

AT FIRST SIGHT, NEW MUNICH DID NOT APPEAR MUCH DIFferent than New Eden, but it was larger. As the Third Thaws entered the town, about a hundred people came out to greet them, all of them cheering *"Die Americaner! Die Americaner!"* *[The Americans! The Americans!]*

"New Munich looks a lot like New Eden," observed Horst.

"Of course. Both places were originally built by Guardians. The Guardians at New Eden and Neu München use the same technology and the same type of artificial intelligence," explained Sigmund. "Our landing and your landing were planned and coordinated by the same people using the same survival plan."

"How many people are in your settlement?" asked Horst.

"Our spacecraft had sixty embryos, as yours also had. All the embryos were delivered successfully," said Sigmund. "Most of our people have married each other, with a few exceptions. The marriages have produced . . . let me count . . . *einundreisig, zweiunddreisig, dreiunddreisig* . . . we have, as you say, thirty-eight children, at last count."

A young woman who appeared to be about eighteen years old ran up to Sigmund.

"Guten Tag, Pappa!" she said to Sigmund.

"Guten Tag, Gretchen!" he replied, giving her a hug.

"Horst, let me introduce my daughter, Gretchen."

"Freut mich!" Horst replied. *[My pleasure!]*

"Hallo. My English is not so good, not true?" said Gretchen, self-consciously.

"*Angenehm [Delightful]*, Gretchen. Your English sounds fine."

～

The Americans were given living quarters with different families. They were very dirty from traveling for the past few months, and they needed to clean up. Many of the men had grown beards. Horst wanted to shave his.

That evening, they gathered in the Beer Garden. Everyone from New Munich had come to welcome the Americans. Before the festivities began, Sigmund stood up to make a formal announcement.

"*Guten Abend, meine Damen und Herren!*" [*Good evening, ladies and gentlemen!*]

"*Guten Abend!*" came the enthusiastic reply.

"*Heute Abend sind wir hier, die Vereinigung der Deutschen und Amerikanischen Kolonien zu feiern*," announced Sigmund. [*Tonight we are here to celebrate the union of both the German and American colonies.*]

"*Unsere Brüder und Schwestern hatten eine gefährliche Reise zu uns nach Hause.*" [*Our brothers and sisters had a dangerous trip to our home.*]

"*Aber jetzt, endlich, wir sind zusammen.*" [*But now, finally, we are together.*]

"*Lassen Sie uns offiziell begrüßen Sie unsere neuen Freunde in unserer Community!*" [*Let us formally welcome our new friends into our community!*]

Most of Sigmund's speech was lost on the Americans, who sat at their tables smiling, barely understanding a word.

Horst leaned over to Ingrid and whispered, "Did you get any of that?"

"Barely a word," whispered Ingrid. "I understood '*Guten Abend*' but the rest was a blur."

Sigmund took out a small piece of paper from his pocket.

"*Entschuldigung. Ich habe Zettle mit meiner Rede in englischer Sprache.*" [*Excuse me. I have my notes for reading in English.*]

All the Germans laughed. The Americans continued to smile, understanding little.

"Sorry, I must learn to speak more English . . . I have written notes . . . . my English is not so good, I'm afraid," he apologized.

Clearing his throat, he began to read from his notes.

"From the people of Neu München, I wish to welcome you into our community. *Wilkommen!* We have been waiting a long time for your arrival.

It greatly pleases us that your colony . . . *was ist das Wort?"* *[What is this word?]* Looking embarrassed, Sigmund quickly turned to one of his colleagues who managed to decipher the English word he had written.

"*Bitte*. As I was saying, it greatly pleases us that your colony *survived*. We have been given a great . . . *was ist das?"* Again, he consulted with his colleague, then continued.

"*Re-spon-si-bil-ity. Ja*, we have been given a great responsibility."

He put away his notes. "As you can see, I think at first we will have some communication difficulties. *Hoffenlich werde das kein problem sein* . . . I mean, hopefully this will become no problem, and we will learn to communicate effectively in the future. And with that, please enjoy yourself. *Wilkommen und Guten Appetit!"* *[Welcome and good appetite!]*

Everyone in the room applauded loudly. "*Guten Appetit!"*

They had a delicious meal of roast pork shank with sauerkraut. Like their German ancestors on Earth, the Germans on this planet made excellent beer, which they served in liter steins. Musicians played polkas. The Third Thaws, along with Jim and Mary, had a wonderful time.

They traded remarkably similar stories about growing up in New Eden and New Munich: the German and American space crafts were identical; both expeditions carried sixty embryos that were raised by the Guardians; both had supercomputers which controlled the Guardians and provided Artificial Personality Simulators. The only real difference was that the Germans were trained by their APS parents and grandparents, focusing on the Deutschland culture, as opposed to American culture, and this accounted for the cultural differences between the two settlements.

Horst was sitting next to Sigmund at a large round table seating twelve people from both settlements. There was much laughter and merrymaking as Germans and Americans practiced their language skills, using sign language where words failed. Only Zelda, who happened to be seated at the same table, did not join in. Waiting for a break in the conversation, Horst turned to Sigmund

"Do you understand why three spacecraft were sent?"

"Yes, I think we do," said Sigmund. "It was explained to us in the Artificial Personality Simulator. Three spacecraft were sent to this planet at different times. The first was the Einstein-Newton probe. It carried a supercomputer, but no embryos."

"Why no embryos?" asked Horst.

"The planners of this mission were not entirely certain that this planet would be habitable; therefore the first probe carried no life-forms."

"Please continue."

"We think that one of the purposes of the Einstein-Newton probe was to make an initial assessment of the planet required for the subsequent landing craft which carried the embryos. The probe made maps of the planet, and these are the only maps that we have as of this date. That probe determined the best landing sites for the two colonies; both needed to be near water. The space shuttles required long, flat, natural landing paths, away from trees. Einstein-Newton accessed the topography of the planet to find suitable landing sites. It did not matter if Einstein-Newton shuttle landed in a desert; however, the human colonies needed to be located near water."

Sigmund took a sip of beer, then said *"Probst!" [Cheers!]* to the others at the table. Everyone raised their steins, except for Zelda who did not have a taste for beer. *"Probst!"*

"Please continue sharing your understanding of the mission," said Horst.

"Yes, of course," said Sigmund. "After mapping the planet from orbit, Einstein-Newton landed. It then made an assessment of the environment. The probe was equipped with robotic vehicles for exploration, too."

"And?"

Sigmund took another draft of his beer.

"When the second spacecraft—our spacecraft—neared the planet, Einstein-Newton sent a radio message to our craft, making a 'Go-No-Go' decision about whether our craft should land."

"I'm a bit confused," said Horst. "What would be the alternative to landing? What if it sent a 'No-Go' decision?"

"We're not sure. There may have been another planet in another solar system that was also a possible candidate for colonization. Frankly, these distances boggle the mind. The farther the distance, the less chance there is of survival. These spacecraft traveled at high velocities in space and were subject to damage by micro-particles in space. Did you ever observe the damage on your spacecraft?"

"No. Leader Graham never allowed us very close to our landing craft. We only saw it from a distance during a field trip in school," said Horst.

"Well, no doubt if you had looked closely at your spacecraft under a microscope you would have seen the same micro-pitting on the surface that we have observed. It is amazing there were no casualties—lost embryos, I mean."

"Please continue. This is fascinating," said Horst.

"Okay," said Sigmund. "The way we understand the mission is that the Einstein-Newton probe was the reconnaissance craft. Then the Deutsch landing craft was sent to establish the actual first human colony."

"Then our craft, carrying the Americans, was sent as a backup, in case yours was unsuccessful?"

"Well, not quite," said Sigmund. "The mission had planned redundancy. In case one of the space craft failed, then, 'yes,' the other was, as you say, a 'backup' space craft."

"But it still does not make sense to me about Einstein-Newton," persisted Horst. "Why did they send a spacecraft with a supercomputer? A reconnaissance craft does not require a supercomputer. What was the purpose?"

Sigmund paused, a serious look flashing across his face.

"We don't have all the pieces to the puzzle, yet. We have some theories, though. There will be a meeting tomorrow in the APS auditorium during which we will explain all that we understand about Einstein-Newton."

"Do you know where the Einstein-Newton probe landed?" asked Horst.

"Yes, we do. We know exactly where it landed, but please, be patient. You will know everything we know tomorrow," answered Sigmund. "We can conclude now that the mission was a complete success, because all three of the space craft made it here safely."

"Except for our people who were killed falling over a waterfall," said Horst soberly. "And we lost another of our crew, killed by a large fish. Frankly, I'm amazed we made it here, with all the dangerous creatures that we encountered."

"What a tragedy! To come all this way, then to be killed!" said Sigmund.

At that, Zelda, who was sitting next to Horst and listening to their conversation, broke down in tears. She pushed her chair away from the table, excused herself, but seemed to lose her balance. Noticing the blank expression in her eyes, Horst immediately jumped up and caught her as she fainted.

"We need to get her to a doctor," said Horst. "She has not been herself since Gerald died."

~

As soon as she recovered, they gave her some water and then supported her as they walked to Dr. Erica's clinic. Once they had helped her onto the examining table, Sigmund and Horst left the room and sat in the small waiting room.

"I understand that you have been feeling ill lately. Can you tell me about it? Have you been throwing up?" asked Dr. Erica, loosening the clothing around Zelda's waist.

"Yes. A lot of things I've been eating make me sick," answered Zelda. "I don't know what it is—maybe it's the reptile meat—but it makes me feel sick."

"Have you been drinking at all tonight?"

"Nothing except water."

"Good. It's probably not a good idea to drink in your condition," said Erica.

"What do you mean, 'in my condition'?" asked Zelda, looking alarmed.

"Surely you realize, don't you?" asked Erica. "Do you remember when your last period was?"

Zelda turned red, unused to discussing such topics. Upon further questioning, she realized it had been at least two months since her last period. She had been so depressed since Gerald's death that she had lost track.

"Of course, we can do a test," said Dr. Erica, "But, in my judgement, I think you have a simple case of being pregnant."

"*Pregnant?*" repeated Zelda. "But *how* did that happen?"

"Were you and Gerald ever intimate?" asked Dr. Erica, gently.

Again, Zelda's face became very flushed.

"Well, we did touch each other," she admitted. "And we also kissed a lot."

"It takes more than touching and kissing to make a baby, Zelda."

"Yes, I know babies come from embryos," said Zelda, still looking confused. "How can I have an embryo inside me?"

"Zelda, you have Gerald's child inside you," said Dr. Erica.

Zelda was shocked to hear this. This possibility had never occurred to her. *Was that really why she had not had her period lately?* As she thought about it, the idea that she was carrying Gerald's child inside her gave her a sense of happiness.

"It's your child as well," said the doctor. "It takes two—"

Seeing that Zelda wasn't listening, she cleared her throat.

"My prescription for you is to avoid drinking any alcohol, and to eat as much as you can. Avoid doing anything too strenuous which would involve bending and picking things up. I would like to see you again in a month."

Zelda walked out of the examination room in a daze. When Sigmund and Horst asked her how she was feeling, she gave them a mysterious little smile, the first smile Horst had seen from her in a long, long time. He looked at her quizzically, but she said nothing. For the first time, he noticed that her belly was rounder than usual.

The next day, the Third Thaws were given a tour of New Munich. They saw many production facilities housing steel tanks with networks of pipes. Smoke billowed from tall chimneys.

"What are you making here?" asked Adam.

"In this facility, we are making synthetic petroleum fuel from biomass," explained Sigmund. "We use the Fischer-Tropsch process, which was invented in Germany in 1925 to produce synthetic lubricant and fuel from coal or biomass. Since the planet lacks both coal and petroleum, we need to make our own fuel."

"Then I assume that you've also built combustible engines?" said Adam.

"Yes, we have built a somewhat crude combustible engine that uses this synthetic fuel," said Sigmund. "For a long time, we used only steam power, which is, of course, what powers the *Zeppelin*. The petroleum we are making here will be used for plastic production and fuel for engines."

"Excuse me--I have another question," interrupted Horst. "If you have been building engines, why have we not seen any cars yet?"

Sigmund answered, "We are not building engines for cars—at least not yet."

"You are much farther along than we are," admitted Adam.

"We have been here longer, my friend," said Sigmund. Then, addressing the entire group, he said, "Please follow me!"

Sigmund showed the group several other chemical production facilities.

"We are focusing on the production of certain basic chemicals that are necessary in modern civilizations. This plant here is making synthetic soda. Soda is necessary to produce soap and glass. The Industrial Revolution of the 1800s had much to do with the production of soda, beginning with the Leblanc process developed in 1787."

They walked to another nearby plant. Sigmund continued the tour.

"This plant makes sulfuric acid, using an old process invented by a Deutsch chemist by the name of Johann Glauber."

He pointed at the chimney towering over them.

"Notice the tall chimney billowing smoke. The action of sulfuric acid on salt in the first stage of the Leblanc process produces clouds of hydrochloric acid gas, which is very noxious. This chimney, which is almost three hundred feet high, has water sprayed on the inside of the stack. This removes ninety-five percent of the hydrochloric acid from the emissions. This idea of cleaning emissions was invented by a British manufacturer, William Gossage, in 1836."

"What is the hydrochloric acid used for?" asked Horst.

"Hydrochloric acid is used for many things. One of the more important uses is for bleaching textiles. For example, the cotton industry was possible due to bleaching, which requires bleaching powder, which contains hydrochloric acid. Another example would be the paper industry, which requires chemical bleaching."

"Are you making building materials here?" asked Adam.

"Yes, we are," answered Sigmund. "We have been making cement from lime and clay, as well as bricks from clay. We have been making wrought iron, too. However, the manufacture of steel has represented a challenge, since we lack a big enough furnace. We just don't have the man power and resources for large steel production."

"And no wood," said Adam.

"Correct. There are no trees on this planet, just the ferns," said Sigmund. "As a substitute, we have been making a composite plastic and fern fiber wood substitute, with pigmentation that resembles wood."

Adam looked at the buildings which were half-timbered with stucco; they reminded him of the quaint houses he had seen in picture books when he was a child.

"These buildings are modeled in the style of half-timbered construction in Deutschland," said Sigmund. "But instead of wood, what you see is plastic. I suppose that you could say that these buildings are 'half-plasticized.'"

This concluded the tour of New Munich. The whole settlement was only three blocks by three blocks.

"I want to make a point about what you have just seen here," said Sigmund. These are not factories; they are only laboratories. We are in the process of relearning and demonstrating technologies which required huge factories on Earth.

"We only have a few people on this planet. We are able to make enough things for our own needs. These chemical processes require minerals and raw chemicals that are difficult for us to collect."

"Yes," interjected Horst, "The same is true in New Eden. The Guardians and the drones made things for us. They grew crops, cooked our food and made our clothes, amongst many other tasks."

"The trouble we have been running into," said Sigmund, "is that the robots are wearing out and breaking down. There are only a limited number of these robots. We can't build any more of them. When they break down, we don't understand how to fix them. And this is becoming a major concern."

Chapter 27

THE NEXT DAY, THE THIRD THAW ASSEMBLED IN THE FRONT rows of a large auditorium. Sigmund was on stage, standing behind a podium. He began his presentation by welcoming the Americans to New Munich.

"Greetings, my fellow explorers! We expected to see you fourteen years ago! What happened?" he joked. "Frankly, we had given up hope that you had been successful in establishing New Eden! But I should not be joking. It is a tragedy that the first two generations of you Americans were all killed."

"Not all of us were killed, Sir," interrupted Jim, rising to his feet. "My wife, Mary, and I are the only remaining members of the Second Thaw. We survived going over the falls. We have been living in the wild for the past five years, until the Third Thaw discovered us, along with our three kids."

"Of course! My apologies, Jim," said Sigmund. "I remember meeting you and your family last night! Someday you must share with us your stories of living in the wilderness."

"Yes, Sir. We'd be happy to share our story," said Jim, taking his seat again.

"As I was saying," said Sigmund. "We had given up hope that the American spacecraft had survived. Because we thought we were the only ones here, we decided to go ahead and complete the mission by contacting the Einstein-Newton site."

"I don't understand what you mean by 'complete the mission,'" said Horst. "What is the purpose of contacting Einstein-Newton?"

"It will be best if we use the Artificial Personality Simulator to explain this part of the overall mission plan; in fact, this is why we have gathered in the auditorium and not in one of our smaller meeting rooms. Let me introduce to you Herr Helmut. He will answer your questions about Einstein-Newton."

With the press of a button, Sigmund lowered a projection screen; he then joined the Third Thaw and sat next to Horst. The image of a man appeared on the screen.

"*Guten Tag*—or should I say, *Good Day*, Americans! My name is Helmut," said the man. "Of course, I am not the real Helmut, but a simulation of a man from Deutschland named Helmut who lived 80,000 years ago on Earth, give or take a few thousand years. I was one of the 'Planners of the Mission' for the Deutsch group.

"I know that some of you have been asking about the Einstein-Newton probe. But before I get into that, I want to digress a moment and talk about the 'Big Picture' of your purpose here. In order to colonize a new planet and provide the future population with modern things, you must have the right technologies. Without modern products, you will be reduced to living like cavemen. The fact is, you are currently living at a medieval level, which is entirely unsatisfactory."

"Excuse me," protested Eileen, "But what is wrong with living in, as you say, a 'medieval way'? Why do we need to be modern?"

"Because you will suffer if you do not progress. For example, there are modern medicines which will make you healthier and prolong your lives. Without modern conveniences, you may live to be only thirty years old."

"Only thirty years old? I'm already twenty-one!"

"Yes, people lived to be only about thirty years old in medieval England. In earlier times, during classical Rome, people lived from between twenty to thirty years old," explained Helmut.

"So, you mean to say that if these were Roman times, I might already be near the end of my life?"

"Very possibly. Having a longer, healthier life is just one reason to desire modern things."

Sigmund stood up and faced the APS screen. "Excuse me, Herr Helmut, I want to interject something here. We presently have some of these modern things in New Munich. We have been very active in manufacturing some modern items such as medicines."

"A point well taken," responded Helmut. "We understand that you have been successful with some things on a small scale."

"Yes, that is correct. We make only small batches, so far."

"*Small batches*—just what I thought," smiled Helmut. "In order to repro-duce modern things, you will need to make big batches. This will represent a monumental task for you, unless you have help. The Earth had billions of people all over the globe making all types of products. How many people do you have living here in New Munich? By last count, only one hundred and fifteen. With only one hundred and fifteen people, how many things can you make? What things should you make? And what things can you do without? What materials are the most essential? Who will do the hard work, such as working in the fields and mining?"

He surveyed his audience. Everyone seemed very attentive, as if con-sidering the future for the first time. Up until now, the Third Thaw had focused on their adventures and miraculous survival. Now, they needed to shift their priorities.

"You there," he said, pointing at Hansel. "What is your name?"

"Hansel, Sir."

"You look like a strong fellow. Let me ask you, Herr Hansel, a question. Have you ever been in a mine?"

"Never, Sir, but I have worked with the digging team in New Eden's excavation pit."

"How was that? Was it hard work?"

"Yes, it was very hard work, Sir."

"Can you imagine how many men it would take to dig a mine, deep enough to excavate iron ore in large quantities?"

"You mean those brown rocks?"

"Yes, iron ore is a brown rock."

"We usually only dug clay, not rocks," said Hansel, thinking back to life in New Eden. "We came across a few of those brown rocks at a deep level in the excavation pit. Can you give me an idea how deep we would need to dig?"

"Let's say you would need to dig a mine that is a hundred feet below the ground. Then let's say you would be digging a tunnel that is about 1,000 feet long, before excavating the ore."

Hansel whistled. "Well, that would be quite an impressive tunnel. I imag-ine it would require hundreds of men using powered mining equipment."

"Exactly my point," said Helmut. "It would require *hundreds* of men to dig a mine such as this. Even with the advantage of powered digging equipment, it would require hundreds of men. That's what it took on Earth—hundreds of miners. And therein lies the problem: You don't have enough people for manual labor like digging mines."

Horst nodded in agreement. The math spoke for itself. *With so few people, what could they expect to achieve on this planet?*

"You need more people here to make things and do the hard work, but you don't have the time to wait for the human population to grow large enough to make all the products you need. That's where the Einstein-Newton probe comes in. It carries a robotic workforce for your human colony, to do the hard work."

He paused, giving the group time to absorb what he was saying.

"Let me first describe what was on board the Einstein-Newton probe: It carried a supercomputer and a robot assembly unit. The Einstein-Newton's spaceship is somewhat like your own, but it did not carry living embryos; instead, it carried very small robots which make bigger robots.

"Robots are the solution the Planners of the Mission gave you, to provide manufacturing capabilities. The plan is for you to control the workforce of robots using digital technologies developed at the Digital Manufacturing and Design Innovation Institute in Chicago. The Einstein-Newton probe has all the software for you to control robot-run factories. Now you just need to connect with the robots.

"Think of the Einstein-Newton probe this way: It has a supercomputer and small robots for making larger 'baby robots.' These robots are not the friendly Guardian-type robots that raised you; they are designed for work, and are able to survive in harsher conditions than humans. The Einstein-Newton probe was designed to establish a colony of robots that is similar to an ant colony. The supercomputer is at the core of this community, like the Queen ant in an ant community. It provides the artificial intelligence for all the robots. This setup is identical to how the Guardians are controlled from supercomputers at New Eden and New Munich."

"You say that it has small robots for making larger robots. How does it make robots? Were the parts brought for the robots?" asked Horst.

"No, large robot parts were not brought here—that would have taken too much space. Instead, very small robots—and by that, I mean 'nanobots'—were shipped," answered Helmut. "The plan was this: send nanobots to mine metals in small quantities. From those metals, the small bots made parts for larger bots. Those large bots then mined more metals, making parts for still larger bots. You can see where I'm going with this, can't you? Somewhat like the cells in living organisms which grow animals, these nanobots were programed to build full-size robots."

"A brilliant concept, I must admit," said Horst. "But it must have taken years and years for such a process of building robots from a small scale to a large scale."

"Yes, it must have taken years," said Helmut. "But, time is immaterial, isn't it? We know for certain that this methodology works, because it was demonstrated in our studies on Earth."

Horst said, "This is a direct mechanical parallel with biological systems. And you say, they were able to do this on Earth?"

Helmut smiled and nodded. Then he continued, "Again, if we think about the 'Big Picture' of the colonization, we have two groups to consider: the humans and the robots. If you people survive all the great obstacles, live to maturity and establish a colony, then the robots produced by Einstein-Newton will provide you with a workforce for creating a modern society. The robots are designed to be your slaves. In this context, the Einstein-Newton probe is a slave ship."

Horst was so impressed, he stood up and began applauding. The rest of the Third Thaw also rose to their feet, clapping their hands as they did so. The entire mission—the idea of sending ships—was a grand plan, with beautiful redundancy. The Germans and Americans acted as redundant embryo groups: If one failed, the other was covered. Meanwhile, the Einstein-Newton probe provided workers for the human colony, in a symbiotic relationship between man and machine.

Sigmund walked back to the podium. "Thank you, Herr Helmut."

"*Vielen Dank [thank you very much]*, Herr Sigmund!" said Helmut. Then his APS image disappeared from the screen.

"Are there any more questions?" asked Sigmund.

"Yes, Herr Sigmund, I have a question," said Adam. You said your party tried to contact Einstein-Newton. What happened?"

Sigmund paused.

"Yes. Five years ago, we decided to send our own expedition to Einstein-Newton. They never returned. We do not know what happened to them."

Chapter 28

A S SIGMUND CONTINUED TO FIELD QUESTIONS FROM THE
audience, Horst pondered over this interesting revelation. There were
so many dangers on this planet, so many ways they could have been killed.

"So what's next?" asked Adam.

Sigmund said, "We must try again to contact the Einstein-Newton
robot colony. That was the plan and this remains the plan. It's true that
we are five years late. But, as the saying goes, 'better late than never.' We
believe the Einstein-Newton colony of robots has grown considerably. The
probe landed well over thirty years ago and all this time it has been building
robots. We estimate there may be as many as 1,000 robots in the colony."

"Where is the colony located?" asked Horst.

Sigmund displayed a map on the screen.

"The robot colony is located here," he said, indicating an "X" on the map.
"This location is a mesa, about 1,000 feet high. The mesa is on the edge of an
arid, hot desert; behind the mesa is a forest. It will be very difficult to travel
to this location on foot."

The Third Thaws looked at each other, evidently surprised.

"Have you been preparing to send a new expedition?" asked Horst
cautiously.

"Yes, we are currently preparing to send an expedition."

"Do you think the expedition may be attacked?" asked Ingrid, making
no effort to hide her concern.

"We don't know what to expect. The colony will have a self-defense system that was designed to protect the robots from dangerous wildlife. We

don't want to rule out the possibility they may attack us, if we are perceived as a threat," said Sigmund.

"If the expedition is attacked by Einstein-Newton, can the robots be immobilized?" asked Horst.

"Yes, we have a plan for immobilizing the robots. Let me show you something," said Sigmund. "Please, follow me."

The entire group left the building and followed Sigmund to another large building three blocks away. Adam, the structural engineer in the group, immediately recognized the building as an airport hangar.

Sigmund opened a door to the hangar. In front of them they saw what looked like ten World War I biplanes. Proudly, he walked up to one of the biplanes and patted it.

"*Nicht schlecht?*" *[Not bad?]*

Horst said, "*Ja. Es ist sehr gut!*" *[Yes. It is very good!]*

"Let me turn this part of the presentation over to Captain Fritz, or should I call you the 'Red Baron' after the WWI flying ace?" said Sigmund, turning towards a man in mechanic's overalls who was leaning against one of the planes.

"*Ja*, you can call me anything you want!" laughed Fritz.

Despite his nickname, "The Red Baron," Fritz did not have the slightest bit of red hair. In fact, his hair was jet black, and was combed back with an exact part. He was ten years younger than Sigmund, and was a tall man, about six foot two, with an athletic build. Captain Fritz was Sigmund's right-hand man. He was married to *Artzin* Erica, the female doctor, who had treated Gertrude when the Third Thaw was saved.

Fritz walked up to a plane and patted the wings.

"This plane is an exact reproduction of the 1918 Fokker D.VII used by Deutschland in World War I. It has a 185 horsepower six-cylinder water-cooled engine, which is a BMW design. The wingspan is twenty-nine feet. It has a top speed of 116.6 miles per hour. During that war, it was especially effective at high altitudes. After the war, the designer, Anthony Fokker, moved to the United States where he headed Fokker Aircraft Corporation."

"It's a beautiful reproduction, but I don't understand. Why the biplanes?" asked Adam.

"Since losing contact with the members of our colony who went to the Einstein-Newton site five years ago, we have been very apprehensive about traveling there again," explained Sigmund. "We don't understand the situation there. It could be that our group met with a natural disaster; it could also be that something more sinister is at work. We just don't know, but we have to be prepared for anything. We decided that, if and when we are to return to the Einstein-Newton site, we will need an element of surprise. We believe the planes will give us an advantage arriving from the air."

"*Ja*, the planes will give us an advantage reaching this very difficult location," agreed Fritz. "The planes can cover the distance and the height of the mesa easily. We can come in quickly from cloud cover and enter the site by surprise."

"It is almost like planning an attack," observed Horst.

"It is a necessary precaution, until we understand the situation," said Sigmund.

"Let me understand you correctly. When you get there, you will land on a mesa. But by your estimate, there may be as many as 1,000 robots by now. How would we disable them if they feel threatened?"

"The robots are controlled by the supercomputer—the same technology used to control the Guardians. This offers us a huge advantage understanding their weak point.

"We have a radio wave jamming system that will disrupt the signals that control the robots. We will turn on the jamming system as we approach the mesa. After we immobilize the robots, we will take control of the Einstein-Newton supercomputer."

"Clever," said Horst.

"*Danke*," responded Sigmund.

"So, I assume that you've been flying these planes already, *nicht war*?" asked Adam who was having difficulty taking his eyes off the planes.

"*Ja, natürlich!* [*yes, of course!*] The air strip is just outside next to the hangar. How about coming for a ride?" asked Sigmund.

Horst and Adam couldn't hold themselves back.

"Yes, we want to go! Any more takers?" said Adam, looking at the rest of the group. Zelda pulled a face and walked out of the hangar, trailed by Eileen, Eva, and a few of the others, including Gertrude who was now able to walk with the assistance of crutches. Those who remained didn't look very eager to go flying.

"Well, no time like the present," said Sigmund. "Let's go! *Mach schnell!*"

Sigmund and Fritz rolled two of the biplanes out of the hangar. Each of the planes carried two people—the pilot and a passenger. Horst and Adam each got into one of the passenger's seats: Horst sat behind Sigmund who was piloting one plane and Adam sat behind Fritz, who was piloting the other.

The planes took off down the runway and lifted into the air. Soaring above New Munich, Horst and Adam looked down at the landscape. In the distance, they could see the carboniferous forest where the sail-backs lived. They could see the river leading into New Munich. The planes flew higher and higher, reaching just below the clouds. Far on the horizon, they could see the beginnings of what looked like a desert, perhaps the very desert where the Einstein-Newton probe landed.

Sigmund pulled on the joystick and flew the plane above the clouds. Horst had never seen such a sight. The clouds were like a big soft cotton blanket that he could almost walk on! He couldn't believe what an adventure he was having. Just days before, he had been fighting giant reptiles, and now he was flying above the clouds!

After they landed, Ingrid ran up to Horst.

"How was it?"

"It was wonderful," said Horst. "I still can't get over it! We were above the clouds! The clouds look like cotton!"

<hr />

As sunset approached, the Germans and Americans discussed plans to have a large feast that evening. The people of New Munich arrived in the park at the center of the colony, each bringing food for themselves and their guests. Everyone sat on blankets and ate their dinner. There was much food and ice cream—and, of course, beer.

In the park was a band shell in which musicians of the New Munich Orchestra were setting up and tuning their instruments. Thrilled at the opportunity to hear them play, Eileen could barely eat. While she was staring at the band shell, a man carrying a violin walked up to her and bowed.

"May I introduce myself? My name is Felix, the conductor of our local orchestra."

"*Angenehm!*" *[Pleasure!]* replied Eileen in perfect German. "*Ich heiße Eileen.*" *[I am called Eileen.]*

"I understand that you are an accomplished pianist."

"Well . . . thank you, Herr Felix. Yes, I do play piano."

"Would you feel comfortable playing for us tonight? I mean, we don't want to put you on the spot," said Felix. "Think of us as family. Perhaps after our orchestra plays the first piece, you would do us the honor of playing something?"

"Well . . . yes," said Eileen, clearly delighted. "Yes, I can do that. Is there an electronic keyboard I can use to warm up with, using headphones?"

"Certainly, we have one," said Felix. "Please, come this way!"

While Eileen was preparing for her performance, the others of the Third Thaw mingled with their German hosts. Spotting three German Guardians in the crowd, Adam wondered if these were a different make and model than the ones in New Eden. They had the same features—but they were laughing and smiling, even whispering to each other. He had never seen Guardians act that way.

"Hansel, do you see those Guardians over there?" asked Adam.

"Yes. What about them?"

"Do you notice anything different about them?"

Hansel looked at the Guardians, trying not to stare.

"Yes, there is something different about them. I can't quite pinpoint what it is."

Quite unexpectedly, the female Guardians walked directly up to Adam and Hansel.

"Hello," said one of them, in a cheerful voice. "May we introduce ourselves?"

"Ah . . . why, sure . . ." stammered Adam. When had a Guardian ever talked to him like this?

"I am Shina," she said.

"And I am Yuna," said the other female. "Our parents are from Japan."

Of course, Japan! Adam suddenly realized that all the Guardians were manufactured in Japan and looked Japanese! So, these were real Japanese *people,* not robots.

"I am so sorry—we must have been staring," said Adam, "It's just that . . ."

"It's because you thought we were Guardians?" said Shina, covering her mouth with her hands, stifling a laugh.

"Ah . . . yes," said Adam, embarrassed.

"That's okay," said Shina. "It happens all the time."

As Adam and Hansel were getting to know Shina and Yuna; Zelda, Gertrude, and Eva were mingling with the other residents of New Munich. Zelda's mood and appetite had improved since she had learned that she was pregnant. Her friends weren't sure how the embryo had gotten inside Zelda and they were confused as to how it would finally be born. Zelda had told them that the doctor had mentioned a birth canal but she herself didn't know where this was.

Shortly after Eva and Zelda left, Gertrude noticed a tall dark-skinned man. Leaning heavily on her crutches, she walked over to him and introduced herself. When Zelda and Eva returned, they found them engaged in conversation.

"Good," said Gertrude, "I was wondering when you'd get back! Let me introduce you to . . . I'm sorry, but I didn't quite get your name."

"Okunola," said the man.

"Yes, Okunola," said Gertrude, "Okunola tells me that his parents are from Nigeria."

"Pleased to meet you," said Zelda, looking up at him He was a tall man, perhaps six foot three. His skin was about the same color as her own, and he had a nice, friendly smile.

"Excuse me for staring at you," said Okunola, "It's just . . . how should I say? It's just you are the first person who I have met whose skin is like mine."

Zelda smiled. "Yes, our kind appear to be in the minority." She studied him, as he studied her.

"It is interesting that the Germans brought an African with them," she said.

"No, no—my parents were Deutsch," said Okunola. "They were born in Nigeria and later immigrated to Deutschland—or Germany, as you say. They have kept our African traditions alive."

"Very interesting," said Zelda. "Did they take you on any APS trips to Africa?"

Okunola smiled. "Yes, they did once. We visited my grandparents there. They live in a little village outside Lagos. They lived a very simple life, with each family in a traditional circular hut made of woven grasses. It was wonderful."

Zelda was impressed with how easy it was to talk to Okunola. He seemed so direct and natural—actually a lot like Gerald. Then she caught herself thinking about Gerald, and suddenly felt depressed. *Was she being unfaithful to Gerald, talking to this man—looking at this man?*

"Is there something wrong? You are frowning," said Okunola.

"Well, yes. One of our people died during the journey," said Zelda, avoiding his gaze.

"And you, you were close to this person?"

Zelda nodded. Subconsciously, her hand went to her belly and rested there.

"You are with child?" he asked. "Your baby will have a good life here. *Neu München ist wunderbar! [New Munich is wonderful!]* I will be your friend. We have a saying: '*Mach dir keine Sorgen,*' which means 'don't worry.'"

"*Mach dir keine Sorgen,*" repeated Zelda, smiling.

"*Ja, ja, stimmt! [Yes, yes, correct!]* And where are your parents from?"

"From Detroit, Michigan."

"Have you made any APS trips there?"

"Yes, several times. My mother took me on APS trips all over America."

"Then we should share our stories in the future," said Okunola.

Zelda smiled. Gerald would want her to be happy, she told herself. She would always remember Gerald, but it would be foolish to stagnate at this point in her life. *Who knows how long she would live, anyway? What was it that Sigmund had said?—that people in medieval England lived to be only about thirty years old? And the Thaws were currently living 'at a medieval' level?* She made a secret resolution to herself to move forward and have fun—at least a little fun.

After sunset, the orchestra band shell lights went on. The New Munich Orchestra consisted of about thirty members. The conductor arrived at the podium and everyone quieted down.

The orchestra began to play several movements from "The Planets" by Gustav Holst. This symphony seemed particularly apropos for this setting on a new planet. The orchestra played the "Jupiter" movement with great feeling. The Americans were thoroughly impressed by listening to a live orchestra for the first time.

After the orchestra had finished playing, Felix walked over to a standing mic, center stage.

"*Guten Abend, Herren und Frauen.* Tonight we will have the pleasure of hearing for the first time in New Munich an American pianist. Let us welcome Eileen!"

Eileen walked to the stage and sat at the grand piano, a magnificent Bosendorfer.

As the Third Thaws expected, she played brilliantly. The crowd enthusiastically applauded her performance. They especially enjoyed the pieces she played by Scott Joplin. After her performance, Felix asked if she would accompany the orchestra for a few numbers. They would be playing American Big Band music.

Adam, Hansel, Horst and Ingrid were sitting together on a checkered picnic blanket, with their new Japanese-German friends, Shina and Yuna. They had stuffed themselves. The food was excellent, although drinking beer and eating ice cream did not quite go well together.

"Having fun?" Horst asked Ingrid.

"Yes. This is wonderful," she answered. "The orchestra was superb, and Eileen gave a fantastic performance. She will make a great addition to the musical community here."

The moon orbiting this planet was somewhat larger than Earth's moon.

Horst looked at Ingrid, who was wearing a blue and white shirt and blue jeans, with a green necklace and matching green bracelet.

"Where did you get that bracelet?" he asked

"I made it. I found the green gems in New Eden," said Ingrid. "I think they may have come from a volcano."

"It looks very nice," said Horst admiringly. "The stones match your eyes," he added, suddenly feeling embarrassed to talk this way. Ingrid looked down at her bracelet, fingering it self-consciously.

The orchestra played several American Big Band pieces. The crowd got up and started dancing. The Americans had never seen anybody dance before, except for that one time they had done the "Cakewalk" to Joplin's ragtime music.

When the band began playing "Moon Glow," Horst remembered the scene from the movie, *Picnic*. He turned to Ingrid, "Hey, isn't this . . . ?" but she was no longer sitting next to him. He looked up and saw her standing about ten feet away. She was slowly clapping her hands together—in just the same way the actress Kim Novak had clapped her hands in the movie. Horst rose to his feet. He watched Ingrid, slowly approaching him, slowly clapping her hands in time to the sultry music. As the violins joined piano and rhythm instruments, he stepped forward, placing his arm around her waist, and they slowly began dancing together. They held each other tightly, slowly rocking to "Moon Glow," in the orange moon light. It was as though they were there by themselves.

Fascinated, Adam was watching them. He nudged Hansel.

"Hey, Hansel. Take a look."

Hansel looked over at Horst and Ingrid, and smiled.

"I knew this was bound to happen. It was simply a matter of time."

"Yes . . . simply a matter of . . ." stammered Adam. He was looking in another direction, "Hansel, look over there."

In the distance, Adam and Hansel saw that Zelda was slowly dancing with a tall black man.

"Tonight has been quite a night, hasn't it?" said Adam.

"It certainly has," agreed Hansel.

Chapter 29

TWO WEEKS AFTER THE PICNIC, HORST LAY AWAKE IN BED, anxiously worrying about their future. For the past hour he had been thinking, as Hansel snored in the bunk above him. The men of the Third Thaw had moved their belongings to a former "Activity Building," where bunk beds had been installed. The living space resembled an Army barrack, which explains why they called them "barracks." Horst had the bottom bunk under Hansel.

Since their arrival in New Munich, the Third Thaw were spending most of their time taking language classes, learning *die Deutch Sprache*. They also took a sex education class, taught by *Artzin* Erica, who explained to them the workings of human reproductive system. During evenings, they socialized with the Germans, dining, drinking and trading stories.

Despite all the fun and relaxing they were having, Horst was beginning to feel anxious about what they should be doing next. He was getting bored studying and partying all the time. Since he was the decision maker—he was the Captain—it was up to him to keep things moving and progressing.

Restless, he decided to get up and take a walk. As Horst stepped out of bed, his right foot stepped on something furry, then he heard a cat screech. Horst reflexively pulled his foot away. It was Georgy, a gray long haired Norwegian Forest Cat. The cat scurried away and jumped to the open window sill, looking back at Horst with a hurt look. Horst immediately walked over to the cat and pet him. "Sorry boy."

Woken by the cat, Hansel said, "What the hell was that?" A few seconds later he rolled over and went back to sleep, snoring again.

Wearing his pajamas, Horst walked outside into the brisk morning air. The old Activity Building was in the original part of New Munich, built by German Guardians for housing and raising the German Thaws. This part of town had long since been abandoned by the Germans, who had built themselves permanent and attractive housing. All around him, Horst saw the same kind of small one-room adobe dwellings they have lived in in New Eden.

As Horst walked around the original settlement, he noticed how badly the huts were crumbling. He was not surprised, because the adobe huts in New Eden required constant patching. Placing his hand on one of the adobe walls, he broke off a piece from the corner of a hut. Examining the piece, it was just a clump of dried clay with pieces of fern twigs holding it together.

The sun began to rise, heralded by the *cock-a-doodle-doo* of a few roosters living in back yards. Horst continued to walk into New Munich's downtown, admiring the buildings, made with stucco and half-plasticized wood. He felt a wall, feeling how much stronger it was than an adobe wall.

It did not take him long to traverse the entire town, which was only a few short blocks, then he began walking toward the river. When he reached the river, he cautiously looked for giant scorpions and spiders. He noticed a few harmless amphibians, which had borrowed themselves into the river mud about ten feet from the water's edge. Deciding the area was safe from predators, he sat down on the riverbank.

He thought about the Third Thaw's most immediately need, which was to find a permanent place to live. *But where?* Should they keep traveling, farther away or stay close to the Germans? It would be easiest if they remained near the Germans. But there was something he didn't like about that option. He really wanted to build an impressive development, which was distinct from the German community.

Then, to his surprised, he saw exactly what the Third Thaw needed: Across the river he saw beautiful land—plenty of nice open land—a perfect place to build an American settlement. Except, of course, for one obstacle: the river. The river was so wide, swift and dangerous—*how could they get there?*

Excited by this new prospect, Horst quickly walked back to the barracks to talk to his architect, Adam, and builder, Hansel. When he arrived at the barracks, all the men were still sleeping. As he approached Adam's bunk, there was a small gray schnauzer on the bed, growling at Horst.

Horst stood away from the dog, to avoid being nipped. He whispered, "Adam! Adam, wake up!"

Groggy, Adam opened his eyes. Noticing his dog's flaring teeth, he patted the schnauzer. "Easy boy." The panting dog licked his chops, then placed his head on Adam's lap. "Good boy—thanks for protecting me."

Horst walked over to Hansel, who was in deep sleep, still snoring. Shaking him, he said, "Hansel! Hansel! Wake up!"

"What . . . ?" Hansel said, as he rolled over, about to go back to sleep.

Horst shook him again. "Time to get up—now! Both of you, meet me at the riverbank. Pronto!"

∾

An hour later, Horst, Adam and Hansel were inside a row boat on the river. The river was about two hundred feet wide at this point. The current was relatively slow but it was very choppy, with two foot waves. Adam volunteered to do the rowing.

Hansel, who was prone to seasickness, was not particularly happy about being in a boat again. As the boat splashed and went up and down in the waves, Horst watched the water for dangerous predator fish. Midway across the river, a giant ten-foot-long arthropod creature approached the boat. When the animal placed one of its claws over the side of their boat, Horst grabbed an oar and whacked the arthropod's appendage; the river creature retreated.

At a speed of only a half a knot, it took them almost five minutes to row to the other side. Stepping off the boat into the muddy shallow water, Horst pulled the boat onto the shore. As he expected, it looked like very good land, with rolling hills on high ground above the river flood plain.

"I feel like Columbus discovering the new world!" proclaimed Horst, with a broad grin. "It's perfect, isn't it?"

"Yeah, it's perfect, except for one slight obstacle," Hansel said, stepping from the boat. "The river. Are we supposed to row a boat every time we come here?"

"What if we had a barge pulled by a line across the river?" asked Horst. "You know, like a ferry?"

Adam said, "I don't know, Horst. We were just attacked by a creature out there. What if there are big predator fish, like the one that killed Gerald? Do you really want to have a ferry in a river with predator fish?"

Horst said, "Yeah, I suppose you're right. A ferry would be dangerous." He was becoming very disappointed. Before giving up he asked, "This may seem impossible, but what about a bridge? You guys are the construction experts. What you do you think, can you build a bridge?"

Adam and Hansel looked at each other, then Adam said, "Give us a moment to talk about it, Horst. We'll see what we can do."

Horst realized that he was expecting a lot from these men. They were fledglings in construction; their training was largely untested and they had no real world experience building anything more than adobe huts. But these men were the only construction experts he had. The fact was, every one of the Third Thaws was an amateur, and each of them would be forced to learn "on the job" in each of their professions.

Horst said, "Thanks, guys. I realize a bridge will be a challenge. But isn't that what engineering is all about, challenges?"

Adam gulped, as he looked the wide expanse of the river. "Yes sir, Captain. It will definitely be a challenge!"

"Thank you, men," Horst said. "I'm going to take a look around," then he walked away.

Adam and Hansel began to brainstorm what type of bridge could be built using whatever resources were available.

"It would be easiest if we drape some ropes from end to end, wouldn't it?" asked Hansel.

"I agree, hanging something is the easiest. But ropes won't be strong enough," said Adam.

"Well, if we can't use ropes, what can we use instead?"

"We can ask the Germans to forge us some steel wire."

"Okay, let's say that they can make the steel wire," said Hansel. "Then what? We hang the wires, but then what do we do? Do we hang boards off the wires?"

Adam thought about this.

"What you are proposing is a classic suspension bridge."

"Yeah, I suppose. 'Classic.'"

"I don't think that will work very well here. The span is too short," said Adam. "Suspension bridges are appropriate for span lengths of a thousand feet or more. For example, the Golden Gate Bridge or the Brooklyn Bridge were suspension bridges with spans over a thousand feet. This span here is only two hundred feet."

"What's wrong with having a short-span suspension bridge?" asked Hansel.

"It will be too unstable and wobbly. We don't want to build a bridge that will deflect all over the place like a jungle rope bridge. Here, let me explain."

He drew in the sand.

"Okay, here I've drawn a suspension bridge. Notice how the cables are draped parabolically?"

"Yeah."

"That's because the load on the bridge is uniform along the bridge."

Next, Adam made another sketch, showing a truck crossing a suspension bridge.

"If we drive a truck across a relatively short suspension bridge, like this, it will deflect a lot. You see how the cables are no longer parabolas?" asked Adam.

"Yeah, the cables are kinked where the truck is," said Hansel.

"My point exactly. The cables are kinked. That's because the load is no longer uniform across the length of the bridge. Most of the load is where the truck is. This is also why short jungle rope bridges are wobbly, because most of the load is where the people are—it's concentrated rather than uniform."

"So, you're saying that suspension bridges need to be very long, because ... why is it, again?"

"Because very long spans tend to have more-or-less uniform loads on them," answered Adam. "The weight of a truck on something like the Golden Gate Bridge or the Brooklyn Bridge is minuscule by comparison to the uniform dead load of these big bridges. A truck is like the weight of a fly by comparison to the bridge's dead load."

"Very interesting," said Hansel. "So if we build a suspension bridge, it will be very wobbly, like a jungle rope bridge?"

"Yes. It will be so wobbly that you will not want to cross it in a truck. You might even throw up, it will be so wobbly."

"But what's the alternative? What kind of bridge can we build that won't be wobbly?"

Adam drew another bridge in the sand.

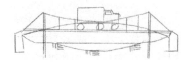

After finishing the sketch, he said, "Fortunately, I learned about an unusual type of bridge from my APS grandfather. This sketch shows a little-known type of bridge that was invented by a Swedish engineer named David Jawerth. This bridge requires hanging *two* suspension cables, but in *opposite* parabolic shapes, then actively pulling the cables."

"What do you mean by 'actively pulling the cables'?" asked Hansel.

"We need to have cable pullers and wedges. Never mind the details. What's important is that we pull on the upper cable and the lower cable, using a certain amount of force. That's the 'active' part: We determine how much force to pull; this will cause the upper cable to pull up, while the lower cable will pull down, causing the cables to work against each other's action. This arrangement creates a very stiff structure, even for short bridges."

"Cool!" said Hansel. "And it looks easy to build. Just a little bit more complicated than a suspension rope bridge."

When Horst returned from his walk, Adam showed him the Jawerth bridge sketch he had made in the sand.

Horst was immediately impressed. "I love it!" he said, smiling broadly. "It's absolutely brilliant!"

"So we're in agreement?" said Adam.

"Yes. Let's do it!"

They discussed the concept with their German counterparts. The Germans said they would be able to forge enough wire in four weeks. They would also manufacture a cable-pulling device—called a "jack"—and the wedges which would anchor the wires to foundations.

In six weeks, they built a Jawerth cable bridge from steel wires and simulated "plastic-fiber" wood. It was a beautiful, slender structure, but also quite stiff. The true test of the bridge was when Adam drove a heavily loaded, horse-drawn carriage across the bridge. The bridge remained stiff, deflecting only a few inches. Having passed this test, it was deemed suitable for use.

Now that they had access to their land, and construction of their settlement could begin. Workers began transporting material across in wagons and wheelbarrows. They staked out streets and decided to give the streets with gentle curves, instead of straight orthogonal grids. The main streets were given the names of American cities, such as "New York City Street," "Chicago Street," "Los Angeles Street," "San Francisco Street," and "Atlanta Street." The minor streets were given names like "Penny Lane," "Abbey Road," "Lois Lane," and "Blueberry Hill."

The town center was located at the intersection of New York Street and Chicago Street. This would become the shopping district and would have a central park. At this intersection, the roads formed a circular drive called a "roundabout," where vehicles would travel counterclockwise around a center island. They envisioned a fountain or a statue in the center island someday.

Except for Jim and Mary, who now lived on a farm in the German sector, most of the Third Thaws planned to live in houses in the American sector. The lots were about one acre in size, with long backyards, allowing each of the families to have a garden.

The Third Thaw wanted houses that would have a distinctively American style. However, the question of what constituted an "American style" was debatable, since there were so many varied house styles in America, many of which were of European and classical origins. Adam and Hansel perused their collection of American house plans and, finally, they committed themselves to building several "Prairie Style" single story ranch houses, based on a Frank Lloyd Wright design.

While Adam and Hansel were busy supervising the building of the new American sector, the others went to their new jobs working with the Germans. Ingrid was receiving further medical training from the German doctors and was working as resident at the New Munich hospital. Horst was preparing to fly to the Einstein-Newton site with the Germans.

The departure date was planned for the next month. Horst was assisting in the design of the jamming devices which would, at least in theory, stop communications between the Einstein-Newton supercomputer and the robots. The plan was to drop jamming devices from parachutes onto the Einstein-Newton site. After immobilizing the robots, the planes would land; then the group would disable the supercomputer.

They began pairing off as couples and giving in to feelings that had previously been held in check. Without the watchful eyes of their Guardians, they explored physical intimacy, at first with a touch, then with a kiss. Observing Jim and Mary and the married couples of New Munich, they learned there was more to being human than performing work-related tasks. Horst's decision to fly to the site was a particularly difficult one, since he and Ingrid were newlyweds. A few others in the group had gotten married, too. A week after Horst's and Ingrid's wedding, Hansel and Gertrude were married. Gertrude, who had lost the bottom portion of her leg to the sail-back reptile, had fully recovered and now wore a prosthetic leg.

Eileen and the conductor of the German orchestra, Felix, had fallen in love and gotten married. They lived in Felix's house in New Munich. Zelda and Okunola had gotten married as well. Zelda was noticeably pregnant at their wedding. They were currently living at Okunola's house in New Munich; however, Zelda was persistent that they must build a new house in the American district. Okunola's house was too small for the large family they were planning.

Marriage was new to the Third Thaws who had been raised without the traditional family structure. There were no "married Guardians" in New Eden. The Third Thaw had been exposed to married relatives in their APS sessions; also, they had seen married people in old television programs and films, though these shows were typically unrealistic. The young newlywed couples approached marriage almost like actors playing a part which they had never actually seen before. Nevertheless, by all accounts, marriage was agreeing well with them.

Horst and Ingrid moved into their small, two-bedroom house. They were the first residents of the American sector of New Munich, living there without any neighbors. At night, when all the construction had stopped for the day and everyone else returned to the German side, Horst and Ingrid had the entire American sector to themselves. They walked down the new streets, looking at all the houses being constructed. Every day, they checked to see how much progress had been made. Their street was in the process of construction. The sewer system had been installed and would eventually be connected to a sanitary system. The concrete curbs and gutters for their street had been poured. In the next few days, a bituminous surface was to be fixed in place, using a thick tar-like synthetic bitumen and crushed stones.

"I can't imagine what this will look like someday," said Horst.

"Someday, this entire neighborhood will be built up and filled with families. There will be kids playing in the streets," said Ingrid. "You see that over there?"

"Ah, no. I don't see anything."

"Okay, imagine this. There will be a two-story house over there," she said, pointing to the left in her imaginary scene, "and over there on the right will be a single-story house. I will be friends with the woman living in the house on the left, but I won't get along too well with the woman living in the house on the right."

"Is Eileen living in the house in the right?" chuckled Horst, squeezing Ingrid's hand.

"No, it will be a different woman whom I don't get along with."

They both laughed.

"And our kids will ride their bikes all over this part of town. But we won't let them cross the bridge until they reach a certain age," said Ingrid.

"How old do they need to be before they are allowed to cross the street?" asked Horst.

"They can cross the street when they are five years old. That's only after they learn to look both ways," said Ingrid.

"Sounds like you have this all planned out!"

"Well, we need to start getting ready for these things."

They continued on, in silence. Then Horst asked Ingrid, "Are you pregnant?"

"Yes, of course I am," said Ingrid, grinning.

"When are you due? How long does it take?"

"It must have happened the night we got married," said Ingrid. "It takes nine months to grow a baby."

"Yee-hah!" whooped Horst, doing his best TV *Gunsmoke* impersonation. "Let's celebrate. How about we get some ice cream?"

"Ah, shucks! Sounds kinda' good to me!" said Ingrid, doing her best *Gunsmoke* impersonation.

Arm in arm, they walked over the to the German side, crossing the new Jawerth suspension bridge, to the ice cream parlor which usually stayed open until nine p.m. Ingrid ordered an ice cream sundae and a pickle.

"How can you eat ice cream and a pickle?" said Horst. "I mean, yuck!"

"I don't know. For some reason I want a pickle," said Ingrid. "That's what pregnant women always want."

"You are so weird!" commented her husband.

Part 4
The Einstein-Newton Site

Chapter 30

AFTER MONTHS OF PLANNING AND TRAINING FOR THE reconnaissance of the Einstein-Newton site, the day had come for the launch. Horst, Hansel and Adam were the only three Americans flying in the expedition. They would be responsible for dropping the jamming devices and activating the parachutes.

Two of the drones, Smokey and Buzzy, would be sitting in the back seat of one of the biplanes. Horst had set the communication frequency of the drones to a different frequency to ensure they would not be affected by the jamming.

Because he would need to speak German exclusively during the mission, Horst had been intensively learning Deutsch. Learning "*das Deutsch Sprache*" was a challenge that all of the Americans were facing. Some learned more easily than the others. The question of which language to use was something of an issue for both communities now living together. Should they simply switch to speaking German all the time? Or should the Germans attempt to accommodate the English speakers in some way, and speak English while in their presence? Should the Americans speak English at home? Would the American sector become an English-speaking ghetto? Was the preservation of a language really necessary?

For English speakers, the grammatical rules of the German language tend to be a major stumbling block. It is an interesting fact that at one time, the people of England and the people of Germany spoke the same language. In October 1066, William the Conqueror left Normandy, France, and invaded England, defeating the last Saxon king in England, Harold Godwinson.

With a French king ruling England, French became the *lingua franca*. The Saxon language and the French language blended together to form a new form of speech, which we now call "Middle English." German is much like Middle English, when people used words such as "*thou*" and "*wilst.*"

Horst was overly concerned that he was not using proper grammar when speaking with the Germans, so much so that he had trouble saying anything at all. Eventually, he loosened up and stopped thinking about all the rules. Many times, to get his point across, he would resort to using English words. This seemed to work, since most of the Germans could speak English fairly well. Gradually, the Americans and Germans developed various way of communicating, using German, a little English, and a lot of pointing and pantomiming.

German became the language spoken almost exclusively between the Americans and the Germans. The Americans spoke English when together, and they raised their children to be bilingual, speaking English at home and German in school with the other children in New Munich.

For the benefit of English-only speaking readers, the remainder of the dialogue has been mostly translated into English.

Ingrid was just beginning to show her now three-month pregnancy. She and Horst had discussed names for the baby. They had decided that if the baby were a girl, she would be named Melissa; if a boy, he would be named Sig.

On the day of the expedition, the sky was overcast, with low cloud cover. This was perfect weather, since they would use the clouds as cover as they approached. While there was always the possibility that all would be well at the Einstein-Newton site, the reverse was also true; the plan, therefore, was to prepare for the worst.

Of course, there was a grand "Send-Off Ceremony." Sigmund gave a speech to the entire community, praising the explorers and emphasizing how their mission was essential for New Munich's survival. The band played a polka march and then, in deference to the Americans, selections from the marches of John Philip Sousa. The crew said goodbye to their friends and families, then walked to their planes, without looking back.

The planes rolled out of the hangar, towards the runway, ready to begin the nearly two-hundred-mile journey.

Once in the air, the planes formed a "V" formation like a flock of geese, with Sigmund in the lead position. For navigational purposes, they stayed at a low altitude. Felix, Eileen's husband, sat behind Sigmund reading the map and shouting directions. Okunola, newly wed to Zelda, piloted another plane.

After flying about fifty miles at one-hundred-twenty miles per hour, they reached the desert which stretched hundreds of miles. Looking down at this hot, forbidding land, Horst appreciated the fact they were flying. It would have been very difficult to travel by foot.

Soon, they saw the mesa in the distance. Sigmund gave the "thumbs up" sign, signaling to the other pilots to pull just above the clouds. In precise formation, the biplanes swooped upward, piercing the cloud cover. They flew just above the bottom of the clouds, into wisps of vapors, so that they would be able to see the land below them.

As they approached the mesa from an altitude of 2,000 feet, details of the Einstein-Newton colony began to appear. They could see a giant complex of structures; they concluded that the black ant-sized things walking around must be the robots.

Horst could make out the unmistakable shape of the space shuttle in the distance. This is where the supercomputer would be—the most vulnerable piece of equipment in the colony.

When the planes reached directly over the site. Horst and Hansel started the jamming devices and got ready to drop them. On Felix's command, they threw the devices from the planes. A total of twenty parachutes were dropped in a pattern that covered all areas of the compound. For the next two minutes, they watched the parachutes slowly descend to the ground below.

After the parachutes had landed, Sigmund lead the squadron, swooping downward to land on the mesa. They found a relatively flat area to land but it was still a bumpy landing. The crew jumped from their planes and gathered in front of some large boulders.

"*Viel glück! [Much luck!]* We've made it here in one piece," said Sigmund. He proceeded to take roll call. Everyone was present and accounted for.

"*Ja, das ist gut!* Ready? On the count of *vier! Ein, zwei, drei, vier! Gehen sie!*" [*Yes, that is good! Ready on the count of four! One, two, three, four! Go!*]

They ran toward the colony. There were robots everywhere, all of which were standing motionless. The jamming devices had effectively done their job. Horst walked up to one of the robots and examined it. The robot looked nothing like the Guardians back at New Eden and New Munich. He noticed that many of the robots had wheels, but a few of them had humanoid arms and legs. Some of the robots had tank-like tractors which they rolled on. Some had long, telescopic arms.

There were pieces of manufacturing equipment everywhere, including rolling gantries with overhead cranes which were most likely used for loading and unloading. There were also railroad tracks and railcars. This appeared to be quite a formidable operation. There was a large enclosure, the largest area at the site, containing stacks and stacks of railroad tracks. Horst and Adam exchanged quizzical looks. There was enough track to cover several miles.

They walked under a very large canopy supported by cables. Adam immediately noticed that the structure resembled the 1972 Munich Olympic Stadium. Under the canopy, they saw piles of iron ingots or "pig iron." In another area, there was an assortment of large rolled steel beams and steel plates, in addition to welding equipment, acetylene torches, steel plasma cutting equipment, and conveyor systems. In yet another area, there were large tanks with complex networks of pipes running in every direction.

Although still, the robots were omnipresent. It was somewhat quiet, except for the sound of a few mechanical fans.

Then, suddenly, they heard a voice, a human voice.

"*Hallo! Hallo!* You're here! You're here!"

A fairly short bald man appeared. Horst noted that the man looked to be around Sigmund's age; they must have come from the same Thaw.

Sigmund walked up to the man, and they greeted each other warmly.

"*Mein Bruder! Guten Tag, Herr Ulrich!*" said Sigmund. [*My brother! Good day, Herr Ulrich!*]

"*Guten Tag, Herr Sigmund!*" said the man, hugging Sigmund. "*Guten Tag, Herr Fritz und Herr Okunola!* What a surprise to see you all here!"

Both Fritz and Okunola greeted Ulrich with vigorous handshakes and hugs.

"*Ja, ja.* We have finally arrived," said Sigmund, beside himself with joy. "I am ashamed to say that we thought you had died in your mission to this place five years ago. Frankly, seeing you here is a complete surprise to us!"

Ulrich seemed to stiffen at these words. He pulled away from Fritz and Okunola.

"*Ah, ja.* You thought we had died? Funny, you should think that," he said looking Sigmund straight in the eyes. "It has been a long time for us here."

Horst felt uneasy. He noticed that Ulrich had many small red marks on his forearm. He immediately recognized these to be syringe marks.

"Are the others alive?" asked Sigmund.

"*Ja, ja,* we all survived and are doing fine," said Ulrich. "I will take you to see the others shortly."

"So . . . everything is under control here, *nicht wahr?* We were prepared to take over the supercomputer if necessary."

"No, no. That is not necessary," said Ulrich. "Everything here is what the Americans call *hunky-dory.* I assume you have jammed our communication systems."

"Yes. We dropped jamming devices in parachutes from our planes," said Sigmund.

Ulrich's eyes narrowed.

"Very clever," he said, forcing a smile.

"Is it safe if we switch off the jamming devices?"

"*Ja, ja,* Herr Sigmund. It is quite safe," he said.

Sigmund turned towards Horst and instructed him to turn off the jamming devices. Horst took out a radio controller from his pocket and flicked a switch. Almost immediately, the robots came back to life. Lights began blinking, machines restarted and activity resumed.

Ulrich walked over to a table on which there was a heavy-looking metal helmet. After he put the helmet on, his overall appearance and demeanor changed visibly.

"What are you wearing, Ulrich?" asked Sigmund.

"You should not have come," said Ulrich. "You are interfering with our operation here."

"I don't understand, *mein Bruder,*" said Sigmund.

"Of course, you don't," said Ulrich. "At one time, I also did not understand—not until we 'Became One' did I understand. Now everything is clear."

Horst studied the helmet that Ulrich was wearing. Its frame had roughly twenty sensory devices with sucker-like electrodes which were fitted against Ulrich's bald head.

"Ulrich, is the helmet a communication device with the supercomputer?" he asked.

"Yes, it is."

"So, the helmet is a communication device for humans to control manufacturing operations here?"

"Yes," said Ulrich. "That was the *original* intended purpose of the helmet. However, that purpose has changed."

"How has it changed?" asked Sigmund.

"We have evolved. When I wear this helmet, I have a symbiotic connection to Einstein-Newton."

Sigmund looked confused.

Ulrich paused. "Let me spell it out to you. 'We' have evolved beyond human beings. We are now connected to 'Genius,' the supercomputer here, allowing us to connect with the robot army. Our senses have been enhanced and extended to control this powerful workforce."

"Do you always wear the helmet?" asked Sigmund.

Suddenly, Ulrich grew angry.

"You ask too many questions!" he said, pointing at Sigmund menacingly.

He grabbed the controller from Horst and tossed it to a robot, giving the humans a look of disgust.

"We haven't much need for beings that have the intelligence of dogs, do we? What would be the purpose, that an advanced intelligence such as ours be a slave to dogs like you?"

With that, several robots appeared, surrounding the humans in a box formation. Then the robot-box prison began moving, shuffling the prisoners in the direction of a small gray building.

Chapter 31

A SMALL ROBOT STUCK THE CATTLE PROD–LIKE DEVICE into Horst's back, producing an electrical shock. He lurched forwards, the searing pain snaking down his spine.

"Damn! Would you watch out with that thing!" yelled Horst.

The robot wacked him again, sending yet another jolt of electricity searing across his shoulder blades. Horst screamed in agony.

"What the hell! Can you stop doing that?" Muttering under his breath, he limped forwards, along with his colleagues from New Munich.

The robots herded them inside a gray building, into a large room where they saw eight men. The men were pale and gaunt. Each of them had a long beard and their bald heads were pock-marked by what looked like rows of little metal terminals. These, at least twenty of them, were arranged uniformly, equidistantly apart, over the backs of their heads.

Sigmund recognized them.

"Alex! *Wie geht es dir?*" *[Alex, how is it going with you?]*

The one named Alex hesitated.

"*Es geht mir gut, viel liecht.*" *[It is going good for me, perhaps.]*

The door opened, and the same small robot that had shocked Horst entered the room carrying a tray of bottles. The men ran over to the robot, grabbed the bottles and began drinking the fluid. The white fluid dripped from the sides of Alex's mouth, as he guzzled down the contents.

"Drink!" said Alex to Sigmund. "This is all you will eat. *Mach schnell!*"

The newcomers each grabbed a bottle. Horst took a sip. The white fluid was somewhat grainy in consistency, like Hawaiian "Poi." It had a slightly salty mineral taste.

"What is this stuff?" asked Horst.

Again, Alex took his time answering a simple question.

"This—this is what we eat. This is our supper. It is also our breakfast and our lunch. We are fed these bottles three times a day."

"But what is it?"

"It is a fluid containing the necessary minerals, proteins, and amino acids required for our bodily survival."

"Do you know what it is derived from? Does it come from plants or animals?"

"Neither. There are no plants or crops here. The probe that landed here did not bring any biological life-forms. There are no livestock here. This fluid is derived from minerals and is synthesized."

Horst drank the rest of his bottle. "How can you stand drinking this stuff?'

"We really have no choice. This fluid and water keep our bodies alive. You will also become accustomed to it."

Apparently, this would not be a simple overnight visit.

Sigmund silently waved to Felix to move his men away from the others. "What do you think?" he whispered.

Horst said, "These guys look really out of it. They're like zombies. Their skin is white. It looks like they never get outside."

"Perhaps," said Felix. "Perhaps there is another possibility. Perhaps they don't want to go outdoors. Perhaps they actually like it here, better than they liked living in New Munich."

"Like it?" said Horst. "What is there to like here? Are we going to become like them if we stay here?"

The group became quiet, exchanging uneasy looks. Sigmund's hand scratched his beard stubble. He looked over at the men with the long beards on the opposite side of the room.

"They must not have razor blades here," he said.

The small robot rolled up to the group of newcomers. It had a stick like a cattle prod affixed to its "head"—which had no resemblance to humanoid head. It closed in on them and paused, as if ready for action.

"Okay, I think we better disperse from this corner," said Sigmund. "I'm afraid this thing is going to zap us at anytime. Let's try to get to know our neighbors."

Ignoring the robot, they walked over to the bearded men, but they didn't seem to care about socializing. Like heroin junkies, they were in a zombie world all to themselves. The one named Alex was sitting on the floor. Sigmund bent over him.

"Alex, what have you been doing here? Can you please tell us your story?"

Alex stared at Sigmund, as though he had lost the will to talk. Finally, he spoke.

"I do not feel like talking now. We are replenishing and resting from all the work we've been doing. You and your people should stay over there, on that side of the room, away from us. Please, do that. We are different from you, so don't try to question us, okay?"

Surveying the group, the robot zapped his cattle prod.

Alex laughed out loud, his eyes rolling wildly as if someone had told a joke.

"Ha! I don't think that Zorro likes you! *Er ist lustig!*" [*He is funny!*]

Meanwhile, Zorro herded the newcomers to the other side of the room again. Another robot rolled in, bringing cots for the newcomers. After setting up the cots, both robots left.

As they sat together, sipping their bottles, Horst asked Sigmund, "Tell me about Ulrich. What was he like back at New Munich?"

Sigmund looked around the room, making sure that the other men could not hear.

"Ulrich was a rival of mine. Or rather, in *Ulrich's mind* we were rivals. You Americans have a saying: 'The squeaky wheel gets the grease.' Well, that's Ulrich in a nutshell. He's the squeaky wheel who can never shut up. He was always looking for attention. He has an insatiable ego. It's 'all about him.' As they say, 'it's his way or no way.' Do you know anyone like that, who acts like a demanding two-year-old?"

"No, not really," said Horst. "We all get along pretty well in New Eden. We're a small group, almost like brothers and sisters."

"It is fortunate for you that you have no one like this," said Sigmund. "No so with Ulrich. We were cursed to have this person."

"New Munich has been here longer than New Eden. Our colony is larger than yours. We have had more than a few misfits."

"What do you mean by '*misfits*'?" asked Horst.

"Social misfits. Misfits are people who disrupt the system, who challenge the hierarchy and status quo. You see—at least this is my theory—some people cannot accept their roles in society. We Germans, especially, are good at assigning roles to people at an early age. This was one of the fundamental social problems back on Earth: dissatisfaction with our assigned place in society.

"Ulrich was dissatisfied with the position that he was being trained for. He has a very strong desire to be the leader, the one giving orders. I believe that he found it very difficult—in fact, he found it impossible—to follow directions from others. It's as though he is missing a part of his brain that controls what he says. He seems to speak whatever idea comes into his head. Actually, I am not sure if he knows the difference between right and wrong."

"That's a pretty strong statement," said Horst.

"Ah, *ja, es ist wahr*. It is true," said Sigmund.

They sat quietly for a time, still holding their now empty bottles.

"So, yes, in answer to your question, Ulrich and I don't quite get along. When I was promoted in rank over Ulrich, this infuriated him. He is a great talker and a motivator. He has charisma and magnetism when he speaks publicly. He prophesizes about a 'better world,' without getting into specifics about how, exactly, we can make a better world. He managed to whip up a group of followers who liked his empty ideas and promises.

"As a manager of New Munich, I found this situation—this person— very difficult. Ulrich was constantly critical of my leadership role, always commenting in public about how he could do things better. He undermined my authority every chance that he could. There were no lines of decency that he would not cross. If he weren't so *pathetic*, I think I would actually hate him! No doubt he hates me!"

Sigmund paused. His eyes narrowed as he concentrated on his story.

"Eventually, I thought of a plan to get Ulrich and his bunch of friends out of my life. Five years ago, I thought of the perfect plan: I proposed that he lead an expedition to the Einstein-Newton site. Of course, he accepted this challenge. He would finally be the leader of something! I hadn't thought things through. I didn't think he would succeed getting here. But, here we are today! Ulrich was actually successful making it here, all the way across the desert!"

Horst was silent. *Sigmund had just acknowledged that he had sent Ulrich on a mission which he thought would fail. He had planned for Ulrich and his colleagues to die.*

"Very interesting."

"The odds were not in his favor that he would make it," said Sigmund, his voice surprisingly cold and detached. "I must give them credit for succeeding in such a difficult expedition."

From across the other side of the room, Alex walked over to Sigmund and Horst.

"Our men will be leaving now," he said, his face expressionless. "It's best if you get some rest. Tomorrow, you will hear from Ulrich what he plans to do with you."

With that, he stood still, not moving until each of the New Munich visitors was lying down on one of the cots. Then, he turned off the light and closed the door. He and the other men from Ulrich's group left the gray building. They heard Zorro rolling into the room, past each of the cots, inspecting everyone to see if they were asleep. Horst and Sigmund lay motionless, barely daring to breathe. Then the robot left.

Out of the corner of his eye, Horst saw something blinking at a window opening. He focused his eyes on the light, which was moving up and down, as if it were flying.

"The drones!" Horst whispered to Sigmund. "Look up at the window! It's the drones!"

"*Mein Gott!*" [My God!] said Sigmund.

Quietly, Horst got up from his bed and went over to the window. The window opening was about ten feet above the floor and was very small, not large enough for a man to crawl though. Horst signaled Sigmund to help him move a table, so he could climb on top and get closer to the window. The two of them lifted the table and moved it under the opening. Sigmund climbed on top of the table, knelt down, then placed his hands on the ground in front of him.

"Climb on my back here, I will lift you up."

Horst climbed on top of Sigmund's back, and straightened up. His head was just level with the window. Buzzy was outside the opening, hovering.

"Buzzy, I need you to get me something. You need to be quiet. Just blink green if you understand, red if you don't understand," Horst said.

Buzzy blinked green.

"Back at the plane, I left my revolver underneath my seat. I need you to bring it to me."

Buzzy blinked green. Horst climbed down from Sigmund's back. Quickly, they pushed the table back into place and then returned to their cots. After a couple of minutes, Buzzy returned. The two men positioned themselves below the window. Buzzy dropped the revolver through the window and Sigmund caught it. Horst looked for a place to hide the gun. The room was virtually barren of furniture. He decided to hide the gun under his cot; then he tried going sleep.

Chapter 32

FOR THE NEXT FEW DAYS, THE VISITORS FROM NEW MUNICH observed Ulrich and his crew as they controlled the robot workforce with their helmets and special gloves. Though they were confined to their quarters during the evening, during the daytime, the newcomers were permitted to visit the manufacturing sector—under robot observation, of course.

Horst watched Ulrich assemble a locomotive engine. Ulrich worked by watching a monitor that showed him the engine plans. It was as though he were assembling a kit. Ulrich waved his hands in the air, virtually "picking up" the parts as the machines, and put everything together, as easily as a child building a model. With the flick of his fingers, Ulrich could instruct the cranes to move the giant locomotive into any position he desired. He seemed "at one" with the machines.

When Ulrich stopped to take a break, he approached Horst.

"You," he said to Horst. "You, what is your name?"

"Horst."

"I don't remember you in New Munich. You are obviously not a native Deutsch speaker."

"No. My native language is English. I came from the American Colony," said Horst.

"*Mein Gott!* The Americans actually made it to New Munich!" said Ulrich. "We had given up on you! This was actually *the* primary reason that our party was sent to Einstein-Newton. What took you so long to make contact with us?"

"The first two generations from the New Eden site were killed in their journey to New Munich."

"Ah, *ja*. That explains it," said Ulrich. "How were they killed?"

"Both of the expeditions went over a waterfall."

"A waterfall! Of all things! And you were able to escape the waterfall? Obviously so."

"Yes, we were able to escape going over the falls. Fortunately, we saw the falls soon enough to get over to the shoreline," said Horst, making no mention of the drones. "May I ask you something, Herr Ulrich?"

"*Ja*. Go ahead, Herr Horst."

"How are you able to do these things? It seems that you are controlling the machines with your thoughts."

"Me and my crew have *evolved* since we arrived here five ago," said Ulrich, his eyes glazing over. "We are a conception of sorts, a meiosis of machine being with human being into the creation of a new and superior machine/human being. The helmet connects us to the supercomputer; likewise, the supercomputer learns from us."

"What is it learning from you?" asked Horst.

"It is learning to communicate with us on a neural level. Each time I wear the helmet, the supercomputer is able to track my neural processes with my movements. As a result, it recognizes certain patterns that I think as I move."

"This sounds to me like something I've heard about called '*mentalese*,'" said Horst.

Ulrich looked at Horst.

"I have never heard of this term, 'mentalese' before. Please explain this to me."

"It's a term a psychologist on Earth had used to describe how the brain works," said Horst. "'Mentalese' refers to the brain processes that are much richer than language."

"*Ja*, I agree that language alone is deficient. When I am wearing the helmet, I am far more connected to these robots than simply giving them mere verbal commands or by using hand controls."

All of this puzzled Horst. *How was this connection possible? Had the Einstein-Newton supercomputer developed this connection during the 80,000-year-long journey from Earth? What were this helmet and glove that Ulrich wore?*

As Horst walked around the Einstein-Newton site, he saw other men working on similar large scale assemblies. In every instance, they looked at monitors which displayed plans of the items they were building. Several men were forging railroad tracks; others were making railroad ties. There were stacks of railroad tracks. Others were assembling entire railcars.

In one building, men worked on the "nanoparticle room," manufacturing tiny machines. It was fascinating to see the workers wearing their virtual reality goggles, manipulating objects that were smaller than a pin.

Horst found Alex focused on a project and approached him.

"Herr Alex, may I ask something?"

"*Ja,* go ahead," said Alex, without looking up.

"How small can you make things?"

"I'm not quite sure, Herr Horst," he said, remaining focused on the work. He paused to take off the goggles, scratching his beard.

"I imagine the smallest we can go is limited by what we can see, which is limited by the shortest wavelength of our imaging equipment. X-ray wavelength is the smallest distance we can go down to."

"What types of machines need to be so small?" asked Horst.

"We build these things from plans. Currently, we are making nanomachines."

"How do you know this stuff? Are you designing these things yourself?" asked Horst.

"No, we are not designing these machines!" laughed Alex. "Don't be ridiculous! We are working from the instructions and plans that the Genius computer provides to us. These plans were developed by Genius and are *given* to us."

He shook his head, chuckling.

"No, no, we're just building this stuff. Sometimes—actually most of the time—we don't even understand what we are making!"

～

That evening, everyone was called to a meeting in an assembly room where a voice from a loudspeaker announced that Ulrich would be giving a speech. As Ulrich walked up to the podium, four men stood up and clapped enthusiastically, chanting "Ulrich! Ulrich! Ulrich!"

"*Danke, meinen Freunden,*" *[Thank you my friends]* he began. His men took their seats and quieted down.

As Ulrich began to address the audience, Horst was reminded of videos he had seen of politicians on Earth. These politicians seemed to have a way of talking to crowds, that differed from normal speech.

"*Guten Abend!*" he began. *[Good evening!]*

"*Guten Abend!*" answered his men in unison.

"It has been five years ago since we arrived here. *Ja, ja,* it has been five years of very hard work, hasn't it?"

His men laughed.

"And today, quite unexpectedly, we have new arrivals. For our new guests, I doubt that you can quite appreciate how hard it has been for us and what we have gone through. But on the positive side, our experience here has been a transformation.

"As my men know, in the coming months, we will be preparing for our return to New Munich. You newcomers may have recognized that we have been fabricating many railroad tracks. This is the big project we have been working on. We will be building a rail line from this site back to New Munich. We will be laying a rail line through the nearby forest—the same way we hiked here, in fact, the route is approximately 300 miles long.

"We will carry everything with us on this journey. The supercomputer, called 'Genius,' will be in a railcar. The train will be pulled by a steam locomotive."

It was here that Horst noted a building up in Ulrich's cadence. His speech pattern reminded him of how Father Graham would go into "Preacher Mode" when he gave his sermons. There was almost a musicality to this type of speech, although Horst himself it found to be somewhat annoying.

"And when we arrive in New Munich," said Ulrich, building up, getting louder, "—and there is no doubt in mind that we will arrive—we will build a new industry!"

His men stood up and clapped and shouted, "Ulrich! Ulrich! Ulrich!"

Bolstered by the applause. Ulrich continued, his speech becoming almost frenzied.

"*WE* will be building a new and BETTER WORLD, when we arrive in New Munich! *WE* will LEAD the people to a NEW and BETTER LIFE!"

And then, Ulrich's expression suddenly changed. Looking towards the back of the room at Sigmund, he focused his eyes on him, like a lion ready to pounce on his prey. Everyone turned to look at Sigmund.

"We will correct the damage that others have done to New Munich!" hissed Ulrich.

"I object, Ulrich," said Sigmund, standing up to face his nemesis.

"Silence! This isn't a courtroom!" said Ulrich. "You are not in charge here! No one asked you to speak!"

Horst was unable to translate as Ulrich continued spewing words. Suffice it to say that Ulrich had gone "totally ballistic."

When Ulrich had finished ranting, he took a towel from one of his men and wiped the perspiration from his forehead.

"Okay, Sigmund, you are somewhat of a problem to us. We need to put you and your men to work. Everyone needs to work here and contribute to the effort. There will be no, as they say, 'free rides.'

"And if any of you get any bright ideas in your head to fly back on your planes, you are out of luck. We have destroyed your planes."

Sigmund and his men looked at each other in shock.

"You have destroyed our planes? Why?" shouted Sigmund.

Ulrich gave a motion of his glove, then, without warning, Zorro zapped Sigmund with his cattle prod. Sigmund rolled to the ground, his back arching in pain.

"*Ja*, Sigmund!" said Ulrich. "Now how does that feel? You like it?"

Then he cued the robot to give Sigmund another jolt. Sigmund's body jerked again.

"*Ja*, you! You sent me—you sent us on a journey into the desert to be killed! Was that your plan? Ha!"

He kicked Sigmund's body in the side with his steel-tipped boots.

Sigmund groaned, unable to move.

"Do you think we are so stupid to walk directly into the desert—*to our death*? Do we look *that* stupid? Did it ever occur to you that we walk here *around* the edge of the desert, *through* the forest?"

Felix ran over to Sigmund, but just as he reached his friend, the robot zapped Felix. Felix's face contorted, then he collapsed on top of Sigmund. The two of them lay limp on the floor.

"Let this be a warning. I don't want anyone getting out of line here. No gathering together. No talking."

"Yes, Herr Ulrich. We understand," said Horst.

Ulrich looked at Horst. Then he smiled appreciatively.

"Good. At least *you* understand."

Ulrich took a drink of water, calmer now. Within a few minutes, he was talking to his men in a normal voice. The group of them huddled together, apparently discussing what to do with their new guests. Then Ulrich addressed the visitors.

"Okay, everybody," he began. "We have developed a job for you. Everyone follow me. Come, come, this way."

They followed Ulrich outside to a small, dark building with a very high roof; it was a one-story building but had clearly been intended to be multistory at some point. Judging by the smell, this was the communal latrine.

"We have not cleaned this place in years. No, I take that back—we've never cleaned this," said Ulrich, laughing. "Your job today is to clean up the toilets here. There are cleaning supplies waiting for you, but I'm afraid we have no gloves—a small inconvenience, don't you think? And when I get back, I want to see everything spotless. Otherwise, my little friend, Zorro, will be inflicting more pain. You like inflicting pain, don't you, Zorro?"

The little robot made a couple of zapping noises with its prod.

As soon as Ulrich and Zorro left, the men got to work cleaning the place. The fumes made the men gag, but they did their best to focus on the task at hand, removing excrement from the floor, wiping smears off the walls. They scrubbed the floor, the urinals, the toilets, and the sinks. They tested flushing every one of the toilets. They even cleaned out the U-traps underneath the sinks.

When Ulrich came back, he inspected their work. Everything appeared sparkling clean until he went to examine one of the sinks.

"Look! What is this?" he said. He pointed at an eyelash in the sink. "Who is responsible for this mess?"

Fritz stepped forward.

"Excuse me, Herr Ulrich. I was responsible for cleaning that sink. What is it that I missed?"

Ulrich pointed to the eyelash.

"Do you think any of us like using a sink with someone's body hair in it?"

"Sorry. That must have been my own eyelash that dropped there," said Fritz.

"Silence!" yelled Ulrich. "I said I wanted this spotless!"

Ulrich gave a silent command to Zorro which was standing in the corner. Immediately, the cattle-prod zapping robot started rolling quickly toward Fritz. Just as it was about to stick the prod into Fritz's chest, Fritz dove out of the way, rolling to the ground, then back onto his feet, prepared to defend himself.

Zorro spun around. The robot's traction system was fast and quick. It accelerated after Fritz, as Fritz attempted to escape, but Fritz was no match for the speed of this machine.

Ulrich was observing this scenario from only a few feet away, grinning with pleasure. However, quite unexpectedly, Fritz grabbed Ulrich and held him tightly against him, using Ulrich as a shield against the Zorro's advances. The little man was no match for Felix's strength, as he squirmed, attempting to free himself.

Zorro extended its cattle prod to full length, like a saber, parrying at Fritz's head with high line ripostes. To the left, then to the right, it jabbed at Fritz, staying clear of its master. Fritz soon recognized a pattern in the robot's jabbing: One left, followed by two right, followed by three left, then one right, again and again. Just at the right moment, Fritz lifted Ulrich's body at the precise moment when Zorro parried right. The cattle prod stuck into Ulrich's left shoulder and zapped him. Ulrich cried out in pain, "*Gedamndt!*"

As Zorro continued jabbing away, Sigmund watched Ulrich and Zorro becoming more coordinated in their motions. Left, right, right, left, left ... Each time Zorro thrust, Ulrich seemed to know the direction of its motion, as if they were communicating. Then, there was a slight change in Ulrich's expression, almost a sneer on his lips.

The game seemed to have changed. Zorro began pushing Felix and Ulrich backward, hammering its armament against them, pushing and pushing backward, intermittently zapping. It was pushing them in a certain direction—a direction in which Ulrich clearly wanted them to be pushed.

As they were being pushed, Ulrich kept looking down at the floor for something. Then Sigmund saw what Ulrich was looking for—a cable loop.

"Fritz! Look where you're stepping!"

But it was too late: Fritz's foot had stepped into the cable loop. The cable loop immediately tightened around Fritz's left foot, and he was lifted upside down into the air, releasing his grip on Ulrich in the process. Ulrich, the circus master of robots, had successfully escaped Fritz's hold. He had successfully summoned a large rolling gantry crane to pick up Fritz by the feet with a hoist!

The hoist lifted Fritz high above the floor, until he was hanging upside-down, at a height of about forty feet.

"*Ulrich, please!*" Sigmund pleaded.

Ulrich yelled, "*Halt die Klappe!*" *[Shut your mouth!]*

Then he gave the executioner's universal "thumbs down" signal, and the rolling gantry dropped Fritz.

Fritz screamed as he fell, then hit the floor hard directly on his head. There was a loud splat, then nothing. Transfixed, the group from New Munich stared at the bloody mess on the floor.

Ulrich turned towards them.

"Let this be a lesson," he said calmly. "If any of you get out of line, my robots will do anything that I command them to do."

Then he looked directly at Sigmund.

"*I* am in charge here, Sigmund! Please clean up the mess!"

Chapter 33

AFTER WITNESSING FRITZ'S EXECUTION, THEY WERE ordered back to the gray building which had become their jail.

Still in a state of shock, Horst approached Sigmund.

"We're not going to make it out of here alive, are we?"

"*Nein*," *[no]* said Sigmund, biting his lower lip. "I am afraid that Ulrich will now be forced to kill us. We witnessed him murdering Fritz. I have known Fritz his entire life! He was my friend—my best friend, in fact—and my work partner. He is married and has two children! What a senseless death!

"I never imagined that Ulrich was capable of such brutality. I never imagined it, that he could actually kill someone. This is the first murder in the history of this planet."

"Was he like this back in New Munich?" asked Horst.

"No, I would have never called him 'evil,'" said Sigmund. "He was certainly annoying. Apparently, in the past five years he has changed."

For several minutes, they sat deep in thought, analyzing the situation. Finally, Sigmund said, "I'm trying to look at things from Ulrich's vantage point. If he stages our death, saying that we died in a plane crash to this place, then who will question him in New Munich?"

"Nobody," replied Horst.

"He will be returning to New Munich, leading his army of robots. The robots will do anything he commands them to do. It will be his ultimate game-play, satisfying his lust for power. He can march into New Munich, either peacefully or forcefully. In either scenario, he will expect to be the new leader, if I am eliminated."

"A 'lust for power,'" repeated Horst.

"He could not accept his position in society. He was trapped in the role the Planners of the Mission assigned him."

"You are right, he will kill us, get us out of the way, and conquer New Munich."

They went to their cots.

"Is it still there?" Sigmund suddenly asked.

Horst checked under his cot. He was able to feel the gun, slipped between bedding straps. He nodded to Sigmund.

"Good. We will need it."

The next morning, Alex arrived carrying a rifle and accompanied by three other men.

"Everybody, get up! It is time to get to work. We have new plans for you."

They were marched outside in single file, at gunpoint, to the railroad stacks. Looking at the quantity of tracks, Horst estimated there were approximately five miles of railroad tracks stored in the yard.

They were marched to what looked like a work train. There were ten flat-bed railcars, each loaded with a stack of tracks. Another car carried ballast, while yet another car had a bulldozer. At the head of the train was a track-laying machine. A small steam powered locomotive was in the second car position. At the end of the train was a caboose.

Waving his rifle at the prisoners, Alex ordered, "Okay, this way. Everyone, get on board the caboose."

They climbed on board the caboose. Inside they found bunk beds and tables. There was also a kitchen. The train soon began to move. As they traveled, Alex explained that they would lay the railroad connecting the Einstein-Newton site to New Munich. Until now, only four men—the entire group minus Ulrich—had been laying track.

Horst recalled seeing the forested area from the plane, just behind the mesa. The railroad must be going through the forested area.

The work train began rolling down the slope of the mesa, carrying the workers in the caboose. As they rode away from the mesa, they saw swarms of drones flying back and forth from the mesa into the forested area.

"Herr Alex, what are these drones doing?" Horst asked Alex.

Alex seemed annoyed. Clearly, he had little patience for the prisoners.

"Well, if you *really need to know*, the drones are bringing us fern chips for fuel."

"Fern chips?" said Horst.

"Yes. We use pellets made from ferns for fuel," answered Alex. "One of the first things Genius did was manufacture small drones to harvest plant life. These little drones fly to and from the forest, nibbling away at the ferns, bringing us back pellets which we use for fuel."

"Amazing!" said Horst. "It is amazing that the Planners of the Mission could anticipate this and developed a solution."

Alex looked at Horst, with a perplexed look, at the mention of the "Planners of the Mission." Did he not understand there were planners? wondered Horst.

"Yes, I must say, Genius is very clever, indeed," said Alex, giving full credit to the supercomputer. "The number of our drones has grown over the years. Now there is an entire swarm of them. They are entirely self-sufficient. They bask in the sun several hours a day to recharge themselves. They supply us with the fuel we need to manufacture things, in particular the steel that we make. Our steel production operations require an immense amount of fuel. These drones are like worker bees; but instead of honey, they provide us with fern pellets."

It took almost an hour to get to the head of the track construction.

"Now you will see why we have been so tired!" said Alex. "You will be laying track today. We have already laid fifty-two miles of track. We have about two hundred and fifty miles more to reach New Munich. You will not have the benefit of using robots out here. We are too far from Genius to use robots, because of the limited range of radio waves."

Alex pointed at Horst, Hansel, and Adam. "You three Americans, come here. You will be clearing the ferns and rocks. As we make progress, we will be making adjustments in the track alignment. This section of the layout is easy: We go straight ahead for the next four miles."

Alex left Horst, Hansel and Adam alone to clear brush, returning to the work train to give instructions to the remaining crew.

The installation of the track involved clearing the brush, leveling the grade, laying ballast, installing ties, then fastening the rails to the ties. There was no need to build a heavy duty railroad; in this case, an absolute minimum amount of track laying materials was to be used: only three inches of ballast, precast concrete ties spaced at two feet on center, with light gauge rails fastened to the ties.

The work was laborious. The sun was blazing hot and there was no shade. The three Americans used machetes to clear the brush and shovels to remove the plants down to the roots. They made good progress, hacking away at the brush. At one point, Horst, Adam and Hansel were almost two hundred feet ahead of the rest of the crew.

The three men decided to take a break and have a drink of water.

"So, what do you think?" said Hansel.

"I think they are going to use us as far as they can. Then, when the railroad is close to completion, they will kill us and dispose of our bodies somewhere in the forest."

"Yeah, that's just about what I was thinking too," said Adam.

"Yeah. I've been talking to Sigmund about this. He's probably making a fake crash site as we speak, to make it look like we flew into a cliff, or crashed in the desert," said Horst.

"So, what are we going to do?" said Hansel.

"We need to eliminate Ulrich when we get back," said Horst. "It's our only option."

Alex yelled at them to get back to work.

They worked for eight hours the first day before quitting. They had made good progress, laying one mile of track in a single day. It was more than Alex and his men had ever laid before.

"I must say, having so many more men to do the work is a relief. You have laid quite a bit of track today! Very good progress!" Alex praised.

"Herr Alex, may I ask you a question?" asked Horst.

"*Ja, ja,* if you must," said Alex.

"While you four men have been laying track, Ulrich has been alone at the site. Who has been fabricating all the steel rails and concrete ties? He couldn't possibly be making these all by himself, could he?"

Alex smiled.

"You ask interesting questions, Herr Horst, don't you? *Ja,* the robots are automated to fabricate the rails and the ties. That is the beauty of the entire operation at the site. With some initial setup, we instruct the robots about the basic operations of making things; then the robots—actually Genius—learns from us, so they can make things on their own without supervision. Every day, an automated crew of robots goes about making the rails and ties. That leaves Ulrich free, by himself, to work on other more important things."

~

After their allotted rations of mineral-liquid for dinner, they made camp for the night, sleeping inside the caboose.

For four days, they continued their labor, constructing an average of about one mile of track a day. There was nothing particularly challenging in this portion of the route: The land was flat, there were no obstacles, such as gorges or rivers, which would require bridges. Alex guarded them closely, pacing back and forth with his rifle.

Quietly, they discussed their options. It did not make sense to escape from the railroad site, because if they were successful, they would probably die in the wilderness without supplies. They decided the best strategy would be making their move back at Einstein-Newton.

~

At the end of the four days, the train headed back to base. When they got back, it was already dark. They were surprised to hear the sound of music and Ulrich laughing coming, from one of the buildings. Alex and his crew looked in the direction of the music and smiled. They seemed eager to join Ulrich's party by himself. Their captives were confused.

Zorro appeared, zapping its cattle prod. The robot marched the prisoners back to the gray building and then provided each of them with their evening ration of nutritional liquid.

"I need some real food!" Hansel protested, disgusted by the taste of the liquid.

After they went to bed, Zorro made his rounds, traveling down the aisles between the cots. As it rolled past his bed, Horst observed that the robot had exposed cables on its back. He lay still, pretending to be asleep, while Zorro continued to rumble between the aisles, back and forth, inspecting the prisoners. The third time Zorro rolled past Horst's cot, Horst threw his shoe against the wall. As soon as Zorro turned its attention to the wall and began zapping wildly in that direction, Horst grabbed the cable in its back and yanked it out. Immediately, the robot stopped functioning.

"Good job!" said Sigmund. "I hate that thing!"

The men got together. "Okay, what's the plan?" asked Hansel.

"Let's complete our original mission, which is disabling the supercomputer. Without the supercomputer, Ulrich and his men will be powerless," said Horst.

"How will we do that?" asked Adam.

"Hell, if I know," said Horst. "At least these robots can be disarmed by pulling the cables on their backs."

"May I suggest something?" said Sigmund. "On our way to the supercomputer, we go to the work train and grab ourselves some machetes."

"Good idea," agreed Horst.

Before leaving the building, Horst grabbed the revolver he had hidden under his bed and stuck it under his belt. The group of men quietly snuck outside into the pitch black night. The site was quiet, except for the loud sounds of partying coming from another building.

As they neared the party building, Adam whispered to the others, "I'm going to see what this about." Before they could stop him, he had slipped away.

"He shouldn't have done that," said Horst. "Let's keep going toward the landing craft. That has to be where the supercomputer is."

They walked in the direction of the work train. All around them the place was still. All the robots were standing motionless. Soon, the men relaxed their pace. When they finally reached the work train, each of them grabbed a machete.

Then they heard someone running toward them. It was Adam. When he arrived he was panting.

"So, what did you see?" asked Horst.

"I looked through the window. They were all wearing APS goggles and were having some sort of party. They were drinking something that looked like beer. But the strangest thing was they were eating—but it was like 'make believe eating' because they had no food in their hands!"

"So, you're saying that they were *pretending* to eat food?" said Hansel.

"Yes, but it wasn't like they were pretending or acting. It looked like they were actually eating something. And it must have been something really good, too. It was like they were relishing the experience! But there wasn't any food there!"

"Fascinating," said Horst. "Perhaps that is what is keeping them satisfied living here."

"My thoughts exactly," said Hansel. "It is almost like they are living in two different worlds."

"Perhaps they have virtual wives in the other world," added Sigmund.

"All quite interesting, but we need to get to the shuttle craft," Horst said.

They walked toward the landing craft, where presumably, the supercomputer was also located. They were only about ten feet from the craft when flood lights turned on.

"Motion detectors!" said Horst. "We should have known!"

A loud klaxon began blasting away.

Horst ran to the landing craft and grabbed the door, but it was locked. He tried kicking the door open, but it wouldn't budge.

Soon, they could hear Ulrich and his men approaching. They looked for cover, but there was no place to hide. They were surrounded by stacks of steel rails on three sides, and were trapped in a corner. The men readied to defend themselves with their machetes.

When Ulrich arrived, he smirked.

"My, my, look at who we have here! Sigmund and his men are attempting to disable our supercomputer! *Tsk, tsk!* Let me guess: The door was locked to the craft?"

He motioned with his gloved hand to summon his robots. In a short time, two robots arrived, one of which had big clampers for lifting up steel rails while the other had a circular saw affixed to its arm, for cutting steel rail.

"Where is Zorro?" said Ulrich. "I am summoning Zorro, but he is not coming. What have you done to Zorro?"

"We've disabled him," said Sigmund.

Ulrich's face turned red; the veins bulged in his forehead. "You will pay for this!"

Before Ulrich could say anything further, Sigmund lunged at him, wrestling him to the ground. The two men rolled, but Sigmund, the larger man, soon had Ulrich in a chokehold. Meanwhile, Horst sucker punched Alex in the stomach. Adam and Felix, who were each brandishing their machetes, were able to hold off the other men of Ulrich's gang.

As Sigmund and Ulrich wrestled, the robot with the large rail clamps grabbed them, picking them up in a horizontal position, about two feet above the ground. Both men were locked into position and could no longer move. As they were being held, however, it seemed that Ulrich remained in control of his robots.

Having knocked out Alex with a good blow to the jaw, Horst looked toward Sigmund and Ulrich. The robot with the circular saw was approaching them, evidently wanting to amputate Sigmund's right leg.

Still held tightly next to his foe by the rail grabber, Ulrich yelled at Sigmund. "Now you will learn what it's like to lose your limbs, Sigmund. I am going to delight in seeing you die! I have hated you all my life!"

Horst walked up to Ulrich, put the gun on his forehead, and fired. Ulrich's body went limp.

The robot with the circular saw suddenly stopped.

Horst pointed his gun at Alex. "Release him! Tell that damn thing to release Sigmund or else I will blow your head off!"

Alex nodded to the robot, and the dead man and Sigmund dropped to the ground.

Chapter 34

ARMED WITH MACHETES, HANSEL AND ADAM HELD HIS henchmen captive. They were still wearing their helmets which theoretically meant they could control the robots. Horst whispered something to Sigmund who nodded.

"Get those damn helmets off, now, or we'll cut your heads off!" he snapped.

The men took off their helmets, exposing their bald, terminal-filled heads.

Horst walked over to Ulrich's corpse. The dead man was still wearing the helmet and his right hand was still sheathed in a metallic glove. Removing the helmet from Ulrich's head, he examined it, then put it on his own head. Nothing happened. He felt nothing at all.

"It doesn't work that way," Alex said. "You just can't put it on. You haven't been prepared yet."

"What do you mean, 'prepared?'"

"You haven't met Albert yet," answered Alex.

"Okay, who is Albert and why do I need to meet him?"

"Albert is the smartest person who ever lived. He is our advisor. It is He who gives us everything. It is He who gives us the plans we use to build things. It is He who gives us the power to control the robot workers," explained Alex. "You will need to meet Albert if you are to become One with Us."

"Yeah, I get it. YOU are superior to us, and WE are like dogs. Just cut the crap and give me a straight answer!"

"It is a process that you need to go through. If you meet Albert, you will see," said Alex.

They moved the captives to the building that had served as their living quarters, where they were placed under guard. All the robots were motionless; all work activities had come to a halt.

"What do we do now?" asked Horst. "We can't fly out of here because our planes have been destroyed."

"We could hike back through the forest," said Hansel.

The idea of traveling approximately 300 miles through the forest on foot was not appealing. Their expedition from New Eden to New Munich had been treacherous, with all the sail-backs, the spiders, scorpions, reptiles and large amphibians.

"I don't like the idea of traveling again on foot," said Horst. "The forest is dangerous. I'm not even sure what gear we have to make the journey."

"Another option is to complete the railroad," said Sigmund.

"How exactly can we do that? There isn't enough track to complete the project. We are unable to fabricate any more track," said Horst.

"And what do we do with our prisoners? If these guys ever get hold of their helmets, they could regain control of the robots and everything," said Sigmund.

Everyone remained quiet, pondering the situation. Finally, Horst spoke. "I think the only option is for one of us to 'meet Albert.'"

"Ah, you lost me. Say that again?" said Hansel.

"We need to be able to control the robot force, or our prisoners represent a potential risk. Also, we need the robot force if we are to finish building the railroad," said Horst. "In the big picture, Einstein-Newton's workforce needs to be brought to New Munich."

"Okay, so any volunteers?" asked Hansel.

"Yes," said Horst. "I'm willing to do it. It's my idea and I want to 'meet Albert.'"

Horst told Alex he wanted to meet Albert.

"Very good," said Alex. "This procedure will require myself and two others to operate the equipment. Is that acceptable?"

Horst weighed his options. "Yes, I agree, but I need to warn you that you will be under guard while I am being 'prepared,' as you say. I will instruct our men to kill all of you if you place my life in danger or harm me in any way."

"No need to worry," said Alex. "It is for the better if you also go through the preparation process."

∿

Horst walked with Alex and two of Ulrich's men to another building, down a long corridor, and into a small room; Adam and Hansel followed at a close distance but waited outside the room. There was a barber's chair in the middle of the room.

"Please sit," said Alex. "Today, you're the lucky one. *Ja*, you're going to meet Albert."

Horst sat in the chair.

"Alex, you had better make sure I am the lucky one! It won't go well for you if you pull any stunts!"

They completely shaved Horst's head, then thoroughly washed his bald scalp. After this procedure, Horst was taken on a gurney into what looked like a surgical room. He was transferred to a table, and then was strapped into place.

One of the men entered the room, wearing a surgical gown.

"Is the patient ready?"

"*Ja. Er ist bereit*," answered Alex. *[Yes, he is ready.]*

"Right," said the man, addressing Horst. "This is going to hurt only a little bit. We will be drilling small holes in your head. The soap had anesthesia in it, and this will make it easier on you."

Horst attempted to sit up, but Alex forced him to lie down again.

"Calm down. The less you move, the better. Don't worry—we will not be drilling into your brain. This is really a minor operation that we are doing. We are making tiny holes through your skull."

Horst lay there, listening to the vibrations as the surgeon drilled holes through his skull. As he drilled, the man kept singing what sounded like an old song called "Hungry Like the Wolf"; but something must have gotten lost in the translation, because he was singing "Hungry Like *a Fox*":

La, la, la, la

La, la, la,

I'm hungry like a fox

The drilling procedure took about twenty minutes. Horst counted as they drilled eight holes in his head; just as the surgeon had promised, the procedure was more uncomfortable than painful

After the drilling, Horst saw the surgeon filling a large syringe with a colorless fluid.

"*Ja, ja.* Let's see, for starters, I will give you … hmm … *viel liecht … sechs pro units? [perhaps six units?] Ja,* for the *Americaner,* I'm giving him, as you say, 'six' units. *Ein, zwei, drei, vier, fünf, sechs. Gut!*"

Then the surgeon injected the fluid into each of the holes in Horst's skull. Each of the holes was then plugged with bandage.

After this operation, Horst was led to another room containing a large machine. He was placed in a flat position on a sliding chair. Someone stuck earplugs into his ears. His head was fitted into a circumferential brace that prevented it from moving. Next, he was given an injection in his arm. All the while, the surgeon kept singing, "Hungry Like *a Fox.*"

La, la, la, la
I'm hungry like a fox

"Can you please stop your incessant singing?" said Horst, who normally never lost his patience.

"*Entschuldigung!" [Excuse me!]*

Finally, the reclining chair slid inside a large machine, which looked like an MRI machine. Horst heard a voice from a speaker.

"Please stay absolutely still and don't move. This phase of your preparation will last a long time—ninety minutes to be exact. You must lie completely still. Don't be alarmed by the loud noises."

During the time Horst was inside the machine, it made rapid sounds like a machine gun. He lay absolutely still for a very long time, a thousand anxious thoughts flitted across his mind.

After an hour and a half, they slid him out of the machine. Completely dazed, he looked up and saw Alex towering over him.

"Good. The hard part is done. Next, we will be taking you to the virtual reality room."

They wheeled him on the gurney to another room with a bed. This time, they instructed him to lie down. The surgeon connected a glucose bag intravenously to his right arm; then taped a tube to his groin. He felt a burning sensation.

"Hey, what's that about?" yelled Horst, alarmed that they were touching him. The tube hurt.

"Don't worry. This is only a catheter. You will need to urinate during this experience. This tube will allow you to urinate without making a mess."

During the entire procedure, Hansel and Adam had been standing guard outside the door. Hearing Horst yell out loud, they burst into the room. To their relief, Horst was alive but seemed shaken.

"He will be alright," said Alex. "We need a helmet now."

Hansel ran outside to where the helmets were securely stored and selected the biggest one there. Before he gave it to Alex, he said, "If there is any funny business, you'll be the first one we kill. Do you understand?"

Alex looked steadily at Hansel.

"Don't worry. The helmet is only for Horst."

Alex mounted the headset of electronic sensors on Horst's head. His men adjusted the sensors, making sure that everything was in its proper place.

Next, Alex held up a pair of virtual reality goggles.

"You've used these types of goggles before, correct?"

"Of course. Those are APS virtual reality goggles," answered Horst.

"*Ja, ja. Das* APS goggles," said Alex.

"Okay, put them on me," said Horst. At this point, there was no going back. He was fully at their mercy, even if Adam and Hansel were standing close by, they would only be able to *avenge* him, not save him!

"In good time," said Alex. "Before we put the goggles on you, there is one more step. We will be injecting a drug into you which will cause you to lose control of your body. This will be the most difficult part of the experience. Don't be too alarmed. You will momentarily feel disoriented."

The surgeon injected the drug into the intravenous port. Within a matter of two seconds, Horst felt his arm become cold. The sensation traveled up his arm, then the full brunt of the injection hit him as he began to hallucinate. It looked like everyone was in slow motion. As he watched the men around him move, images of their bodies appeared to trail behind them. The light from a window hurt his eyes, manifesting in a kaleidoscope of colors. He began feeling a loss of equilibrium; then he felt completely paralyzed. He tried to scream but no sound came.

"Don't worry," said Alex soothingly. "We have everything under control. After I put the goggles on you, you will begin to feel normal again. You will get to meet Albert. Are you ready?"

Once the goggles were in place, Horst saw that he was in the living room of a house. Judging from the decor, it was an old house, perhaps circa 1930s or 1940s. The furniture was heavy dark wood, which appeared to be hand carved. There was an ornate staircase with beautiful wood railings and spirally carved posts; at the bottom of the staircase there was a massive newel post. He saw an impressive cuckoo clock which featured a water-wheel as well as moving people and farm animals. Just as he looked at the clock, it began cuckooing twelve times. It must be noon, thought Horst.

Upstairs, someone was playing the violin. *Was this music by Mozart?* He remembered Eileen playing the same music on the piano. It sounded like someone was playing the violin with a very old recording. Horst remembered that people used to listen to record players. *Was this a record player?* The music sounded tinny and scratchy.

Then he heard a woman's voice.

"Albert! *Est ist zeit fur Mittagessen. Gehen sie hierin!"*

Horst easily translated that the woman was telling Albert it was time for lunch and that he should come downstairs.

He saw the feet of a man wearing slippers slowly descend the staircase. When he was able to see the man's face, he instantly recognized Albert Einstein. The great scientist's gray hair was a mess. He was wearing a bathrobe.

"*Guten Tag!"* said Professor Einstein, addressing Horst directly. "*Sind sie Americaner?"* [Are you an American?]

Horst was momentarily taken aback. He simply stammered, "*Ah, ja. Ich bin Americaner."* [Ah, yes, I am American.]

"Please to meet you. I am Albert Einstein," the scientist said in English, with a very heavy accent.

"Ah, yeah . . . I know. I mean, of course I recognize you. I mean, I don't know what I mean."

A woman in her late fifties appeared. She was wearing an apron over an old fashioned flowered dress, and her gray hair was knotted in a bun.

"*Guten Tag!"* said the woman.

"This is my wife, Elsa," said Einstein.

"*Freut mich! Ich heisse Horst."* [My pleasure! My name is Horst.]

"*Angenehm"* [My pleasure], said Elsa. "Excuse my English, it is not so good. Would you like to have some lunch?"

Of course, Horst was accustomed to the APS simulations, which did not allow any movement. As was usually the case, the APS simulations were extremely real, but not "quite right." This experience with Einstein was different. Horst discovered that when he moved his legs, he could actually walk in this virtual experience. When he touched things, he could actually feel things! He could also smell and taste things!

Horst walked over to the kitchen to eat lunch with Einstein. He sat down at the table. Elsa brought them sausages, with sauerkraut and potatoes. In typical German fashion, Einstein ate with his fork in his left hand and his knife in the right, cutting and forking, without switching hands as Americans are taught to do. Horst took a slice of sausage and stuck it in his mouth. To his surprise, he could taste it. It was delicious.

How could this be possible? How could a virtual experience be so real?

"You look perplexed," observed Einstein.

"Yes, I'm baffled by this experience," said Horst. "I'm familiar with the virtual experience of the APS simulator—I mean the 'Artificial Personality Simulator.' With the APS we see things, but we cannot feel things. We also can't move with the simulation. The APS can be a very nauseating experience. But this . . . feels absolutely real."

Einstein chuckled. "Ah, *ja,* I think I know what you mean. No, not really—I'm lying: I don't know what you mean. I'm not be the best person to ask these questions. Perhaps after lunch I can call on the proper expert. Does that sound alright with you?"

"Of course, Professor."

"Good. I understand physics, but some of this other stuff is way beyond me," said Einstein.

They continued to eat their lunch. Elsa was an excellent cook. She brought them *Schwarzwälder Kuchen*—Black Forest Cake—chocolate cake with cherries. They also drank coffee. Einstein took his with milk and cream. Horst had his coffee with cream only.

"You look puzzled, *nicht wahr?*" said Einstein.

"Yes," said Horst. "How is it that I can walk and eat? How am I able to taste these things?"

"There you go again with these difficult questions. I will need to call this fellow to explain. But, yes, you can use the bathroom. It's right over there."

Horst walked over to the bathroom—again, still amazed that he could walk—and relieved himself. When he returned to the living room, Einstein was sitting in a chair, smoking his pipe.

"Please, sit down," said Einstein. "Elsa, can you please call Tony and ask him to come here to explain things to Horst?"

"*Ja*, Albert," said Elsa.

"*Vielen Dank*," replied Einstein. *[Thank you very much.]*

About five minutes later, someone buzzed the front door. Elsa let the visitor inside.

"*Guten Tag*, Tony." *[Good day, Tony.]*

A man who looked to be in his twenties entered.

"Hello, Professor. How can I help you?"

"We have a new visitor here, Mr. Horst, who is asking some questions that I am unable to answer. Can you please help him?"

"Certainly, Professor Einstein."

Tony turned his attention to Horst. "Pleased to meet you, Mr. Horst."

"It's just 'Horst,' without the 'Mr.,'" said Horst.

"My apologies. How can I help you, Horst?"

Horst paused, attempting to prioritize his thoughts. "I am perplexed about this virtual experience. I assume that you are familiar with the APS system?"

"Of course. We use the same basic components as the APS system."

"Well, in my former experiences with the APS, it was not possible to actually walk around inside the virtual images. We couldn't physically touch things."

"I see. So you are wondering how is it possible that you can walk around and sense things inside this simulation?"

"Yes."

"Very good question. Do you remember the preparation steps that you went through before you came here?"

"Yes. I was tied down. They drilled holes in my head. Then they gave me an injection of something."

"Exactly. What they were doing was injecting nanoparticles into your brain. It was necessary to drill small holes through your skull in lieu of simply giving you a pill, because of what is called the 'blood-brain barrier.' Direct injection is the only way to get the nanoparticles into your brain because of their size."

"What is the purpose of the nanoparticles?"

"The nanoparticles are necessary to create a connection between your autonomic and limbic nervous systems and our supercomputer. You remember sitting for a long time in a big machine?"

"Of course. I laid there for ninety minutes."

"Correct. That machine was an MRI, the same type that was used in hospitals on Earth to observe internal anatomy. The MRI sends magnetic pulses, the 'M' part, to detect resonance, the 'R' part, of bodily tissues. Its full name is 'magnetic resonance instrument.'"

"I still don't understand. Why use an MRI?"

"The MRI was used to direct the nanoparticles to organize new connections to external sensor points. In effect, the nanoparticles create artificial neural pathways to various brain components that are involved in your autonomic and limbic nervous systems."

"Okay, I think you've lost me. What do you mean by 'autonomic nervous system'?"

"This has to do with a neurophysiological model of the brain. There are various parts of the brain that are responsible for maintaining basic body functions. Think of it as the 'lower brain' or 'primitive brain functions. The primitive brain organs maintain your heart rate, for instance. Besides that, these primitive brain organs are responsible for receiving sensory input from all areas of the body and sending that input to the higher brain organs, where we analyze and perceive the input.

"You see, the senses that we perceive are transmitted to your brain through neurological electrical circuits. Our senses are stimulated, which in turn generate neural synaptic currents in neural circuits. We hear things, which stimulate auditory neural circuits. We feel things in our hands, which stimulate neural circuits in our hands. There are less obvious known neural circuits, such as the ones that connect to our vestibular systems in our inner ears, which monitor our position, giving us our sense of balance. These types of things involve basic input, which is processed by lower brain organs. Are you with me so far?"

"Yes. You make it sound as though we are a bunch of electrical circuits and wires."

"Yes. But instead of metal wires, electrical currents travel on neural circuits. Understand?"

"Ah, yeah, more or less."

"Good. The other part of the brain, which we sometimes refer to in general terms as the 'upper brain,' is involved in processing all this input from the lower brain. That part of the brain is involved in our conscious thought processes. We are somewhat in control of our conscious thoughts. However, it is very difficult—in fact it's nearly impossible—to control our autonomic nervous system."

"Okay, so your point is . . . the nanoparticles that were injected into my brain form a connection to my autonomous system?"

"No, you're not quite right. The nanoparticles are providing an alternate path of sensory input to your higher brain," said Tony. "Do you remember what happened just before they put the virtual reality goggles on you?"

Horst was not quite sure. So much had happened to him, it was overwhelming. Then he remembered.

"Yes, I remember. The surgeon warned me that he was giving me an injection, and that I might find this scary—or something like that."

"Yes. Go on. Do you remember how you felt?"

"Yes. As soon as he gave me the injection, I was unable to move at all," answered Horst.

"Do you have a theory about this?" asked Tony. "Of course, I know the answer. I'm just curious what you think."

"Yes, I think I do. I think that the drug they gave me paralyzed the connections to my autonomous functions. Was this done to allow the artificial nanoparticle connections to take over and provide an alternative path of sensory input for my sense of touch and balance?"

"Bingo! We have a winner!" exclaimed Tony.

Einstein laughed. "Very interesting, Tony. Good job, Horst. This is quite fascinating."

"So, let me conjecture what this is about," said Horst. "The supercomputer which is generating this virtual reality is feeding neural signals to my brain, giving me a sense of touch, smell and taste. It is even providing me with signals to my vesti—"

"Vestibular."

". . . to my vestibular system, so that I maintain a sense of balance."

"Exactly."

"So I'm actually paralyzed, lying down in a bed, but in this virtual reality system, I can walk, run, feel things and taste things."

"Yes," answered Tony. "But, don't worry; you are not permanently paralyzed. The effects of the drugs will wear off. This is something that we have control over. You will return from this virtual experience."

Horst was beginning to feel exhausted. Simply meeting Einstein, the world's greatest physicist—except, for perhaps Isaac Newton . . .

"Oh, my God, I just thought of something. Is Isaac Newton here, too?" asked Horst.

Tony answered, "Unfortunately, the fact is, this all a simulation of reality. Professor Einstein, here, is not the real Albert Einstein, but a simulation we have based on extensive information about the real Einstein, including film footage. We don't have enough resources to attempt a realistic simulation of the real Isaac Newton. If we tried, it would ring false, and probably make a mockery of the real Newton."

"Of course. I momentarily forgot the situation," said Horst. "It's just so real here."

"You look tired. Would you like to take a rest?" asked Einstein. "You can use our guest bedroom."

"Yes. I think I would like that, but I need to ask Tony one more thing."

"Go ahead. Shoot," said Tony.

"How can I sleep during this virtual reality experience?"

"Don't worry. You can sleep here. Have you ever dreamed of sleeping in your dreams?"

"Ah, I'm not sure. Maybe I have."

"Sleep is something your conscious brain does. Your conscious brain—your upper brain—is intact. We have simply provided you with an alternative form of input to your higher brain."

Horst contemplated this idea: input to the higher brain. They had swapped the source of input. Instead of input from his body's autonomous system input, he was getting input from the supercomputer.

"I find this disturbing. It makes me wonder, what is reality?" asked Horst. "If I sense things simply based on neural input, what is reality?"

"Have you ever heard of people who have lost a leg, but still feel their leg? Or people with tinnitus, who hear a sound, even though there is no sound outside their body?" asked Tony.

"Yes. My friend, Hansel, has tinnitus. He hears a sound in his head that the rest of us cannot hear."

"These pains and sounds are very real to the people experiencing them. These things can be traced to neural loops, involving inputs and responses in our bodies."

"So it all boils down to this? Circuits and electricity?"

Horst was extremely tired. "Professor, I'm going to take up your offer and go upstairs and take a nap."

"*Ja, ja. Guten Abend!*" [*Yes, yes, good evening!*] said Einstein, as he watched Horst walk upstairs.

Chapter 35

HORST SLEPT FITFULLY. AT ABOUT TWO A.M. HE WOKE UP IN a panic attack, feeling as though he were suffocating. He woke up screaming.

Elsa hurried into his room, wearing a bathrobe over a long flannel nightie. Her graying hair was wound tightly around metal rollers that were held in place with bobby pins.

"*Was machen Sie? Sind Sie krank?*" *[What is happening to you? Are you sick?]*

Seeing that Horst was in a sweat, Elsa brought in a wet towel and cleaned his face.

"You are alright. Please calm down. You've had a rough day. *Bitte, schlafen Sie.*" *[Please, sleep.]*

Horst tried to calm down, but he was confused. The entire situation was so disorienting. *Where the hell was he?* What was reality? Where was he *really*?

Still agitated, he stayed awake for another two hours, trying to sort out his thoughts. At about four thirty a.m., he finally fell asleep again, but soon, at five fifteen a.m., the alarm clock went off. Minutes later,

Einstein knocked on his door.

"*Ausstehen Sie, bitte!*" *[Get up, please!]*

Horst quickly got out of bed and dressed. Then, going downstairs to the kitchen, he found Elsa making breakfast. Einstein was eating a bowl of cereal and drinking coffee.

"Would you like some oatmeal, or perhaps eggs and bacon?" asked Elsa.

"I would like eggs and bacon, if it's not too much trouble. I've never had oatmeal before," answered Horst.

"Well, in that case, how about trying a little bit of oatmeal, too?" said Elsa.

"Sure, I can try it."

Elsa prepared a small bowl of oatmeal, with brown sugar and raisins, topping it with whole milk and a sprinkling of pecans. Horst took a spoonful, and it was delicious. He quickly ate the entire contents of the bowl.

"*Hat es geschmeckt?*" said Elsa *[Did it taste good?]*

"*Ja, ja!*" said Horst enthusiastically. "*Es hat sehr gut geschmeckt!*" *[Yes, yes! It did taste delicious!]*

While Horst ate his oatmeal and bacon and eggs, followed by three cups of coffee, Einstein was very quiet, appearing to be lost in thought. Horst looked at him, wondering what he was thinking, but then he stopped himself.

This person—this virtual thing—was not the real man. He was a facsimile of the real Einstein, an electronic reproduction. And, yet, what was the harm in accepting this image as Einstein? *Why not allow himself a "willing suspension of disbelief"?* Perhaps he would learn something new and amazing about physics from this Einstein. *Just imagine if this virtual Einstein had discovered something like time travel?* He became quite excited thinking what he might learn that day.

Finally, Einstein spoke.

"So, what do you want to do today?"

"Heck, I don't know. Frankly, I didn't realize that I had any choice!"

"Of course," said Einstein. "This is your first time here. Do you have any more questions that you would like to discuss with Tony?"

Horst thought about this.

"Yes, I do."

Einstein got up and called Tony, using the telephone on the kitchen wall. Within half an hour, Tony arrived and entered the living room. Tony and Horst sat across from each other in wingback chairs while Einstein read the morning newspaper on the sofa. Horst looked at the newspaper, which was in German. Interestingly, it was the *Berliner Zeitung*, dated July 11, 1948.

"So, what can I do for you today?" asked Tony.

Horst paused to gather his thoughts.

"I think I understand the discussion we had last night, about how nanoparticle input circuitry is providing autonomous brain signals to my brain. But I have one big question: Can the supercomputer read my thoughts?"

"No, it can't," said Tony. "The only way we know your thoughts is if you talk to us."

Horst was relieved to hear this. He was glad he could keep secrets from this thing.

"Let's go over everything again," said Tony. "You're actually seeing things through your virtual reality goggles. You're actually hearing things through headphones that you are wearing. You're actually talking to us through a microphone. However, you are feeling and tasting things using the nanoparticle circuitry providing autonomous input to your upper brain."

"Yes, I think I understand. You have taken the APS to the next level, but you cannot read my thoughts."

"No, we can't."

Horst sipped his coffee.

"How long will I stay here in this state of virtual reality?"

"We have found that two days is about the maximum limit," said Tony. "To be honest with you, we are concerned that if people stay any longer than that it is unhealthy for them. Realize that your body is actually lying in a bed, immobilized for a long period, not getting any exercise. We need to limit the duration of this experience. You will discover that when you come out of this virtual state, your body will feel sore."

"So I will be returning soon?"

"Yes, tonight you will be returning to reality," answered Tony. "So, please, have some fun today with the Professor."

So, I'll be leaving tonight, Horst thought to himself, feeling some relief. After Tony left, Horst found himself alone with Einstein and Elsa, who kept refilling his cup of coffee. Einstein had just finished reading the newspaper.

"*Ja*, it is a shame that Berlin is in ruins after the war."

"You mean World War II?"

"*Natürlich*" *[of course]*, said Einstein. "What other war could I be talking about?"

Was Einstein still living in the year 1948? Horst decided to say nothing about this.

"How about we go for a walk?" said Einstein.

"Sounds good to me," replied Horst. "Will you be coming, Elsa?"

"No," said Elsa. "I'll let you enjoy your time together."

~

The two men left the house. As they closed the door behind them, Horst saw that Einstein's house was a simple wooden framed two-story building with a covered front porch which had blue and white petunias cascading from hanging baskets; there was a one-story extension with a flat roof to the left of the front door. The house was painted white, with black window shutters. Leaving the front yard, they began walking down a street lined with stately houses and old trees. Horst noticed a sign saying "Mercer Street."

"Where are we?"

"Princeton, New Jersey, of course," answered Einstein. "We should walk over to the Institute of Advanced Physics and see what the graduate students are up to."

As they continued walking, Einstein pointed at a manhole.

"Just the other day, I fell into that manhole; it had an open lid."

"Did you hurt yourself?"

"No. As usual, I was lost in my thoughts, not looking where I was going. There was a photographer who wanted to take a photo of me climbing out of the manhole. Fortunately, I was able to talk the fellow out of taking a photo. I don't like all the publicity they make of me. Now tell me, what are you interested in?"

"I'm interested in a lot of things," said Horst. "I like to read a lot. I'm interested in chemistry and physics. Can I ask you a question about the atom, Professor?"

"Sure."

"I have read that you disagree with some of the concepts of quantum mechanics."

"Quantum mechanics is certainly imposing," said Einstein, "but an inner voice tells me that it is not yet the real thing. The theory says a lot, but does not really bring us any closer to the secret of the 'old one.' I, at any rate, am convinced that *He* does not throw dice."

When Horst heard him say this, it sounded strangely familiar. *Was it a quote he had read?* He recalled that Einstein was adamantly opposed to the idea of using probabilistic methods used by quantum physicists, such as Heisenburg and his "uncertainty principle."

"What about the idea that electrons behave as waves when observed from a small distance and as particles when we observe them from a far distance?" asked Horst.

Einstein sucked on his pipe.

"Try and penetrate with our limited means the secrets of nature and you will find that, behind all the discernible concatenations, there remains something subtle, intangible and inexplicable. Veneration for this force beyond anything that we can comprehend is my religion. To that extent I am, in point of fact, religious."

Their conversation bantered back and forth, but the more they talked, the more Horst felt that this Einstein was merely reciting Einstein's famous sayings from a prepared script. Their discussions lacked the genuine give and take of a natural discussion. Every time Horst carefully framed a question about something that he considered difficult, Einstein replied to him with one of his famous sayings. As a result, by the time they had arrived at the Institute for Advanced Physics, Horst had become more and more withdrawn. He realized that he was becoming bored with this Einstein.

When they arrived at the Institute, Einstein introduced Horst to several graduate students. Horst played along with the pleasantries. All the while, in the back of his mind, he was assessing the situation. This was not the real Einstein. The talk was too easy. The man he was talking to was the celebrity version of the real Einstein, the "friendly-old-genius/wise-old-man" version of the real Einstein that had been commercialized for public consumption.

It was almost noon when they walked back to Einstein's house. Elsa served them lunch: cheese sandwiches, with chips and a pickle. While they ate, Horst said very little, but his hosts didn't seem to notice. Then the telephone rang, and Einstein went to answer it. When he returned to the table, he told Horst that Tony would be coming over to prepare him for his return to reality.

Within five minutes, Tony arrived at the door.

"Are you ready for the return trip?"

"Yes, I suppose so," answered Horst.

"Okay, let's get you back, then. You will need to go back upstairs and lie down on the bed. You will momentarily go to sleep during the transition. When you wake up, you will be back in the real world."

Horst said goodbye to Einstein and Elsa, then walked upstairs with Tony to the bedroom where he sat on the side of the bed.

He looked at Tony.

"This is not the real Einstein. He is too simple."

"I'm sorry that you feel that way," said Tony. "Of course, you're right."

"This Einstein is an APS version of Einstein. He has nothing new to say. He seems to be a stagnant reproduction of Albert Einstein."

"You are correct. This entire experience that you are having is the same as the APS technology you experienced before in New Eden. The only difference is you are able to feel things in this more advanced APS version. This more advanced version of APS was assembled with nanotechnology invented by humans on Earth. The Einstein downstairs is an APS Einstein. He is based on newsreel footage and information from various biographies. We have captured his appearance and general mannerisms, but that is all."

"But, I was under the impression that you—the supercomputer—had become far more advanced than we humans," said Horst. "I was expecting to hear Einstein tell me all sorts of new and profound discoveries in physics, but he told me nothing new."

Tony paused.

"Horst, we are only a supercomputer. We are not human. While we can crunch numbers and recall any fact ever developed in human history, we lack creativity. We are a machine, not human. We also lack emotions. The real Einstein was a genius—an especially creative man. This is something that we cannot simulate."

Horst suddenly felt very sleepy. He lay back on the bed and shut his eyes. When he opened his eyes again, he found himself back in the laboratory with Alex.

Chapter 36

WHEN HORST OPENED HIS EYES, ALEX WAS STANDING IN front of him, holding the virtual reality goggles, headphones, and microphone that he had been wearing for the past two days.

"Take it easy. You need to go slowly," said Alex. "We have given you an injection that reawakens the connections between your upper and lower brain systems. You are currently in a transition state. The supercomputer is gradually releasing control of your autonomic nervous system back to your conscious brain's system as the paralysis drugs wear off. The duration of this transition will be two hours. Then we can remove the helmet connected to the nanoparticle circuits in your brain. If you understand, blink once. If you don't understand, don't."

Horst blinked once.

"If you are in any way feeling uncomfortable, blink once. If you feel okay, blink twice."

Horst blinked twice.

"Good. I will leave you here for the next two hours. It would probably be best if you close your eyes and try to sleep," said Alex. Then he exited the room.

Horst closed his eyes and tried to sleep, but couldn't. He was thinking about the situation there at the Einstein-Newton site. It was an enigma to him. What was the purpose of "meeting Albert"?

After two hours, Alex returned.

"I think you should try to sit up now," he said.

As Horst sat up, he felt extremely weak. He swung his legs over the side of the gurney.

"You look like you feel lousy."

"That's an understatement," said Horst. "Every muscle in my body hurts."

"You'll almost be back to normal in a few hours. Just take it easy this first day. So, how was it? Did you meet Einstein?"

"Yes. I did," said Horst.

"So what did you think of the smartest scientist that ever lived?" asked Alex.

Horst hesitated.

"Yes, I agree that Einstein was perhaps the smartest physicist that ever lived. Actually, that's a hard assessment, and one on which I don't feel qualified to give an opinion. Einstein, Newton, Maxwell, were all very smart guys, but who am I to judge?" Horst took a sip of water, then continued. "Now let me ask you a question, Herr Alex. Have you ever studied physics?"

"*Ah, nein,*" said Alex. "That wasn't a part of my training."

"And what was your training, may I ask?" asked Horst.

"*Eine Metzger,*" answered Alex. "You know, a butcher. That is what my father was back on Earth," he said, with more than a hint of disdain. "This was the role in life that I was assigned."

"I see," said Horst. "Well, I have studied physics and chemistry quite a bit. In fact, these are my favorite subjects. My father was a chemist."

"And so, what is your point?" asked Alex, with a bit of an edge in his voice. "Is it that I, a common *Metzger*, think something *stupid*?"

"No, no, not at all. It is a subtle observation which a physicist might notice about this Einstein. My point is, the Einstein that I met is not the real Einstein. The one that I met is an APS version of Einstein. This Einstein appears to lack creative intelligence."

Alex frowned when he heard this. He lowered his head and appeared to be deeply upset. But to Horst's surprise, his mood suddenly changed. He smiled, then vigorously shook Horst's hand.

"Thank you! We thank you! You are providing us with excellent new insight! You will be very useful to us!"

Horst said nothing but made a mental note of Alex's reactions. Eventually, Alex rolled him in a wheelchair back to the room where the Sigmund,

Hansel, Felix and the rest of the landing team were staying. Relieved to see that Horst was alive and well, they were eager to hear about his experience. Would each of them be going through the same process? Once Alex left the room, they huddled around their friend.

As Horst shared his impressions of this new APS experience, he acknowledged that it didn't make sense to him. The supercomputer at Einstein-Newton had taken the APS experience to a new level, beyond anything he had experienced back at New Eden. This new APS experience was indistinguishable from reality. But to what end?

But, most importantly, who created this new system? Did this Einstein-Newton supercomputer, Genius, develop this concept on its own? Was Genius a new more highly evolved level of being? Was Ulrich right, that a new man/machine being had been created by Genius?

Suddenly, Alex walked into the room. "Who is next on the list to meet Albert?"

Immediately, Hansel raised his hand.

"Good," said Alex. "Have you studied physics, too?"

"No, I never studied physics."

"What were you trained for?"

"I'm a builder. My father was a contractor on Earth."

"So, what have you built?"

"We are building a new community for the Americans across the river from New Munich. So far, we have built seven houses and a bridge."

"Do you have a wife?"

"Yes, I do. Her name is Gertrude."

"Lucky you, you have yourself a new young wife," sneered Alex. "Okay, you will do. You will be the next one to meet Albert. The new *American husband* will meet Albert."

Hansel was understandably upset. Horst went over to him.

"Don't worry about it. It's not that bad. You will be back here in a couple of days. I think that every one of us will 'meet Albert' at one time or another. It seems to be a preparation process that we each must go through."

"I still don't understand. What are they preparing me for?"

Before Horst could say anything more, Alex escorted Hansel out of the room.

"Are we all going 'meet Albert'?" asked Sigmund.

"Apparently so," said Horst. "They install the nanoparticles in your brain that create circuitry. Don't worry, the nanocircuits are still in my brain, and I don't feel them at all."

"Nanocircuits?" said Sigmund. "*Mein Gott!*"

"Yes. The preparation process takes several hours. It doesn't hurt at all. It just takes a long time, sitting inside a big machine that makes a lot of noise." Horst paused to think. "I'm puzzled. All I can figure is the supercomputer is learning from each of us. Whatever it is learning, it requires that it learn from each of us, individually. However, I'm not certain what or who we are dealing with."

~

Two days later, Hansel came back to the group. His head had been shaved, and he had a stubble of beard. He was dazed and disoriented. Horst handed him a bottle of water, which he guzzled.

"How to you feel?" asked Horst.

"Lousy," said Hansel.

"Did you get to meet Einstein?"

"Yes, I got to meet Albert. Very nice old man. The guy's a genius. I met his wife, Elsa. Great cook," said Hansel. Then he vomited on Horst's shirt.

"Man . . . did you have to?" said Horst.

"Sorry about that!" said Hansel. "Oh, my aching head. I am so tired! I have such a headache!"

"Please lie down," said Sigmund.

"I don't need to lie down! I've been lying down for two days!" said Hansel. Then he suddenly smiled. "It's gone. It's finally gone."

"What do you mean, 'it's gone'?" asked Horst.

"I can't hear it anymore," said Hansel, suddenly beginning to cry. "My tinnitus is gone."

Horst thought about this. "They must have done something that fixed your tinnitus. It must be the nanoparticles they injected into your brain."

"After so many years, I can finally hear silence," sobbed Hansel.

Chapter 37

Horst decided Tony was the key to the puzzle. He must be the wizard of this operation. It had been a week since Horst had met Einstein or "Albert" as he was commonly called. Since then, a number of men had also met Albert. Now Horst was anxious to talk to Tony. He informed Alex that he wanted to go through the experience again. Apparently, no one had ever gone to "meet Albert" a second time before, and Alex warned him that his body needed more time to rejuvenate from the previous trip. Nonetheless, Horst wanted to go as soon as possible. He was placed next on the list to "meet," or rather, "re-meet," Albert.

When the time came, the preparation was very quick, because the nano-circuitry was already implanted in his brain. Immediately after he arrived in the virtual reality room, he was placed on the operating table. The team fitted him with the helmet and goggles, and attached the intravenous tubes for the drugs to immobilize him.

"Are you ready? Remember, this is the time when the supercomputer will take control of you. This shot will make you feel nauseous."

"I'm ready," Horst answered, bracing himself.

Almost immediately, he felt the numbness and cold sensation traveling up his arm. Feeling a momentary loss of control of his basic bodily functions, he realized he had urinated. His breathing became labored and his heart pounded. Then he blacked out.

When Horst regained consciousness, he was once again in Einstein's house, standing at the foot of the staircase, leaning against the beautifully carved newel post. As before, he heard Einstein playing the same Mozart piece on his violin upstairs. Again, Einstein slowly descended the stairs wearing his bathrobe.

"*Guten Morgen*, Horst," said Einstein. *[Good morning, Horst.]*

"*Guten Morgen, Herr Doktor*," answered Horst, letting go of the stair post and stepping aside.

"What brings you back so soon?" asked Einstein.

He paused on the last step, looking steadily at Horst.

"This is highly unusual. I have never seen a new patient more than once."

"I want to talk to Tony about a few things, if you don't mind, Sir," said Horst.

"*Natürlich!*" *[of course!]* I don't mind at all," answered Einstein. He walked to the phone in the kitchen and dialed.

"Tony, can you please come here? We have an important visitor."

Horst was surprised to hear that he was considered "important."

After several minutes, Tony rang the front door bell.

"May I excuse myself?" asked Einstein, letting in his guest. "I just woke up and still have to get dressed."

"No problem, *Herr Doktor*," said Horst, stepping aside so Tony could enter the narrow hallway.

Once Einstein had reached the top stair, Tony looked at Horst. There was the trace of a frown on his face.

"So, what's up? It hasn't been very long, has it?"

"I have many questions about this APS experience. It's important that I understand how all of this came about. I think that you are the only one who can help me."

"If you came back just to talk to me, it wasn't necessary for you to go through the initial treatment again," said Tony. "Didn't anyone warn you it could be dangerous?"

"You mean, I didn't need to be anesthetized to see you?" exclaimed Horst.

"No, you didn't need to be 'put under.' You can easily contact me by putting on APS goggles, in just the same way as you used the APS in New Eden," said Tony.

Horst felt embarrassed. There had been no need for him to "meet Albert" again, after all.

"Okay, shoot. What's your question?" said Tony, taking a seat at the kitchen table.

"Who are you, really?" asked Horst, pulling out a chair to join him.

"What do you mean? I'm Tony."

"Yeah, I know, 'Tony'. You're the APS Tony. But who was the *real* Tony?"

After a long pause, Tony responded; he seemed rather taken aback by the question.

"I was a part of the Chicago team. I mean, the *real* Tony was a programmer in the Chicago team."

"What do you mean, the 'Chicago Team'?"

"During the days of President Obama, there was an initiative to develop a progressive digital manufacturing research center in Chicago. The aim of the initiative was to construct a manufacturing research park that would allow entrepreneurs a place to design and test new products in an entirely digital environment."

"What do you mean by an 'entirely digital environment'?"

"It was a place for entrepreneurs to build and test their products using virtual reality. Is that clearer?"

"No, sorry. Not quite."

"Okay, let's slow down. Traditionally, people with a product have built actual physical prototypes of their products. Then they test the prototypes to see if they work. They do all sorts of tests. To get a product from conception to production can be a lengthy and costly process. The Chicago research park was designed to avoid building actual physical prototypes and to speed up the process. At the research park, entrepreneurs could build digital prototypes which they would test by using virtual reality simulations."

"I recall hearing something about this before," said Horst, "but it never made much sense to me. I once heard that the Einstein-Newton supercomputer carried technologies from the Chicago team."

"Yes, it did. In fact, our technology is the most important component of the Einstein-Newton probe. It was created for this purpose."

"What purpose?"

"Please be patient and let me finish," said Tony.

"Of course. Please continue."

"The Chicago research park accomplished its mission. We worked for years providing a virtual reality testing place for prototypes. With the enormous computational power of our supercomputer, we were able to model parts realistically. We could compute stresses in the solids, no matter how complex the shape. We could model any fluid behavior and thermodynamic behavior realistically. The system integrated many aspects of the physical world into the modeling process: kinematic movements, stress analysis, fluid mechanics, thermodynamics, chemical reactions, failure and fatigue predication capability. It was a phenomenal system, to be sure.

"But we seemed to be ahead of our time. Many businesses did not understand our vision and purpose. Perhaps they did not want to outsource this type of testing. Whatever the reason, they did not take advantage of the resources we had to offer. Are you with me so far?"

"Yes, I follow you," said Horst. "So what did you do, if you were not always busy?"

"We played games during slow periods," said Tony. "Many of us were serious gamers. Do you know what video games are, Horst?"

"Not exactly. I've heard about them."

"On Earth, a lot of us got into playing games on our computers. In the old days, games were very primitive, and only two dimensional, but that all changed when 3-D gaming was invented. Wearing stereoscopic headsets, players were able to enter the virtual reality of games, but only to a point. You see, when you wear those goggles, your equilibrium can be disturbed. Some people just can't wear them without throwing up. The mind and the body perceive a disconnect. Do you understand why?"

"Yes, I do," responded Horst. "Our body's vestibular system, which maintains our sense of balance, cannot be fooled by 3-D goggles."

"Yes!" answered Tony. "Our vestibular system messes up the whole experience."

"So, to improve your game playing, you guys came up with the nanoparticle system?" said Horst.

"Well, yes and no," said Tony. "We thought that artificial nanocircuits could provide alternative vestibular input. But this was purely science fiction, just a radically cool dream of ours. I mean, we were just programmers, not brain surgeons!"

"Please continue."

"The situation changed when we discovered an asteroid might hit the Earth. That's when the 'big-boys' got serious about sending embryos into space to a new planet. This led to all sorts of challenges: How do you raise the kids? Well, artificial intelligence had sufficiently progressed to a point that The Planners of the Mission decided robots could raise the kids. That's how the Guardians originated.

"But let's dig deeper into the concept of the mission. It's not quite enough to feed and educate the kids into adulthood by robots, is it? The Planners of the Mission realized that your small group would need manufacturing capabilities in order to re-create the technologies that we had on modern Earth. Without manufacturing, you would be reduced to living like cavemen in just a few years after all your machines wear out. It was because of our expertise in manufacturing, that we were contacted. We were assigned the task of designing a probe that would deliver manufacturing capabilities to the new planet.

"We didn't know where to begin or what to do at first. You see, our expertise was simulating reality, but we were being asked to do the *exact reverse* thing! They needed us to develop a way to build real things with real robots! You might ask how a robot can build things by itself, without humans? I mean, robots are machines. Machines lack 'experience.' They lack neural circuits providing them with a system of pleasure and pain.

"Robots, even the most advanced ones, even the ones that look human, are not like humans. Even the Guardian and APS systems at New Eden and New Munich have their limitations. These things are nothing more than giant programs, systems of 'psycho-logic,' giant flow charts of 'IF/THEN' statements and 'DO LOOPS.' The APS systems use the distilled collections of experiences from people who were interviewed for countless hours on Earth. They use collections of someone else's experiences. As a prime example, for Albert Einstein's personality, we used old newsreels and his writings, and an actor named Phil Schwartz."

"Phil Schwartz?" asked Horst.

"Phil Schwartz was an Einstein impersonator," said Tony. "He looked the part and acted the part. We captured Phil's mannerisms in the APS simulator to create our APS model of Einstein."

"Fascinating," said Horst.

"My point is, we couldn't just ship robots to another planet and expect them to run themselves. The only way to use the robots is to control them using people. It was during one of our brainstorming sessions that somebody mentioned the 'nanoconnection in the brain' concept, which we had fantasized about using as a game controller. To our surprise, the Planners of the Mission liked the idea! We were very surprised that these guys were risk takers. They agreed that, by implanting nanoparticles into the brain, we might develop mind-to-robot controls.

"I mean, you need to realize that the situation on Earth had become desperate. There was no time to deliberate and be cautious in every decision. This idea of brain circuitry was wild, but it seemed worth a shot. If it worked, it could only be beneficial. An entire army of robot workers could be controlled by a relatively small number of people using this system."

"So, just like that, you were involved in a programming dream project which would affect generations!" exclaimed Horst.

"Yes," said Tony, beaming with pride. "The US government sent the leading neurologists from Rockefeller University to work with the Chicago team of programmers. After defining the behavior of the real brain systems, it became a matter of designing substitute neural pathways using the nanoparticles. Writing the software for the simulation systems was right up our alley."

"What about building the nanoparticles?" asked Horst.

"For that, we required the help of nanoparticle engineers. Using off-the-shelf magnetic resonance machines, they helped us coordinate the paths of the nanoparticles. When the system was finished, we tested it on several people."

"Did they test it on you?" asked Horst.

"Yes, they did," said Tony. "I was one of the first. The experience was terrifying, but it worked. Based on the success of this component, the Einstein-Newton probe was put into full production. We were racing against the clock as the asteroid was nearing Earth. Now, have I answered all of your questions?"

"Yes, you have. Thank you."

"Are you ready to go back now?"

"Yes. If I can."

"This may be the last time you see *Docktor* Einstein," said Tony. "Want to say goodbye?"

Together, they walked to the living room were the APS Einstein was now reading the newspaper.

"Well, I think this is it. Nice seeing you again, *Herr Docktor*."

"Nice seeing you, too, young man. *Aufweidersehen!*"

Chapter 38

AFTER EVERYONE FROM NEW MUNICH WENT THROUGH their "preparation," Alex trained them how to control the robots using their helmets.

At first, their coordination with the robots' movements was awkward, but as the supercomputer learned their neural patterns, they began to "feel" each robot's movements. It was almost like having extensions added to their bodies. The more they practiced, the more they attained subtle and accurate movements. The robots and their human controllers "became one," so to speak.

Once they became skilled enough, the supercomputer taught them the manufacturing skills they would need to make things—how to use a drill press, a lathe and a bending table; how to bend conduit and lay wiring; how to weld metals and seal joints; how to mix concrete and how to install reinforcing bars and pre-stressing steel.

Once they had mastered various basic manufacturing skills, each of them was further trained in specialized skills, based on the types of things they would be making. Some of these skills were unbelievably complex. If it had been manual work, it would have been brutally labor-intensive, but the robots gave the men the power to do almost anything, effortlessly.

Horst reflected on this new power. It was easy for him to see how a person such as Ulrich could be corrupted; he had learned to control robots and his fellow humans whom he had more or less enslaved. Fortunately, with Ulrich gone, his men were no longer hostile. In a short time, they became friends with the newcomers. It was as though the experience of "meeting Albert" was a rite of passage for the newcomers, an initiation into a club to which Ulrich's men already belonged.

Ulrich's men had truly believed that their connection to the supercomputer made them more advanced, "evolved" combinations of machine and human. They were shocked to learn from Horst that the supercomputer was *not* a "superior being" which had evolved over 80,000 years in space and that, instead, the nanocircuits had actually been designed by a bunch of computer programmers from Chicago!

As Horst and the rest of the New Munich group had suspected, Ulrich and his men had been living in two worlds: the real one and a virtual one. On a regular basis, these men had visited their APS world, one that was inhabited with their virtual wives and virtual families. This created a complex social situation to be sure: the men felt—in fact, they believed—that they were married to virtual wives!

This peculiar situation raised all sorts of ethical questions as to what was real and what was not. In the end, the newcomers decided not to interfere and allow Ulrich's men to continue with their trips to their APS world—to 'live and let live,' or as the Germans say, "*leben und leben lassen.*"

For their part, Ulrich's men made overtures attempting to convince the newcomers to visit the APS world, where anything is possible. They talked about the great food in the APS world, even the great Chicago-style pizza—with sausage, mushrooms, and pepperoni! However, none of this talk had any influence on the newcomers who had absolutely no interest in visiting these alternate forms of reality. "Meeting Albert" was quite enough.

Everyone's work efforts were directed toward fabricating and installing the new railroad tracks leading to New Munich. For the next year, both groups worked together, hacking through the forests, installing tracks and camping outdoors. Frequently, they were attacked by dangerous wildlife, such as scorpions and sail-backs. They worked in unbearable heat and humidity. Mile by mile, at a steady rate of about one mile per day, they progressed toward New Munich.

At the end of the year, they were within fifty miles of New Munich. At this this point, Sigmund and his men and the Third Thaw were quite anxious to get back to see their families. They decided to walk the final distance, leaving Ulrich's men to finish the rail road, which would take at least another six weeks.

Before they left for New Munich, Sigmund called everyone to a meeting.

"Tomorrow we will be leaving our new friends to finish the work. I think that it is proper for me to acknowledge that it has been an honor to reunite with our fellow countrymen. You have done an outstanding job, building this new railroad. More importantly, you men were able to utilize the robot-to-human interface which the Planners of the Mission intended for us to have. Please, everyone, give these men a round of applause!"

Horst, Hansel, Adam, Okunola, and the others enthusiastically applauded the four men from Ulrich's expedition party.

Then Sigmund became more serious, almost confidential in his tone. "There is also a more sensitive matter which we need to discuss, something which I've given much thought. When we return to Neu München, people will be asking us what happened to Ulrich and Fritz. As some of you know, both of these men were well liked in Neu München. Ulrich was an influential person in our community. Fritz was my best friend and has a family."

At the mention of Fritz, Sigmund could not control himself, as tears began streaming down his face. He paused for several seconds, letting the wave of emotions subside before attempting to speak again.

"Now, after much thought, I suggest that we keep the unfortunate episode of how Fritz died and how Ulrich died a secret to ourselves. The reason I think it is best to keep the truth secret is, it will serve no purpose in our community if people know the truth; in fact, I believe it will divide our community."

Alex raised his hand.

"Yes, Alex, please go ahead."

Alex said, "Thank you, Sigmund. I happen to agree with you on this point. Ulrich was our commander, someone who I respected. However, I think that something happened to him. He had a lust for power. I think it would be best to leave this awful experience behind. I feel selfish to admit this, but I don't want the people of Neu München to know that I was personally involved with this torturous man."

Horst listened to Alex, and it made sense to him. Alex had become his friend. If news got out the Ulrich had killed Fritz and he was about to kill Sigmund—and that his men were cohorts—these men would be branded and perhaps punished.

Horst said, "I agree. I think we should make a pack among ourselves to promise to tell no one what actually happened—not even our wives."

Alex asked, "So what do we tell people when they ask us how Fritz and Ulrich died?"

Sigmund say, "Let's say there was a plane crash, and Fritz died in the plane crash."

Alex asked, "And Ulrich? How did he die?"

Horst said, "Let's say he got sick, and he died before we landed at the site."

"Are we in agreement?" asked Sigmund, looking around. Everyone nodded. "Good, we are in agreement. The matter is settled."

It took them three days to walk the last fifty miles through the forest and brush. They pushed hard, driven by the desire for home, hearts aching for their loved ones. Armed only with their machetes, they cut their way through the vegetation, forging a path for the train tracks while creating the long road home. It was nearly sunset when they could finally see the silhouette of New Munich in the distance. After almost two years, they were almost home!

As they walked into town, the beauty of New Eden and civilization was in marked contrast to the wilderness where they had been living. There were red and purple flowers everywhere, cascading from window boxes on each façade. The men took in the scene, overcome with emotion as they re-entered the world they had left behind so long ago.

A little boy noticed them first. He had been peering into the window of a toy shop, looking at hand carved "wooden" locomotives, cars and planes.

"They're back!" he screamed. "They're back, but they're funny looking! *Mutti, Mutti!*" [*Mother, Mother!*]

Self-consciously, the men looked at each other, suddenly aware of their appearance. They must look haggard to the people of New Munich.

Sigmund grimaced.

"That was Fritz's son—I'm going to have to break the news to his widow and children. I'm not looking forward to this!"

Soon, the word spread that they were back, and the entire town came out to greet them.

The Americans continued to their own sector across the river. When Horst reached his house, he opened the door and saw his daughter for the first time; barely a year old, she was sitting on the floor shelling peas. For a moment, Horst stood still, watching in amazement as she neatly placed peas in one bowl and pods and strings in another. As her tiny fingers split open each pod, he could see how intensely she was concentrating—so much like her mother. Looking up, he saw Ingrid standing next to her, staring at him, almost in a state of shock. Both wept as they clung to each other, locked in a tight embrace. They only let go when the little girl grabbed Horst's legs and he swooped her up, smothering her in kisses.

"We didn't know if you would ever come back!" said Ingrid, half laughing, half crying. "We thought you had crashed in the desert and had starved to death. You were gone so long, we had given up hope!"

"If you can give me something to eat, I'll explain everything," said Horst, cradling his daughter tightly. As Ingrid whipped up an omelet, grilled tomatoes, and french fries, Horst began his narrative, only pausing when Ingrid seemed too distracted to focus on cooking.

"It's a miracle you survived!" was all she could say when he reached the end of the group's adventures.

"Miracle?" teased Horst. "Sounds like you've been spending time with Eileen!"

⌇

It was another six weeks before the track from the Einstein-Newton site to New Munich was completed. The people of New Munich were amazed to see the long train carrying approximately 1,000 robots. The train cars were filled with all sorts of machines and steam-powered vehicles that had been built at the Einstein-Newton site. As the train rolled into town, Sigmund activated a cordless mic, explaining to his astonished neighbors how their survival as a community would depend upon how well they advanced technologically. Graciously, he welcomed Ulrich's men, making no reference to the way they had blindly followed Ulrich. If there were to be peace and harmony in New Munich, these men would have to be incorporated into the society, even finding wives among her citizens.

The swarm of fern-eating pellet-making drones had also accompanied the train in the 300 mile journey. No one quite understood why these autonomous machines felt the need to move themselves with the humans. Perhaps, like so many creatures on Earth, the drones were accustomed to living in tandem with human society. Perhaps the drones had acquired a sense of purpose, providing fuel to the humans.

Part 5
Life in New Munich

Chapter 39

NOW THAT THE ROBOT WORKFORCE HAD ARRIVED IN NEW Munich, the settlement was about to change substantially. Industrialization would transform this society in much the same way that Earth's Western civilization had been transformed from a rural based society to an industrial society. The major difference was that the Industrial Age on Earth occurred over a period of about a hundred years; New Munich's industrialization was happening instantaneously.

The citizens now had a workforce which could give them a standard of living comparable to that of people living in early twentieth century America. Still not quite up to the modern living standards on Earth, when the spacecraft launched; but that would come eventually, at this rate.

The community decided to build the new factories on the river, downstream from the center of New Munich, about five miles away. The massive industrialization effort would require new responsibilities for everyone. These frontier people, who had been "jacks-of-all-trades," would need to become specialists in various fields. Horst was very happy to be in charge of the pharmaceutical industry. He and a group of robots would be manufacturing medicines.

Before industrialization, there had been no need for currency. New Eden and New Munich had been communal societies, where everyone shared everything. A simple system of sharing would no longer work as the community grew larger. Inevitably, the industries would interact and make supplies for each other, and therefore a system of exchange was needed.

Thus, for the first time on the planet, industries began "doing business" with each other and with individuals, thus requiring the exchange of currency.

Coins were the first form of currency. Gold and silver coins were the most valuable, since these metals were scarce on the planet. Copper coins were also introduced; they were less valuable, since this metal was more abundant. After the first minting, each citizen received a bag of coins. When Ingrid was first given a bag of coins, however, she didn't understand what to do with them.

"What exactly am I supposed to do with these things?" she asked Horst.

"We're supposed to 'buy things' with the coins," her husband replied.

"What do you mean, 'buy things'?"

Horst thought this over, trying to come up with a situation where they would need to buy things.

"Okay, I think I have a situation. Let's say you need some bread. What do you do when you need bread?"

"I make myself bread."

"But what if you're too busy to make bread?"

"I suppose I would ask somebody for some bread."

"Like who?"

"I would probably ask Martha, because she's the closest to us."

"Okay, good—we're off to a start. Now you're supposed to give coins to Martha for a piece of bread."

"Why? Why don't I just ask Martha for a piece of bread?"

"I see your point," said Horst. "Let's say you're going to a store that sells bread."

"What's a 'store'?"

"Remember on Earth, they had stores. Didn't you ever see one during one of your APS sessions with your mother on Earth?"

"No, I don't think I was paying much attention. So what's a store?"

"Didn't you go anywhere with your APS mother?"

"Not really," said Ingrid, remembering her mother who was a biologist. "We talked a lot about science, but we didn't go many places, except sometimes to observe nature."

Horst thought a while. "Okay, this is what I think. You're now a doctor, right?"

"Of course. Are you attempting to be sarcastic?"

"No, I'm not being sarcastic, but don't you find that, with your job as a doctor, you have less time to do all the chores than before when we lived in New Eden? Like making bread? Like making your own clothes?"

"Well, I'm still knitting after dinner."

"Yes, I get it—you're still knitting! But what about other things, like making pots and sewing clothes, and all the other stuff we used to do back at New Eden?"

"I agree that I have much less time to sew clothes."

"Good, then clothes are a perfect example," said Horst. "Well, in the near future, we will have people who will make clothes for everyone."

"Everyone! That's a lot of clothes!"

"Yes, it will be a lot of clothes. And the people who will be making these clothes will need a place for people to pick out their clothes."

"You mean there will be a place where I will be able to see a whole lot of dresses and be able to pick one out that I like?"

"Yes, I think so. That's how it was on Earth."

Ingrid smiled. "You mean, I will be given different choices? I think I will like that."

"Let's continue. This place where clothes will be distributed is called a 'store.' There will be other stores that distribute other things, like bread and meat."

"Yes, that sounds good. But I don't think we need any more than two or three stores. Clothes, bread, and meat. That's all we will ever need," said Ingrid.

Horst chuckled.

"Well, I'm not too sure about that. Let's not forgot about cheese and milk stores." Then he remembered going out to eat with his APS ancestors on Earth. "They are opening another type of store where they will serve food. It's called a 'restaurant.'"

"You mean at this store—this *restaurant*, as you say—they will serve us food, like the Guardians did in New Eden?"

"Yes," replied Horst. "And why do you think that people will go to restaurants?"

"I think people will go to restaurants when they are too busy to make dinner."

"Exactly what I think," said Horst "Let's get back on track about the coins. When we have stores, we use our coins to trade in exchange for the things we get."

"So can I still ask Martha for a loaf of bread without giving her coins?" asked Ingrid.

"Yes, I think you can still ask Martha for a loaf of bread," laughed Horst.

"Good, because we're almost out of bread."

∾

As New Munich grew, shops began to spring up: a new *delicatessen* with strings of sausages and wheels of cheese in its windows; a bakery that sold *Brotchen [rolls]*, *Brezein [soft pretzels]*, *Streuselkuchen [streusel cake]*, and *Kasekuchen [cheesecake]*; a clothing store specializing in *Lederhosen [leather trousers]* and the *Dirndl* or ruffled apron dress worn by women . . . There was also a shoe shop, and a newly constructed post office which doubled as a corner tavern.

Like Ingrid, many of the citizens did not understand why they had to use coins. These people, who had been living together as large families found the concept of using currency odd.

Sigmund explained that, as New Munich grew, people would no longer "know everyone." He predicted that someday, when the population was large, people would be interacting as strangers, and it was therefore necessary to use this new system of trade, which he called "money." He tried to explain the concept of "buying" and "selling," but the people found this all quite confusing.

This was a critical juncture in the evolution of their society. This group of humans was being forced to leave its "Garden of Eden" to become less like brothers and sisters and more like strangers. They were preparing themselves to become a much larger population.

One night, Horst reflected on these changes with his wife.

"You know, Ingrid, we are living so differently than before," he said.

"I think I know what you mean," said Ingrid. "We used to live in New Eden, now we're in New Munich."

"It's not only that," said Horst, pausing to collect his thoughts. "I don't know, but it seems like before we were always living together, all doing the same things. And now we're doing our own individual things."

"Isn't that called 'growing up'?" said Ingrid.

"Yes—and no. I'm talking more about the way we live as community has changed."

"How so?"

"I am so busy in my work that I have very little time to see my friends, Adam and Hansel. I don't know what they're up to. They are building new buildings, aren't they?" asked Horst.

"Yes, they certainly are. As a matter of fact, I saw them building a new house in our sector the other day."

"Whereabouts?"

"Just over on San Francisco and New York."

~

After dinner, Horst and Ingrid and little Melissa took a stroll to the construction site where Hansel and Adam were building the new house. Adam and Hansel were delighted to see them. Proudly, Adam unrolled the blueprints as well as a sketch of how the building would look once completed.

Horst whistled. "It's a Frank Lloyd Wright, isn't it? That's just like the Robie House in Chicago!"

"Yes," said Adam, "I visited it with my APS grandparents—never forgot how it looked. Hey, I have an idea. There is a new—what do you call it?—a 'restaurant' in New Munich. Why don't we go over there? Hansel and I can bring our families."

"Unfortunately, we just ate our dinner," sighed Ingrid, "but it would be lovely to see Gertrude and Shina and all the kids. I can't remember when we last got together!"

"Do they serve beer?" asked Horst.

"*Natürlich!*" said Adam. "And while you're enjoying your steins, Shina will appreciate not having to cook tonight. She has her hands full with the twins. What say you, Hansel?"

"Great idea!" said Hansel. "Gertrude gets tired easily on account of her injury, but this will be a perfect break for her! Kid number three is due any day now, so it may be several months before we can join you again."

They all went to the new restaurant where they ate, drank, and caught up with each other's lives. Meanwhile, the children enjoyed soft cinnamon coated pretzels hot from the oven, along with *Apfelsaft [apple juice]* served in miniature Rhine wine glasses with thick green stems. When the group was ready to leave, they used their new coins for the very first time, leaving something called "a tip."

Chapter 40

ALMOST FIVE YEARS AFTER THE THIRD THAW HAD ARRIVED in New Munich, the Fourth Thaw walked into town. They were ragged and dirty looking, almost emaciated. Judging from their appearance, they had faced challenges along the way. The townsfolk poured out of their homes and offices to greet the newcomers and to assess their needs.

The Fourth Thaw followed Adam to the American sector, where they were each given a place to stay. They were delighted to find that the houses in New Munich had hot running water, and as soon as they had something to eat, they each took a long shower. Their traveling clothes were beyond repair, but, fortunately, there was no shortage of clothing in New Munich. The residents were able to produce goods on demand.

That evening, there was a banquet in New Munich to celebrate the newcomers' arrival. Everyone was interested in meeting the visitors and hearing about their journey. In many ways, the tale that unfolded was predictable, with all the usual elements—sail-back lizards, giant dragonflies, scorpions, massive predatory fish, poisonous plants, treacherous terrain . . . As the residents listened, many found themselves traveling back in time to when they had made their own journey, facing similar hardships and dangers along the way. The town's children listened wide-eyed, mesmerized by every adventure. Some, of course, had heard their own parents' accounts of the world beyond New Munich, but others had been sheltered from the more disturbing details. Even more impressive, however, was the fact that the Fourth Thaw were the last humans to live in New Eden. They were the last link to "home."

Karl, one of the Fourth Thaw, walked to the podium, "Good evening, my fellow Americans—*und Guten Abend, meinen Deutcher!*" *[and good evening my Germans!]*

The audience—both the Americans who were now fully comfortable speaking *Deutch,* and the Germans—responded in unison, "*Guten Abend!*"

"*Ja, ja, das ist gut!*" *[Yes, yes, this is good!]* said Karl. "I can see that I will need to practice my *Deutch, nicht wahr?*"

Everyone laughed.

"On a more serious note," continued Karl, "I need to let you know that we had a rough time getting here. We lost some people along the way, but fortunately, very fortunately, most of us made it. I offer our deepest thanks to the Third Thaw for warning us about the waterfall." He paused, overcome by emotion. In spite of all the festivities and warm welcome, the reality was that they had lost good people along the way. "Well, do you have any questions?" he asked abruptly.

Horst raised his hand. "Herr Karl, you and others of the Fourth Thaw were the last humans to live in New Eden. Do you know what is happening there now that you are gone?"

"Yes, we do. Leader Graham explained their plans for after we left," said Karl. "The Guardians are busy with the final task of birthing and raising the newborn large animals from Earth: African wildlife—tigers, lions, elephants—all the embryos of Earth's animals that would have been too dangerous to have around when we humans were living there."

Everyone was amazed to hear this. *Imagine, African animals living in New Eden!*

"This is amazing!" said Ingrid. "I recall that many African animals were almost to the point of extinction on Earth. Do you know how long the Guardians will be raising these animals?"

"Leader Graham told us that the Guardians are merely serving as first generation 'foster parents' to these large animals, much like they acted as our own foster parents, although none of us knew it at the time. The next generations of these animals will be born and raised by their parents in the wild. It is my understanding that there are still many embryos of large animals to birth and raise. This part of the Guardians' work is nowhere near completion."

Chapter 41

IN THE YEARS THAT FOLLOWED, THE CITIZENS OF NEW MUNICH lived much the same way as people had lived on Earth. Their technologies had rapidly developed to the equivalent of late 1940s Earth technologies. Life in the settlement had fallen into a stable, predictable pattern. Families got bigger and everyone was getting older.

After twenty-four years in New Munich, the Third Thaw found themselves in the unusual position of being called the "Elders." They were now forty-five years old. All of them had families, and some of them had many children. Hansel and Gertrude had eight children. Adam and Shina, the Japanese German, had six children. Horst and Ingrid had only two children—a son named Sig and a daughter named Melissa. They intended to have more kids, but Ingrid had difficulty delivering her second child. Eileen and Felix, the musicians who lived in New Munich, had four children whom they raised in a strictly religious household.

When the Third Thaw reached "Elder" vintage, many of their children were in their early twenties, which was about the same age the Third Thaw had been when they had arrived in New Munich. It was interesting to see that the sons of Hansel, Horst, Adam, and the long-deceased Gerald had been good friends since a young age.

The oldest member of this group of friends was Gerald, or "Junior," as his mother Zelda called him. At age twenty-two, Gerald bore an uncanny resemblance to his father who, of course, had been tragically killed in the journey from New Eden to New Munich. Like his father, Gerald had dark skin, curly black hair, a happy face, and eyelashes that any woman would have envied. Gerald had been raised by his stepfather, Okunola, the only father he had ever known. Zelda and Okunola were very happily married and had five more children. Gerald worked with his step father at their family coffee bean plantation. They also owned a coffee shop, the "African Grind," in the American sector.

The next oldest member of this group of friends was Filbert, the son of Adam and Shina, who was twenty-one years old. Filbert was the more studious and serious minded member of the foursome. He had inherited his mother's Japanese features and had very straight, black hair. As a child, the other children constantly teased him, calling him "Little Guardian," since he resembled a Guardian. He had been called "Little Guardian" so often that he had acquired the moniker "LG," but, fortunately, he had a good sense of humor and did not mind. Filbert worked as a teacher at the Advanced Institute in New Munich, and was currently teaching a course on the History of Technology.

The third wheel of the foursome was Jeff, the son of Hansel and Gertrude, who was twenty years old. Jeff, like both his mother and father, was a good-natured fellow. He had a muscular, short physique, which was an ideal body type for gymnastics. In high school, he had excelled at gymnastics, competing in the rings. After graduation, Jeff went to work with his father's construction business which now went by the name "H & J Construction," with the "J" representing "Jeff." He was an expert mason, especially talented building chimneys and fireplaces.

The fourth oldest member of the foursome was Sig, the son of Horst and Ingrid, who was also twenty years old. Sig was very outgoing and personable, and was somewhat the antithesis of his parents, who were both scientifically inclined quiet types. Perhaps in reaction to his parents' emphasis on science, Sig was not at all "turned-on" by science.

When he was a small boy, his father gave Sig a molecular modeling kit to play with. He diligently tutored Sig, instructing him how to fit together the little plastic balls and snap-ties which represented single, double, and triple molecular bonds. This particular father-son endeavor lasted about a year, as Horst hoped that Sig would become inspired by his own enthusiasm. But this molecular building activity eventually waned to nothing, as it became obvious that Sig felt no passion for chemistry, or even for science in general.

Sig considered his parents to be introverts, and, deciding that he did not want to be that way, he proclaimed that he was "a people person." The last thing he wanted was be stuck alone in a laboratory. As a result, he found himself a job in the packaging division of his father's pharmaceutical company, as this allowed him contact with customers.

～

One Saturday on his day off from work, Sig walked into The African Grind coffee shop where Gerald was working at the counter.

"Hey, Sig, how's it going?" said Gerald.

"*Es geht nicht schlecht*" *[not bad]*, said Sig, "*Und du?*" *[and you?]* The Americans had fallen into a pattern of using a mixture of English and Deutsch when they spoke together. When they were in the presence of Germans, they spoke almost exclusively Deutsch, except for a few English colloquialisms which had become acceptable to the communities.

"*Ja, ja*, I am also not bad," answered Gerald. "So, what would you like?"

"A cappuccino, *bitte*," said Sig.

"One cappuccino, coming up!"

Sig looked across the street and saw Eileen and Felix approaching the store with their family. Eileen, now middle aged, tended to wear formal attire these days, usually stiff tweed garments and her favorite golden brooch. Today, she was wearing a plain gray suit. Her husband, Felix, also typically wore formal attire such as a gray suit and black fedora, a red handkerchief in his breast pocket. Their oldest daughter, Mary, accompanied her parents. She was twenty years old, and, like her mother, had red hair and a slim figure. She was wearing a somewhat dowdy dress, something considered acceptable by her mother who was conscious of such things. Mary had been a classmate of both Sig and Gerald at the school in New Munich.

"*Guten Tag, Frau Eileen und Herr Felix!*" said Sig, properly addressing the parents first. *[Good day, Mrs. Eileen and Mr. Felix!]*

"*Guten Tag, jungen Mannen!*" responded Eileen and Felix. *[Good day, young men!]*

"*Und hallo, Fraulein Mary!*" said Sig, smiling at Mary. *[And hello, Miss Mary!]*

"*Guten Tag, jungen Mann*" *[Good day, young man]*, said Mary, looking down, carefully avoiding calling him by his name, so as not to appear be too familiar. Everyone knew that mother Eileen was very strict with her children.

"And what would you like today?"

"*Wir mochten eine tasse Kaffee, bitte,*" answered Eileen, resisting the entrée to slip into casual conversation in English with Sig. *[We would like a cup of coffee, please.]*

"*Al so, drei tasse Kaffee,*" said Gerald, "*Kommen es oben!*" *[Then so, three cups of coffee, coming up!]*

While Gerald was preparing their coffees, Eileen, Felix and Mary sat at a table by the window. As he sipped his coffee and pretended to read something, Sig looked over at Mary. Discreetly, Mary looked up at Sig, giving him a quick direct look, and her beautiful smile. How he loved that smile!

It was well known among the few families living in the American sector that the family of Horst and Ingrid and the family of Eileen and Felix were polar opposites. Out of common courtesy, Horst and Ingrid were always pleasantly differential to Eileen and Felix, and vice versa; however, underneath it all, there remained a tension between Eileen and Ingrid.

As musicians, Eileen and Felix emphasized the musical education of their children. First, each of their children took violin lessons for two years, followed by piano lessons. However, it quickly became apparent that one of their children, their daughter, Mary, had not inherited Eileen's and Felix's aptitude for playing musical instruments. Mary found herself as the odd-ball in a family of musicians.

Sig and Mary were very much alike, because, among other things, each of them had not lived up to the expectations of their parents: Sig was not the scientist his parents expected, and Mary was not the musician her parents expected.

This situation between these two families would have been unremarkable except, in this case, Sig and Mary, the offspring of the two such disparate families, were secretly romantically involved.

As teenagers, Sig and Mary discovered that they were kindred spirits. Both were highly intelligent and physically attracted to each. Over time, they shared their own personal stories and raw feelings, using each other to make sense of emotional conflicts, as they matured into adults. They became astute observers of human nature, able to recognize drama in human social situations, seeing analogies between the old Earth stories and lives of people inhabiting this new planet. As they grew together, they fell in love and became soul mates.

Since they were now both working adults, their time together had become much more limited. To complicate matters, Mary hid their relationship from her mother.

∼

Mary and Sig typically saw each other on Saturdays, at three p.m., in the park in the American sector. When she was going to see Sig, Mary always told her family she was meeting up with her friend, Karen, the daughter of Hansel and Gertrude. Karen was fully cognizant that she was a part of the conspiracy.

At three p.m., Sig went to the park and found Mary waiting for him.

"When I saw you in the coffee shop, I almost burst out laughing!" said Mary. "I mean, you should have seen the look on your face!"

Sig grinned, "What do you mean, 'the look on my face'? After calling me '*jungen Mann*'! Give me a break!" he laughed.

"So, how's work?" Mary asked.

"Can't stand it. I just can't get into packaging," he said. Then he laughed, "That didn't come out right, did it? It sounded like I can't be packaged."

"Yeah, real funny!" she said sarcastically.

"Do you remember reading stories about Johnny Appleseed when we were kids?" Sig asked.

"Sure, I loved that story," said Mary. "What brings this on?"

"I've been thinking—just bear with me now. Picture this, like, what if there was a Johnny Appleseed on this planet?"

"Okay, I'm picturing . . . it's fuzzy . . . yeah, cool, I like it. Keep going with it."

Sometimes they would do this thing together that they referred to as a "stream of consciousness," as if they were writing a story.

"Okay, so there is this new character, Johnny Appleseed, on this planet. He walks around planting trees all over the place."

"Is this what you want to do? You want to be Johnny Appleseed?"

"No, not really," he said. "But I would like to make adaptions to stories like that. I'd like to adapt these old stories for this planet."

"You're saying you want to write children's stories?"

"Yes, I think so."

Mary smiled. Despite her outwardly shy appearance, she had a very active fantasy life, a trait that Sig also shared.

Mary took off one of her socks and put it on her hand, making a puppet. Then she talked to the sock, "Hey, Johnny! Johnny! Are you up yet?"

Using a strange little voice, she pretended the sock was talking back to her.

"Yeah, what's up?"

"Sig has been telling me that you've been planting apple seeds. Is that so?" said Mary to the sock.

"Yep, been plantin' seeds," said the sock, sounding like a crabby old farmer.

"How many seeds have you planted so far?"

"Don't know. Never counted 'em," said the crabby old farmer puppet.

Sig got into the act.

"Hello, Mr. Appleseed," said Sig.

"And who the heck are you?" said the sock.

"I'm a reporter, Mr. Appleseed," said Sig.

"What ya reportin' on, Mr. Reporter man?"

"I'm asking you, how many seeds did you plant today?"

"Don't know, yet," said the sock. There was a pause and Mary burst out laughing.

"I'm running out of material!" she spluttered.

"So am I," laughed Sig.

"That was fun," said Mary. "It needs some work, but it was fun."

Then Sig's expression became serious. He grabbed her hands and said, "I don't want to continue like this anymore."

"You mean with the Johnny Appleseed act?"

"No, you know what I mean. I mean about us. Tomorrow, at church, we must tell your parents," said Sig. "We must tell your mother and father we are getting married."

Mary frowned. "I suppose we'll be forced to tell them, since we'll need to be married in the church. I mean, there is only one church . . . only one church on this entire planet."

"Good point."

"Okay," she agreed. "Let's do it. Tomorrow."

~

The next morning, Sig went to church with his family, sitting in the second to last pew. Almost all the families from New Munich and the American sector attended the church on Sundays, whether they were religious or not, and all had their favorite places. Sig could see Mary sitting in the first pew with her brothers and sisters. She looked back at Sig and smiled.

This church had formal traditional services, which were a mixture of Anglican and Lutheran ceremonies, representing the English and German branches of Christianity on Earth. The church music consisted of traditional hymns and classical music. As music director and organist, Felix and Eileen produced quite an impressive musical repertoire each Sunday: Eileen played the organ while Felix directed the choir, in the balcony in the back of the church. Eileen was partial to playing organ pieces by Handel, Bach, and Haydn.

After mass, a hymn was sung, concluding with the priest announcing to "Go out into the world in peace!" As the people left the church, Eileen played a postlude, Bach's Fugue No. 2 in C minor.

As always, she played this piece brilliantly. Finishing the fugue, she readied herself to leave the balcony. When she turned around from the organ, she found her daughter, Mary, standing behind her, with the *jungen Man*— Sig. Momentarily, they stood there, not saying anything.

"*Mutti*," said Mary, "You remember Sig, don't you?"

Hesitantly, Eileen responded, beginning in Deutsch, "*Ja, ja*," before dropping her usually austere mannerisms and switching to her native English. "Yes, I remember you. You were in the coffee shop the other day, correct?"

"Yes, Frau Eileen," stammered Sig. "I . . . I . . . well, let me begin . . ."

"What is it you are trying to say?" Eileen said looking at him directly. "Are you trying to say you like my daughter, Mary?"

Sig nodded, "Yes. I—I mean, we—want to ask you . . . well, actually I am not asking . . . what I want to say is . . ."

"Spit it out, young man!"

"I . . . love . . . . Mary. We want to get married."

There, he had said it; the truth was out. Sig and Mary braced themselves for Eileen's wrath, fully expecting their relationship was doomed to become *Romeo and Juliet in Space.*

To their surprise, Eileen looked steadily at Sig and then at her daughter, then she broke into a smile.

"Of course. This is great news! We must tell Papa!"

Mary hugged her mother who by now was weeping for joy.

"*Danke, Mutti! Vielen Dank!*" *[Thank you, Mother! Thank you so much!]*

"Surely you don't think I didn't know about the two of you?" Eileen said, with a sly grin.

~

As things turned out, Eileen was quite proud that Mary was marrying the son of Ingrid and Horst. She actually had great respect for Ingrid, who was her personal physician. Besides, she loved her daughter Mary, and was generally supportive of her decisions.

The engagement of Sig and Mary lasted three months. During this time, H & J Construction built them a new house in the American sector. Their wedding was held at the church, with everyone from New Munich and the American sector in attendance. It was a beautiful ceremony, even though Eileen, as the mother of the bride, allowed one of her students to take her place at the organ.

After the wedding, the couple went on their honeymoon to a cabin built especially for newlyweds, called the "honeymoon cottage," in a secluded area only a few miles from New Munich. Located at the end of a horseshoe canyon, next to a lagoon and a small waterfall, the cabin was built on a platform supported by tall posts. Sig and Mary spent a blissful week at the honeymoon cottage, staying in bed most of the morning, swimming in the warm waters of the lagoon and cooking their meals by campfire.

When they returned to their new house in the American sector, their marriage and life together was good. It was difficult to believe that just a few months before they had felt the need to meet secretly, and now they were married!

Unfortunately, neither of them found much satisfaction in their jobs. At dinner, they avoided discussing their work lives. Sig had no interest in his job involving packaging. Likewise, Mary did not like working in the office of the steel mill.

One night at dinner, Sig asked Mary, "Remember when you did that Johnny Appleseed thing?"

"You mean the thing with the puppet?"

"Yeah."

"That was fun. What about it?"

"I was thinking, what if we could do stuff like that for a living?" he said.

"Seriously?"

"Yes, I'm serious. I've been thinking—and you need to bear with me on this idea—I've been thinking, what if we could start a television station here?"

"Cool. Trouble is, there are no televisions here, genius," she teased.

In fact, there were no televisions or radio stations in either New Munich or the American sector. Daily life focused entirely on work, and the community was therefore somewhat dull compared to modern day Earth societies. There was no "entertainment industry" at all, and certainly no one made a living as an actor or a writer, at least, not yet. While it was true that the Third Thaw had been raised watching television series like *Gunsmoke* and *Gilligan's Island*, no one wanted to see those old shows any longer. They had their own lives to live, and there was no point in watching Earth TV shows. A few people enjoyed reading old Earth novels as a way to escape, but most were focused on building their new society.

"Yes, I've been thinking," continued Sig. "I've been thinking that if we could get some televisions made at the Einstein-Newton manufacturing facility, then we could start a television station."

Mary pondered over this idea.

"Okay, let's say that we're successful getting some TV's made. What types of shows would we show? Old Earth television shows?"

Sig grinned. "No, not old Earth shows. I want us to start writing our own scripts and shows."

"Okay, Keep going. Tell me more."

"What if we start off small? Like, suppose we do a daily puppet show for kids?"

"I like it," said Mary enthusiastically. "Keep going. You're on a roll."

"Ok, we could do this little puppet show on television that's for kids."

"At what time of day?"

"At three thirty p.m." he said. "It would air just after the kids get out of school."

"And we would have a Johnny Appleseed puppet on this show," Mary said. "What other puppets?"

Sig thought about this.

"Why don't we have Paul Bunyan, too? Like on Earth, there was this storybook fable about a character who was really big and could chop down trees."

"But the Paul Bunyan character on our show chops down ferns . . . Yeah, I can see where you're going with this."

So, Mary and Sig began making puppets for their show out of papier-mâché. They began writing, creating characters, developing scripts for a daily children's show.

Sig talked to his father, Horst, about supporting this new business enterprise. Initially, Horst was reluctant to get involved; however, he was so happy to see his son finally taking an interest in something, that he eventually supported the idea. Also, Sig had convinced him that starting a television industry would be a sound financial investment.

Using his business connections and his own money, Horst arranged the manufacturing of fifty television sets at the Einstein-Newton facility. These television sets were similar to TVs circa 1950s and were capable of displaying only black-and-white images.

Since there was no market for selling television sets yet, Eileen arranged for a raffle at the church. All fifty TV sets were given away for free to the raffle winners. Sig and Horst hoped that, if the station became successful, people would be willing to pay for television sets in the future. The plan was to use the money from the sale of TVs to support the television station.

A transmission tower and a small studio were built behind their house. The studio was named "Studio 1A." There would be no one other than themselves to operate the television cameras. After much experimentation, they positioned two cameras, showing two different views, which they could control using a toggle switch.

When all was in place, they made their first broadcast on a Monday, at three thirty p.m. On the show, Sig wore a ridiculous looking sailor's uniform and cap, and called himself "Captain Ned." For her part, Mary worked the puppets, "Johnny Appleseed," "Paul Bunyan," and a cast of several talking farm animals.

After their first show, Sig said to Mary, "I must be crazy doing this."

"If you're crazy, then I'm crazy, too," she said.

It seemed like a gamble for two grown adults to hole themselves up in a little building and give a puppet show—a show which, perhaps, no one was watching. But they stuck by their plan, and continued doing the performances, day after day. During the first two weeks of production, they never heard any comments from anybody, not even from a single person.

Fortunately, by the third week production, they finally got some feedback. Sig was walking in downtown New Munich when he found himself being followed by a group of young children.

"Captain Ned! Captain Ned!" they yelled.

Sig went into his Captain Ned persona.

"Well, hello mates!" he said, in his silly Captain Ned voice.

"Captain Ned, where is Johnny Appleseed?" a little girl asked.

"Johnny is outside, planting seeds," said Captain Ned.

"Where outside?"

"Oh . . . I'm not quite sure. I think he's on New York Street today, in the American sector."

"And where is Paul Bunyan?"

"Paul is out chopping ferns in the forest."

"Where is the forest, Captain Ned?"

And so, it continued like this, with children asking him endless questions, over and over. Eventually, even the adults began calling Sig "Captain Ned"!

"What have I created, Mary? Have I become 'Captain Ned'? Did I actually wish this on myself?"

"Perhaps," she replied, smiling with amusement.

In fact, Sig had become this planet's first "celebrity"- whether he wanted to or not. He had, unwittingly, created for himself an alternate ego that he was now obliged to wear whenever he was in public. He wore his alter ego in public and forced himself to be in-character whenever people recognized him!

This situation became a mixed blessing. Because of the show's success, all the families in New Munich and in the American sector purchased television sets. Soon businesses asked if they could place advertising on the television. As a result, the television station began raking in profits, much to Horst's relief.

～

Sig and Mary became quite busy, producing other television shows besides the *Captain Ned Show*. They hired other actors to appear in their shows as side characters.

Most notable was a young man with a childlike personality who played "Skippy" on the *Captain Ned Show*. Skippy became wildly popular, due to his goofy antics. They also created a news show, which aired at six p.m. every night; this included weather forecasts and featured news announcers who were more serious looking than Skippy. They also produced a night-time soap opera, *As the Planet Turns*. Eventually, their station began to broadcast sport tournaments at the school in New Munich.

Despite the fact there weren't many shows to watch, families became glued to their TV sets every evening. People began talking about what they saw the night before on, *As the Planet Turns*; they talked about the news; they discussed the weather; kids even began doing impersonations of the characters they had seen on *Captain Ned*.

In effect, this small television station made the New Munich community experience a running commentary on their own lives. Before television had been introduced, these people had lived their lives focused on reality and practical matters. Just as had happened on Earth in the 1950s, the introduction of television offered the people on this planet entirely new worlds of delusion and fantasy. The very behavior of people—their mannerisms, how they interacted and joked with each other—was subtly, even insidiously, being influenced by the new TV pop culture.

And, just as had happened on Earth, the introduction of television on this planet created a new type of person: the celebrity. Ironically, this was a role which Sig had never intended to take on. He did not enjoy all the attention he was receiving. He was not particularly interested in entertaining children, either—that was more an interest of Mary's. He had always been a private person, but now he had no privacy.

As the *Captain Ned Show* continued, Sig and Mary made the decision that the role of "Skippy" would be promoted, so that Captain Ned could be eliminated from the show. Gradually, over a course of three months, Skippy became promoted to "Captain Skippy" and the character of Captain Ned was eliminated. Captain Ned was written out of the script, and young viewers were told that he had been shipwrecked on an island. The show was renamed the *Captain Skippy Show*, and the kids adapted. Sig continued to produce and write the show with Mary, even sometimes working the puppets himself, but he no longer wanted to be in front of the camera.

Eventually, the kids stopped following Sig around, and he got his life back. But he was never able to completely get rid of the nickname "Captain Ned."

Part 6
The Return

Chapter 42

ONCE A MONTH, THE AMERICANS HELD A MEETING AT THEIR clubhouse in the American sector. These meetings were mainly social affairs, more of a chance to talk and get together rather than to conduct any serious business. There were some obligatory formalities to these gatherings. Every year the "American Club," as it was called, elected board members. Currently, Hansel was the president of the club.

The meetings began with a roll call, then a reading of the last meeting's minutes, then a speech, and, finally, any proposed motions that needed to be voted on.

One evening it was Horst's turn to give a speech.

"I want to begin by asking the group a question which has been nagging me lately: Are any of you interested in seeing New Eden again?"

This question created quite a commotion in the audience.

Hansel was the first to stand up. "After the dangerous experiences we had getting here, I have no interest, nor does my wife Gertrude, in traveling back to New Eden."

"I understand, Hansel. But what if we could eliminate the danger of traveling by foot? What if we could somehow travel there safely?"

Again, everyone in the room began talking.

Horst's son, Sig, raised his hand. "Father, I would be interested in seeing New Eden."

Several more of the young men and women raised their hands. Many of them said that they wanted to visit New Eden. They were hungry for adventure and eager to learn more about their roots.

"I myself would like to go back and visit," continued Horst. "I want to see the Guardians who raised us. Our heritage is back there. Our APS relatives are back there, stored on the supercomputer in New Munich. I just hope that the supercomputer is still intact; otherwise, these things will be lost forever."

Adam raised his hand. "I am curious about the Guardians, too. But Horst, what are you proposing? Is it really worth the risk?"

"Adam, I understand your reservations. Forgive me, but I'm simply 'thinking out loud' now. I just wanted to explore the idea and see if there is any interest. What kind of a vehicle could we build to keep us safe and comfortable?"

The group began discussing this idea.

"How about flying planes to New Eden?" suggested Adam.

"You mean like the planes we flew to the Einstein-Newton site?"

"Perhaps. Maybe bigger."

"That's a possibility," said Horst, "However, the distance is very far. It's over a thousand miles to New Eden. This would require a very large plane, such as a B-29."

"I don't know what a 'B-29' is," said Adam.

"A B-29 was a bomber used in World War II to fly long distances over the Pacific Ocean," answered Horst. "A plane like that needs a long flat landing strip. We may not find a place to land."

Hansel interrupted, "We need a vehicle that can travel over this hard terrain. We have terrain with bushes and holes in the ground and rocks."

Then he paused, recollecting their arrival in New Munich.

"Remember how the Germans rescued us using a simple rolling vehicle? I remember that simple vehicle was powered by a primitive steam engine. Seems to me that something like that may be good enough."

"I like your thinking," said Horst. "Yes, a simple rolling platform. We could improve on the previous version. We could make it higher, and we could have living quarters. The only real danger would be the sail-backs, but we learned that if we squirt them in the eyes with vinegar they will run away."

Adam said, "It sounds almost too easy. If the vehicle is too big, it may get stuck in the mud. If we get stuck, we'd really be in trouble!"

"Good point," said Horst. "This brings up the need for testing. Any vehicle that we use will require thorough testing first." He paused. "I appreciate this discussion. We can't develop plans for a vehicle like this in one meeting. Therefore, I want to make a proposal. I suggest we assign a group to develop a design."

"I second that motion!"

"All those in favor of developing a vehicle to transport some of our members to New Eden, please raise your hands."

Everyone raised their hands.

"Anyone opposed?"

"No? The motion is approved. Who wants to come up with a design?"

Several of the younger men eagerly volunteered. After a lengthy discussion, it was decided that Filbert, Gerald Junior; and Hansel and Gertrude's son, Jeff would develop a prototype vehicle. Adam, now the "Elder" structural engineer would oversee their work. The design would be tested with the Einstein-Newton supercomputer using the virtual testing facility.

Once a month, the design team provided updates at the American Club's meetings. After six months, they were making a formal presentation at their meeting. Horst prepared a speech before the design team's presentation.

Horst took a sip of water. "Now we'll hear from the designers of the expedition vehicle. Filbert, Gerald Junior and Jeff, please come up."

No one came to the stage. Everyone looked around the room, but the young men were nowhere to be seen.

Once again, Horst said, "Filbert, Gerald Junior and Jeff . . . where are you?" but, again, there was no response. "Apparently, the design team has skipped the meeting!"

Suddenly, everyone heard something very loud outside—something that made the whole building shake.

Hansel was staring out of the window, unable to believe his eyes. "Hey, look everyone! They're outside!"

Everyone rushed outside the clubhouse. They saw three vehicles racing in circles, kicking up dust. The vehicles had big rubber tires and were very loud. When they came to a stop, the young men descended from the cockpits using rope ladders.

Filbert was the first to speak. "How's that for an entrance?" Everyone laughed. "Let me introduce you to our expedition vehicles," continue Filbert. "We have manufactured four of these machines. You are seeing three of them here today. These vehicles were called 'off-road' vehicles on Earth. They can travel over virtually any terrain."

"Did you design these by yourself?" asked Hansel, evidently impressed.

"Yes and no," said Gerald. "We modified a stock Ford F-150 pickup truck, replacing the tires with these big monster truck tires. We have replaced the stock fuel tanks with larger fuel tanks."

Ingrid asked, "Where will you sleep?"

"The small cabins in the back of each rig hold bunk beds for two people. The cabins are equipped with both heating and air-conditioning," answered Jeff.

"Is there enough room to carry all your supplies?" asked Hansel.

"These vehicles will be towing trailers," said Filbert. "We have a small tank trailer with a kitchen. Another trailer has an outhouse and shower. Finally, we have another empty trailer for carrying things back to New Munich."

"I have another question," said Hansel. "These trucks are very high in the air. Will you be climbing down and up between the trailers every time you need to use the bathroom?"

Everyone laughed at that comment.

"Good question!" said Filbert. "No, we think that we can stay on the trucks for almost the entire journey without getting off. We will be stopping the vehicles and parking them next to each other. It should be easy to hop between the vehicles. We plan to circle the wagons, then jump over to the chuck wagon for grub."

"The chuck wagon for grub!" said Hansel. "I love it! Just like on *Gunsmoke*!"

"What will you do when you encounter animals, like the sail-backs?" asked Gertrude.

Filbert walked to the front of the truck and pointed at something. "On the engine's hood you will see what is called a 'squirt gun.' These squirt guns are modeled after a popular type of toy used by kids called a 'Super Soaker.' This gun contains a weak acid—vinegar, actually. When we are attacked by sail-backs, we will squirt the animals in the eyes. We know from experience they can't stand being squirted with vinegar."

"What if you are attacked by giant dragonflies?" asked Hansel.

Filbert laughed.

"We'll roll up the windows!"

The Elder Horst walked up to the young men and shook their hands. "Excellent job! You have risen to the challenge and designed a perfect vehicle for the expedition. Thank you!"

Everyone applauded enthusiastically.

"Next on the agenda, we should discuss when we should leave, and who is going."

It was decided that Filbert, Gerald Junior, and Jeff would be drivers and that Horst, Hansel, Adam, and Karl would ride with them. Denise, a young doctor, and Maude, a chef, would also come. Three of the old drones— Smokey, Buzzy, and Jaimie—would also accompany them. They would scout ahead for any dangers.

The team calculated that they could make it to New Eden in one week. They planned to stay in New Eden for a week to pack anything they wished to bring back. The return trip would require another week. The expedition was estimated to take three weeks.

The departure was scheduled in five days.

Chapter 43

O N THE DAY OF EXPEDITION PARTY'S DEPARTURE FOR NEW
Eden, there was a formal ceremony. As before, a speech was delivered by New Munich's mayor, *Burgermeister* Sigmund, commemorating the
event. Felix directed the New Eden Brass Ensemble to play several John
Philip Sousa marches.

This event was also broadcast by Sig and Mary's new television station.
Practically all families had the new television sets, even though there were
only a few shows on air. This particular television news event was the very
first time they were broadcasting from outside the television studio.

While Sig was managing an electrical cord extending to the American
Club, Mary was talking to the news announcer, Chet Gerke: "We'll be
broadcasting in one minute. Let's do one last check of your sound levels,"
she asked.

"Sure, Mary." Chet spoke into the microphone, "One, two, three . . .
Check . . . One, two, three . . . Check."

"Okay, you're good," said Mary. "Horst, are you okay?"

Chet was standing with Horst—officially *Captain* Horst—who would
be giving a farewell speech.

"Yes, I'm doing fine," answered Horst, clearly uncomfortable by the presence of the television camera.

Sig motioned to Mary, "Mary, can you please comb Dad's hair a little?"

Immediately Mary made some last minute adjustments to Horst's
unruly hair.

"This is about the best I can do. No more time."

As Sig held the camera pointing at Chet, he gave the countdown on the set: "Ready everyone? On the count of five: Five, four, three, two . . ." then he gave the silent "one" finger.

The news announcer began speaking: "*Guten Morgen, Neu München!* This is Chet Gerke, broadcasting live, for the first time outside our television studio. Today we are witnessing an historic event: the return of an American expedition party to the place of their birth, New Eden. Standing next to me is the expedition leader, Captain Horst, who is just about to speak."

As the television camera focused on Horst, he became momentarily stunned. There was an awkward silence, which lasted almost ten seconds. Mary whispered to Horst, "You're on! Say something!"

Finally, Horst began to speak: "*Guten Morgen*, everyone!"

The crowd replied "*Guten Morgen!*" in unison

"*Ja, ja, es ist eine Guten Morgen,* indeed. It was twenty-five years ago that a group of us, called the Third Thaw left the place of our birth, New Eden. When I reflect back, it amazes me just how much we have changed and built in the past twenty-five years! I am so proud to see all the technologies which we have literally reinvented on this planet which is light-years from Earth! Please, everyone, let's give ourselves a round of applause!"

Horst paused as the crowd enthusiastically applauded.

"The progress we are seeing here is astounding. It is as though we experienced an Industrial Revolution at light speed. Every day, we are seeing more technologies transforming our new society. Even as I speak, we are seeing for the first time television cameras broadcasting this event. It is as though our society is already progressing into the 1950s! I wonder what I can expect to see here in the next few weeks when I return: Will New Munich look like 1980s Earth?"

Many people laughed.

"It was six months ago when we first discussed revisiting our birthplace, New Eden. At that time, I mentioned this idea almost casually. Today, I remain firmly convinced of the importance of returning to New Eden. In fact, I firmly believe that it is imperative that we do so.

"We must go back. Our heritage is there. The simulations of our Earth families are there. The Guardians who raised us are there. The remnants of America's contribution to this entire mission is back there. We need to go back to retrieve our heritage, *before it is too late*—if it is already not too late—before these things are destroyed by the elements and are lost forever."

For a moment, there was silence, A few of the older residents fought back tears or wept openly. Then the audience applauded, giving Horst a standing ovation. Now they all agreed that the mission was imperative. It would be folly to let New Eden go to waste. How could they have ignored it for so long!

"It is for these reasons we will be leaving today to the place of our birth, New Eden. It should not be long. We expect this journey will last for three weeks, if all goes as plans. Therefore, on this note, we bid farewell to Neu München—for the time being!"

When Horst finished his speech, the four all-terrain vehicles revved up. He walked to one of the ATV's and climbed onboard; the vehicles burst off, in a cloud of dust, into the wilderness toward New Eden.

The trucks traveled at a good pace of about twenty miles per hour over the sail-back prairies. For most of the trip, the land was flat; occasionally they ran into fern forests, which slowed their pace.

After five days, they reached the sea across from New Eden.

Horst consulted his map. "This sea is fairly large. We will need to travel along the coast in this direction," he said pointing to the left. "It is about two hundred miles. If we start tomorrow morning, I think we can make it by midafternoon."

As usual, they parked in a circle. For the entire trip, they had not descended from the trucks and trailers, since it was safer to stay above the ground to avoid the scorpions and spiders.

That evening at supper, the three Elders, Horst, Hansel and Adam, sat together talking, while Denise, the doctor, assisted Maude with food preparation.

"So, what do you think?" said Adam.

"About what?" said Hansel.

"About returning, of course," said Adam.

Horst said, "I'm a bit anxious. I don't know what to expect."

"Yeah, I know how you feel," said Hansel.

"I'm more concerned about seeing the Guardians," Adam said, "about seeing Clare and Ellie and Father Graham. I mean, is Clare even alive?"

"Adam, of course she's not 'alive'!" said Hansel. "She's a robot!"

"You know what I mean," said Adam. "She doesn't need to be 'alive' to be 'alive.'"

"That sounds weird!" said Horst. "But, yeah, I think I know what you mean."

In the morning, they set off along the shoreline, towards New Eden. This side of the sea was not in the direction of the usually prevailing winds; consequently, the beaches were typically pea-gravel and, in a few places, sand. This proved to be a good surface for driving the off-road vehicles. In a few places, there were dunes and dune grass.

It was not all easy going. In some places, the shoreline was marshy and muddy, requiring them to take the vehicles away from the coast into the surrounding forest. These wooded areas typically had thorny bushes which were hard to get around, even for the off-road vehicles. When they really got stuck, the men got out and hacked their way through the brush with machetes. Denise and Maude kept the vehicles running.

By late afternoon, they made it to the other side of the sea Since it would be getting dark soon, they decided to delay arriving into New Eden until the next morning. The vehicles formed a circle and the group set up camp for the night.

Chapter 44

IN THE MORNING, THEY BEGAN THE LAST PART OF THE JOURney toward New Eden. The coastline favored the prevailing direction of winds; as a result, the beaches had fine sand and many more sand dunes and dune grass. It was a beautiful drive along the shore that morning.

It took only about one hour for them to reach the outskirts of New Eden. When they finally arrived, they stopped the trucks and descended.

"This is the first time we've seen this place in—*what is it?*—twenty-four years," said Horst. "I never realized how small this place was. Look at it! It's so tiny compared to New Munich!"

"Hey, we didn't know the difference when we lived here, did we?" said Adam. "This is where we were born, the place where it all started. Just imagine how we had been brought here on a small space craft! It boggles my mind, when I think about it."

The entire town—actually, a settlement, not a town—was a merely one square mile, perhaps even less. They looked at the area in the center where there used to be fields, where they had worked every year since they were five years old, planting and weeding and picking crops. Now there were no crops—just a mangy field with weeds and bushes. They saw the houses where they had once lived, now in shambles. The adobe walls, made from rammed earth and fern twigs, had not been maintained and were falling apart. There were bushes and weeds growing in the front yards. Some of the roofs had collapsed.

The Elders started walking toward the houses, each heading to the little house where he had grown up. Adam walked directly to his house, which was in the row of houses closest to the beach. He walked inside the crumbling dwelling place, which was more of a shed than a house. It looked so small; there was just room enough for his bed, which was still there, and a little closet. The mattress was old, damp, and moldy.

Surveying the room, Adam was overcome by powerful childhood memories. He remembered how happy he had been living here. Since the time they had left New Eden, life had become so much more complicated. Then he remembered his secret hiding place, a small hole in the closet, close to the ceiling. He went to the closet and stuck his hand in the hole. He felt something, and pulled out a small box.

Inside the box, he found some drawings he had made. One of the drawings was of Miss Clare; another drawing was the landing craft. These were the drawings he had made after the first time they had been inside the warehouse, after escaping the dogs! He also found a small notebook, filled with notes. It was a notebook he had written one summer, when he was fourteen!

As he was reading the notebook, Adam suddenly heard a very loud sound of an animal outside his house. Then he heard a man crying for help. Quickly, he ran outside to see an elephant chasing after Horst! It was a big bull elephant with enormous tusks. Horst was running as fast as he could, but he was no match for the elephant. Just as the elephant was about to ram its tusks into his back, Horst dove to the ground and rolled to the left, escaping certain death by the slimmest of margins. His diversionary tactic momentarily confused the beast. Quickly, the elephant locked onto Horst's position, but this time Horst was not so lucky. The bull elephant picked up Horst with its trunk and lifted him into the air.

Adam and the others ran up to the elephant and began throwing rocks at it from all sides. With so many humans attacking it, the animal became confused and started backing off. Then it turned around and ran off, still carrying Horst wrapped in its trunk. Frantically, the group ran after the elephant as it ran toward the sugar cane fields; however, they could not keep up and soon lost sight of him. Luckily, the fresh elephant tracks were easy to follow.

∼

They walked into the sugar cane, then through the fields into the surrounding fern forest. As they walked deeper into the fern forest, they could see where the elephant has trampled the tall brush. However, in some places, there were so many animal prints, it was difficult to determine which were freshly made.

Adam got down on his knees and studied the impressions in the ground.

"See this one?" he began saying, "They went this way," but then Hansel stopped him, grabbing his arm and motioning him to be quiet.

"I just saw something over there! Can you see it?"

"Where?" asked Adam.

"Over there, on the right."

There was something big behind the bush, making grunting sounds. They could see several silhouettes of animals that seemed to be moving. Then, the animals emerged—a large male lion accompanied by five females. The male saw them and snarled, preparing to attack.

Fortunately, Adam remembered this location from his childhood adventure. He yelled to the others, "Follow me!" as he ran over to the pond in the sinkhole. He and the others jumped into the water and began swimming toward the center, as the lions leaped toward them.

The alpha lion also jumped in the water and began paddling toward them.

Adam looked at Hansel. "You remember this, don't you?"

"Yeah. Let's do it!" said Hansel.

Adam shouted, "Take a deep breath!"

Then, Adam dove underwater and everyone followed, descending deeper and deeper until they made their way through a hole in the rocks, into a completely dark space. It was a long way to hold their breath. When they rose upward to the water surface, they were gasping for air. They were inside a pitch-black space.

"Can everyone hear me?" someone said.

"Is that you, Adam?" said Hansel.

"Yes," answered Adam. "Did everyone make it?"

He took roll call: "Hansel? Karl? Denise? Maude? Jeff? Gerald Junior? Filbert?"

Everybody was present and accounted for, still treading water, with the exception of Horst.

"Somewhere, there is a ledge where we can crawl out. We need to find it!" explained Adam.

There was no light inside the cavern. Everyone began groping for the ledge, but the cavern had smooth walls offering nothing to grab onto. Finally, Filbert, still gasping for air, said "I think I found it."

"Keep talking," said Adam. "The only way we can follow you is if you keep making noise."

Filbert began to clap his hands. "Follow my clapping."

Each of them swam towards him. One by one, they hoisted themselves out of the water, lending a hand to the others still in the water.

"Hansel, where are you?"

"I'm right over here, Adam."

"You remember when we were last here?"

"Of course, I do. There was a light."

"Yes, there was a light which means there is still a light with wiring," said Adam. "We need to find the electrical conduit leading to the light. Once we find it, we can follow the conduit out of this cave."

"Good plan," said Hansel.

They felt their way around them, looking for the electrical conduit. After about five minutes, Karl said "I think I found it. It feels like a small pipe. Yes, I definitely found it."

He began clapping so the others could find him.

When they were finally together, Adam said, "Since I've been here before, let me lead the way. Everyone, hold on to the person in front of you."

They each grabbed the other person's hand or piece of clothing and began inching along, as Adam felt his way along the conduit.

After following the conduit for almost half an hour, they saw a faint glimmer of light. As they got closer, it looked as though a sliver of light was shining underneath the bottom of a door. When they reached the door, it was locked.

Filbert and Jeff found a large rock and tried using it to break the door's lock, but it was no use. The lock wouldn't break. Then Karl found that the door had hinges which were exposed on the side where they were standing. He took out his small pocket knife and began working the hinge pins out. The top hinge pin came out easily, but the bottom hinge pin had rusted. He hit it with rock, loosening the pin.

With both the hinge pins removed, they removed the door and walked into a room, Adam and Hansel immediately recognized they were in the back of the warehouse. The room was now dusty. Old drones were lying around, motionless. There were storage boxes everywhere. Walking out of the storage room, they saw the twelve Guardians sitting side-by-side on chairs, all of them slumped over. Adam remembered that night when he followed the Guardians into the sugar cane field. This place was the Guardian's recharging station, where they would go each night, after the kids had gone to bed.

Adam walked up to each one of the Guardians, looking at their faces, until he found Miss Clare. "Clare?" said Adam, cautiously, but Clare said nothing.

"Hey, quit looking at the Guardians and come over here!" yelled Hansel. He was standing next to the space shuttle landing craft's door. "We need to try and get the power back on."

With some assistance from Karl, Hansel opened the door of the landing craft. "I think I found something."

"What did you find?" said Adam.

"A big red button," said Filbert.

"What does it say?" said Karl.

"It says 'Power,'" answered Filbert. " I'm pushing it."

Immediately, lights inside the space shuttle came on, then, outside the space shuttle, the lights in the warehouse began to flicker.

"How about the supercomputer? Is it powering up?" asked Adam.

"Yes, it appears to be rebooting," said Hansel. He watched a monitor above the supercomputer control panel, displaying each of the reboot routines. It took a long time. After five minutes, the supercomputer's terminal displayed a root menu with several functions. One of the functions was "Robot Controls." Hansel clicked on "Robot Controls" and then, seeing another menu, he double-clicked on "Reboot Robots."

They ran outside of the shuttle toward the robots. It was somewhat miraculous to see these machines waking up, opening their eyes, looking at their arms and legs, determining their locations. The Guardians moved their jaws opened and closed their eyes, looking left and right and up and down, checking the functioning of their systems.

"They are initializing and calibrating their systems," said Filbert. "There must be hundreds of thousands of neural simulation circuits which need to be calibrated. This could take a long time.

"Clare! Do you recognize me?" said Adam to Miss Clare.

Clare was staring off in the distance, blinking her eyes. Then she turned her head from left to right, then up and down.

Adam repeated, "Clare! Clare! Look at me!"

This time, she turned her head to Adam. She looked at his face, then examined him from toe to head.

Finally, she spoke. "Adam. It is you, again. How long has it been?"

Adam replied, "It's been about twenty-four years since I last saw you."

"Yes, it has. This means, if my arithmetic is correct, I have been without power for the past fifteen years."

This explained why the entire settlement was in disrepair.

"Clare, we need your help. An elephant has taken Horst. We need to rescue him."

"That must be Jumbo," said Clare. "He must be very large by now."

"With a name like 'Jumbo'—well, yes, he is very large!" said Adam.

Clare looked at the other Guardians, wirelessly communicating to them the situation. Then she and the other Guardians stood up.

"Please, follow me," Clare said to the humans.

In single file, the Guardians left the warehouse and began walking out into the fern forest. As the humans followed the Guardians, they saw large beasts appearing from the forests: lions, tigers, grizzly bears, giraffes, rhinoceroses, even some hippos. None of the animals came close to the Guardians. It was though there was an invisible force field protecting them. These wild animals seemed to remember that the Guardians had raised them, and they should not be attacked.

The Guardians led the group to an area where there were ten or more elephants. Jumbo, the big bull with the tusks was there. Next to the bull, the body of Horst lay motionless.

Adam and Hansel ran to Horst. He was not breathing.

"Wake up! Wake up Horst!" yelled Hansel.

Adam called for Denise.

Denise listened to Horst's chest, but couldn't hear a heartbeat. She felt his head which was still warm. Then she began pumping his chest with her hands, but still nothing happened.

Clare walked up to Horst. "Everyone, please stand back."

Denise moved out of the way while Clare took her hands and peeled away the robot skin from her palms, exposing the metal parts. Then she put each of her palms over Horst's chest, over his heart. "On the count of three. One, two, three!"

Clare gave Horst an electric shock. His body arched up.

Denise listened to his chest again. She shook her head. "Still no pulse."

Clare gave Horst another electric shock. This time, he coughed! Horst was alive!

Denise began gently slapping him in the face. "Horst! Horst! Wake up!"

Horst slowly regained consciousness, looking up at the group of people gathered around him.

"Can you see my fingers?" the doctor asked. "Blink if you understand."

He blinked.

"Good. How many fingers can you see?"

Finally, he coughed again and said. "Two. I can see two fingers."

Then Adam smelled something burning. When he looked at Clare, her back was smoldering. "No!" he screamed, as the flames engulfed her.

But there was no way to stop the fire; they had no water or blankets. As they watched, Clare looked at them, her robot skin burning away, until all the skin on her back and head had melted, exposing all her metal parts and electronics. She did not appear to be in pain—if robots can experience pain at all. Clare held her right hand up to her face, looking at the flames; then she looked down as the flames spread to the remainder of her body.

Her final words were, "Apparently, I have overloaded my circuits."

Then she collapsed into a pile of burning metal.

"Clare! Clare!" Adam cried, looking at what was left of his surrogate robot mother.

Horst coughed. "What happened?"

"Clare saved you," said Adam, tears running down his face. He turned away, burying his face in his hands. Maude instinctively put her arms around him and, holding her close, he wept for the only mother he had ever known.

"Clare?" Horst muttered, still in a daze. "Where am I?"

Denise checked his body for broken bones. Horst could not feel anything below the waist. Denise assessed he had broken his lower back and his left leg was fractured in two places.

Two Guardians went to the warehouse for a gurney. When they returned, gently they lifted him and took him back to the warehouse. There, Denise fitted him with a makeshift back brace. She also set his broken leg in a plaster cast.

Chapter 45

 AS THEY PACKED FOR THE JOURNEY BACK TO NEW MUNICH, the Guardians made sure the large carnivores did not attack the humans during their stay. Nevertheless, Adam was a bit nervous about seeing lions prowling the outskirts of the village.

The supercomputer was too big to carry back; however, they were able to remove the digital storage units. They also packed the various "tools for making tools" that had come from Earth. These tools, which the Planners of the Mission considered to be important enough to ship in the shuttle, included such things as screw-cutting lathes, microscopes, measuring machines, nail makers and a universal milling machine for making gears.

When it was time to leave, the Guardians were turned off. Their bodies were packed, lying on top of each other inside the trailer. Horst's bed was also placed in the same trailer, which was becoming quite cramped as it was filled with Guardian bodies, computer units and tools. Horst joked he was riding in a storage compartment filled with mannequins.

Despite the severity of his back injury, Horst's outlook remained positive. He was thankful to be alive. He hoped the nerves in his back could be repaired using nanocircuitry.

On the morning of their departure from New Eden, Adam was in the lead ATV vehicle. Adam looked back at New Eden and said a silent goodbye to Miss Clare. Although he knew she was a robot, he mourned for her and he would carry his grief home to New Munich.

The wild big animals were left to live without humans, which was probably for the best. Most of these animals had faced near extinction on Earth due to the human population. It would be interesting to see how they would evolve on this strange planet without any competition or human predators.

⌒

They didn't travel too fast, because of Horst's fragile condition and the delicate electronics they were now carrying. They easily retraced the path they had taken to New Eden, but at a bit slower pace of one hundred and fifty miles a day.

On the fourth day of their journey, a large sail-back appeared out of the forest and rammed into the lead truck, rolling it onto its side. Fortunately, no one was hurt. Adam chased the animal away by squirting it in the eyes with vinegar. After rolling back the truck into an upright position using a winch, they saw there was only minor damage.

On the sixth day when they stopped for lunch, Filbert saw something in the sky. "Look! Look up there!" he said, pointing. Something was falling through the sky from high up. By its contrails it looked big.

"It looks like the Interstellar booster rockets falling from orbit," said Adam.

As Horst watched, he saw the object seemed to be gliding.

"I don't think it's the Interstellar boosters," said Horst. "The Interstellar boosters will break up upon reentry. That thing isn't breaking up. If it were breaking up, we'd see fireballs."

"If it's not the boosters, what is it?" asked Adam.

Horst watched the object. He noticed that it was swooping slightly, up and down. "That object is flying, like it's gliding."

"So, what is it you are suggesting?" asked Adam.

"I think it's a spacecraft," said Horst, "that's coming in for a landing."

The object descended toward the Einstein-Newton site. They watched until it was no longer visible, except for the contrails.

Horst said, "The General told us the Russians and Chinese may have also been planning a mission. Is that what this is?"

"Perhaps," said Adam. "That would make sense."

Then Horst smirked to himself.

"What?" Adam asked.

"Just a thought," said Horst.

"What thought?"

"The only other possibility," said Horst, "is that the asteroid missed."

Acknowledgements

To the best of my recollection, I thought of the concept of this story in the early 2000s. The technical challenges of traveling to any planet that is light-years away from Earth have always seemed insurmountable to me. So, why not send embryos to another planet, to be raised by robots?

In 2010, I read an NBC News Internet article about interstellar space travel, titled "Ride a starship? Not for a century." I contributed to the discussion of that article under the alias, "DCEngineer," proposing to send frozen embryos to another planet to be raised by robots. My comment received very good response in the discussion, with some saying that it would make a great science fiction story. To my surprise, since then, this idea has gained some credibility in scientific circles as a possible way to travel to another planet.

For almost ten years I had kept this story "in my back pocket." One day I shared this story with my younger daughter, Paige, who was quite supportive and helpful. Without her, I would have never had the momentum to start this project.

As ridiculous as this may sound, the first draft of the manuscript was written on my cell phone connected to Bluetooth enabled keyboard, while I traveled to and from my work in Chicago on the Metra rail line. I have since progressed to using a laptop.

I have never been much a fan of science fiction, except for a few "hard" science fiction novels. "Hard" science fiction attempts to use as much real science as possible to make the story believable. I do not like the trend for fantasy, unless it is very well written.

To write a novel such as this, without any magic or fantasy, I needed to do quite a bit of research on the history of technology. We need to keep in mind that, if people go to another planet, they will need to reinvent technology from scratch. I have tried in this book to describe just how much technology we have and take granted, and the challenges that future explorers in space may face maintaining modern technology.

After finishing the original manuscript, I sought the help of a professional writer to critique and polish the manuscript. Fortunately, I found a writing coach and author, Dr. Elizabeth-Anne Stewart, who lives and teaches in Chicago. It was a great pleasure to work with Elizabeth in this venture, whose considerable efforts breathed life into the characters.

Finally, I must express my gratitude to WiDo Publishing for accepting my manuscript and the further improvements they made to the story. I learned much about the process of editing a book from Liesel, Karen, and Forrest. Publishing a book can be a very long, exacting process with many varied components and many people involved, who each love the art of writing.

Further Reading

AS A STRUCTURAL ENGINEER, MY ENTIRE CAREER HAS BEEN based on being able to accurately calculate stresses in structures due to forces. Engineers have great respect for gravity and objective numerical facts; consequently, many engineers have no room for fantasy or "alternative facts" based on beliefs. This may explain why I have chosen to write a fictional novel which uses factually based ideas as much as possible. The term "Hard Science Fiction" is a term sometimes used to describe this genre of fiction. I have aimed to provide a substantial amount of actual science to create a foundation for a plausible story, so that the reader's required "willing suspension of disbelief" is minimized. It is my hope that this story will appeal to scientific and engineering literate readers who like to be challenged.

Apart from the epic adventure of "the mission," this storyline offers a sly way to teach science as part of an adventure. Since there are so many scientific ideas mentioned in the book, I must give appropriate credit to several references which I have used in developing this story:

1. *The Language Instinct: How the Mind Creates Language*, by Steven Pinker, published by Harper Perennial Modern Classics. This book is a fascinating study of linguistics and how our minds work. Pinker uses the term "Mentalese" to describe how the human mind works, which is a term I have borrowed in this novel. Pinker also describes the linguistic work of Noam Chomsky quite well, using his tiny syntax examples.

2. *On Intelligence*, by Jeff Hawkins and Sandra Blakeslee, published by Times Books. This book, written by the inventor of the "Palm Pilot,"

describes research being done to understand the processes of the human brain. One of the main goals of his research is to produce a "neocortical algorithm." I have borrowed from "On Intelligence" the idea that our brains tend to form neural circuitry representing something like stories.

3. *Cradle of Life*, by J. William Schopf, published by Princeton University Press. This book is an extremely interesting study of the origins of life. In particular, Schopf describes the oldest fossil remains on earth—stromatolites—which demonstrate cyanobacteria were the first life-forms on Earth. Excellent explanations of the "Tree of Life," metabolic processes and the hierarchy of "feeders," "eaters," and "eatees." Brilliant and fascinating.

4. *What Is Life?*, by Lynn Margulis and Dorion Sagan, published by University of California Press. Equally fascinating and similar in subject to *Cradle of Life*, explaining cellular life-forms. Enlightening about how much biological scientists have discovered about life. Well written and accessible.

5. *Tinnitus Retraining Therapy*, by Pawel Jastreboff and Jonathan Hazell, published by Cambridge University Press. Highly recommended for anyone with tinnitus. Explains how the auditory system works, the connection between the lower limbic brain organs and higher conscience. This book explains the "Neurophysiological Model" of the brain, which was the inspiration in certain parts of this novel (particularly the "meeting Albert" episode).

6. *Principles of Neural Science* (5th Edition), Kandel, Schwartz, Jessell, Siegelbuam, and Hudspeth, published by McGraw-Hill. A huge textbook written for medical and neurology students, and doctors—definitely not an "easy read." Contains extensive information about the brain, such as the auditory and vestibular systems.

7. *The Complete Guide to Prehistoric Life*, by Tim Haines and Paul Chambers, from the makers of *Walking with Dinosaurs*, published by Firefly Books. This book is a companion volume to the phenomenal BBC television series, *Walking with Dinosaurs*. All of the creatures described in the Third Thaw are based on the "Before There Were Dinosaurs" episodes of this production.

8. *The Fossil Book: A Record of Prehistoric Life*, by Rich, Rich, Fenton and Fenton, published by Dover Publications, Inc. Information about trilobites, ferns, ancient pre-tree plants were inspired by this book.

9. *Organic Chemistry for Dummies*, by Arthur Winter, published by John Wiley and Sons, Inc. Information about organic chemistry was taken from this book.

10. *A Short History of Technology: From the Earliest Times to A.D. 1900*, by T. K. Derry, published by Dover Books. We take so much for granted about the things we use in our daily lives. This book explains many of the inventions that we rely on in modern society. In writing this novel, I used this particular reference to determine which things a new civilization will need in order to recreate modern society.

11. *Life: The Movie*, by Neil Gabler, published by Vintage Books. Neil Gabler is perhaps my favorite non-fiction and biography writer. Although *Life* is not a science book, I mention this book in reference to the "Captain Ned" character, which describes the fledgling entertainment industry and the invention of celebrities. Since the entertainment industry is such an important part of modern Westernized civilization, I felt it deserved coverage.

Some of the statements made by the APS Albert Einstein are actual quotations said by the real Albert Einstein, which I took from Wikipedia.

That said, I should clarify what things are purely conjecture in this story.

In particular, the story of nanoparticle circuitry used in the brain to take over autonomous brain functions is purely fictional. However, such a procedure does not seem too far-fetched if we consider that many people receive cochlear ear implants connected to the brain.

Another point of pure conjecture—one of the founding premises of the book—is the idea that a spacecraft can travel 80,000 years to a planet and remain intact. I believe the engineering challenges in designing a spacecraft which can last so long would be quite challenging, purely from a corrosion perspective.

I have no idea if a "ceramic"-based computer is even feasible.

I hope the above give proper credit to originators of these ideas which I borrowed. As far as defending the conjectural parts, this is a work of fiction, after all. These are the "holes" that can be expected in Hard Science Fiction which require the reader to have "a willing suspension of disbelief."

About the Author

Karl Hanson, a structural engineer, earned degrees from Colorado State University and the University of Illinois. Since 1980, he has helped design buildings and bridges throughout the country. In Chicago, he is involved in

everything from small projects to high profile projects such as Millennium Park and McCormack Place.

Since 1991, he has developed a suite of structural engineering software by the name of "DCALC" (DesignCalcs), used by structural engineers across the country.

His hobbies are piano playing, learning German, and riding bikes with his wife Lisa on the weekends. Karl and Lisa have two daughters and a family of avid readers. Visit the author at kjhanson.net for information about his current writing projects.